**Praise for *New York Times* bestselling author
RaeAnne Thayne**

"RaeAnne has a knack for capturing those emotions
that come from the heart."

—*RT Book Reviews*

"Thayne, once again, delivers a heartfelt story of a
caring community and a caring romance between
adults who have triumphed over tragedies."

—*Booklist* on *Woodrose Mountain*

"Thayne's series starter introduces the Colorado town
of Hope's Crossing in what can be described as a cozy
romance… [A] gentle, easy read."

—*Publishers Weekly* on *Blackberry Summer*

**Praise for *USA TODAY* bestselling author
Patricia Davids**

"Patricia Davids is one of the best writers in the Amish
fiction genre. She's now on my must-read list!"

—Shelley Shepard Gray, *New York Times* bestselling author

"Davids' deep understanding of Amish culture is
evident in the compassionate characters and beautiful
descriptions."

—*RT Book Reviews* on *A Home for Hannah*

RaeAnne Thayne finds inspiration in the beautiful northern Utah mountains, where the *New York Times* and *USA TODAY* bestselling author lives with her husband and three children. Her books have won numerous honors, including RITA® Award nominations from Romance Writers of America and a Career Achievement Award from *RT Book Reviews*. RaeAnne loves to hear from readers and can be contacted through her website, www.raeannethayne.com.

After thirty-five years as a nurse, **Patricia Davids** hung up her stethoscope to become a full-time writer. She enjoys spending her free time visiting her grandchildren, doing some long-overdue yard work and traveling to research her story locations. She resides in Wichita, Kansas. Patricia always enjoys hearing from her readers. You can visit her online at patriciadavids.com.

New York Times Bestselling Author

RaeAnne THAYNE

HIS SECOND-CHANCE FAMILY

**HARLEQUIN
BESTSELLING
AUTHOR
COLLECTION**

**HARLEQUIN®
BESTSELLING
AUTHOR
COLLECTION**

Recycling programs
for this product may
not exist in your area.

ISBN-13: 978-1-335-20995-5

His Second-Chance Family
First published in 2008. This edition published in 2021.
Copyright © 2008 by RaeAnne Thayne

Katie's Redemption
First published in 2010. This edition published in 2021.
Copyright © 2010 by Patricia MacDonald

This edition published by arrangement with Harlequin Books S.A.

For questions and comments about the quality of this book, please contact
us at CustomerService@Harlequin.com.

Harlequin Enterprises ULC
22 Adelaide St. West, 40th Floor
Toronto, Ontario M5H 4E3, Canada
www.Harlequin.com

MIX
Paper from
responsible sources
FSC® C021394

Printed in Lithuania

CONTENTS

HIS SECOND-CHANCE FAMILY   7
RaeAnne Thayne

KATIE'S REDEMPTION   211
Patricia Davids

Also by RaeAnne Thayne

Harlequin Special Edition

The Cowboys of Cold Creek

The Cowboy's Christmas Miracle
A Cold Creek Homecoming
A Cold Creek Holiday
A Cold Creek Secret
A Cold Creek Baby
Christmas in Cold Creek
A Cold Creek Reunion
A Cold Creek Noel
A Cold Creek Christmas Surprise
The Christmas Ranch
A Cold Creek Christmas Story
The Holiday Gift
The Rancher's Christmas Song

The Women of Brambleberry House

A Soldier's Secret
His Second-Chance Family
The Daddy Makeover

HQN

Haven Point

Riverbend Road
Snowfall on Haven Point
Serenity Harbor
Sugar Pine Trail
The Cottages on Silver Beach
Season of Wonder

Visit her Author Profile page at Harlequin.com,
or www.raeannethayne.com for more titles!

HIS SECOND-CHANCE FAMILY

RaeAnne Thayne

For the staff and donors
of The Sunshine Foundation, for five days of
unimaginable joy. Sometimes wishes do come true!

Chapter 1

As signs from heaven went, this one seemed fairly prosaic.

No choir of angels, no booming voice from above or anything like that. It was simply a hand-lettered placard shoved into the seagrass in front of the massive, ornate Victorian that had drifted through her memory for most of her life.

Apartment For Rent.

Julia stared at the sign with growing excitement. It seemed impossible, a miracle. That *this* house, of all places, would be available for rent just as she was looking for a temporary home seemed just the encouragement her doubting heart needed to reaffirm her decision to pack up her twins and take a new teaching job in Cannon Beach.

Not even to herself had she truly admitted how worried she was that she'd made a terrible mistake moving here, leaving everything familiar and heading into the unknown.

Seeing that sign in front of Brambleberry House seemed

an answer to prayer, a confirmation that this was where she and her little family were supposed to be.

"Cool house!" Maddie exclaimed softly, gazing up in awe at the three stories of Queen Anne Victorian, with its elaborate trim, cupolas and weathered shake roof. "It looks like a gingerbread house!"

Julia squeezed her daughter's hand, certain Maddie looked a little healthier today in the bracing sea air of the Oregon Coast.

"Cool dog!" her twin, Simon, yelled. The words were barely out of his mouth when a giant red blur leaped over the low wrought-iron fence surrounding the house and wriggled around them with glee, as if he'd been waiting years just for them to walk down the beach.

The dog licked Simon's face and headbutted his stomach like an old friend. Julia braced herself to push him away if he got too rough with Maddie, but she needn't have worried. As if guided by some sixth sense, the dog stopped his wild gyrations and waited docilely for Maddie to reach out a tentative hand and pet him. Maddie giggled, a sound that was priceless as all the sea glass in the world to Julia.

"I think he likes me," she whispered.

"I think so, too, sweetheart." Julia smiled and tucked a strand of Maddie's fine short hair behind her ear.

"Do you really know the lady who lives here?" Maddie asked, while Simon was busy wrestling the dog in the sand.

"I used to, a long, long time ago," Julia answered. "She was my very best friend."

Her heart warmed as she remembered Abigail Dandridge and her unfailing kindness to a lonely little girl. Her mind filled with memories of admiring her vast doll collection, of pruning the rose hedge along the fence with her, of shared confidences and tea parties and sand dollar hunts along the beach.

"Like Jenna back home is my best friend?" Maddie asked.

"That's right."

Every summer of her childhood, Brambleberry House became a haven of serenity and peace for her. Her family rented the same cottage just down the beach each July. It should have been a time of rest and enjoyment, but her parents couldn't stop fighting even on vacation.

Whenever she managed to escape to Abigail and Brambleberry House, though, Julia didn't have to listen to their arguments, didn't have to see her mother's tears or her father's obvious impatience at the enforced holiday, his wandering eye.

Her fifteenth summer was the last time she'd been here. Her parents finally divorced, much to her and her older brother Charlie's relief, and they never returned to Cannon Beach. But over the years, she had used the image of this house, with its soaring gables and turrets, and the peace she had known here to help center her during difficult times.

Through her parents' bitter divorce, through her own separation from Kevin and worse. Much worse.

"Is she still your best friend?" Maddie asked.

"I haven't seen Miss Abigail for many, many years," she said. "But you know, I don't think I realized until just this moment how very much I've missed her."

She should never have let so much time pass before coming back to Cannon Beach. She had let their friendship slip away, too busy being a confused and rebellious teenager caught in the middle of the endless drama between her parents. And then had come college and marriage and family.

Perhaps now that she was back, they could find that friendship once more. She couldn't wait to find out.

She opened the wrought-iron gate and headed up the walkway feeling as if she were on the verge of something oddly portentous.

She rang the doorbell and heard it echo through the house. Anticipation zinged through her as she waited, wondering what she would possibly say to Abigail after all these years. Would her lovely, wrinkled features match Julia's memory?

No one answered after several moments, even after she rang the doorbell a second time. She stood on the porch, wondering if she ought to leave a note with their hotel and her cell phone number, but it seemed impersonal, somehow, after all these years.

They would just have to check back, she decided. She headed back down the stairs and started for the gate again just as she heard the whine of a power tool from behind the house.

The dog, who looked like a mix between an Irish setter and a golden retriever, barked and headed toward the sound, pausing at the corner of the house, head cocked, as if waiting for them to come along with him.

After a wary moment, she followed, Maddie and Simon close on her heels.

The dog led them to the backyard, where Julia found a couple of sawhorses set up and a man with brown hair and broad shoulders running a circular saw through a board.

She watched for a moment, waiting for their presence to attract his attention, but he didn't look up from his work.

"Hello," she called out. When he still didn't respond, she moved closer so she would be in his field of vision and waved.

"Excuse me!"

Finally, he shut off the saw and pulled his safety goggles off, setting them atop his head.

"Yeah?" he said.

She squinted and looked closer at him. He looked familiar. A hint of a memory danced across her subconscious and she was so busy trying to place him that it took her a moment to respond.

"I'm sorry to disturb you. I rang the doorbell but I guess you couldn't hear me back here with the power tools."

"Guess not."

He spoke tersely, as if impatient to return to work, and Julia could feel herself growing flustered. She had braced herself to see Abigail, not some solemn-eyed construction worker in a sexy tool belt.

"I…right. Um, I'm looking for Abigail Dandridge."

There was an awkward pause and she thought she saw something flicker in his blue eyes.

"Are you a friend of hers?" he asked, his voice not quite as abrupt as it had been before.

"I used to be, a long time ago. Can you tell me when she'll be back? I don't mind waiting."

The dog barked, only with none of the exuberance he had shown a few moments ago, almost more of a whine than a bark. He plopped onto the grass and dipped his chin to his front paws, his eyes suddenly morose.

The man gazed at the dog's curious behavior for a moment. A muscle tightened in his jaw then he looked back at Julia. "Abigail died in April. Heart attack in her sleep. I'm sorry to be the one to tell you."

Julia couldn't help her instinctive cry of distress. Even through her sudden surge of grief, she sensed when Maddie stepped closer and slipped a small, frail hand in hers.

Julia drew a breath, then another. "I…see," she mumbled.

Just one more loss in a long, unrelenting string, she thought. But this one seemed to pierce her heart like jagged driftwood.

It was silly, really, when she thought about it. Abigail hadn't been a presence in her life for sixteen years, but suddenly the loss of her seemed overwhelming.

She swallowed hard, struggling for composure. Her friend was gone, but her house was still here, solid and reassuring, weathering this storm as it had others for generations.

Somehow it seemed more important than ever that she bring her children here.

"I see," she repeated, more briskly now, though she thought she saw a surprising understanding in the deep blue of the man's eyes, so disconcertingly familiar. She knew him. She knew she did.

"I suppose I should talk to you, then. The sign out front says there's an apartment for rent. How many bedrooms does it have?"

He gave her a long look before turning away to pick up another board and carry it to the saw. "Three bedrooms, two of them on the small side. Kitchen's been redone in the last few months and the electricity's been upgraded but the bathroom plumbing's still in pretty rough shape."

"I don't care about that, as long as everything works okay. Three bedrooms is exactly the size my children and I need. Is it still available?"

"Can't say."

She pursed her lips. "Why not?"

He shrugged. "I don't own the place. I live a few houses down the beach. I'm just doing some repairs for the owners."

Something about what he said jarred loose a flood of

memories and she stared at him more closely. Suddenly everything clicked in and she gasped, stunned she hadn't realized his identity the instant she had clapped eyes on him.

"Will? Will Garrett?"

He peered at her. "Do I know you?"

She managed a smile. "Probably not. It's been years."

She held out a hand, her pulse suddenly wild and erratic, as it had always been around him.

"Julia Blair. You knew me when I was Julia Hudson. My parents rented a cottage between your house and Brambleberry House every summer of my childhood until I was fifteen. I used to follow you and my older brother, Charlie, around everywhere."

Will Garrett. She'd forgotten so much about those summers, but never him. She had wondered whether she would see him, had wondered about his life and where he might end up. She never expected to find him standing in front of her on her first full day in town.

"It's been years!" she repeated. "I can't believe you're still here."

At her words, it took Will all of about two seconds to remember her. When he did, he couldn't understand why he hadn't seen it before. He had yearned for Julia Hudson that summer as only a relatively innocent sixteen-year-old boy can ache. He had dreamed of her green eyes and her dimples and her soft, burgeoning curves.

She had been his first real love and had haunted his dreams.

She had promised to keep in touch but she hadn't called or answered any of his letters and he remembered how his teenage heart had been shattered. But by the time school started a month later, he'd been so busy with football practice and school and working for his dad's carpentry business on Saturdays that he hadn't really had much time to wallow in his heartbreak.

Julia looked the same—the same smile, the same auburn hair, the same appealing dimples—while he felt as if he had aged a hundred years.

He could barely remember those innocent, carefree days when he had been certain the world was his for the taking, that he could achieve anything if only he worked hard enough for it.

She was waiting for a response, he realized, still holding her hand outstretched in pleased welcome. He held up his hands in their leather work gloves as an excuse not to touch her. After an awkward moment, she dropped her arms to her side, though the smile remained fixed on her lovely features.

"I can't believe you're still here in Cannon Beach," she repeated. "How wonderful that you've stayed all these years! I remember how you loved it here."

He wouldn't call it wonderful. There were days he felt like some kind of prehistoric iceman, frozen forever in place. He had wondered for some time if he ought to pick up and leave, go *anywhere,* just as long as it wasn't here.

Someone with his carpentry skills and experience could find work just about any place. He had thought about it long and hard, especially at night when the memories overwhelmed him and the emptiness seemed to ring through his house but he couldn't seem to work past the inertia to make himself leave.

"So how have you been?" Julia asked. "What about family? Are you married? Any kids?"

Okay, he wasn't a prehistoric iceman. He was pretty certain they couldn't bleed and bleed and bleed.

He set his jaw and picked up the oak board he was shaping for a new window frame in one of the third-floor bedrooms of Brambleberry House.

"You'll have to talk to Sage Benedetto or Anna Galvez about the apartment," he said tersely. "They're the new owners. They should be back this evening."

He didn't quite go so far as to fire up the circular saw but it was a clear dismissal, rude as hell. He had to hope she got the message that he wasn't interested in any merry little trips down memory lane.

She gave him a long, measuring look while the girl beside her edged closer.

After a moment, she offered a smile that was cool and polite but still managed to scorch his conscience. "I'll do that. Thank you. It's good to see you again, Will."

He nodded tersely. This time, he did turn on the circular saw, though he was aware of every move she and her children made in the next few moments. He knew just when they walked around the house with Abigail's clever Irish Setter mix Conan following on their heels.

He gave up any pretense of working when he saw them head across the lane out front, then head down the beach. She still walked with grace and poise, her chin up as if ready to take on the world, just as she had when she was fifteen years old.

And her kids. That curious boy and the fragile-looking girl with the huge, luminescent blue eyes. Remembering those eyes, he had to set down the board and press a hand to the dull ache in his chest, though he knew from two years' experience nothing would ease it.

Booze could dull it for a moment but not nearly long enough. When the alcohol wore off, everything rushed back, worse than before.

He was still watching their slow, playful progress down the beach when Conan returned to the backyard. The dog barked once and gave him a look Will could only describe as peeved. He planted his haunches in front of the worktable and glared at him.

Abigail would have given him exactly the same look for treating an old friend with such rudeness.

"Yeah, I was a jerk," he muttered. "She caught me off guard, that's all. I wasn't exactly prepared for a ghost from the past to show up out of the blue this afternoon."

The dog barked again and Will wondered, not for the first time, what went on inside his furry head. Conan had a weird way of looking at everybody as if he knew exactly what they might be thinking and he managed to communicate whole diatribes with only a bark and a certain expression in his doleful eyes.

Abigail had loved the dog. For that reason alone, Will would have tolerated him since his neighbor had been one of his favorite people on earth. But Conan had also showed an uncanny knack over the last two years for knowing just when Will was at low ebb.

More than once, there had been times when he had been out on the beach wondering if it would be easier just to walk out into the icy embrace of the tide than to survive another second of this unrelenting grief.

No matter the time of day or night, Conan would somehow always show up, lean against Will's legs until the despair eased, and then would follow him home before returning to Brambleberry House and Abigail.

He sighed now as the dog continued to wordlessly reprimand him. "What do you want me to do? Go after her?"

Conan barked and Will shook his head. "No way. Forget it."

He *should* go after her, at least to apologize. He had been unforgivably rude. The hell of it was, he didn't really know why. He wasn't cold by nature. Through the last two years, he had tried to hold to the hard-fought philosophy that just because his insides had been ripped apart and because sometimes the grief and pain seemed to crush the life out of him, he hadn't automatically been handed a free pass to hurt others.

Lashing out at others around him did nothing to ease his own pain so he made it a point to be polite to just about everybody.

Sure, there were random moments when his bleakness slipped through. At times, Sage and Anna and other friends had been upset at him when he pushed away their efforts to comfort him. More than a few times, truth be told. But he figured it was better to be by himself during those dark moments than to do as he'd just done, lash out simply because he didn't know how else to cope.

He had no excuse for treating her poorly. He had just seen her there looking so lovely and bright with her energetic son and her pretty little daughter and every muscle inside him had cramped in pain.

The children set it off. He could see that now. The girl had even looked a little like Cara—same coloring, anyway, though Cara had been chubby and round where Julia's daughter looked as if she might blow away in anything more than a two-knot wind.

It hadn't only been the children, though. He had seen Julia standing there in a shaft of sunlight and for a moment, long-dormant feelings had stirred inside him that he wanted to stay dead and buried like the rest of his life.

No matter how screwed up he was, he had no business being rude to her and her children. Like it or not, he would have to apologize to her, especially if Anna and Sage rented her the apartment.

He lived three houses away and spent a considerable amount of time at Brambleberry House, both because he was busy with various remodeling projects and because he considered the new owners—Abigail's heirs—his friends.

He didn't want Julia Hudson Blair or her children here at Brambleberry House. If he were honest with himself, he could admit that he would have preferred if she had stayed a long-buried memory.

But she hadn't. She was back in Cannon Beach with her children, looking to rent an apartment at Brambleberry House, so apparently she planned to stay at least awhile.

Chances were good he would bump into her again, so he was going to have to figure out a way to apologize.

He watched their shapes grow smaller and smaller as they walked down the beach toward town and he rubbed the ache in his chest, wondering what it would take to convince Sage and Anna to find a different tenant.

Chapter 2

"Will we get to see inside the pretty house this time, Mommy?"

Julia lifted her gaze from the road for only an instant to glance in the rearview mirror of her little Toyota SUV. Even from here, she could see the excitement in Maddie's eyes and she couldn't help but smile in return at her daughter.

"That's the plan," she answered, turning her attention back to the road as she drove past a spectacular hotel set away from the road. Someday when she was independently wealthy with unlimited leisure time, she wanted to stay at The Sea Urchin, one of the most exclusive boutique hotels on the coast.

"I talked to one of the owners of the house an hour ago," Julia continued, "and she invited us to walk through and see if the apartment will work for us."

"I hope it does," Simon said. "I really liked that cool dog."

"I'm not sure the dog lives there," she answered. "He

might belong to the man we talked to this morning. Will Garrett. He doesn't live there, he was just doing some work on the house."

"I'm glad he doesn't live there," Maddie said in her whisper-soft voice. "He was kind of cranky."

Julia agreed, though she didn't say as much to her children. Will had been terse, bordering on rude, and for the life of her she couldn't figure out why. What had she done? She hadn't seen him in sixteen years. It seemed ridiculous to assume he might be angry, after all these years, simply because she hadn't written to him as she had promised.

They had been friends of a sort—and more than friends for a few glorious weeks one summer. She remembered moonlight bonfires and holding hands in the movies and stealing kisses on the beach.

She would have assumed their shared past warranted at least a little politeness but apparently he didn't agree. The Will Garrett she remembered had been far different from the surly stranger they met that afternoon. She couldn't help wondering if he treated everyone that way or if she received special treatment.

"He was simply busy," she said now to her children. "We interrupted his work and I think he was eager to get back to it. We grown-ups can sometimes be impatient."

"I remember," Simon said. "Dad was like that sometimes."

The mention of Kevin took her by surprise. Neither twin referred to their father very often anymore. He had died more than two years ago and had been a distant presence for some time before that, and they had all walked what felt like a million miles since then.

Brambleberry House suddenly came into view, rising above the fringy pines and spruce trees. She slowed, savoring the sight of the spectacular Victorian mansion sil-houetted against the salmon-colored sky, with the murky blue sea below.

That familiar sense of homecoming washed over her again as she pulled into the pebbled driveway. She wanted to live here with her children. To wake up in the morning with that view of the sea out her window and the smell of roses drifting up from the gardens and the solid comfort of those walls around her.

As she pulled into the driveway and turned off the engine, she gave a silent prayer that she and the twins would click with the new owners. The one she'd spoken with earlier—Sage Benedetto—had seemed cordial when she invited Julia and her children to take a look at the apartment, but Julia was almost afraid to hope.

"Mom, look!" Simon exclaimed. "There's the dog! Does that mean he lives here?"

As she opened her door to climb out, she saw the big shaggy red dog waiting by the wrought-iron gates, almost as if he somehow knew they were on their way.

"I don't know. We'll have to see."

"Oh, I hope so." Maddie pushed a wisp of hair out of her eyes. She looked fragile and pale. Though Julia would have liked to walk from their hotel downtown to enjoy the spectacular views of Cannon Beach at sunset, she had been afraid Maddie wouldn't have the strength for another long hike down the beach and back.

Now she was grateful she had heeded her motherly instincts that seemed to have become superacute since Maddie's illness.

More than anything—more than she wanted to live in this house, more than she wanted this move to work out, more than she wanted to *breathe*—she wanted her daughter to be healthy and strong.

"I hope we can live here," Maddie said. "I really like that dog."

Julia hugged her daughter and helped her out of her seat belt. Maddie slipped a hand in hers while Simon took his sister's other hand. Together, the three of them walked through the gate, where the one-dog welcoming committee awaited them.

The dog greeted Simon with the same enthusiasm he had shown that morning, wagging his tail fiercely and nudging Simon's hand with his head. After a moment of attention from her son, the dog turned to Maddie. Julia went on full mother-bear alert, again ready to step in if necessary, but the dog showed the same uncanny gentleness to Maddie.

He simply planted his haunches on the sidewalk in front of her, waiting as still as one of those cheap plaster dog statues for Maddie to reach out with a giggle and pet his head.

Weird, she thought, but she didn't have time to figure it out before the front door opened. A woman wearing shorts and a brightly colored tank top stepped out onto the porch. She looked to be in her late twenties and was extraordinarily lovely in an exotic kind of way, with blonde wavy hair pulled back in a ponytail and an olive complexion that spoke of a Mediterranean heritage.

She walked toward them with a loose-hipped gait and a warm smile.

"Hi!" Her voice held an open friendliness and Julia instinctively responded to it. She could feel the tension in her shoulders relax a little as the other woman held out a hand.

"I'm Sage Benedetto. You must be the Blairs."

She shook it. "Yes. I'm Julia and these are my children, Simon and Maddie."

Sage dropped her hand and turned to the twins. "Hey kids. Great to meet you! How old are you? Let me guess. Sixteen?"

They both giggled. "No!" Simon exclaimed. "We're seven."

"Seven? Both of you?"

"We're twins." Maddie said in her soft voice.

"Twins? No kidding? Cool! I've always wanted to have a twin. You ever dress up in each others' clothes and try to trick your mom?"

"No!" Maddie said with another giggle.

"We're not *identical* twins," Simon said with a roll of his eyes. "We're *fraternal*."

"Of course you are. Silly me. 'Cause one of you is a boy and one is a girl, right?"

Sage obviously knew her way around children, Julia thought as she listened to their exchange. That was definitely a good sign. She had observed during her career as an elementary school teacher that many adults didn't really know how to talk to kids. They either tried too hard to be buddies or treated them with obvious condescension. Sage managed to find the perfect middle ground.

"I see you've met Conan," Sage said, scratching the big dog under the chin.

"Is he your dog?" Simon asked.

She smiled at the animal with obvious affection. "I guess you could say that. Or I'm his human. Either way, we kind of look out for each other, don't we, bud?"

Oddly, Julia could swear the dog grinned.

"Thank you again for agreeing to show the apartment to us tonight," she said.

Sage turned her smile to Julia. "No problem. I'm sorry

we weren't here when you came by the first time. You said on the telephone that you knew Abigail."

That pang of loss pinched at her again as she imagined Abigail out here in the garden, her big floppy straw hat and her gardening gloves and the tray of lemonade always waiting on the porch.

"Years ago," she answered, then was compelled to elaborate.

"Every summer my family rented a house near here. The year I was ten, my brother and I were running around on the beach and I cut my foot on a broken shell. Abigail heard me crying and came down to help. She brought me back up to the house, fixed me a cookie and doctored me up. We were fast friends after that. Every year, I would run up here the minute we pulled into the driveway of our cottage. Abigail always seemed so happy to see me and we would get along as if I had never left."

The other woman smiled, though there was an edge of sorrow to it. Julia wondered again how Sage had ended up as one of the two new owners of Brambleberry House after Abigail's death.

"Sounds just like Abigail," Sage said. "She made friends with everyone she met."

"I've been terrible about keeping in contact with her," Julia admitted with chagrin as they walked into the entryway of the house, with its sweeping staircase and polished honey oak trim. "I was so sorry to hear about her death—more sorry than I can say that I let so much time go by without calling her. I suppose some foolish part of me just assumed she would always be here. Like the ocean and the seastacks."

The dog—Conan—whined a little, almost as if he understood their conversation, though Julia knew that was impossible.

"I think we all felt that way," Sage said. "It's been four months and it still doesn't seem real."

"Will said she died of a heart attack in her sleep."

"That's right. I find some comfort in knowing that if she could have chosen her exit scene, that's exactly how she would have wanted to go. The doctors said she probably slept right through it."

Sage paused and gave her a considering kind of look. "Do you know Will, then?"

Julia could feel color climb her cheekbones. How foolish could she be to blush over a teenage crush on Will Garrett, when the man he had become obviously wanted nothing to do with her?

"Knew him," she corrected. "It all seems so long ago. The cottage we rented every year was next door to his. We socialized a little with his family and he and my older brother, Charlie, were friends. I usually tried to find a way to tag along, to their great annoyance."

She had a sudden memory of mountain biking through the mists and primordial green of Ecola National Park, then cooling off in the frigid surf of Indian Beach, the gulls wheeling overhead and the ocean song a sweet accompaniment.

Will had kissed her for the first time there, while her brother was busy body surfing through the baby breakers and not paying them any attention. It had just been a quick, furtive brush of his lips, but she could suddenly remember with vivid clarity how it had warmed her until she forgot all about the icy swells.

"He was my first love," she confessed.

Oh no. Had she really said that out loud? She wanted to

snatch the words back but they hung between them. Sage turned around, sudden speculation sparking in her exotic, tilted eyes, and Julia could feel herself blushing harder.

"Is that right?"

"A long time ago," she answered, though she was certain she had said those words about a million times already. So much for making a good impression. She was stuttering and blushing and acting like an idiot over a man who barely remembered her.

To her relief, Sage didn't pursue it as they reached the second floor of the big house.

"This is the apartment we're renting. It's been vacant most of the time in the five years I've lived here. Once in a while Abigail opened it up on a short-term basis to various people in need of a comfortable place to crash for a while. Since Anna and I inherited Brambleberry House, we've kept Will busy fixing it up so we could rent out the space."

Will again. Couldn't she escape him for three seconds? "Convenient that he lives close," she said.

"It's more convenient because he's the best carpenter around. With all the work that needs to be done to Brambleberry House, we could hire him as our resident carpenter. Good thing for us he likes to stay busy."

She remembered again the pain in his eyes. She wanted to ask Sage the reason for it, but she knew that would be far too presumptuous.

Anyway, she wasn't here to talk about Will Garrett. She was trying to find a clean, comfortable place for her children.

When Sage opened the door to the apartment, Julia felt a little thrill of anticipation.

"Ready to take a look?" Sage asked.

"Absolutely." She walked through the door with the oddest sense of homecoming.

The apartment met all her expectations and more. Much, much more. She walked from room to room with a growing excitement. The kitchen was small but had new appliances and what looked like new cabinets stained a lovely cherry color. Each of the three bedrooms had fresh coats of paint. Though two of them were quite small, nearly every room had a breathtaking view of the ocean.

"It's beautiful," she exclaimed as she stood in the large living room, with its wide windows on two sides that overlooked the sea.

"Will did a good job, didn't he?" Sage said.

Before Julia could answer, the children came into the room, followed by the dog.

"Wow. This place is so cool!" Simon exclaimed.

"I like it, too," Maddie said. "It feels friendly."

"How can a house feel friendly?" her brother scoffed. "It's just walls and a roof and stuff."

Sage didn't seem to mind Maddie's whimsy. Her features softened and she laid a hand on Maddie's hair with a gentleness that warmed Julia's heart.

"I think you're absolutely right, Miss Maddie," she answered. "I've always thought Brambleberry House was just about the friendliest house I've ever been lucky enough to live in."

Maddie smiled back and Julia could see a bond forming between the two of them, just as the children already seemed to have a connection with Conan.

"When can we move in?" Simon asked.

Julia winced at her son's bluntness. "We've still got some details to work out," she said quickly, stepping in to avoid Sage feeling any sense of obligation to answer before she was completely comfortable with the idea of them as tenants. "Nothing's settled yet. Why don't the two of you play with Conan for a few moments while I talk with Ms. Benedetto?"

He seemed satisfied with that and headed to the window seat, followed closely by his sister and Sage's friendly dog.

Her children were remarkably adept at entertaining themselves. Little wonder, she thought with that echo of sadness. They had spent three years developing patience during Maddie's endless string of appointments and procedures.

When they seemed happily settled petting the dog, she turned back to Sage. "I'm sorry about that. I understand that you need to check references and everything and talk to the co-owner before you make a decision. I'm definitely interested, at least through the school year."

Sage opened her mouth to answer but before she could speak, the dog gave a sudden sharp bark, his ears on alert. He rushed for the open door to the landing and she could hear his claws scrabbling on the steps just an instant before the front door opened downstairs.

Sage didn't even blink at the dog's eager behavior. "Oh, good. That's Anna Galvez. I was hoping she'd be home before you left so she could have a chance to meet you. Anna took over By-the-Wind, Abigail's old book and giftshop in town."

"I remember the place. I spent many wonderful rainy afternoons curled up in one of the easy chairs with a book."

"Haven't we all?" Sage said with a smile, then walked out to the stairs to call down to the other woman.

A moment later, a woman with dark hair and petite, lovely features walked up the stairs, her hand on Conan's fur.

She greeted Julia with a smile slightly more reserved than Sage's warm friendliness. "Hello."

Her smile warmed when she greeted the curious twins. "Hey, there," she said.

Sage performed a quick introduction. "Julia and her twins are moving to Cannon Beach from Boise. Julia's going to be teaching fifth grade at the elementary school and she's looking for an apartment."

"Lovely to meet you. Welcome to Oregon!"

"Thank you," Julia said. "I used to spend summers near here when I was a child."

"She's one of Abigail's lost sheep finally come home," Sage said with a smile that quickly turned mischievous. "Oh, you'll be interested to know that Will was her first love."

To Julia's immense relief, Sage added the latter in an undertone too low for the children to hear, even if they'd been paying attention. Still, she could feel herself blush again. She really *had* to stop doing that every time Will Garrett's name was mentioned.

"I was fifteen. Another lifetime ago. We barely recognized each other when I bumped into him earlier today outside. He seems…very different than he was at sixteen."

Sage's teasing smile turned sober. "He has his reasons," she said softly.

She and Anna gave each other a quick look loaded with layers of subtext that completely escaped Julia.

"Thank you for showing me the apartment. I have to tell you, from what I see, it would be perfect for us. It's exactly what I'm looking for, with room for the children to play, incredible views and within walking distance to the school. But I certainly understand that you need to check references and credit history before renting it to me. Feel free to talk to the principal of the elementary school who hired me, and any of the other references I gave you in our phone conversation. If you need anything else, you have my cell number and the number of the hotel where we're staying."

"Or we could always talk to Will and see what he remembers from when you were fifteen."

Julia flashed a quick look to Sage and was relieved to find the other woman smiling again. She had no idea what Will Garrett remembered about her. Nothing pleasant, obviously, or he probably would have shown a little more warmth when she encountered him earlier.

"Will may not be the best character reference. If I remember correctly, I still owe him an ice-cream cone. He bet me I couldn't split a geoduck without using my hands. I tried for days but the summer ended before I could pay him back."

"Good thing you're sticking around," Anna said. "You can pay back your debt now. We've still got ice cream."

"And geoducks," Sage said. "Maybe you're more agile than you used to be."

She laughed, liking both women immensely. As she gathered the children and headed down the stairs to her car, Julia could only wish for a little more agility. Then she would cross her toes and her fingers that Sage Benedetto and Anna Galvez would let her and her twins rent their vacant apartment.

She couldn't remember when she had wanted anything so much.

"So what do you think?" Sage asked as she and Anna stood at the window watching the schoolteacher strap her children into the backseat of her little SUV.

She looked like she had the process down to a science,

Sage thought, something she still struggled with when she drove Chloe anywhere. She could never figure out how to tighten the darn seat belt over the booster chair with her stepdaughter-to-be. She ought to have Julia give her lessons.

"No idea," Anna replied. "I barely talked to her for five minutes. But she seems nice enough."

"She belongs here."

Anna snorted. "And you figured that out in one quick fifteen-minute meeting?"

"Not at all." Sage grinned. She couldn't help herself. "I figured it out in the first thirty seconds."

"We still have to check her references. I'm sorry if this offends you, but I can't go on karma alone on this one."

"I know. But I'm sure they'll check out." Sage couldn't have said how she knew, she just did. Somehow she was certain Abigail would have wanted Julia and her twins to live at Brambleberry House.

"Did you see her blush when Will's name came up?"

Anna shook her head. "Leave it alone, Sage. You engaged women think you have to match up the entire universe."

"Not the entire universe. Just the people I love, like Will."

And you, she added silently. She thought of the loneliness in Anna's eyes, the tiny shadow of sadness she was certain Anna never guessed showed on her expression.

Their neighbor wasn't the only one who deserved to be happy, but she decided she—and Abigail—could only focus on one thing at a time. "Will has had so much pain in his life. Wouldn't you love to see him smile again?"

"Of course. But Julia herself said she hadn't seen him in years and they barely recognized each other. And we don't even know the woman. She could be married."

"Widowed. She told me that on the phone. Two years, the same as Will."

Compassion flickered in Anna's brown eyes. "Those poor children, to lose their father at such a young age." She paused. "That doesn't mean whatever scheme you're hatching has any chance of working."

"I know. But it's worth a shot. Anyway, Conan likes them and that's the important thing, isn't it, bud?"

The dog barked, giving his uncanny grin. As far as Sage was concerned, references or not, that settled the matter.

Chapter 3

Sage and Anna apparently had a new tenant.

Will slowed his pickup down as he passed Brambleberry House coming from the south. He couldn't miss the U-Haul trailer hulking in the driveway and he could see Sage heading into the house, her arms stacked high with boxes. Anna was loading her arms with a few more while Julia's children played on the grass not far away with Conan. Even from here he could see the dog's glee at having new playmates.

Damn. This is the price he paid for his inaction. He should have stopped by a day or two earlier and at least tried to dissuade Anna and Sage from taking her on as a tenant.

It probably wouldn't have done any good, he acknowledged. Both of Abigail's heirs could be as stubborn as crooked nails when they had their minds made up about something. Still, he should have at least made the attempt.

But what could he have said, really, that wouldn't have made him sound like a raving lunatic?

Yeah, she seems nice enough and I sure was crazy about her when I was sixteen. But I don't want her around anymore because I don't like being reminded I'm still alive.

He sighed and turned off his truck. He wanted nothing more than to drive past the house and hide out at his place down the beach until she moved on but there was no way on earth his blasted conscience would let him leave three women and two kids to do all that heavy lifting on their own.

He climbed out of his pickup and headed to the trailer. He reached it just as the top box on Anna's stack started to slide.

He lunged for it and plucked the wobbly top box just before it would have hit the ground, earning a surprised look from Anna over the next-highest box.

"Wow! Good catch," she said, a smile lifting her studious features. "Lucky you were here."

"Rule of thumb—your stack of boxes probably shouldn't exceed your own height."

She smiled. "Good advice. I'm afraid I can get a little impatient sometimes."

"Is that it? I thought you just like to bite off more than you can chew."

She made a wry face at him. "That, too. How did you know we needed help?"

He shrugged. "I was driving past and saw your leaning tower and thought you might be able to use another set of arms."

"We've got plenty of arms. We just need some arms with muscle. Thanks for stopping."

"Glad to help." It was a blatant lie but he decided she didn't need to know that.

She turned and headed up the stairs and he grabbed

several boxes from inside the truck and followed her, trying to ignore the curious mingle of dread and anticipation in his gut.

He didn't want to see Julia again. He had already dreamed about her the last two nights in a row. More contact would only wedge her more firmly into his head.

At the same time, part of him—maybe the part that was still sixteen years old somewhere deep inside—couldn't help wondering how the years might have changed her.

Anna was breathing hard by the time they reached the middle floor of the house, where the door to the apartment had been propped open with a small stack of books.

"I could have taken another one of your boxes," he said to Anna.

She made a face. "Show-off. Are you even working up a sweat?"

"I'm sweating on the inside," he answered, which was nothing less than the truth.

The source of his trepidation spoke to Anna an instant later.

"Thanks so much," Julia Blair said in her low, sexy voice. "Those go in Simon's bedroom."

Will lowered his boxes so he could see over them and found her standing in the middle of the living room directing traffic. She wore capris and a stretchy yellow T-shirt. With her hair pulled back into a ponytail, she looked fresh and beautiful and not much older than she'd been that last summer together.

He didn't miss the shock in her eyes when she spied him behind the boxes. "Will! What are you doing here?"

He shrugged, uncomfortable at her obvious shock. Why *shouldn't* he be here helping? It was the neighborly thing to do. Had he really been such a complete jerk the other day that she find his small gesture of assistance now so stunning?

"Do these go into the same room?"

She looked flustered, her cheeks slightly pink. "Um, no. Those are my things. They go in my bedroom, the big one overlooking the ocean."

He headed in the direction she pointed, noting again no sign of a Mr. Blair. On some instinctive level, he had subconsciously picked up the fact that she wore no wedding ring when he had seen her the other day and she had spoken only of herself and her children needing an apartment. Was she widowed, divorced, or never married?

He only wondered out of mild curiosity about the road she might have traveled in the years since he had seen her. Or at least that's what he told himself.

In her bedroom, he found stacks of boxes, some of them open and overflowing with books. The queen-size bed was already made up with a cozy-looking comforter in soft blue tones, with piles of pillows against the headboard.

An image flashed in his head of her tousled and welcoming, her auburn hair spread out on those pillows and a soft, aroused smile teasing the edges of those lovely features.

He dropped the boxes so abruptly he barely missed his toe.

Whoa. Where the hell did that come from?

He had no business thinking about her at all, forget about in some kind of sultry, welcoming pose.

When he returned to the living room, her cheeks were still flushed and she didn't meet his gaze, as if she were embarrassed about something. It was a damn good thing she couldn't know the inappropriate direction of his thoughts.

"I'm sorry." She fidgeted with a stack of books in her hand. "I probably sounded terribly ungracious when you first came in. I just didn't expect you to show up and start hauling my boxes inside."

"No problem."

He started to head toward the door, but she apparently wasn't content with his short response. "Why, again, are you helping me move in?"

He shrugged. What did it matter? He was here, wasn't he? Did they really have to analyze the reasons why? "I was heading home after a job south of here and saw your U-Haul out front. I figured you could use a hand."

"How...neighborly of you."

"Around here we look out for each other." It was nothing less than the truth.

"I remember." She smiled a little. "That's one of the reasons I wanted to come back to Cannon Beach. I remembered that sense of community with great affection."

She set the stack of books down on the coffee table, then turned a searching gaze toward him. "Forgive me, Will, but...for some reason I had the impression you weren't exactly overjoyed to see me the other day."

And he thought he'd been so careful at hiding his reaction. He shifted his weight, not sure how to answer. Any apology would only lead to explanations he was eager to avoid at all costs.

"You took me by surprise, that's all," he finally said.

"A mysterious stranger emerging from your distant past?"

"Something like that. Sixteen seems like a long, long time ago."

She nodded solemnly but said nothing. After an awkward moment, he headed for the door again.

"Anyway, I'm sorry if I seemed less than welcoming." It needed to be said, he decided. Apparently, she was going to be his neighbor and he disliked the idea of this uneasiness around her continuing. That didn't make the words any easier to get out. "You caught me at a bad moment, that's all. But I'm sorry if I gave you the impression I didn't want you here. It was nothing personal."

"I must say, that's a relief to hear."

She smiled, warm and sincere, and for just an instant he was blinded by it, remembering the surge of his blood every time he had been anywhere close to her that last summer.

Before he could make his brain work again, Sage walked up carrying one bulky box.

"What do you have in these, for Pete's sake? Did you pack along every brick from your old place?"

Julia laughed, a light, happy sound that stirred the hair on the back of his neck.

"Not bricks, but close, I'm afraid. Books. I left a lot in storage back in Boise but I couldn't bear to leave them all behind."

So that hadn't changed about her. When she was a kid, she always seemed to have her nose in a book. He and her brother used to tease her unmercifully about being a bookworm.

That last summer, he had been relentless in his efforts to drag her attention away from whatever book she was reading so she would finally notice him....

He dragged his mind away from the past and the dumb, self-absorbed jerk he'd been. He didn't want to remember those times. What was the damn point? That stupid, eager, infatuated kid was gone, buried under the weight of the years and pain that had piled up since then.

Instead, he left Sage and Julia to talk about books and headed back down the sweeping Brambleberry House stairs. On the way, he passed Anna heading back up, carrying a suitcase in each hand. He tried to take them from her but she shook him off.

"I've got these. There are some bulkier things in the U-Haul you could bring up, though."

"Sure," he answered.

In the entryway on the ground floor, he heard music coming from inside Anna's apartment. Through the open doorway, he caught a glimpse of her television set where a Disney DVD was just starting up.

Julia's twins must have finished playing and come inside. He spotted Julia's boy on the floor in front of the TV, his arm slung across Conan's back. Both of them sensed Will's presence and looked up. He started to greet them but the boy put a finger to his mouth and pointed to Abigail's favorite armchair.

Will followed his gaze and found the girl—Maddie—curled up there, fast asleep.

She looked small and fragile, with her too-pale skin and thin wrists. There was something going on with her, but he was pretty sure he was better off not knowing.

He waved to the boy, then headed down the porch steps to the waiting U-Haul.

It was nearly empty now except for perhaps a half-dozen more boxes, a finely crafted Mission-style rocking chair and something way in the back, a bulky-looking item wrapped in an old blanket that had been secured with twine.

He went for the rocking chair first. Might as well get the tough stuff out of the way. It was harder to carry than he expected—wide and solid, made of solid oak—but more awkward than really heavy.

He made it without any trouble up the porch steps and was trying to squeeze it through the narrow front door without bunging up the doorframe moldings when Sage came down the stairs.

"Okay, Superman. Let me help you with that."

"I can handle it."

"Only because of your freakish strength, maybe."

He felt his mouth quirk. Sage always managed to remind him he still had the ability to smile.

"I had my can of spinach just an hour ago so I think I've got this covered. There are a few more boxes in the U-Haul. Those ought to keep you busy and out of trouble."

She stuck her tongue out at him and he smiled at the childish gesture, with a sudden, profound gratitude for the friendship of those few people around him who had sustained him through the wrenching pain of the last two years.

"Which is it? Are you Popeye or Superman?"

"Take your pick."

"Or just a stubborn male, like the rest of your gender?" She lifted the front end of the chair. "Even Popeye and Superman need help once in awhile. Besides, we wouldn't want you to throw your back out. Then how would all our work get done around here?"

He knew when he was defeated. With a sigh, he picked up the other end. They had another minor tussle about who should walk backward up the stairs but he won that one simply by turning around and starting up.

She didn't let him gloat for long. "I understand you know our new tenant."

His gaze flashed to hers. *Uh-oh. Here comes the inquisition,* he thought. "Knew. Past tense. A long time ago."

The words were becoming like a mantra since she showed up again in Cannon Beach. *A long time ago.* But not nearly long enough. Like a riptide, the memories just

seemed to keep grabbing him out of nowhere and suck-
ing him under.

"She's lovely, isn't she?" Sage pressed as they hit the
halfway mark on the stairs. "And those kids of hers are
adorable. I can't wait until Eben and Chloe finish up their
trip to Europe in a few weeks. Chloe's going to be over the
moon at having two new friends."

"How are the wedding plans?" he asked at her mention
of her fiancé and his eight-year-old daughter. The question
was aimed more at diverting her attention than out of much
genuine interest to hear about her upcoming nuptials, but
it seemed to work.

Sage made a face. "You know I'm not good at that kind
of thing. If I had my way, I would happy with something
simple on the beach, just Eben and me and Chloe and the
preacher."

"I guess when you marry a gazillionaire hotel magnate,
sometimes you have to make sacrifices."

"It's still going to be small, just a few friends at the ceremony then a reception later at the Sea Urchin. I'm leaving
all the details to Jade and Stanley Wu."

"Smart woman."

She went on about wedding plans and he listened with
half an ear.

In a million years, he never would have expected a hip-
pie-chick like Sage to fall for a California businessman like
Eben Spencer but somehow they seemed to fit together.

Sage was more at peace than he'd ever known her, settled in a way he couldn't explain.

She was one of his closest friends and had been since she
moved to town five years ago and found herself immediately drawn into Abigail's orbit. He loved her as a little sister and he knew she deserved whatever joy she could find.

He wanted to be happy for her—and most of the time he was—but every once in a while, seeing the love and happiness that seemed to surround her and Eben when they were together was like a slow, relentless trickle of acid on an open wound.

Despite knowing Julia was inside, he was relieved as hell when they reached the top of the stairs and turned into the apartment.

"Oh, my Stickley! We bought that when I was pregnant with the twins. I know the apartment is furnished but I couldn't bear to leave it behind. Thank you so much for carrying that heavy thing all that way! That goes right here by the window so I can sit in it at night and watch the moonlight shining on the ocean."

He set it down, his mind on the rocking chair he had made Robin when she was pregnant with Cara. It was still sitting in the nursery along with the toddler bed he had made, gathering dust.

He really ought to do something with the furniture. Sage would probably know somebody who could use it....

Not today, he thought abruptly. He wasn't ready for that yet.

He turned on his heel and headed back down the stairs to retrieve that mysterious blanket-wrapped item. When he reached the U-Haul, he stood for a moment studying it, trying to figure out what it might be—and how best to carry it up the Brambleberry House stairs—when the enticing scent of cherry blossoms swirled around him.

"It's a dollhouse." Julia spoke beside him in a low voice and he automatically squared his shoulders, though what he was bracing for, he wasn't quite sure.

"My father made it for me years ago. My...late husband

tried to fix it up a little for Maddie but I'm afraid it's still falling apart. I really hope it survived the trip."

So she was a widow. They had that in common, then. He cleared his throat. "Should we take the blanket off?"

She shrugged, which he took for assent. He unwrapped the cord and heard a crunching kind of thud inside. Uh-oh. Not a good sign. With a careful look at her and a growing sense of trepidation, he pulled the blanket away and winced as Julia gasped.

Despite her obvious efforts to protect the dollhouse, the piece hadn't traveled well. The construction looked flimsy to begin with and the roof had collapsed.

One entire support wall had come loose as well and the whole thing looked like it was ready to implode.

"I'm sorry," he said, though the words seemed grossly inadequate.

"It's not your fault. I was afraid it wouldn't survive the trip. Oh, this is going to break Maddie's heart. She loved that little house."

"So did you," he guessed.

She nodded. "For a lot of reasons." She tilted her head, studying the wreckage. "You're the carpentry expert. I don't suppose there's any way I can fix this, is there?"

He gazed down at her, at the fading rays of the sun that caught gold strands in her hair, at the sorrow marring those lovely features for a lost treasure.

He gave an inward groan. Dammit, he didn't want to do this. But he was such a sucker for a woman in distress. How could he just walk away?

He cleared his throat. "If you want, I could take a look at it. See what I can do."

"Oh, I couldn't ask that of you."

"You didn't ask," he said gruffly.

She sent him a swift look. "No. I didn't."

"I'm kind of slammed with projects right now. It might take me a while to get to it. And even then, I can't make any guarantees. That's some major damage there. You might be better just starting over."

She forced a smile, though he could see the sadness lingering in her eyes. Her father had made it for her, she had said. He didn't remember much about her father from their summers in Cannon Beach, mostly that the man always seemed impatient and abrupt.

"I can't make any promises," he repeated. "But I'll see what I can do."

"Oh, that would be wonderful. Thank you so much, Will."

Together, they gathered up the shattered pieces of the dollhouse and carried them to his truck, where he set them carefully in the back between his toolbox and ladder.

"I'm happy to pay you for your time and trouble."

As if he would ever accept her money. "Don't worry about it. Let's see if I can fix it first."

She nodded and looked as if she wanted to say something more. To his vast relief, after a moment, she closed her mouth, then returned to the U-Haul for the last few boxes.

Chapter 4

Between the two of them, they were able to carry all but a few of the remaining boxes from the U-Haul up the stairs, where they found Sage and Julia pulling books out of boxes and placing them on shelves.

"You're all so wonderful to help me," Julia said, gratitude coursing through her as she smiled at all three of them. "I have to tell you, I never expected such a warm welcome. I thought it would be weeks before I would even know a soul in Cannon Beach besides Abigail. I haven't even started teaching yet but I feel as if I have instant friends."

Sage smiled. "We're thrilled to have you and the twins here. And I think Abigail would be, too. Don't you think, Will?"

He set down the boxes. "Sure. She always loved kids."

"She was nothing but a big kid herself. Remember how she used to sit out on the porch swing for hours with Cara, swinging and telling stories and singing."

"I remember," he said, his voice rough.

Color flooded Sage's features suddenly. "Oh, Will. I'm sorry."

He shook his head. "Don't, Sage. It's okay. I'd better get the last load of boxes."

He turned and headed down the stairs, leaving behind only the echo of his workboots hitting the wooden steps. Julia turned her confused gaze to Anna and Sage and found them both watching after Will with identical expressions of sadness in their eyes.

"I missed something, obviously," she said softly.

Sage gave Anna a helpless look and the other woman shrugged.

"She'll find out sooner or later," Anna said. "She might as well hear it from us."

"You're right," Sage said. "It just still hurts so much to talk about the whole thing."

"You don't have to tell me anything," Julia said quickly. "I'm sorry if I've wandered into things that are none of my business."

Sage glanced down the stairs as if checking to see if Will was returning. When she was certain he was still outside, she turned back, her voice pitched low. "Will had a daughter. She would have been a couple years younger than your twins. Cara. That's who I was talking about. Abigail adored her. We all did. She was the cutest little thing you've ever seen, just full of energy, with big blue eyes, brown curls and dimples. She was full of sugar, our Cara."

Had a daughter. Not has. An ache blossomed in her chest and she knew she didn't want to hear any more.

But she had learned many lessons over the last few years—one of the earliest was that information was empowering, even if the gaining of it was a process often drenched in pain.

"What happened?" she forced herself to ask.

Sage shook her head, her face inexpressibly sad. Anna squeezed her arm and picked up the rest of the story.

"Cara was killed along with Will's wife, Robin, two years ago." Though Anna spoke in her usual no-nonsense tone, Julia could hear the pain threading through her words.

"They were crossing the street downtown in the middle of the afternoon when they were hit by a drunk tourist in a motorhome," she went on. "Robin died instantly but Cara hung on for two weeks. We all thought—hoped—she was going to pull through but she caught an infection in the hospital in Portland and her little body was too weak and battered to fight it."

She wanted to cry, just sit right there in the middle of the floor and weep for him. More than that, she wanted to race down the stairs and hug her own precious darlings to her.

"Oh, poor Will. He must have been shattered."

"We all were," Sage said. "It was like a light went out of all of us. Will used to be so lighthearted. Like a big tease of an older brother. It's been more than two years since Robin and Cara died and I can count on one hand the number of times I've seen him genuinely smile at something since then."

The ache inside her stretched and tugged and her eyes burned with tears for the teenage boy with the mischievous eyes.

Sage touched her arm. "I'm so glad you're here now."

"Me? Why?"

"Well, you've lost someone, too. You understand, in a way the rest of us can't. I'm sure it would help Will to talk to someone who's experienced some of those same emotions."

Julia barely contained her wince, feeling like the world's biggest fraud.

"Grief is such a solitary, individual thing," she said after an awkward moment. "No one walks the same journey."

Sage smiled and pressed a cheek to Julia's. "I know. But I'm still glad you're here, and I'm sure Will is, too."

Julia was saved from having to come up with an answer to that when she again heard his footsteps on the stairs. A moment later, he came in, muscles bulging beneath the cotton of his shirt as he carried in a trio of boxes.

He had erased any trace of emotion from his features, any sign at all that he contained any emotions at all. Finding out about his wife and daughter explained so much about him. The hardness, the cynicism. The pain in his eyes when he looked at Maddie.

She had a wild urge to take the boxes from him, slip her arms around his waist and hold him until everything was all right again.

"This is the last of it. Where do these go?"

Her words tangled in her throat and she had to clear her throat before she could speak. "The top one belongs in my bedroom. The others are Simon's."

With an abrupt nod, he headed first to her room and then to the one down the hall where Simon slept.

He returned to the living room just as the doorbell downstairs rang through the house.

"Hey, Mom!" Simon yelled up the stairs an instant later. "The pizza guy's here!"

Conan started barking in accompaniment and Julia rolled her eyes at the sudden cacophony of sound. "Are you sure about this? The house was so quiet before we showed up. If you want that quiet again, you'd better speak now while I've still got the U-Haul."

Sage shook her head with a laugh. "No way. I'm not lugging those books back down the stairs. You're stuck here for a while."

Right now, she couldn't think of anywhere she would rather be. Julia flashed a quick smile to the other two women and Will, grabbed her purse, and headed down the stairs to pay for the pizza.

Simon stood at the door holding on to Conan's collar as the dog wriggled with excitement, his tail wagging a mile a minute.

Her son giggled. "I think he really likes pizza, Mom."

"I guess. Maybe you had better take him into Anna's apartment so he doesn't attack the pizza driver."

With effort, he wrangled the dog through the door and closed the door behind him. Finally, Julia opened the door and found a skinny young man with his cap on backward and his arms full of pizza boxes.

She quickly paid him for the pizza—adding in a hefty tip. She closed the door behind him and backed into the entry, her arms full, and nearly collided with a solid male.

Strong arms came around her to keep her upright.

"Oh," she exclaimed to Will. "I didn't hear you come down the stairs."

"You were talking to the driver," he answered. He quickly released her—much to her regret. She knew she shouldn't have enjoyed that brief moment of contact, but it had been so very long...

She couldn't help noticing the boy she had known now had hard strength in his very grown-up muscles.

"I thought you said the trailer was empty," she said with some confusion as he headed for the door.

"It is. You're done here so I'm heading home."

"You can't leave!" she exclaimed.

He raised an eyebrow. "I can't?"

She held out the boxes in her arms. "You've got to stay

for pizza. I ordered way too much for three women and two children."

"Don't forget Conan," he pointed out. "He's crazy about pizza, even though all that cheese is lousy for him."

"Knowing my kids, I'm sure he'll be able to sneak far more than is good for him."

The scent of him reached her, spicy and male and far more enticing than any pizza smells. "I still have too much. Please stay."

He gazed at the door with a look almost of desperation in his eyes. But when he turned back, she thought he might be weakening.

"Please, Will," she pressed.

He opened his mouth to answer but before he could, the door to Abigail's apartment opened and Maddie peeked her head out, looking tousled and sleepy.

"Can we come out now?" she asked.

"As long as the dog's not going to knock me down to get to the Canadian bacon."

At Maddie's giggle, Julia saw a spasm of pain flicker across Will's features and knew the battle was lost.

"I really can't stay." He reached for the doorknob. "Thanks anyway for the invitation, but I've got a lot of work to do at home."

She couldn't push him more, not with that shadow of pain clouding his blue eyes. Surrendering to the inevitable, she simply nodded. "You still need to eat. Take some home with you."

She could see the objections forming on his expression and decided not to take no for an answer. Will Garrett didn't know stubborn until he came up against her.

"What's your pleasure? Pepperoni or Hawaiian? I'd offer you the vegetarian but I think Sage has dibs on that one."

"It's not necessary, really."

"It is to me," she said firmly. "You just spent forty-five minutes helping me haul boxes up. You have to let me repay you somehow. Here, I hope you still like pepperoni and olive."

His eyes widened that she would remember such a detail. She couldn't have explained why—it was just one of those arcane details that stuck in her head. Several times that last summer, they'd gone to Mountain Mike's Pizza in town with her brother and Will always had picked the same thing.

"Maddie, can you hold this for a second?"

She gave the box marked pepperoni to her daughter, then with one hand she opened it and pulled out half the pizza, which she stuck on top of the Hawaiian.

He looked as if he wanted to object, but he said nothing when she handed him the box with the remaining half a pizza in it.

"Here you go. You should have enough for dinner tonight and breakfast in the morning as well. Consider it a tiny way to say thank you for all your hard work."

He shook his head but to her vast relief, he didn't hand the pizza back to her.

"Mom, I can't hold him anymore!" Simon said from behind the door. "He's starving and so am I!"

"You'd better get everyone upstairs for pizza," Will said.

"Right. Good night, then."

She wanted to say more—much more—but with a rambunctious dog and two hungry children clamoring for her attention, she had to be content with that.

Blasted stubborn woman.

Will sat on his deck watching the lights of Cannon Beach flicker on the water as he ate his third piece of pizza.

He had to admit, even lukewarm, it tasted delicious—

probably a fair sight better than the peanut butter sandwich he would have scrounged for his meal.

He didn't order pizza very often since half of it usually went to waste before he could get to the leftovers so this was a nice change from TV dinners and fast-food hamburgers.

He really needed to shoot for a healthier diet. Sage was always after him to get more vegetables and fewer preservatives into his diet. He tried but he'd never been a big one for cooking in the first place. He could grill steaks and burgers and the occasional chicken breast but he usually fell short at coming up with something to go alongside the entree.

He fell short in a lot of areas. He sighed, listening to the low rumble of the sea. He spent a lot of his free time puttering around in his dad's shop or sitting out here watching the waves, no matter what the weather. He just hated the emptiness inside the house.

He ought to move, he thought, as he did just about every night at this same time when the silence settled over him with like a scratchy, smothering wool blanket.

He ought to just pick up and make a new start somewhere. Especially now that Julia Hudson Blair had climbed out of the depths of his memories and taken up residence just a few hundred yards away.

She knew.

Sometime during the course of the evening, Sage or Anna must have told her about the accident. He wasn't quite sure how he was so certain, but he had seen a deep compassion in the green of her eyes, a sorrow that hadn't been there earlier.

He washed the pizza down with a swallow of Sam Adams—the one bottle he allowed himself each night.

He knew it shouldn't bother him so much that she knew.

Wasn't like it was some big secret. She would find out sooner or later, he supposed.

He just hated that first shock of pity when people first found out—though he supposed when it came down to it, the familiar sadness from friends like Sage and Anna wasn't much easier.

Somehow seeing that first spurt of pity in Julia's eyes made it all seem more real, more raw.

Her life hadn't been so easy. She was a widow, so she must know a thing or two about loss and loneliness. That didn't make him any more eager to have her around—or her kids.

He shouldn't have made a big deal out of the whole thing. He should have just sucked it up and stayed for pizza with her and Sage and Anna. Instead, his kneejerk reaction had been to flee and he had given into it, something very unlike him.

He sighed and took another swallow of beer. From here, he could see her bedroom light. A dark shape moved across the window and he eased back into the shadows of his empty house.

Why was he making such a big deal about this? Julia meant nothing to him. Less than nothing. He hadn't thought about her in years. Yeah, years ago he had been crazy about her when he was just a stupid, starry-eyed kid. He had dreamed about her all that last summer, when she came back to Cannon Beach without her braces and with curves in all the right places.

First love could be an intensely powerful thing for a six-teen-year-old boy. When she left Cannon Beach, his dreams of a long-distance relationship were quickly dashed when she didn't write to him as she had promised. He had tried to call the phone number she'd given him and left several messages that were never returned.

He was heartbroken for a while but he'd gotten over it. By spring, when he'd taken Robin Cramer to the prom, he had completely forgotten about Julia Hudson and her big green eyes.

Life had taught him that a tiny little nick in his heart left by a heedless fifteen-year-old girl was nothing at all to the pain of having huge, jagged chunks of his soul ripped away.

Now, sixteen years later, Julia was nothing to him. He just needed to shake this weird feeling that the careful order of the life he had painstakingly managed to piece together in the last two years had just been tossed out to sea.

He could think of no earthly reason he shouldn't be able to treat her and her children with politeness, at least.

He couldn't avoid interacting with Julia, for a dozen reasons. Beyond the minor little fact that she lived three houses down, he was still working on renovating several of the Brambleberry House rooms. He couldn't avoid her and he sure as hell couldn't run away like a coward every time he saw her kids.

He looked up at Brambleberry House again and his gaze automatically went to the second-floor window. A shape moved across again and a moment later the light went out and somehow Will felt more alone than ever.

"Thank you both again for your help today." Julia smiled at Sage and Anna across the table in her new apartment as they finished off the pizza. "I don't know what I would have done without you."

Anna shook her head. "We only helped you with the easy part. Now you have to figure out where to put everything."

"We have dishes in the kitchen and sheets on the beds. Beyond that, everything else can wait until the morning."

"Looks like some of us need to find that path there sooner than others," Sage murmured, gesturing toward Maddie.

"Not me," Maddie instantly protested, but Julia could clearly see she was drooping tonight, with her elbow propped on the table and her head resting on her fist.

Even with her short nap, Maddie still looked tired. Julia sighed. Some days dragged harder than others on Maddie's stamina. They had spent a busy day making all the arrangements to move into Brambleberry House. Maddie had helped carry some of her own things to her bedroom and had delighted in putting her toys and clothes away herself.

With all the craziness of moving in, Julia hadn't been as diligent as usual about making sure Maddie didn't overextend herself and now it looked as if she had reached the limit of her endurance.

"Time for bed, sweetie. Let's get your meds."

"I'm not ready for bed," she protested, sending a pleading look to Anna and Sage, as if they could offer a reprieve. "I want to stay up and help move in."

"I'm tuckered myself," Julia said. "I'll leave all the fun stuff for tomorrow when we're all rested, okay?"

Maddie sighed with a quiet resignation that never failed to break her heart. She caught herself giving in to the sorrow and quickly shunted it away. Her daughter was still here. She was a miracle and Julia could never allow herself to forget that.

Before she brought in any other boxes, she had made sure to put Maddie's pill regimen away in a cabinet by the kitchen sink. She poured a glass of water and handed them to her. With the ease of long, grim practice, Maddie downed the half-dozen pills in two swallows, then finished the water to flush down the pills.

Because her daughter seemed particularly tired, Julia helped her into her pajamas then did a quick set of vitals. Everything was within normal ranges for Maddie so Julia pushed away her lingering worry.

"Good night, sweetie," she said after a quick story and kiss. "Your first sleep in the new house!"

"I like this place," Maddie said sleepily as Julia pulled the nightgown over her thin shoulders.

"I like it, too. It feels like home, doesn't it?"

Maddie nodded. "And the lady is nice."

Julia smiled. "Which one? Sage or Anna? I think they're both pretty nice."

Maddie shook her head but her eyes drooped closed before she could answer.

Julia watched her sleep for a moment, marveling again at the lessons in courage and strength and grace her daughter had taught her these last few years.

A miracle, she thought again. As she stood watching over her, she felt the oddest sensation, almost like feather-light fingers touching her cheek.

Weird, she thought. Sage and Anna had warned her Brambleberry House was a typical drafty old house. She would have to do her best to seal up any cracks in Maddie's room.

When she returned to the other room, she found only Simon, curled up in the one corner of the couch not covered in boxes. He had a book in one hand and was petting Conan absently with the other.

What a blessing her son loved to read. Books and his Game Boy had sustained him through many long, boring doctor appointments.

"Did Sage and Anna go downstairs?" she asked.

"I think they're still in the kitchen," Simon answered without looking up from his book.

She heard low, musical laughter before she reached the kitchen. For a moment, she stood in the doorway watching them as they unloaded her grandmother's china into the built-in cabinet.

Here was another blessing. She was overflowing with them. She had come back to Cannon Beach with only a teaching position and her hope that everything would work out. Now she had this great apartment overlooking the sea and, more importantly, two unexpected new friends who were already becoming dear to her.

She didn't think she made a sound but Sage suddenly sensed her presence. She glanced toward her, her exotic tilted eyes lighting in welcome.

"Our girl is all settled for the night?"

Julia nodded. "It was a hectic day. She wore herself out."

"Is she all right?" Anna asked, her features tight with concern.

"Yes. She's fine. She just doesn't have the stamina she used to have." She paused, deciding it was time to reveal everything. "It's one of the long-term side effects of her bone marrow transplant."

"Bone marrow transplant?" Anna exclaimed, her eyes wide with a shock mirrored on Sage's features.

Julia sighed. "Yes. And a round of radiation and two rounds of chemotherapy. I probably should have told you this earlier but Maddie is in remission from acute lymphocytic leukemia."

Chapter 5

Saying the words aloud always left her feeling vaguely queasy, as if she were the one who had endured months of painful treatments, shots, blood draws, the works.

She found it quite a lowering realization that Maddie had faced her cancer ordeal with far more courage than Julia had been able to muster as her mother.

"Oh, Julia." Sage stepped forward and wrapped her into a spontaneous hug. "I'm so sorry you've all had to go through this."

"It's been a pretty bumpy road," she admitted. "But as I said, she's in remission and she's doing well. Much better since the bone marrow transplant. Simon was the donor. We were blessed that they were a perfect match."

"You've had to go through this all on your own?" Anna's dark eyes looked huge and sad.

She knew Anna was referring to Kevin's death and the timing of it. She decided she wasn't quite ready to delve into those explanations just yet so she chose to evade the question.

"I had a strong support network in Boise," she said instead. "Good friends, my brother and his wife, my co-workers at the elementary school there. They all think I'm crazy to move away."

"Why did you?" Anna asked.

"We were all ready for a change. A new start. Three months ago, Maddie's oncologist took a new job at the children's hospital in Portland. Dr. Lee had been such a support and comfort to us and when she moved, it seemed like the perfect time for us to venture back out in the world."

She sometimes felt as if their lives had been on hold for three years. Between Maddie's diagnosis, then Kevin's death, she and her children had endured far too much.

They needed laughter and joy and the peace she had always found by the ocean.

She smiled at the two other women. "I have to tell you both, I was still wondering if I had made a terrible mistake leaving behind our friends and the safe cushion of support we had in Boise, until we saw the for-rent sign out front of Brambleberry House. It seemed like a miracle that we might have the chance to live in the very house I had always loved so much when I was a little girl, the house where I had always found peace. I took that sign as an omen that everything would be okay."

"We're so glad you found us," Anna said.

"You belong here," Sage added. She squeezed Julia's fingers with one hand and reached for Anna's hand with the other, linking them all together and Julia had to fight back tears, overwhelmed by their easy acceptance of her.

She realized she felt happier standing in this warm

kitchen with these women than she could remember being in a long, long time.

"Thank you," she said softly. "Thank you both."

"You smell that?" Sage demanded after a moment.

Anna rolled her eyes. "Cut it out, Sage."

"Smell what?" Julia asked.

"Freesia," Sage answered. "You smelled it, too, didn't you?"

"I thought it was coming from the open window."

Sage shook her head. "Nope. As much as she loved it, Abigail could never get any freesia bulbs to survive in her garden. Our microclimate is just not conducive to them."

"I hope you're not squeamish about ghosts," Anna said after a long sigh. "Sage insists Abigail is still here at Brambleberry House, that she flits through the house leaving behind the freesia perfume she always wore."

Julia blinked, astonished. It seemed preposterous—until she remembered Maddie's words that the lady was nice, and that soft brush against her skin when she had been standing in Maddie's room looking over her daughter almost as if someone had touched her tenderly.

She fought back a shiver.

"You don't buy it?" she said to Anna.

Anna laughed. "I don't know. I usually tend to fall on the side of logic and reason. My intellect tells me it's a complete impossibility. But then, I can't put anything past Abigail. It wouldn't surprise me at all if she decided to defy the rules of metaphysics and stick around in this house she loved. If it's at all within the realm of possibility, Abigail would find a way."

"And Conan is her familiar," Sage added. "You probably ought to know that up front, too. I think the two of them are a team. If Abigail is the brains of the outfit, he's the muscle."

"Okay, now you're obviously putting me on."

Sage shook her head.

"Conan. The dog."

Sage grinned. "Don't look at me like I'm crazy. Just watch and see. The dog is spooky."

"On that, at least, we can agree," Anna said, setting the last majolica teacup in the cupboard. "He's far smarter than your average dog."

"I've seen that much already," Julia admitted. "I'm sorry, but it's a bit of a stretch for me to go from thinking he's an uncommonly smart dog to buying the theory that he's some kind of conduit from the netherworld."

Sage laughed. "Put like that, it does sound rather ridiculous, doesn't it? Just keep your eyes open. You can judge for yourself after you've been here awhile. I wanted to put a disclosure in the rental agreement about Abigail but Anna wouldn't let me."

Anna made a face. "It's a little tough to find an attorney who will add a clause that we might have a ghost in the house."

"There's no *might* about it. You wait and see, Julia."

A ghost and a dog/medium. She supposed there were worst things she could be dealing with in an apartment. "I hope she is still here. I can't imagine Abigail would be anything but a benevolent spirit."

Sage grinned at her. Anna shook her head, but she was smiling as well. "I see I'm outnumbered in the sanity department."

"You're just better at being a grown-up," Sage answered. Her teasing slid away quickly, though, replaced with concern. "And on that note, is there anything special we need to worry about with Maddie? Environmental things she shouldn't be exposed to or anything?"

Julia sighed. She would much rather ponder lighthearted theories of the supernatural than bump up against the harsh reality of her daughter's illness and recovery.

"It's a tough line I walk between wrapping her up in cotton wool to protect her and encouraging as normal a life as possible. Most of the time she's fine, if a little more subdued than she once was. You probably wouldn't know it but she used to be the spitfire of the twins. When they were toddlers, she was always the one leading Simon into trouble."

She gave a wobbly smile and was warmed when Anna reached out and squeezed her hand.

A moment passed before she could trust her voice to continue. "Right now we need to work on trying to regain the strength she lost through the month she spent in the hospital with the bone marrow transplant. I hope by Christmas things will be better."

Sage smiled. "Well, now you've got two more of us— four, counting Abigail and Conan—on your side."

"Thank you," she whispered, immeasurably touched at their effortless acceptance of her and her children.

After Simon was finally settled in bed, Julia stood in her darkened bedroom gazing out at the ripples of the sea gleaming in the moonlight. Though she had a million things to do—finding bowls they could use for cereal in the morning hovered near the top of her list—she decided she needed this moment to herself to think, without rushing to take care of detail after detail.

Offshore some distance, she could see the moving lights of a sea vessel cutting through the night. She watched it for a moment, then her gaze inexorably shifted to the houses along the shore.

There was the cottage where her family had always stayed, sitting silent and dark. Beyond that was Will Garrett's house. A light burned inside a square cedar building set away from the house. His father's workshop, she remembered. Now it would be Will's.

She glanced at her watch and saw it was nearly midnight. What was he working on so late? And did he spend his time out in his workshop to avoid the emptiness inside his house?

She pressed a hand to her chest at the ache there. How did he bear the pain of losing his wife and his child? She remembered the vast sorrow in his gaze when he had looked at Maddie and she wanted so much to be able to offer some kind of comfort to him.

She sensed he wouldn't want her to try. Despite his friendship with Sage and Anna, Will seemed to hold himself apart, as if he had used his carpentry skills to carefully hammer out a wall between himself and the rest of the world.

She ached for him, but she knew there was likely very little she could do to breach those walls.

She could try.

The thought whispered through her head with soft subtlety. She shook her head at her own subconscious. No. She had enough on her plate right now, moving to a new place, taking on a new job, dealing with twins on her own, one of whom still struggled with illness.

She didn't have the emotional reserves to take on anyone else's pain. She knew it, but as the peace of the house settled around her, she had the quiet conviction that she could at least offer him her friendship.

As if in confirmation, the sweet, summery scent of free-sia drifted through the room. She smiled.

"Abigail, if you are still here," she whispered, "thank you. For this place, for Anna and Sage. For everything."

For just an instant, she thought she felt again the gentle brush of fingers against her cheek.

Will managed to avoid his new neighbors for several days, mostly because he was swamped with work. He was contracted to do the carpentry work on a rehab project in Manzanita. The job was behind schedule because of other subcontractors' delays and the developer wanted the car-pentry work done yesterday.

Will was pouring every waking moment into it, leav-ing his house before the sun was up and returning close to midnight every night.

He didn't mind working hard. Having too much work to do was a damn sight better than having too little. Building something with his hands helped fill the yawning chasm of his life.

But his luck where his neighbors were concerned ran out a week after he had helped carry boxes up to the second-floor apartment of Brambleberry House.

By Friday, most of the basic work on the construction job was done and the only thing left was for him to install the custom floor and ceiling moldings the developer had ordered from a mill in Washington State. They hadn't been delivered yet and until they arrived, he had nothing to do.

Finally he returned to Cannon Beach, to his empty house and his empty life.

After showering off the sawdust and sweat from a hard day's work, he was grilling a steak on the deck—his nightly beer in hand—watching tourists fly kites and play in the sand in the pleasant early evening breeze when he suddenly heard excited barking.

A moment later, a big red mutt bounded into view, trailing the handle of his retractable leash.

As soon as he spied Will, he switched directions and bounded up the deck steps, his tongue lolling as he panted heavily.

"You look like a dog on the lam."

Conan did that weird grin thing of his and Will glanced down the beach to see who might have been on the other end of the leash. He couldn't see anyone—not really surprising. Though he seemed pondeorus most of the time, Conan could pour on the juice when he wanted to escape his dreaded leash and be several hundred yards down the beach before you could blink.

When he turned back to the dog, he found him sniffing with enthusiasm around the barbecue.

"No way," Will muttered. "Get your own steak. I'm not sharing."

Conan whined and plopped down at his feet with such an obviously feigned morose expression that Will had to smile. "You're quite the actor, aren't you? No steak for you tonight but I will get you a drink. You look like you could use it."

He found the bowl he usually used for Conan and filled it from the sink. When he walked back through the sliding doors, he heard a chorus of voices calling the dog's name.

Somehow, he supposed he wasn't really surprised a moment later when Julia Blair and her twins came into view from the direction of Brambleberry House.

Conan barked a greeting, his head hanging over the deck railing. Three heads swiveled in their direction and even from here, he could see the relief in Julia's green eyes when she spotted the dog.

"There you are, you rascal," she exclaimed.

With her hair held back from her face in a ponytail, she looked young and lovely in the slanted early evening light. Though he knew it was unwise, part of him wanted to just sit and savor the sight of her, a little guilty reward for putting in a hard day's work.

Shocked at the impulse, he set down Conan's bowl so hard some water slopped over the side.

"I'm so sorry," Julia called up. Though he wanted to keep them off the steps like he was some kind of medieval knight defending his castle from assault, he stood mutely by as she and her twins walked up the stairs to the deck.

"We were taking him for a walk on the beach," Julia went on, "but we apparently weren't moving quickly enough for him."

"It's my fault," the boy—Simon—said, his voice morose. "Mom said I had to hold his leash tight and I tried, I really did, but I guess I wasn't strong enough."

"I'm sure it's not your fault," Will said through a throat that suddenly felt tight. "Conan can be pretty determined when he sets his mind to something."

Simon grinned at him with a new warmth. "I guess he had his mind set on running away."

"We were going to get an ice cream," the girl said in her whispery voice. He had no choice but to look at her, with her dark curls and blue eyes. A sense of frailty clung to her, as if the slightest breeze would pick her up and carry her out to sea.

He didn't know how to talk to her—didn't know if he could. But he had made a pledge not to hurt others simply because he was in pain. He supposed that included little dark-haired sea sprites.

"That sounds like fun. A great thing to do on a pretty summer night like tonight."

"My favorite ice cream is strawberry cheesecake," she announced. "I really hope they have some."

"Not me," Simon announced. "I like bubblegum. Especially when it's blue bubblegum."

To his dismay, Julia's daughter crossed the deck until she was only a few feet away. She looked up at him out of serious eyes. "What about you, Mr. Garrett?" Maddie asked. "Do you like ice cream?"

Surface similarities aside, she was not at all like his roly-poly little Cara, he reminded himself. "Sure. Who doesn't?"

"What kind is your favorite?"

"Hmmm. Good question. I hate to be boring but I really like plain old vanilla."

Simon hooted. "That's what my mom's favorite flavor is, too. With all the good flavors out there—licorice or coconut or chocolate chunk—why would you ever want plain vanilla? That's just weird."

"Simon!" Julia's cheeks flushed and he thought again how extraordinarily lovely she was—not much different from the girl he'd been so crazy about nearly two decades ago.

"Well, it is," Simon insisted.

"You don't tell someone they're weird," Julia said.

"I didn't say *he* was weird. Just that eating only vanilla ice cream is weird."

Will found himself fighting a smile, which startled him all over again. "Okay, I'll admit I also like praline ice cream and sometimes even chocolate chip on occasion. Is that better?"

Simon snickered. "I guess so."

He felt the slightest brush of air and realized it was Maddie touching his arm with her small, pale hand. Suddenly he couldn't seem to catch his breath, aching inside.

"Would you like to come with us to get an ice-cream cone, Mr. Garrett?" she asked in her breathy voice. "I bet if you were holding Conan's leash, he couldn't get away."

He glanced at her sweet little features then at Julia. The color had climbed even higher on her cheekbones and she gave him an apologetic look before turning back to her daughter.

"Honey, I'm sure Mr. Garrett is busy. It smells like he's cooking a steak for his dinner."

"Which I'd better check on. Hang on."

He lifted the grill and found his porterhouse a little on the well-done side, but still edible. He shut off the flame, using the time to consider how to answer the girl.

He shouldn't be so tempted to go with them. It was an impulse that shocked the hell out of him.

He had spent two years avoiding social situations except with his close friends. But suddenly the idea of sitting here alone eating his dinner and watching others enjoy life seemed unbearable.

How could he possibly go with them, though? He wasn't sure he trusted himself to be decent for an hour or so, the time it would take to walk to the ice-cream place, enjoy their cones, then walk home.

What if something set him off and brought back that bleak darkness that always seemed to hover around the edges of his psyche? The last thing he wanted to do was hurt these innocent kids.

"Thanks for the invitation," he said, "but I'd better stay here and finish my dinner."

Conan whined and butted his head against Will's leg, almost as if urging Will to reconsider.

"We can wait for you to eat," Simon said promptly. "We don't mind, do we, Mom?"

"Simon, Mr. Garrett is busy. We don't want to badger him." She met his gaze, her green eyes soft with an expression he couldn't identify. "Though we would love to have you come along. All of us."

"I don't want you to have to wait for me to eat when you've got strawberry cheesecake and bubblegum ice-cream cones calling your name."

Julia nodded rather sadly, as if she had expected his answer. "Come on, kids. We'd better be on our way."

Conan whined again. Will gazed from the dog to Julia and her family, then he shook his head. "Then again, I guess there's no reason I can't warm my steak up again when we get back from the ice-cream parlor. I'm not that hungry right now anyway."

His statement was met with a variety of reactions. Conan barked sharply, Julia's eyes opened wide with surprise, Simon gave a happy shout and Maddie clapped her hands with delight.

It had been a long time since anyone had seemed so thrilled about his company, he thought as he carried his steak inside to cover it with foil and slide it in the refrigerator.

He didn't know what impulse had prompted him to agree to go along with them. He only knew it had been a long while since he had allowed himself to enjoy the quiet peace of an August evening on the shore.

Maybe it was time.

Chapter 6

This was a mistake of epic proportions.

Will walked alongside Julia while her twins moved ahead with Conan. Simon raced along with the dog, holding tightly to his leash as the two of them scared up a shorebird here and there and danced just out of reach of the waves. Maddie seemed content to walk sedately toward the ice-cream stand in town, stopping only now and again to pick something up from the sand, study it with a serious look, then plop it in her pocket.

Will was painfully conscious of the woman beside him. Her hair shimmered in the dying sunlight, her cheeks were pinkened from the wind, and the soft, alluring scent of cherry blossoms clung to her, feminine and sweet.

He couldn't come up with a damn thing to say and he felt like he was an awkward sixteen-year-old again.

Accompanying her little family to town was just about the craziest idea he had come up with in a long, long time.

She didn't seem to mind the silence but he finally decided good manners compelled him to at least make a stab at conversation.

"How are you settling in?" he asked.

She smiled softly. "It's been lovely. Perfect. You know, I wasn't sure I was making the right choice to move here but everything has turned out far better than I ever dreamed."

"The apartment working out for you, then?"

"It's wonderful. We love it at Brambleberry House. Anna and Sage have become good friends and the children love being so close to the ocean. It's been a wonderful adventure for us all so far."

He envied her that, he realized. The sense of adventure, the willingness to charge headlong into the unknown. He had always been content to stay in the house where he had been raised. He loved living on the coast—waking up to the sound of scoters and grebes, sleeping to the murmuring song of the sea—but lately he sometimes felt as if he were suffocating here. It was impossible to miss the way everyone in town guarded their words around him and worse, watched him out of sad, careful eyes.

Maybe it was time to move on. It wasn't a new thought but as he walked beside Julia toward the lights of town, he thought perhaps he ought to do just as she had—start over somewhere new.

She was looking at him in expectation, as if she had said something and was waiting for him to respond. He couldn't think what he might have missed and he hesitated to ask her to repeat herself. Instead, he decided to pick a relatively safe topic.

"School starts in a few weeks, right?" he asked.

"A week from Tuesday," she said after a small pause. "I plan to go in and start setting up my classroom tomorrow."

"Does it take you a whole week to set up?"

"Oh, at least a week!" Animation brightened her features even more. "I'm way behind. I've got bulletin boards to decorate, class curriculum to plan, students' pictures and names to memorize. Everything."

Her voice vibrated with excitement and despite his discomfort, he almost smiled. "You can't wait, can you?"

She flashed him a quick look. "Is it that obvious?"

"I'm glad you've found something you enjoy. I'll admit, back in the day, I wouldn't have pegged you for a schoolteacher."

She laughed. "I guess my plans to be a rich and famous diva someday kind of fell by the wayside. Teaching thirty active fifth-graders isn't quite as exciting as going on tour and recording a platinum-selling record."

"I bet you're good at it, though."

She blinked in surprise, then gave him a smile of such pure, genuine pleasure that he felt his chest tighten.

"Thank you, Will. That means a lot to me."

Their gazes met and though it had been a long, long time, he knew he didn't mistake the currents zinging between them.

A gargantuan mistake.

He was almost relieved when they caught up with Maddie, who had slowed her steps considerably.

"You doing okay, cupcake?" Julia asked.

"I'm fine, Mommy," she assured her, though her features were pale and her mouth hung down a little at the edges.

He wondered again what the story was here—why Julia watched her so carefully, why Maddie seemed so frail—but now didn't seem the appropriate time to ask.

"Do you need a piggyback ride the rest of the way to the ice-cream stand?" Julia asked.

Maddie shook her head with more firmness than before, as if that brief rest had been enough for her. "I can make it, I promise. We're almost there, aren't we?"

"Yep. See, there's the sign with the ice-cream cone on it."

Somehow Maddie slipped between them and folded her hand in her mother's. She smiled up at Will and his chest ached all over again.

"I love this place," Maddie announced when they drew closer to Murphy's Ice Cream.

"I do, too," Will told her. "I've been coming here for ice cream my whole life."

She looked intrigued. "Really? My mom said she used to come here, too, when she was little." She paused to take a breath before continuing. "Did you ever see her here?"

He glanced at Julia and saw her cheeks had turned pink and he wondered if she was remembering holding hands under one of the picnic tables that overlooked the beach and stealing kisses whenever her brother wasn't looking.

"I did," he said gruffly, wishing those particular memories had stayed buried.

Maddie looked as if she wanted to pursue the matter but by now they had reached Murphy's.

He hadn't thought this whole thing through, he realized as they approached the walk-up window. Rats. Inside, he could see Lacy Murphy Walker, who went to high school with him and whose family had owned and operated the ice-cream parlor forever.

She had been one of Robin's best friends—and as much as he loved her, he was grimly aware that Lacy also happened to be one of the biggest gossips in town.

"Hi, Will." She beamed with some surprise. "Haven't seen you in here in an age."

He had no idea how to answer that so he opted to stick with a polite smile.

"We're sure loving the new cabinets in the back," she went on. "You did a heck of a job on them. I was saying the other day how much more storage space we have now."

"Thanks, Lace."

Inside, he could see the usual assortment of tourists but more than a few local faces he recognized. The scene was much the same on the picnic tables outside.

His neck suddenly itched from the speculative glances he was getting from those within sight—and especially from Lacy.

She hadn't stopped staring at him and at Julia and her twins since he walked up to the counter.

"You folks ready to order?"

He hadn't been lumped into a *folks* in a long time and it took him a moment to adjust.

Sometimes he thought that was one of the things he had missed the most the last two years, being part of a unit, something bigger and better than himself.

"Hang on," he said, turning back to Julia and her twins. "Have you decided?" he asked, in a voice more terse than he intended.

"Bubblegum!" Simon exclaimed. "In a sugar cone."

Lacy wrote it down with a smile. "And for the young lady?"

Maddie gifted Lacy with a particularly sweet smile. "Strawberry cheesecake, please," she whispered. "I would like a sugar cone, too."

"Got it." Again Lacy turned her speculative gaze at him and Julia, standing together at the counter. "And for the two of you?"

The two of you. He wanted to tell her there was no *two*

of you. They absolutely were *not* a couple, just two completely separate individuals who happened to walk down the beach together for ice cream.

"Two scoops of vanilla in a sugar cone," he said.

"Make that two of those." Julia smiled at Lacy and he felt a little light-headed. It was only because he hadn't eaten, he told himself. Surely his reaction had nothing to do with the cherry blossom scent of her that smelled sweeter than anything coming out of the ice cream shop.

Lacy gave them the total and Will pulled out his wallet.

"My treat," he said, sliding a bill to Lacy.

She reached for it at the same time Julia did.

"It is not!" Julia exclaimed. "You weren't even planning to come along until we hounded you into it. Forget it, I'm paying."

Even more speculative glances were shooting their way. He could see a couple of his mother's friends inside and was afraid they would be on the phone to her at her retirement village in San Diego before Lacy even scooped their cones.

Above all, he wanted to avoid attention and just win this battle so they could find a place to sit, preferably one out of view of everyone inside.

"Nobody hounded anybody. I wanted to come." *For one brief second of insanity,* he thought, but didn't add. "I'm paying this time. You can pick it up next time."

The minute the words escaped his mouth, he saw Lacy's eyes widen. *Next time,* he had said. Rats. He could just picture the conversation that would be buzzing around town within minutes.

You hear about Will Garrett? He's finally dating again, the new teacher living in Abigail's house. The pretty widow with those twins. Remember, her family used to rent the old Turner place every summer.

He grimaced to himself, knowing there wasn't a darn thing he could do about it. When a person lived in the same town his whole life, everybody seemed to think they had a stake in his business.

"Are you sure?" Julia still looked obstinate.

He nodded. "Take it, Lace," he said.

To his vast relief, she ended the matter by stuffing the bill into the cash register and handing him his change.

"It should just be a minute," she said in a chirpy kind of voice. She disappeared from the counter, probably to go looking for her cell phone so she could start spreading the word.

"Thank you," Julia said, though she still looked uncomfortable about letting him treat.

"No problem."

"It really doesn't seem fair. You didn't even want to come with us."

"I'm here, aren't I? It's fine."

She looked as if she had something more to say but after a moment she closed her mouth and let the matter rest when Lacy returned with the twins' cones.

"Here you go. The other two are coming right up."

"Great service as always, Lacy," he said when she handed him and Julia their cones. "Thanks."

"Oh, no problem, Will." She smiled brightly. "And let me just say for the record that it's so great to see you out enjoying…ice cream again."

Heat soaked his face and he could only hope he wasn't blushing. He hadn't blushed in about two decades and he sure as hell didn't want to start now.

"Right," he mumbled, and was relieved when Simon spoke up.

"Hey, Mom, our favorite table is empty. Can we sit out there and watch for whales?"

Julia smiled and shook her head ruefully. "We've been here twice and sat at the same picnic table both times. I guess that makes it our favorite."

She studied Will. "Are you in a hurry to get back or do you mind eating our cones here?"

He would rather just take a dip in the cold waters of the Pacific right about now, if only to avoid the watching eyes of everyone in town. Instead, he forced a smile.

"No big rush. Let's sit down."

He made the mistake of glancing inside the ice-cream parlor one time as he was sliding into the picnic table across from her—just long enough to see several heads swivel quickly away from him.

With a sigh, he resigned himself to the rumors. Nothing he could do about them now anyway.

She was quite certain Conan was a canine but just now he was looking remarkably like the proverbial cat with its mouth stuffed full of canary feathers.

Julia frowned at the dog, who settled beside the picnic table with what looked suspiciously like a grin. Sage and Anna said he had an uncanny intelligence and some hidden agenda but she still wasn't sure she completely bought it.

More likely, he was simply anticipating a furtive taste of one of the twins' cones.

If Conan practically hummed with satisfaction, Will resembled the plucked canary. He ate his cone with a stoicism that made it obvious he wasn't enjoying the treat—or the company—in the slightest.

She might have been hurt if she didn't find it so terribly sad.

She grieved for him, for the boy she had known with the teasing smile and the big, generous heart. His loss was staggering, as huge as the Pacific, and she wanted so desperately to ease it for him.

What power did she have, though? Precious little, especially when he would only talk in surface generalities about mundane topics like the tide schedule and the weather.

She tried to probe about the project he was working on, an intriguing rehabilitation effort down the coast, but he seemed to turn every question back to her and she was tired of talking about herself.

She was also tired of the curious eyes inside. Good heavens, couldn't the poor man go out for ice cream without inciting a tsunami of attention? If he wasn't being so unapproachable, she would have loved to give their tongues something to wag about.

How would Will react if she just grabbed the cone out of his hand, tossed it over her shoulder into the sand, and planted a big smacking kiss on his mouth, just for the sheer wicked thrill of watching how aghast their audience might turn?

It was an impulse from her youth, when she had been full of silly dreams and impetuous behavior. She wouldn't do it now, of course. Not only would a kiss horrify Will but her children were sitting at the table and they wouldn't understand the subtleties of social tit-for-tat.

The idea was tempting, though. And not just to give the gossips something to talk about.

She sighed. It would be best all the way around if she just put those kind of thoughts right out of her head. She had been alone for two years and though she might have longed for a man's touch, she wasn't about to jump into anything with someone still deep in the grieving process.

"What project are you working on next at Brambleberry House?" she asked him.

"New ceiling and floor moldings in Abigail's old apartment, where Anna lives now," he answered. "On the project I'm working on in Manzanita, the developer ordered some custom patterns. I liked them and showed them to Anna and she thought they would be perfect for Brambleberry House so we ordered extra."

"What was wrong with the old ones?"

"They were cracking and warped in places from water damage a long time ago. We tried to repair them but it was becoming an endless process. And then when she decided to take down a few walls, the moldings in the different rooms didn't match so we decided to replace them all with something historically accurate."

He started to add more, but Maddie slid over to him and held out her cone.

"Mr. Garrett, would you like to try some of my strawberry cheesecake ice cream? It's really good."

A slight edge of panic appeared around the edges of his gaze. "Uh, no thanks. Think I'll stick with my vanilla."

She accepted his answer with equanimity. "You might change your mind, though," she said, with her innate generosity. "How about if I eat it super slow? That way if decide you want some after all, I'll still have some left for you to try later, okay?"

He blinked and she saw the nerves give way to astonishment. "Uh, thanks," he said, looking so touched at the small gesture that her heart broke for him all over again.

Maddie smiled her most endearing smile, the particularly charming one she had perfected on doctors over the years. "You're welcome. Just let me know if you want a taste. I don't mind sharing, I promise."

He looked like a man who had just been stabbed in the heart and Julia suddenly couldn't bear his pain. In desperation, she sought a way to distract him.

"What will you do on Brambleberry House after you finish the moldings?" she finally asked.

He looked grateful for the diversion. "Uh, your apartment is mostly done but the third-floor rooms still need some work. Little stuff, mostly, but inconvenient to try to live around. I figured I would wait to start until after Sage is married and living part-time in the Bay Area with Eben and Chloe."

"I understand they're coming back soon from an extended trip overseas. We've heard a great deal about them from Sage and Anna. The twins can't wait to meet Chloe."

"She's a good kid. And Eben is good for Sage. That's the important thing."

He was a man who loved his friends, she realized. That, at least, hadn't changed over the years.

He seemed embarrassed by his statement and quickly returned to talking about the repairs planned for Brambleberry House. She listened to his deep voice as she savored the last of her cone, thinking it was a perfect summer evening.

The children finished their treats—Maddie's promise to Will notwithstanding—and were romping with Conan in the sand. Their laugher drifted on the breeze above the sound of the ocean.

For just an instant, she was transported back in time, sitting with Will atop a splintery picnic table, eating ice-cream cones and laughing at nothing and talking about their dreams.

By unspoken agreement, they stood, cones finished, and

started walking back down the beach while Conan herded the twins along ahead of them.

"I'm boring you to tears," Will said after some time. "I'm sorry. I, uh, don't usually go on and on like that about my work."

She shook her head. "You're not boring me. On the contrary. I enjoy hearing about what you do. You love it, don't you?"

"It's just a job. Not something vitally important to the future of the world like educating young minds."

She made a face. "My, you have a rosy view of educators, don't you?"

"I always had good teachers when I was going to school."

"Good teachers wouldn't have anywhere to teach those young minds if not for great carpenters like you," she pointed out. "The work you've done on Brambleberry House is lovely. The kitchen cupboards are as smooth as a satin dress. Anna told me you made them all by hand."

"It's a great old house. I'm trying my best to do it justice."

They walked in silence for a time and Julia couldn't escape the grim realization that she was every bit as attracted to him now as she had been all those years ago.

Not true, she admitted ruefully. Technically, anyway. She was far *more* aware of him now, as a full-grown woman— with a woman's knowledge and a woman's needs—than she ever would have been as a naive, idealistic fifteen-year-old girl.

He was bigger than he had been then, several inches taller and much more muscled. His hair was cut slightly shorter than it had been when he was a teenager and he had a few laugh lines around his mouth and his eyes, though she had a feeling those had been etched some time ago.

She was particularly aware of his hands, square-tipped and strong, with the inevitable battle scars of a man who used them in creative and constructive ways.

She didn't want to notice anything about him and she certainly wasn't at all thrilled to find herself attracted to him again. She couldn't afford it. Not when she and her children were just finding their way again.

Hadn't she suffered enough from emotionally unavailable men?

"Look what I found, Mom!" Maddie uncurled her fingers to reveal a small gnarled object. "What is it?"

As she studied the object, Julia held her daughter's hand, trying not to notice how thin her fingers seemed. It appeared to be an agate but was an odd color, greenish gray with red streaks in it.

"We forgot to bring our rocky coast field book, didn't we? We'll have to look it up when we get back to the house."

"Do you know, Mr. Garrett?" Maddie presented the object for Will's inspection.

"I'm afraid I'm not much of a naturalist," he said, rather curtly. "Sage is your expert in that department. She can tell you in a second."

"Oh. Okay." Maddie's shoulders slumped, more from fatigue than disappointment, Julia thought, but Will didn't pick up on it. Guilt flickered in his expression.

"I can look at it," he said after a moment. "Let's see."

Will reached for her hand and he examined the contents carefully. "Wow. This is quite a find. It's a bloodstone agate."

"I want to see," Simon said.

"It's pretty rare," Will said. He talked to them about some of the other treasures they could find beachcombing on the coast until they reached his house.

"I guess this is your stop," Julia said as they stood at the steps of his deck.

He glanced up the steps, as if eager to escape, then looked back at them. "I'll walk you the rest of the way to Brambleberry House. It's nearly dark. I wouldn't want you walking on your own."

It was only three houses, she almost said, but he looked so determined to stick it out that she couldn't bring herself to argue.

"Thank you," she said, then gave Maddie a careful look. Her daughter hadn't said much for some time, since finding the bloodstone.

"Is it piggyback time?" Julia asked quietly.

Maddie shrugged, her features dispirited. "I guess so. I really wanted to make it the whole way on my own this time."

"You made it farther this time than last time. And farther still than the time before. Come on, pumpkin. Your chariot awaits." Julia crouched down and her daughter climbed aboard.

"I can carry her," Will said, though he looked as if he would rather stick a nail gun to his hand and pull the switch.

"I've got her," she answered, aching for him all over again. "But you can make sure Simon and Conan stay away from the surf."

They crossed the last hundred yards to Brambleberry House in silence. When they reached the back gate, Will held it open for them and they walked inside where the smells of Abigail's lush late-summer flowers surrounded them in warm welcome.

She eased Maddie off her back. "You two take Conan inside to get a drink from Anna while I talk to Mr. Garrett, okay?"

"Okay," Simon said, and headed up the steps. Maddie followed more slowly but a moment later Julia and Will were alone with only the sound of the wind sighing in the tops of the pine trees.

"What's wrong with Maddie?"

His quiet voice cut through the peace of the night and she instinctively bristled, wanting to protest that nothing was wrong with her child. Absolutely nothing. Maddie was perfect in every way.

The words tangled in her throat. "She's recovering from a bone marrow transplant," she answered in a low voice to match his. It wasn't any grand secret and he certainly deserved to know, though she didn't want to go through more explanations.

"It's been four months but she hasn't quite regained her strength. She's been a fighter through everything life has thrown at her the last two and a half years, though—two rounds of chemo and a round of radiation—so I know it's only a matter of time before she'll be back to her old self."

Chapter 7

He heard her words as if she whispered them on the wind from a long distance away.

Bone marrow transplant. Chemotherapy. Radiation. Cancer.

He had suspected Maddie was ill, but *cancer*. Damn it. The thought of that sweet-faced little girl enduring that kind of nightmare plowed into him like a semitruck and completely knocked him off his pins.

"I'm sorry, Julia."

The words seemed horrifyingly inadequate but he didn't have the first idea what else to say in this kind of situation. Besides, hadn't he learned after the dark abyss of the last two years that sometimes the simplest of sentiments meant the most?

The sun had finally slipped beyond the horizon and in the dusky twilight, she looked young and lovely and as fragile as her daughter.

"It's been a long, tough journey," she answered. "But I have great hope that we're finally starting to climb through to the other side."

He envied her that hope, he realized. That's what had been missing in his world for two years—for too long there had seemed no escape to the unrelenting pain. He missed Robin, he missed Cara, he missed the man he used to be.

But this wasn't about him, he reminded himself. One other lesson he had learned since the accident that stole his family was that very few people made it through life unscathed, without suffering or pain, and Julia had obviously seen more than her share.

"A year and a half, you said. So you must have had to cope with losing your husband in the midst of dealing with Maddie's cancer?"

In the twilight, he saw her mouth open then close, as if she wanted to say something but changed her mind.

"Yes," she finally answered, though he had a feeling that wasn't what she intended to tell him. "I guess you can see why I felt like we needed a fresh start."

"She's okay now, you said?"

"She's been in remission for a year. The bone marrow transplant was more a precaution because the second round of chemo destroyed her immune system. We were blessed that Simon could be the donor. But as you can imagine, we're all pretty sick of hospitals and doctors by now."

He released a breath, his mind tangled in the vicious thorns of remembering those last terrible two weeks when Cara had clung to life, when he had cried and prayed and begged for another chance for his broken and battered little girl.

For nothing.

His prayers hadn't done a damn bit of good.

"It's kind of surreal, isn't it?" Julia said after a moment. "Who would have thought all those summers ago when we were young that one day we'd be standing here in Abigail's garden together talking about my daughter's cancer treatment?"

He had a sudden, savage need to pummel something—to yank the autumn roses up by the roots, to shatter the porch swing into a million pieces, to hack the limbs off Abigail's dogwood bushes.

"Life is the cruelest bitch around," he said, and the bitter words seemed to scrape his throat bloody and raw. "Makes you wonder what the hell the point is."

She lifted shocked eyes to his. "Oh, Will. I'm so sorry," she whispered, and before he realized her intentions, she reached out and touched his arm in sympathy.

For just a moment the hair on his arm lifted and he forgot his bitterness, held captive by the gentle brush of skin against skin. He ached for the tenderness of a woman's touch—no, of *Julia's* touch— at the same time it terrified him.

He forced himself to take a step back. Cool night air swirled between them and he wondered how it was possible for the temperature to dip twenty degrees in a millisecond.

"I'd better go." His voice still sounded hoarse. "Your kids probably need you inside."

Her color seemed higher than it had been earlier and he thought she looked slightly disconcerted. "I'm sure you're right. Good night, then. And…thank you for the ice cream and the company. I enjoyed both."

She paused for the barest of moments, as if waiting for him to respond. When the silence dragged on, an instant's disappointment flickered in her eyes and she began to climb the porch steps.

"You're welcome," he said when she reached the top step. She turned with surprise.

"And for the record," he went on, "I haven't enjoyed much of anything for a long time but tonight was…nice."

Her brilliant smile followed him as he let himself out the front gate and headed down the dark street toward his home, a journey he had made a thousand times.

He didn't need to think about where he was going, which left his mind free to wander through dark alleys.

Cancer. That cute little girl. Hell.

Poor thing. Julia said it was in remission, that things were better except lingering fatigue. Still, he knew this was just one more reason he needed to maintain his careful distance.

His heart was a solid block of ice but if it ever started to melt, he knew he couldn't let himself care about Julia Blair and her children. He couldn't afford it.

He had been through enough pain and loss for a hundred lifetimes. He would have to be crazy to sign up for a situation with the potential to promise plenty more.

When he was ready to let people into his life again—if he was ever ready—it couldn't be a medically fragile little girl, a boy with curious eyes and energy to burn, and a lovely auburn-haired widow who made him long to taste life again.

She didn't see Will again for several days. With the lead-up to the start of school and then the actual chaos of adjusting to a new classroom and coming to know thirty new students, she barely had time to give him more than a passing thought.

But twice in the early hours of the morning as she graded math refresher assignments and the obligatory essays about how her students had spent the summer, she had glimpsed the telltale glimmer of lights in his workshop through the pines.

Only the walls of Abigail's old house knew that both times she had stopped what she was doing to stand at the window for a few moments watching that light and wondering what he was working on, what he was thinking about, if he'd had a good day.

It wasn't obsession, she told herself firmly. Only curiosity about an old friend.

Other than those few silent moments, she hadn't allowed herself to think about him much. What would be the point?

She had seen his reaction to the news of Maddie's cancer, a completely normal response under the circumstances. He had been shocked and saddened and she certainly couldn't blame him for the quick way he distanced himself from her.

She understood, but it still saddened her.

Now, the Friday after school started, she pulled into the Brambleberry House driveway to find his pickup truck parked just ahead of her SUV. Before she could contain the instinctive reaction, her stomach skittered with anticipation.

"Hey, I think that's Mr. Garrett's truck," Simon exclaimed. "See, it says Garrett Construction on the side."

"I think you must be right." She was quite proud of herself for the calm reply.

"I wonder what's he doing here." Simon's voice quivered with excitement and she sighed. Her son was so desperately eager for a man in his life. She couldn't really blame him—except for Conan, who didn't really count, Simon was surrounded by women in every direction.

"Do you think he's working on something for Sage and Anna? Can I help him, do you think? I could hand him tools or something. I'm really good at that. Do you think he'll let me?"

"I don't know the answer to any of your questions, kiddo. You'll have to ask him. Why don't we go check it out?"

Both children jumped out of the vehicle the moment she put it in Park. She called to them to wait for her but either they didn't hear her or they chose to ignore her as they rushed to the backyard, where the sound of some kind of power tool hummed through the afternoon.

She caught up with them before they made it all the way.

"I don't want you bothering Will—Mr. Garrett—if he's too busy to answer all your many questions. He has a job to do here and we need to let him."

The rest of what she might have said died in her throat when they turned the corner and she spotted him.

Oh mercy. He wore a pair of disreputable-looking jeans, a forest green T-shirt that bulged with muscle in all the right places, and a leather carpenter's belt slung low like a gunfighter's holster. The afternoon sun picked up golden streaks in his brown hair and he had just a hint of afternoon stubble that made him look dangerous and delectable at the same time.

Oh mercy.

Conan was curled under the shade nearby and his bark of greeting alerted Will's to their presence.

The dog lunged for Simon and Maddie as if he hadn't seen them in months instead of only a few hours and Will even gifted them with a rare smile, there only for an instant before it flickered away.

He drew off his leather gloves and shoved them in the back pocket of his jeans. "School over already? Is it that late?"

"We have early dismissal on Fridays. It's only three o'clock," Julia answered.

"We've been out for a few hours already," Maddie informed him. "Usually we get to stay at the after-school club until Mama finishes her work in her classroom."

"Is that right?"

"It's really fun," Simon answered. "Sometimes we have to stay in Mom's room with her and do our homework if we have a lot, but most of the time we go to extracurriculars. Today we played tetherball and made up a skit and played on the playground for a long time."

"Sounds tiring."

"Not for me," Simon boasted. "Maybe for Maddie."

"I'm not tired," Maddie protested.

His gaze met Julia's in shared acknowledgment that Maddie's claim was obviously a lie.

"What's the project today?" she asked.

"Last time I was here I noticed the back steps were splintering in a few places. I had a couple of hours this afternoon so I decided to get started on replacing them before somebody gets hurt."

Simon looked enthralled. "Can we help you fix them? I could hand you tools and stuff."

That subtle panic sparked in his eyes, the same uneasiness she saw the day they went for ice cream, whenever she or the children had pushed him for more than he was willing to offer.

She could see him trying to figure a way out of the situation without hurting Simon and she quickly stepped in.

"We promised Sage we would pick a bushel of apples and make our famous caramel apple pie, remember? You finally get to meet Chloe in a few hours when she and her father arrive."

Simon scowled. "But you said in the car that if Mr. Garrett said it was okay, we could help him."

She sent a quick look of apology to Will before turning back to her son. "I know, but I could really use your help with the pies."

"Making pies is for girls. I'd rather work with tools and stuff," Simon muttered.

Will raised an eyebrow at this blatantly chauvinistic attitude. "Not true, kid. I know lots of girls who are great at using tools and one of my good friends is a pastry chef at a restaurant down the coast. He makes the best brambleberry pie you'll ever eat in your life."

"Brambleberry, like our house?" Maddie asked.

"Just like."

"Cool!" Simon said. "I want some."

"No brambleberries today," Julia answered. "We're making apple, remember? Let's go change our clothes and get started."

Simon's features drooped with disappointment. "So I don't get to help Mr. Garrett?"

"Simon—"

"I don't mind if he stays and helps," Will said.

"Are you sure?"

He nodded, though she could still see a shadow of reluctance in his eyes. "Positive. I'll enjoy the company. Conan's a good listener but not much of a conversationalist."

She smiled at the unexpected whimsy. "Conversing is one thing Simon does exceptionally well, don't you, kiddo?"

Simon giggled. "Yep. My dad used to say I could talk for a day and a half without needing anybody to answer back."

"I guess that means you probably talk in your sleep, right?"

Simon giggled. "I don't, but Maddie does sometimes.

It's really funny. One time she sang the whole alphabet song in her sleep."

"I was only five," Maddie exclaimed to defend herself.

"And you're going to be fifteen before we finish this pie if we don't hurry. We all need to change out of school clothes and into apple-picking and porch-fixing clothes."

Simon looked resigned, then his features brightened. "Race you!" he called to Maddie and took off for the house. She followed several paces behind with Conan barking at their heels, leaving Julia alone with Will.

"I hope he doesn't get in your way or talk your ear off."

"Don't worry. We'll be fine."

"Feel free to send him out to play if you need to."

They lapsed into silence. She should go upstairs, she knew, but she had suddenly discovered she had missed him this last week, silly as that seemed after years when she hadn't given the man a thought.

She couldn't seem to force herself to leave. Finally she sighed, giving into the inevitable.

She took a step closer to him. "Hold still," she murmured.

Wariness leapt into the depths of his blue eyes but he froze as if she had just cast his boots in concrete.

He smelled of leather and wood shavings, and hot, sun-warmed male, a delicious combination, and she wanted to stand there for three or four years and just enjoy it. She brushed her fingers against the blade of his cheekbone, feeling warm male skin.

At her touch, their gazes clashed and the wariness in his eyes shifted instantly to something else, something raw and wild. An answering tremble stirred inside her and for a moment she forgot what she was doing, her fingers frozen on his skin.

His quick intake of breath dragged her back to reality and she quickly dropped her hand, feeling her own face flame.

"You, um, had a little bit of sawdust on your cheek. I didn't want it to find its way into your eye."

"Thanks." She wasn't sure if it was her imagination or not but his voice sounded decidedly hoarse.

She forced a smile and stepped back, though what she really wanted to do was wrap her arms fiercely around his warm, strong neck and hold on for dear life.

"You're welcome," she managed.

With nothing left to be said, she turned and hurried into the house.

She tried hard to put Will out of her mind as she and Maddie plucked Granny Smith apples off Abigail's tree. She might have found it a bit easier to forget about him if the ladder didn't offer a perfect view of the porch steps he was fixing.

Now she paused, her arm outstretched but the apple she was reaching to grab forgotten as she watched him smile at something Simon said. She couldn't hear them from here but so far it looked as if Simon wasn't making too big a pest of himself.

"Is this enough, Mama?" Maddie asked from below, where she stood waiting by the bushel basket.

Julia jerked her attention back to her daughter and the task at hand. "Just a moment." She plucked three more and added them to the glistening green pile in the basket.

"That ought to do it."

"Do we really need that many apples?"

"Not for one pie but I thought we could make a couple of extras. What do you think?"

She thought for a moment. "Can we give one to Mr. Garrett?"

Maddie looked over at the steps where Simon was trying his hand with Will's big hammer and Julia saw both longing and a sad kind of resignation in her daughter's blue eyes.

Maddie could be remarkably perceptive about others. Julia thought perhaps her long months of treatment—enough to make any child grow up far too early—had sensitized her to the subtle behaviors of others toward her. The way adults tried not to stare after she lost her hair, the stilted efforts of nurses and doctors to befriend her, even Julia's attempts to pretend their world was normal. Maddie seemed to see through them all.

Could Maddie sense the careful distance Will seemed determined to maintain between them?

Julia hoped not. Her daughter had endured enough. She didn't need more rejection in her life right now when she was just beginning to find her way again.

"That's a good idea," she finally answered Maddie, hoping her smile looked more genuine than it felt. "And perhaps we can think of someone else who might need a pie."

She lifted the bushel and started to carry it around the front of the house. She hadn't made it far before Will stepped forward and took the bushel out of her hands.

"Here, I'll carry that up the stairs for you."

She almost protested that it wasn't necessary but she could tell by the implacable set of his jaw that he wouldn't accept any arguments from her on the matter.

"Thank you," she said instead.

She and Maddie followed him up the stairs.

"Where do you want this?" he asked.

"The kitchen counter by the sink."

"We have to wash every single apple and see if it has a

worm," Maddie informed him. "I hope we don't find one. That would be gross."

"That's a lot of work," he said stiffly.

"It is. But my mama's pies are the best. Even better than brambleberry. Just wait until you try one."

Will's gaze flashed to Julia's then away so quickly she wondered if she'd imagined the quick flare of heat there.

"Good luck with your pies."

"Good luck with your stairs," she responded. "Send Simon up if you need to."

He nodded and headed out the door, probably completely oblivious that he was leaving two females to watch wistfully after him.

Chapter 8

About halfway through helping Julia peel the apples, Maddie asked if she could stop for a few minutes and take a little rest.

"Of course, baby," Julia assured her.

Already Maddie had made it an hour past the time when Julia thought she would give out. School alone was exhausting for her, especially starting at a new school and the effort it took to make new friends. Throw in an hour of after-school activities then picking the apples and it was no wonder Maddie was drooping.

A few moments later, Julia peered through the kitchen doorway to the living room couch and found her curled up, fast asleep.

Julia set down the half-peeled apple, dried her hands off on her apron, and went to double-check on her. Yes, it might be a bit obsessive, but she figured she had earned the right the last few years to a little cautious overreaction.

Maddie's color looked good, though, and she was breathing evenly so Julia simply covered her with her favorite crocheted throw and returned to the kitchen.

Her job was a bit lonely now, without Maddie's quiet observations or Simon's bubbly chatter. With nothing to distract her, she found her gaze slipping with increasing frequency out the window.

She couldn't see much from this angle but every once in a while Will and Simon would pass into the edge of her view as they moved from Will's power saw to the porch.

She had nearly finished peeling the apples when she suddenly heard a light scratch on the door of her apartment over the steady hammering and the occasional whine of power tools.

Somehow she wasn't surprised to find Conan standing on the other side, his tail wagging and his eyes expectant.

"Let me guess," she murmured. "All that hammering is interfering with your sleep."

She could swear the dog dipped his head up and down as if nodding. He padded through the doorway and into the living room, where he made three circles of his body before easing down to his stomach on the floor beside Maddie's couch.

"Watch over her for me, won't you?"

The dog rested his head on his front paws, his attention trained on Maddie as if the couch where she slept was covered in peanut butter.

"Good boy," Julia murmured, and returned to the kitchen.

She finished her work quickly, slicing enough apples for a half-dozen pies.

She assembled the pies quickly—cheating a little and using store-bought pie shells. She had a good pie crust recipe but she didn't have the time for it today since Eben and Chloe would be returning soon.

Only two pies could cook at a time in her oven and they took nearly forty minutes. After she slid the first pair in, she untied her apron and hung it back on the hook in the kitchen.

Without giving herself time to consider, she grabbed the egg timer off the stovetop, set it for the time the pies needed and stuck it in her pocket, then headed down the stairs to check on Simon.

It was nearly five-thirty but she couldn't see any sign of Anna or Sage yet. Sage, she knew, would be meeting Eben and Chloe at the small airstrip in Seaside, north of Cannon Beach. As for Anna, she sometimes worked late at her store in town or the new one in Lincoln City she had opened earlier in the summer.

She followed the sound of male voices—Will's lower-pitched voice a counterpoint to Simon's mile-a-minute higher tones.

She stepped closer, still out of sight around the corner of the house, until she could hear their words.

"My mom says next year I can play Little League baseball," Simon was saying.

"Hold the board still or we'll have wobbly steps, which won't do anyone any good."

"Sorry."

"Baseball, huh?" Will said a moment later.

"Yep. I couldn't play this year because of Maddie's bone transplant and because we were moving here. But next year, for sure. I can't wait. I played last year, even though I had to miss a lot of games and stuff when Mad was in the hospital."

She closed her eyes, grieving for her son who had suffered right along with his sister. Sometimes it was so easy to focus on Maddie's more immediate needs that she forgot Simon walked each step of the journey right along with her.

"Yeah, I hit six home runs last year. I bet I could do a lot more this year. Did you ever play baseball?"

"Sure did," Will answered. "All through high school and college. Until a few years ago, I was even on a team around here that played in the summertime."

"Probably old guys, huh?"

Julia cringed but Will didn't seem offended, judging by his quick snort of laughter—the most lighthearted sound she had heard from him since she'd been back.

"Yeah. We have a tough time running the bases for all the canes and walkers in the way."

Julia couldn't help herself, she laughed out loud, drawing the attention of both Will and Simon.

"Hi, Mom," Simon chirped, looking pleased to see her. "Guess what? Mr. Garrett played baseball, too."

"I remember," she said. "Your Uncle Charlie dragged me to one of his summer league games the last time I was here and I got to watch him play. He hit a three-run homer."

"Trying to impress you," Will said in a laconic tone.

She laughed again. "It worked very well, as I recall."

That baseball game had been when she first starting thinking of Will as more than just her brother's summer-vacation friend. She hadn't been able to stop thinking about him.

What, exactly, had changed since she came back? she wondered. She still couldn't seem to stop thinking about him.

"My mom likes baseball, too," Simon said. "She said maybe next month sometime we can go to a Mariners game, if they're in the playoffs. It's not very far to Seattle."

His eyes lit up with sudden excitement. "Hey, Mr. Garrett, you could come with us! That would be cool."

Will's gaze met hers and for an instant she imagined sharing hot dogs and listening to the cheers and sitting beside him for three hours, his heat and strength just inches away from her.

"I do enjoy watching the Mariners," Will said, an unreadable look in his eyes. "I'm pretty busy next month but if you let me know when you're going, I can see how it fits my schedule."

"We haven't made any definite plans," Julia said, hoping none of the longing showed in her expression.

She hadn't realized until this moment that Simon wasn't the only one in their family who hungered for a man in their lives.

And not just any man, either. Only a strong, quiet carpenter with callused hands and a rare, beautiful smile.

She decided to quickly change the subject. "The stairs look wonderful. Are you nearly finished?"

Before he could answer, they heard sudden excited barking from the front of the house.

Julia laughed. "I guess Conan needed to go out. It's a good thing he has his own doggy door."

"Hang on a minute," Will said. "That's his *somebody's home* bark."

A moment later they heard a vehicle pull into the driveway.

"Conan!" a high, excited voice shrieked and the dog woofed a greeting.

"That would be Chloe," Will said.

By tacit agreement, the three of them walked together toward the front of the house. When they rounded the corner, Julia saw a dark-haired girl around the twins' age with her arms around the dog's neck.

Beside her, Sage—glowing with joy—stood beside a man with commanding features and brilliant green eyes.

"Hey, guys!" Sage beamed at them. "Julia, this is Chloe Spencer and her dad, Eben."

Julia smiled, though she would have known their identities just from the glow on Sage's features—the same one that flickered there whenever she talked about her fiancé and his daughter.

"Eben, this is Julia Blair."

The man offered a smile and his hand to shake. "The new tenant with the twins. Hello. It's a pleasure to meet you finally. Sage has told me a great deal about you and your children the last few weeks."

Sage had told her plenty about Eben and Chloe as well. Meeting them in person, she could well understand how Sage could find the man compelling.

It seemed an odd mix to her—the buttoned-down hotel executive who wore an elegant silk power tie and the free-thinking naturalist who believed her dog communicated with her dead friend. But Julia could tell in an instant they were both crazy about each other.

Eben Spencer turned to Will next and the two of them exchanged greetings. As they spoke, she couldn't help contrasting the two men. Though Eben was probably more classically handsome in a *GQ* kind of way, with his loosened tie and his rolled up shirt sleeves, she had to admit that Will's toolbelt and worn jeans affected her more.

Being near Eben Spencer didn't make her insides flutter and her bones turn liquid.

"And who's this?" Eben was asking, she realized when she jerked her attention back to the conversation.

Color soaked her cheeks and she hoped no one else noticed. "This is one of my kiddos. Simon, this is Mr. Spencer and his daughter, Chloe."

"I'm eight," Chloe announced. "How old are you?"

Simon immediately went into defensive mode. "Well," he said slowly, "I won't be eight until March. But I'm taller than you are."

Chloe made a face. "*Everyone* is taller than me. I'm a shrimp. Sage says you have a twin sister. How cool! Where is she?"

He looked to Julia for an answer.

"Upstairs," she answered. "I'll go wake her, though. She's been anxious to meet you."

As if on cue, her timer beeped. "Got to run. That would be my pies ready to come out of the oven."

"You're making pie?" Chloe exclaimed. "That's super cool. I just *love* pie."

She smiled, charmed by Sage's stepdaughter-to-be. "I do, too. But not burnt pie so I'd better hurry."

She tried to be quiet as she slid the pies from the oven and carefully set them on a rack to dry, but she must have clattered something because Maddie began to stir in the other room.

She stood in the doorway and watched her daughter rise to a sitting position on the couch. "Hey, baby. How are you feeling?"

Maddie gave an ear-popping yawn and stretched her arms above her head. "Pretty good. I'm sorry, Mama. I said I would help you make pies and then I fell asleep."

"You helped me with the hard part, which was picking the apples and washing them all."

"I guess."

She still looked dejected at her own limitations and Julia walked to her and pulled her into a hug. "You helped me a ton. I never would have been able to finish without you. And while you were sleeping soundly, guess who arrived?"

Her features immediately brightened. "Chloe?"

"Yep. She's outside with Simon right now."

"Can I go meet her?"

She smiled at her enthusiasm. One thing about Maddie, even in the midst of her worst fatigue, she could go from full sleep to complete alertness in a matter of seconds.

"Of course. Go ahead. I'll be down in a minute—I just have to put in these other pies."

A few moments later, she closed her apartment door and headed down the stairs. The elusive scent of freesia seemed to linger in the air and she wondered if that was Abigail's way of greeting the newcomers. The whimsical thought had barely registered when Anna's door—Abigail's old apartment—slowly opened.

She instinctively gasped, then flushed crimson when Will walked out, a measuring tape in hand.

What had she expected? The ghostly specter of Abigail, complete with flashy costume jewelry and a wicked smile?

"Hi," she managed.

He gave her an odd look. "Everything okay?"

"Yes. Just my imagination running away with me."

"I was double-checking the measurements for the new moldings in Anna's apartment. I'm hoping to get to them in a week or so."

"All done with the stairs, then?"

"Not quite. I'm still going to have to stain them but the bulk of the hard work is done."

"You do good work, Will. I'm very impressed."

"My dad taught me well."

The scent of freesia seemed stronger now and finally

she had to say something. "Okay, tell me something. Can you smell that?"

Confusion flickered across his rugged features. "I smell sawdust and your apple pie baking. That's it."

"You don't smell freesia?"

"I'm not sure I know what that is."

"It's a flower. Kind of light, delicate. Abigail used to wear freesia perfume, apparently. I don't remember that about her but Anna and Sage say she did and I believe them."

He still looked confused. "And you're smelling it now?"

She sighed, knowing she must sound ridiculous. "Sage thinks Abigail is sticking around Brambleberry House."

To her surprise, he laughed out loud and she stared, arrested by the sound. "I wouldn't put it past her," he said. "She loved this old place."

"I can't say I blame her for that. I'm coming to love it, too. There's a kind of peace here—I can't explain it. Maddie says the house is friendly and I have to tell you, I'm beginning to believe her."

He shook his head, but he was smiling. "Watch out or you'll turn as wacky as Sage. Next thing I know, you'll be balancing your chakras every five minutes and eating only tofu and bean sprouts."

She gazed at his smile for a long moment, arrested by his light-hearted expression. He looked young and much more relaxed than she had seen him in a long time, almost happy, and her heart rejoiced that she had been able to make him smile and, yes, even laugh.

His smile slid away after a moment and she realized she was staring at his mouth. She couldn't seem to look away, suddenly wildly curious to know what it would be like to kiss him again.

Something hot kindled in the blue of his eyes and she caught her breath, wanting his touch, his kiss, more than she had wanted anything in a long time.

He wasn't ready, she reminded herself, and eased back, sliding her gaze from his. No sooner had she made up her mind to step away and let the intense moment pass when she could swear she felt a determined hand between her shoulderblades, pushing her forward.

She whirled around in astonishment, then thought she must be going crazy. Only the empty stairs were behind her.

"What's wrong?" Will asked. Though his words were concerned, that stony, unapproachable look had returned to his expression and she sighed, already missing that brief instant of laughter.

"Um, nothing. Absolutely nothing. My imagination seems to be in overdrive, that's all."

"That's what you get for talking about ghosts."

She forced a smile and headed for the door. Just before she walked through it, she turned and aimed a glare at the empty room.

Stay out of my love life, Abigail, she thought. *Or any lack thereof.*

She could almost swear wicked laughter followed behind her.

Damn it. He wasn't at all ready for this.

Will followed Julia out the door, still aware of the heat and hunger simmering through him.

He had almost kissed her. The urge had been so strong, he had been only seconds away from reaching for her.

She wouldn't have stopped him. He sensed that much— he had seen the warm welcome in her eyes and had known she would have returned the kiss with enthusiasm.

He still didn't know why he had stopped or why she had leaned away then looked behind her as if fearing her children were skulking on the second-floor landing watching them.

He didn't know why they hadn't kissed but he was enormously grateful they had both come to their senses.

He didn't want to be attracted to another woman. Sure, he was a man and he had normal needs just like any other male. But he had been crazy about his wife. Kissing another woman—even *wanting* to kiss another woman—still seemed like some kind of betrayal, though intellectually he knew that was absurd.

Robin had been gone for more than two years. As much as he had loved her, he sometimes had to work hard to summon the particular arrangement of her features and the sound of her voice.

He was forgetting her and he hated it. Sometimes his grief seemed like a vast lake that had been frozen solid forever. Suddenly, as if overnight, the ice was beginning to crack around the edges. He wouldn't have expected it to hurt like hell but everything suddenly seemed more raw than it had since the accident.

He pressed his fist to the ache in chest for just a moment then headed for the backyard, where he had set up his power tools. His gaze seemed to immediately drift to Julia and he found her on the brick patio, laughing at something Sage had said, the afternoon sunlight finding gold strands in her hair. He could swear he felt more chunks of ice break free.

She must have sensed the weight of his stare—she turned her head slightly and their gazes collided for a brief moment before he broke the connection and picked up his power saw and headed for his truck.

On his next trip to get the sawhorses, he deliberately

forced himself not to look at her. He was so busy *not* looking at her that he nearly mowed down Eben.

"Sorry," he muttered, feeling like an ass.

Eben laughed. "No problem. You look like your mind's a million miles away."

He judged her to be only about twenty-five feet, but he wasn't going to quibble. "Something like that," he murmured.

He hadn't expected to like Eben Spencer. When Sage had first fallen for the man, Will had been quite certain he would break her heart. As he had come to know him these last few months, he had changed his mind. Eben was deeply in love with Sage.

The two of them belonged together in a way Will couldn't have explained to save his life.

"You look like you could use a hand clearing this up."

He raised an eyebrow. "No offense, but you're not really dressed for moving my grimy tools."

"I don't mind getting a little dirty once in a while." The other man hefted two sawhorses over one shoulder, leaving Will only his toolbox to carry.

"Thanks," he said when everything had been slid into the bed of his pickup truck.

"No problem," Eben said again. "You're staying for dinner, aren't you? Sage has decided to throw an impromptu party since Chloe and I are back in town for a few days. I really don't want to be the only thing around here with a Y chromosome. Beautiful as all these Brambleberry women are, they're a little overwhelming for one solitary man."

"Don't forget you've got Simon Blair around now."

Eben laughed. "Well, that does help even the scales a little, but I have a feeling Sage and the others will be lost in wedding plans. I wouldn't mind company while I'm manning the grill."

He was tempted. He knew he shouldn't be but his empty house had become so oppressive sometimes he hated walking inside it.

"Got anything besides veggie burgers?"

"Sage talked to Jade and Stanley and they're sending over some choice prime-cut steaks from The Sea Urchin—the kind you can't buy at your average neighborhood grocery store."

"Sage *must* be in love if she's chasing down steaks for you," Will said, earning a chuckle from Eben.

"She might be a vegetarian but she's very forgiving of those of us who aren't quite as enlightened yet."

"Maybe she's just biding her time until you're married, then she'll start substituting your bacon for veggie strips and your hamburgers for mushroom, bean-curd concoctions."

Eben smiled, his expression rueful. "I'm so crazy about her, I probably wouldn't mind." He paused. "Stay, why don't you? Anna and Sage would love to have you."

What about Julia? He wondered. His attention shifted to her and that longing came out of nowhere again, knocking him out at the knees.

"Sure," he said, before he could give himself a chance to reconsider. "I just need to run home and wash off some of this sweat and sawdust."

"Great. We'll see you in a few minutes then."

He drove away, already regretting the momentary impulse to accept the invitation.

Chapter 9

An hour later, after taking a quick shower and changing his clothes, Will stood beside Eben at the grill, beer in hand, asking himself again why he had possibly thought this might be a good idea.

It was a lovely evening, he had to admit that. A breeze blew off the ocean, cool enough to be refreshing but not cold enough to have anybody reaching for a sweater.

The sweet sound of children's laughter rang through the Brambleberry House yard as Chloe and the twins threw a ball for Conan. Sage, Julia and Anna were sitting at a table on the weathered brick patio looking over wedding magazines.

Abigail would have adored seeing those she loved most enjoying themselves together. This casual, informal kind of gathering was exactly the kind of thing she loved best.

He only wished he could enjoy himself as he used to do, that he didn't view the whole scene with his chest aching and this deep sense of loss in his gut.

"My people at The Sea Urchin tell me the work you've done on the new cabinetry in the lobby is spectacular," Eben said as he turned the steaks one last time.

Will forced a smile. "I had great bones to work with. That helps on any project."

"She's a beautiful old place, isn't she?" Eben's smile was much more genuine. "I'm sorry I haven't had the opportunity yet to see what you've accomplished there. I'm looking forward to tomorrow when I have a chance to check out the progress of the last three weeks while Chloe and I have been overseas. I've been getting daily reports but it's not the same as seeing it firsthand."

"I think you'll be happy with it. You've got some real craftsmen working on The Sea Urchin."

"Including you." He took a sip of his beer, then gave Will an intent look. "In fact, I've got a proposition for you."

Will raised an eyebrow, curiosity replacing the ache, if only temporarily. Another job? he wondered. As far as he knew, The Sea Urchin was the only Spencer Hotels property along the coast.

"Spencer Hotels could always use a master carpenter. We've got rehab projects going in eight different properties right now alone. There's always something popping. What would you say to signing on with us, traveling a little? You could take your pick of the jobs, anywhere from Tokyo to Tuscany. We've got more than enough work to keep you busy, with much more in the pipeline."

He blinked, stunned at the offer. He was just a journeyman carpenter in piddly little Cannon Beach. What the hell did he know about either Tokyo or Tuscany?

"Whoa," he finally managed through his shock. "That's certainly…unexpected."

"I've been thinking about it for a while. When I received

the glowing report from my people here, it just seemed a confirmation of what had already been running around my head. I think you'd be perfect for the job. I usually try to hire workers from the various communities where my hotels are located—good business practice, you know—but I also like to have my own man overseeing the work."

"I don't know what good I would be in that capacity. I don't speak any language except good old English and a little bit of Spanish."

"The Spanish might help. But we always have translators on site, so that's not really a concern. I'm looking for a craftsman. An artisan. From what I've seen of your work, you definitely qualify. I also want someone I can trust to do the job right. And again, you qualify."

He had to admit, he was flattered. How could he not be? He loved his work and took great pride in it. When others saw and acknowledged a job well done, he found enormous satisfaction.

For just a moment, he allowed himself to imagine the possibilities. He had lived his entire life in Cannon Beach—in the very same house, even. Though he loved the town and loved living on the coast, maybe it was time to pick up and try something new, see the world a little.

On the other hand. he wasn't sure the ghosts that haunted him were ready for him to move on.

"You don't have to give me any kind of answer tonight," Eben said at his continued silence. "Just think about it. If you decide you're interested, we can sit down while I'm here and talk details."

"I'll think about it," he agreed. "I…it's a little over-whelming. It would be a huge change for me."

"But maybe not an unwelcome one," Eben said, showing more insight than Will was completely comfortable with.

"Maybe not." He paused. "I've got a buddy up in Ketchikan who's been after me to come up and go into business with him. I've been tossing the idea around."

"That might be good for you, too. Look at all your options. Take all the time you need. As far as I'm concerned, you can consider the Spencer Hotels offer an indefinite one with no time limit."

"What offer?"

He hadn't even noticed Sage had joined them until she spoke. Now she slipped her arm through the crook of Will's elbow and gave his arm an affectionate squeeze. Of all his friends, Sage was the most physical, and he always appreciated her hugs and kisses on the cheek and the times, like now, when she squeezed his arm.

He didn't like to admit it, but he sometimes ached for the soft comfort of a woman's touch, even the touch of a woman he considered more in the nature of a little sister than anything else.

"You won't like it," Eben predicted.

She made a face. "Try me. Believe it or not, I can be remarkably open-minded sometimes."

"Good. It might be a good idea for you to keep that in mind," Eben said with a wary expression.

"What are you up to?"

"I'm trying to steal Will away from Cannon Beach to come work for Spencer Hotels."

She dropped her arm and glared with shock at both of them. "You can't leave! We need you here."

"Says the woman who's going to be moving to San Francisco herself in a few months," Will murmured.

She tucked a loose strand of wavy blonde hair behind her ear, flushing a little at the reminder. "Not full-time. We'll be here every summer so I can still run the nature center camps. And we're planning to spend as much time up here as we can—weekends and school holidays."

"But you'll still be in the Bay Area most of the time, right?"

"Yes." She made a face. "I'm selfish, I know. I just don't want things to change."

"Things change, Sage. Most of the time we have no choice but to change, too, whether we want to or not."

She squeezed his arm again, her eyes suddenly moist. He saw memories of Robin and Cara swimming there and he didn't want to ruin her night by bringing up the past.

"I'm not going anywhere right now," he said. "Let's just enjoy the evening while we can."

Eben kissed his fiancée on the tip of her nose, an intimate gesture that for some reason made Will's chest ache. "These steaks are just about ready and I think your bean burger is perfect, though I believe that statement is a blatant oxymoron."

She laughed and headed off to tell the others dinner was ready.

"Give my offer some thought," Eben said when Sage was out of earshot. "Like I said, you don't have to answer right away. Maybe you could try it for six months or so to see how the traveling lifestyle fits you."

"I'll think about it," he agreed, which was an understatement of major proportions.

They ate on the brick patio, protected from the wind blowing off the sea by the long wall of Sitka spruce on the seaward edge of the yard.

While he and Eben had been grilling, the women had set out candles of varying heights around the patio and turned on the little twinkling fairy lights he had hung in the trees for Abigail a few summers earlier.

It seemed an odd collection of people but somehow the mix worked. Sage, with her highly developed social conscience. Anna with her quiet ambition and hard work ethic. Eben, dynamic businessman, and Julia, warm and nurturing, making sure plates were full, that the potato salad was seasoned just so, that drinks were replenished.

A group of very different people brought together because of Abigail, really.

Conversation flowed around him like an incoming tide finding small hidden channels in the sand and he was mostly content to sit at the table and listen to it.

"You're not eating your steak."

He looked up to find Julia watching him, her green eyes concerned. Though she sat beside him, he hadn't been ignoring her for the last hour but he hadn't exactly made any effort to seek her out, still disconcerted by that moment in the hallway when he had wanted to kiss her more than he wanted oxygen.

"Sorry," he mumbled and immediately applied himself to the delicious cut in front of him.

"You don't have to eat it just because I said something." She pitched her voice low so others didn't overhear. "I was just wondering if everything is okay. You seem distracted."

He was distracted by *her*. By the cherry blossom scent of her, and her softness so close to him and the inappropriate thoughts he couldn't seem to shake.

"You don't know me anymore, Julia. For all you know, maybe I'm always this way."

As soon as the sharp words left his mouth, a cold wind suddenly forced its way past the line of trees to flutter the edges of the tablecloth and send the lights shivering in the treetops.

He didn't miss the hurt that leapt into her eyes or the way her mouth tightened.

He was immediately contrite. "I'm sorry. I'm not really fit company tonight."

"No, you're not. But it happens to all of us." She turned away to talk to Eben, on her other side, and the prime-cut steak suddenly had all the appeal of overdried beef jerky.

He would have to do a better job of apologizing for his sharp words, he realized. She didn't deserve to bear the brunt of his temper.

His chance didn't come until sometime later when everyone seemed to have finished dinner. Julia stood and started clearing dishes and Will immediately rose to help her, earning a surprised look and even a tentative smile from her.

"Where are we taking all this stuff?" he asked when he had an armload of dishes.

"My apartment. My dishwasher is the newest and the biggest. Most of the dishes came out of my kitchen anyway and I can make sure those that belong to Sage or Anna are returned to their rightful homes."

He followed her up the stairs, then headed down for another load. When he returned, she was rinsing and loading dishes in the dishwasher and he immediately started helping.

She flashed him one quick, questioning look, then smiled and made room for him at the sink.

The sheer domesticity of it stirred that same weird ache in his throat and he could feel himself wanting to shut down, to flee to the safety and empty solitude of his house down the beach.

But he had come this far. He could tough it out a little longer.

"I owe you an apology for my sharpness," he said after

a moment. "A better one than the sorry excuse I gave you outside."

Her gaze collided with his for just a moment before she returned her attention to the sink. "You don't owe me anything, Will. I overstepped and I'm sorry. I've been overstepping since I came back to Cannon Beach."

She sighed and turned around, her hip leaning against the sink. "You were absolutely right, we don't have any kind of…anything. We were friends a long time ago, when we were both vastly different people. That was in the past. Somehow I keep forgetting that today we're simply two people who happen to live a few houses apart and have the same circle of friends."

"That's not quite true."

She frowned. "Which part isn't true?"

"That we were friends so long ago."

Hurt flickered in her eyes but she quickly concealed it and turned back to the sink. "My mistake, then. I guess you're right. We didn't know each other well. Just a few weeks every summer."

He should just stop now before he made things worse. What was the point in dragging all this up again?

"That's not what I meant. I only meant that the way we left things was definitely more than just friends."

She stared at him, sudden awareness blossoming in the green of her eyes.

"It took me a long time to get over you," he said, and the admission looked as if it surprised her as much as it did him. "When you didn't answer my letters, I figured everything I thought we had was all in my head. But it still hurt."

"Oh, Will." She dried her hands on a dish towel. "I would have written you but…things were so messed up. I was messed up. The day we returned home from our last summer in Cannon Beach, my parents told us they were divorcing. This was only two weeks before school started. My dad ended up with Charlie and the house in Los Angeles, and my mom took me to Sacramento with her. I had to start a new school my junior year, which was terrible. I didn't even get your letters until almost the end of the school year when my dad finally bothered to forward them from L.A."

She touched his arm, much the way Sage had earlier, but Sage's touch hadn't given him instant goosebumps or make him want to yank her into his arms.

"I should have written to explain to you what was going on," she went on. "I'm sorry I didn't, but I never forgot you, Will. This probably sounds really stupid, but the time I spent with you that summer was the best thing that happened to me in a long time, either before it or after, and I didn't want to spoil the memory of it."

She smiled, her hand still on his arm. He was dying here and he doubted she even realized what effect she was having on him. "You have no idea how long it took me to stop comparing every other boy to you."

"What can I say? I'm a hell of a kisser."

He meant the words as a flippant joke and she gave him a startled laugh, then followed up with a sidelong glance. "I do believe I remember that about you," she murmured.

The intimacy of the room seemed to wrap around them. For one wild moment, he felt sixteen again, lost in the throes of first love, entranced by Julia Hudson.

He could kiss her.

The impulse to taste her, touch her, poured through him and he was powerless to fight it. He took a step forward, expecting her to back away. Instead, her gaze locked with his and he saw in her eyes an awareness—even a longing—to match his own.

Still he hesitated, the only sound in the kitchen their mingled breathing. He might have stayed in an eternity of indecision if she hadn't leaned toward him slightly, just enough to tumble the last of his defenses.

In an instant, his mouth found hers and captured her quick gasp of surprise.

So long. So damn long.

He had forgotten how soft a woman's mouth could be, how instantly addictive it could be to taste desire.

Part of him wanted to yank back and retreat to his frozen lake where he was safe. But he was helpless to fight the tide of yearning crashing over him, the heat and sensation and pure, delicious pleasure of her softness against him.

It seemed impossible, but he tasted better than she remembered, of cinnamon and mint and coffee.

She should be shocked that he would kiss her, after being quite blunt that he wasn't interested in starting anything. But it seemed so right to be here in his arms that she couldn't manage to summon anything but grateful amazement.

She slid her arms around his neck, letting him set the pace and tone of the kiss. It was gentle at first, sweet and comfortable. Two old friends renewing something they had once shared.

Just as it had so many years earlier, being in his arms felt right. Completely perfect.

Their bodies had changed over the years—he was much broader and more muscled and she knew giving birth to twins had softened her edges and given her more curves.

But they still seemed to fit together like two halves of the same planed board.

She was aware of odd, random sensations as the kiss

lingered—the hard countertop digging into her hip where he pressed her against it, the silk of his hair against her fingers, the smell of him, leathery and masculine.

And freesia.

The smell of flowers drifted through her kitchen so strongly that she opened one eye to make sure Abigail wasn't standing in the doorway watching them.

An instant later, she forgot all about Abigail—or any other ghosts—when Will pulled her closer and deepened the kiss, his tongue playing and teasing in a way that demonstrated quite unequivocally that he had learned more than a few things in the intervening years since their last kiss on the beach.

Heat flared, bright and urgent, and she dived right into the flames, holding him closer and returning the kiss.

She had no idea how long they kissed—or just how long they might have continued. Both of them froze when they heard the squeak of the entry door downstairs.

Will wrenched his mouth away, breathing hard, and stared at her and her heart broke at the expression on his face—shock and dismay and something close to anguish.

He raked a hand through his hair, leaving little tufts looking as if he'd just walked into a wind tunnel.

"That was... I shouldn't have..."

He seemed so genuinely upset, she locked away her hurt and focused on trying to ease his turmoil. "Will, it's okay."

"No. No, it's not. I shouldn't have done that. I've... I've got to go."

Without another word, he hurried out of the kitchen and her apartment and she heard the thud of his boots as he rushed down the wooden stairway and out the door.

She leaned against the counter, her breathing still ragged. She felt emotionally ravaged, wrung out and hung to dry.

She was still trying to figure out what just happened when she heard a knock on her door.

She wasn't sure she was at all ready to face anyone but when the knock sounded again, she knew she wouldn't be able to hide away there in her kitchen forever.

"It's open," she called.

The door swung open and a moment later Anna Galvez walked into the apartment.

"What's up with Will? He passed me on the stairs and didn't even say a word before he headed out the door like the hounds of hell were nipping at his heels."

She gave Julia a careful look. "Are you okay? You look flushed. Did you and Will have a fight or something?"

"That blasted *or something* will get you every time," Julia muttered under her breath.

"You're going to have to give me a break here. I've been working all day on inventory and my brain is mush. Do you want to explain what that means?"

"Not really." She sighed, not at all comfortable talking about this. But right now she desperately needed a friend and Anna definitely qualified. "He kissed me," she blurted out.

Surprise then delight flickered across Anna's features. "Really? That's wonderful!"

"Is it? Will obviously didn't think so."

"Will doesn't do anything he doesn't want to do. If he hadn't wanted to kiss you, he wouldn't have."

"He was horrified afterward."

"A little overdramatic, don't you think?"

"You should have seen his face! I don't think he's ready. He's lost so much."

"So have you. I don't hear you saying you're not ready."

But their situations were vastly different, a point she

wasn't prepared to point out to Anna. Will had been happily married when his wife died. She, on the other hand, had let Kevin go long before his fatal car accident.

"He will figure things out in his own time. Don't worry," Anna went on. "He's a wonderful man who's been through a terrible tragedy. But he'll get through it. Have a little faith."

Right now faith was something Julia had in very short supply. She could tumble hard and fast for Will Garrett. It wouldn't take a hard push—she had been in love with him when she was fifteen years old and she could easily see herself falling again.

But what would be the point, if he had his heart so tightly wrapped in protective layers that he wouldn't let anyone in?

Chapter 10

It was just a damn kiss.

Three weeks later, Will backed his truck into the Brambleberry House driveway, fighting a mix of dread and unwilling anticipation.

He knew both reactions were completely ridiculous. What the hell was he worrying about? She wouldn't even be here—he had finally managed to work the molding job into his schedule only after squeezing in a time when he could be certain Julia and her children were safely tucked away at the elementary school.

The very fact that he had to resort to such ridiculous manipulations of his own schedule simply to avoid seeing a certain woman bugged the heck out of him.

He ought to be tougher than this. He should have been completely unfazed by their brief encounter, instead of brooding about it for the better part of three weeks.

So he had kissed her. Big deal. The world hadn't stopped

spinning, the ocean hadn't suddenly been sucked dry, the Coast Range hadn't suddenly tumbled to dust.

Robin hadn't come back to haunt him.

He knew his reaction to the kiss had been excessive. He had run out of her apartment at Brambleberry House like a kid who had been caught smoking in the boy's room of the schoolhouse.

Yeah, he had overreacted to the shock of discovering not all of him was encased in ice—that he could desire another woman, could long to have her wrapped around him.

He still wanted it. That was what had bothered him for three weeks. Even though he hadn't seen her in all that time, she hadn't been far from his thoughts.

He remembered the taste of her, sweet and welcoming, the softness of her skin under his fingers, the subtle peace he had so briefly savored.

He couldn't seem to shake this achy sense that with that single kiss, everything in his world had changed, in a way he couldn't explain but knew he didn't like.

He didn't want change. Yeah, he hated his life and missed Robin and Cara so much he sometimes couldn't breathe around the pain. But it was *his* pain.

He was used to it now, and somewhere deep inside, he worried that letting go of that grief would mean letting go of his wife and baby girl, something he wasn't ready to face yet.

He knew his reaction was absurd. Plenty of people had lost loved ones and had moved ahead with their lives. His own mother had married again, just a few years after his father died, when Will was in his early twenties. She had moved to San Diego with her new husband, where the two of them seemed to be extremely happy together. They played golf, they went sailing on the bay, they enjoyed an active social life.

Will didn't begrudge his mother her happiness. He liked his stepfather and was grateful his mother had found someone else.

Intellectually, he knew it was possible, even expected, for him to date again sometime. He just wasn't sure he was ready yet—indeed, that he would ever be ready.

It had just been a kiss, he reminded himself. Not a damn marriage proposal.

As he sat in the driveway, gearing himself to go inside, the moist sea breeze drifted through his cracked window and he could suddenly swear he smelled cherry blossoms.

It was nearing the end of September, for heaven's sake, and was a cool, damp morning. He had absolutely no business smelling the spring scent of cherry blossoms on the breeze.

No doubt it was only the power of suggestion at work— he was thinking about Julia and his subconscious somehow managed to conjure the scent that always seemed to cling to her.

He closed his eyes and for just a moment allowed his mind to wander over that kiss again—the way she had responded to him with such warm enthusiasm, the silky softness of her mouth, the comfort of her hands against his skin.

Just a damn kiss!

His sigh filled the cab of the pickup and he stiffened his resolve and reached for the door handle.

Enough. Anna and Sage weren't paying him to sit on his butt and moon over their tenant. He had work to do. He'd been promising Anna for weeks he would get to her moldings and he couldn't keep putting it off.

A Garrett man kept his promises.

He climbed out and strapped on his tool belt with a dogged determination he would have found amusing under other circumstances, then grabbed as many of the moldings out of the back as he could lift.

He carried them to the porch and set them as close to the house as he could, then went back to his pickup for the rest. Judging by the steely clouds overhead, they were in for rain soon and he needed to keep the custom-cut oak dry.

He nearly dropped his second load when the front door suddenly swung open. A second later, Conan bounded through and barked with excitement.

He set the wood down with the other pile and gave the dog the obligatory scratch. "You're opening the door by yourself now? Pretty soon you're going to be driving yourself to the store to pick up dog food. You won't need any of us anymore."

"Until that amazing day arrives, he'll continue to keep us all as willing slaves. Hi, Will."

His entire insides had clenched at the sound of that first word spoken in a low, musical voice, and he slowly lifted his gaze to find Julia standing in the doorway.

She looked beautiful, fresh and lovely, and he could almost feel the churn of his heart.

"What are you doing here?" he said abruptly. "I figured you'd be at school."

Too late, he realized all that his words revealed—that he had given her more than a minute's thought in the last three weeks. She wasn't a stupid woman. No doubt she would quickly read between the lines and figure out he had purposely planned the project for a time when he was unlikely to encounter her.

To his vast relief, she didn't seem to notice. "I should be. At school, I mean. But Maddie's caught some kind of a bug. She was running a fever this morning and I decided I had better stay home and keep an eye on her."

"Is it a problem, missing your class?"

She shook her head. "I hate having to bring in a substitute this early in the school year but it can't be helped. The school district knew when they hired me that my daughter's health was fragile. So far they've been amazingly cooperative."

"She's okay, isn't she?"

All he could think about even as he asked the question was the irony of the whole thing. Above all else, he had tried his best to avoid bumping into her. So how, in heaven's name, had he managed to pick the one day she was home to finish the job?

"I think she's only caught a little cold," Julia answered. "At least that's what I hope it is. She's sniffly and coughing a bit but her fever broke about an hour ago. I hope it's just one of those twenty-four hour bugs."

"That's good."

"Her night was a little unsettled but she's sleeping soundly now. I figured rest was the best thing for her so I'm letting her sleep as long as she needs to beat this thing."

"Sounds like a smart plan."

"I guess you're here to do the moldings in Anna's apartment."

He nodded curtly, not knowing what else to say.

"Do you have more supplies in your truck that need to come in? I can help you carry things."

"This is it." His voice was more brusque than he intended and Conan made a snarly kind of growl at him.

Will just barely managed not to snarl back. He didn't need a dog making him feel guilty. He could do that all on his own.

It wasn't Julia's fault she stirred all kinds of unwelcome feelings in him and it wasn't at all fair of him to take out his bad mood on her.

He forced himself to temper his tone. "Would you mind holding the door open for me, though? It's going to rain soon and I'd hate for all this oak to get wet."

"Oh! Of course." She hurried to open the door. The only tricky part now was that he would have to move past her to get inside, he realized. He should have considered that little detail.

Too late now.

He let out a sigh of defeat and picked up several of the moldings and squeezed past her, doing his best not to bang the wood on the doorway on his way inside.

Going in wasn't so tough. Walking back out for a second load with his arms unencumbered was an entirely different story. He was painfully aware of her—that scent of spring, the heat of her body, the flicker of awareness in her green eyes as he passed.

Oh, he was in trouble.

His only consolation was that she seemed just as disconcerted by his presence.

"I guess you probably have a key to Anna's apartment, don't you?" she asked.

He nodded. "I have keys to the whole house so I can come and go when I'm working on something. All but your apartment. I gave it back to Anna and Sage when I finished up on the second floor."

"Good to know," she murmured.

He cleared his throat, set down the moldings in the entry and fished in his pocket, then pulled out the Brambleberry keyring. Of course, his hands seemed to fumble as he tried to find the right one to fit the lock for Anna's apartment, but he finally located it and opened her door.

"Would you mind holding the apartment door open as well? I need to be careful not to hit the wood on the frame. If you could guide it through, that would be great."

"Sure!" She hurried to prop open the door with an eagerness that made him blink. Even though it was akin to torture, he had to walk past her all over again and he forced himself to put away this sizzle of awareness and focus on the job.

She followed him inside as he carried the eight-foot-long moldings in and set them behind Anna's couch.

"Can I give you a hand with anything else?" Julia asked. "To be honest, I'm a bit at loose ends this morning and was looking for a distraction. I've already finished my lesson plans for the next month and I'm completely caught up with my homework grading. I was just contemplating rearranging my kitchen cabinets in alphabetical order, just to kill the boredom. I'd love the chance to do something constructive."

That was just about the last thing on earth he needed right now, to have to work with Julia looking on. She was the very definition of distraction. With his luck, he'd probably be so busy trying not to smell her that he would glue his sleeve to the wood.

His hesitation dragged on just a moment too long, he realized as he watched heat soak her cheeks.

"You're used to working alone and I would probably only get in the way, wouldn't I? Forget I said anything."

He hated her distress, hated making her think he didn't want her around. Was he a coward or was he a man who could contain his own unwanted desires?

"I *am* used to working alone," he said slowly, already

regretting the words. "But I guess I wouldn't mind the company."

It was almost worth his impending discomfort to see her face light up with such delight. She must really be bored if she could get so excited about handing him tools and watching him nail up moldings.

"I'll just run up and grab the walkie-talkie I let the kids use when they're sick to call out to me when they need drinks and things. That way Maddie will be able to find me when she wakes up."

He nodded, though she didn't seem to expect much of an answer as she hurried out the door and up the stairs.

What the hell had he just done? he wondered. The whole point of scheduling this project during this time had been to avoid bumping into her. He certainly didn't expect to find himself inviting her to spend the next hour or so right next to him, crowding his space, posing far too much of a temptation for his peace of mind.

"What are you grinning at?" he growled to Conan.

The dog just woofed at him and settled onto the rug in front of the empty fireplace. When Abigail was alive, that had always been his favorite place, Will remembered.

He supposed it was nice to see a few things didn't change, even though he felt as if the rest of his life was a deck of cards that had suddenly been thrown into the teeth of the wind.

She was a fool when it came to Will Garrett.

Up in her apartment, Julia quickly ran a brush through her hair. She thought about touching up the quick makeup job she'd done that morning but she figured Will would probably notice—and wonder—if she put on fresh lipstick.

Would he really notice? The snide voice in her head

asked. He had made it plain he wasn't interested in her. Or at least that he didn't want to be interested in her, which amounted to the same thing.

More reason she was a fool for Will Garrett. Some part of her held out some foolish hope that this time might be different, that this time he might be able to see beyond the past.

Her conversation with Anna seemed to play through her head again. *He's a wonderful man who's been through a terrible tragedy. But he'll get through it. Have a little faith.*

She understood grief. Understood and accepted it. Despite their marital problems toward the end, she had mourned Kevin's death for the children's sake and for the sake of all those dreams they had once shared, the dreams that had been lost along the way somewhere.

She understood Will's sorrow. But she also accepted that she had missed him these last few weeks.

He hadn't been far from her thoughts, even as she went about the business of living—settling into the school year, getting to know her new students and co-workers at the elementary school, helping Simon and Maddie with their schoolwork.

She glanced out the window at his workshop, tucked away behind his house beneath the trees. How many nights had she stood at the window, watching the lights flicker there, wondering how he was, what he was thinking, what he might be working on?

She was obsessed with the man. Pure and simple. Perhaps they would both be better off if she just stayed up here with her daughter and pushed thoughts of him out of her head.

She sighed. She wasn't going to, because of that whole being-a-fool thing again. She couldn't resist this chance to talk to him again, to indulge herself with his company and perhaps come to know a little more about the man he had become.

She opened Maddie's door and found her daughter still sleeping, her skin a healthy color and her breathing even. Julia scribbled a quick note to tell her where she was.

"I have the other walkie-talkie so just let me know when you wake up," she wrote and slipped the note under the other wireless handset on Maddie's bedside table where she couldn't miss it.

She spent one more moment watching the miracle of her daughter sleeping.

It was exactly the reminder she needed to wake her to the harsh reality of just how cautious she needed to be around Will Garrett.

Girlhood crushes were one thing, but she had two children to worry about now. She couldn't risk their feelings, couldn't let them come to care any more about a man who quite plainly wasn't ready to let anyone else into his life.

She would walk downstairs and be friendly in a polite, completely casual way, she told herself as she headed for the door. She wouldn't push him, she wouldn't dig too deeply.

She would simply help him with his project and try to bridge the tension between them so they could remain on friendly terms.

Anything else would be beyond foolish, when she had her children's emotional well-being to consider.

Chapter 11

When she returned to Anna's apartment, she found Conan sleeping on his favorite rug but no sign of Will. His tools and the boards he had brought in were still in evidence but Will wasn't anywhere to be found so Julia settled down to wait.

A moment later, she heard the front door open. Conan opened one eye and slapped his tail on the floor but didn't bother rising when Will came in carrying a small tool box and a container of nails.

He faltered a little when he saw her, as if he had forgotten her presence, or, worse, had maybe hoped it was all a bad dream. She was tempted again to abandon the whole idea and return upstairs to Maddie. But some part of her was still intensely curious to know why he seemed so uncomfortable in her presence.

He obviously wasn't completely impervious to her or he wouldn't care whether she hung around or not, any more than it bothered him to have Conan watching him work.

Was that a good sign, or just more evidence that she ought to just leave the poor man alone?

"Are you sure there's not anything else I can bring in-side for you?" she asked. "I'm not good for much but I can carry tools or something."

"No. This should be everything I need."

He said nothing more, just started laying out tools, and she might have thought he had completely forgotten her presence if not for the barest clenching of muscle along his jawline and a hint of red at the tips of his ears.

She knew she shouldn't find that tiny reaction so fasci-nating but she couldn't seem to stop staring.

She found *everything* about Will Garrett fascinating, she acknowledged somewhat grimly.

From the tool belt riding low on his hips to the broad shoulders he had gained from hard work over the years to the tiny network of lines around his eyes that had probably once been laugh lines.

She wanted to hear him laugh again. The strength of her desire burned through her chest and she would have given anything just then to be able to come up with some kind of hilarious story that would be guaranteed to have him in stitches.

"Since you're here, can you do me a favor?" he spoke suddenly as she was wracking her brain trying to come up with something.

"Of course." She jumped up, pathetically grateful for any task, no matter how humble.

"I need to double-check my measurements. I've checked them several times but I want to be sure before I make the final cuts."

"I guess you can't be too careful in your line of work."

"Not when you're dealing with oak trim that costs an arm and a leg," he answered.

"It's gorgeous, though."

"Worth every penny," he agreed, and for one breathless moment, he looked as if he wanted to smile. Just before the lighthearted expression would have broken free, his features sobered and he held out the end of the tape measure to her.

He was a man who devoted scrupulous attention to detail, she thought as they measured and re-measured the circumference of the room. He had kissed her the same way, thoroughly and completely, as if he couldn't bear the idea of missing a single second.

Her stomach quivered at the memory of his arms around her and the intensity of his mouth searching hers.

Maybe this hadn't been such a grand idea, the two of them alone here in the quiet hush of a rainy day morning with only Conan for company.

"What do you do when you don't have a fumbling and inept—but well-meaning—assistant to help you out with things like this?" she asked, to break the sudden hushed intimacy.

He shrugged. "I usually make do. I have a couple of high school kids who help me sometimes. Most jobs I can handle on my own but sometimes an extra set of hands can definitely make the work a lot easier."

She was grateful again that she had offered help, even if he still seemed uneasy about accepting.

"Well, I can't promise that my hands are good for much, but I'm happy to use them for anything you need."

As soon as the words left her mouth, she realized how they could be misconstrued. She flushed, but to her vast relief he didn't seem to notice either her blush or her unintentionally provocative statement.

"Thanks. I appreciate that."

He paused after writing down one more measurement then retracting the tape measure. "Robin was always after me to hire a full-time assistant," he said after a moment.

This was the first time he had mentioned his wife to her on his own. It seemed an important step, somehow, as if he had allowed himself to lower yet another barrier between them.

Julia held her breath, not wanting to say anything that might make him regret bringing up the subject.

"You didn't do it, though?"

He shrugged. "I like working on my own. I can pick the music I want, can work at my own pace, can talk to myself when I need to. Yeah, I guess that probably makes me a little on the crazy side."

She laughed. "Not crazy. I talk to myself all the time. It helps to have Conan around, then I can at least pretend I'm talking to him."

He smiled. One moment he was wearing that remote, polite expression, then next, a genuine smile stole over his handsome features. She stared at it, her pulse shivering.

She wanted to leap up and down and shriek with glee that she had been able to lighten his features, even if only for a moment, but then he would definitely think *she* was the crazy one.

"Maybe I need a dog to take on jobs with me, just so I don't get a reputation as the wild-eyed carpenter who carries on long conversations with himself."

"I'm sure Sage and Anna would consider renting Conan out by the hour," she offered.

He smiled again—twice in as many minutes!—and turned to the dog. "What do you say, bud? Want to be my permanent assistant?"

Conan snuffled and gave a huge yawn that stretched his jaws, then he flopped over on his other side, turning his back toward both of them.

Julia couldn't help laughing. "Sorry, Will, but I think that's a definite no. You wouldn't want to interfere with his strenuous nap schedule. I guess you'll have to make do with me for now. I just hope I haven't messed up your rhythm too much."

"No. You're actually helping."

"You don't have to sound so surprised!" she exclaimed. "I do occasionally have my uses."

"Sorry. I didn't mean it that way."

She managed a smile. "No problem. Believe it or not, I've got a pretty thick skin."

They worked in silence and Will seemed deep in thought. When he spoke some time later, she realized his mind was still on what he'd said about hiring an assistant.

"Sometimes Robin would come with me on bigger jobs to lend a hand, until Cara came along, anyway," he said. "She started to crawl early—six months or so—and was into everything. She barely gave Robin a second to breathe for chasing her."

Again, she sensed by the stiff set of his shoulders that he wasn't completely comfortable talking about his family. She wasn't sure why he had decided to share these few details but she was beyond touched that he was willing to show her this snapshot of their life together.

"I can imagine it was hard to get any work done while you were chasing a busy toddler," she said.

He nodded. "She wasn't afraid of anything, our Cara. If Robin or I didn't watch her, she'd be out the back door and halfway to the ocean before we figured out where she had gone. We had to put double child-locks on every door."

He smiled a little at the memory but she could still sense the pain around the edges of his smile. She couldn't help herself, she reached out and touched his forearm, driven only by the need to comfort him.

His skin was warm, covered in a layer of crisp dark hair. He looked down at her fingers on his darker skin and she thought she saw his Adam's apple move as he swallowed.

"Maddie was like that, too," she said after a moment, lifting her hand away.

"Maddie?"

"I know. Hard to believe. She was a much busier toddler than Simon. She was always the ringleader of the two of them."

She smiled at the memory. "When they still could barely walk, they used to climb out of their cribs in the night to play with their toys. I couldn't figure out how they were doing it so I set up the video camera with a motion sensor and caught Maddie moving like a little monkey to climb out of hers. She didn't need any help but Simon apparently wasn't as skilled so Maddie would climb out and then push a half-dozen stuffed animals over the top railing of his crib so he could use them to climb out. It was quite a system the little rascals came up with."

He paused in the middle of searching through his toolbox, his features far more interested than she might have expected. "So what did you do? Take out all the stuffed animals from the room?"

She made a face. "No. Gave in to the inevitable. We bought them both toddler beds so they wouldn't break their necks climbing out"

"Did they still get up in the night?"

"Not as much. I think it was the lure of the forbidden that kept them trying to escape."

He laughed—a real, full-fledged laugh. She watched the shadows lift from his eyes for just a moment, saw in that light expression some glimmer of the Will she had known, and she could swear she felt the tumble and thud of her heart.

She was an idiot for Will Garrett, only now she didn't have the excuse of being fifteen, flush with the heady excitement of first love.

After entirely too short a time, his laughter slid away and he turned his attention back to the project. "How do you feel about heights?"

"Moderately okay, within reason."

"It would help if you could hold the trim up while I nail it, as long as you don't mind climbing the ladder."

"Not at all."

For the next twenty minutes, they spoke little as they worked together to hang the trim. They finished two walls quickly but the other two weren't as straightforward. One had a fireplace and chimney flue that Will needed to work the trim around and the other had a jog that she thought must contain ductwork.

As she waited for Will to figure out the angles for the cuts, Julia sat on the couch, enjoying the animation on his features as he calculated. She wondered if he knew how his eyes lit up while he was working, how he seemed to vibrate with an energy she didn't see there at other times.

At last he figured out the math involved to make sure the moldings matched up correctly. He left for a moment and she heard his power saw out on the porch.

"You love this, don't you?" she asked when he returned carrying the cut pieces of trim.

He shrugged. "It's a living."

"It's more than that to you. I can tell. I keep remembering how much you complained about your dad making you go out on jobs with him that summer."

His laugh was rueful, tinged with embarrassment. "I was a stupid sixteen-year-old punk without a brain in my head. All I wanted to do was hang out with my friends and try to impress pretty girls."

She shook her head. "You were *not* a punk. You were by far the most decent boy I knew."

The tips of his ears turned that dusky red again. "Funny, you always seemed like such a sensible kind of girl."

"I was sensible enough to know when a boy is different from the others I'd met. All they wanted to do was flirt and see how many bases they could steal. They weren't interested in talking about serious things like the political science class they had taken the year before or the ecological condition of the shoreline."

"Did I do that?"

"You don't remember?"

He slanted her a sidelong look. "All I remember is trying to figure out whether I dared try sliding in to second base."

She blushed, though she couldn't help smiling, too. "I guess you were just more subtle about that particular goal than the other boys, then."

"Either that or more chicken."

She laughed. She couldn't help herself. To her delight, he laughed along with her and the unexpected sound of it even had Conan lifting his head to watch the two of them with what looked suspiciously like satisfaction.

She remembered Sage's assertion that the dog was working in cahoots with Abigail.

Just now—with the rain pattering softly against the window and this peculiar intimacy swirling around them—the idea didn't seem completely ludicrous.

"Okay, I think I've finally got this figured out," he said after a moment. "I think I'm ready for my assistant."

She pushed her ladder closer to his since they were working with a much smaller length of trim.

As he was only a few feet away from her, she was intensely aware of him—his scent, leathery and masculine, and the heat that seemed to pulse from him.

He wasn't smiling or laughing now, she noted. In fact, he seemed tense suddenly and in a hurry to finish this section of the job.

"I can probably handle the rest on my own," he said, his voice suddenly sounding strained. "None of the remaining lengths of trim are very long so I shouldn't need your help holding them in place."

"I can stick around, just in case you need me."

His gaze met hers and she thought he would tell her not to bother but he simply nodded. "Sure. Okay."

She was so relieved he wasn't going to send her away that she wasn't paying as close attention to what she was doing as she should have been while she descended the ladder at the same time Will descended his own ladder next to her.

In her distracted state, she misjudged the last rung and stumbled a little at the bottom.

"Whoa! Careful there," he exclaimed, reaching out instinctively to catch her.

For one moment, they froze in that suspended state, with his strong arms around her and her arms trapped between their bodies. Her startled gaze flew to his and she thought she saw awareness and desire and the barest shadow of resignation there.

Will stared at her, his heart pumping in his chest like an out-of-control nail gun. A desperate kind of hunger prowled through him, wild and urgent. Though he knew she was far from it, she felt small and fragile in his arms.

He could feel the heat of her burning his skin, could smell that soft, mouthwatering scent of cherry blossoms.

He closed his eyes, fighting the inevitable with every ounce of strength he had left. But when he opened his eyes, he found her color high, her lips parted slightly, her eyes a deep and mossy green, shadowed with what he was almost positive was a heady awareness to match his own.

He should stop this right now, should just release her, push her from Anna's apartment and lock the door snugly behind her. The tiny corner of his brain that could still manage to string together a coherent thought told him that was exactly the course of action he ought to follow.

But how could he? She was so soft, so sweetly, irresistibly warm, and he had been cold for so damn long.

He heard a groan and realized it came from his own throat just an instant before he lowered his mouth and kissed her.

She sighed his name, just a whispered breath between their mouths, but the sound seemed to sink through all the layers of careful protection around his heart.

She wrapped her arms around his neck, responding eagerly to his kiss. Tenderness surged through him, raw and terrifying. He wanted to hang on tight and never let go, wanted to stand in Abigail's old living room for the rest of his life with a soft rain clicking against the windows and Julia Hudson Blair in his arms.

They kissed for a long time, until he was breathing hard and light-headed, until her mouth was swollen, until his body cried out for more and more.

He didn't know how long they would have continued—forever if he'd had his way—when suddenly he heard the one thing guaranteed to shatter the moment and the mood like a hard, cold downpour.

"Mama? Are you there? I woke up."

The sweet, high voice cut through the room like a buzz saw. He stiffened, his insides cold suddenly, and frantically looked to the doorway, aghast at what he had done and that her daughter had caught them at it.

He only knew a small measure of relief when he realized the voice was coming from the walkie-talkie she had brought downstairs.

Julia was breathing just as hard as he was, her eyes wide and dazed and her cheeks flushed.

Even through his dismay, he had to clench his fists at his side to keep from reaching for her again.

She drew in a deep, shuddering breath, then walked to the walkie-talkie and picked it up.

"I'm here, baby," she said, her voice slightly ragged. "How are you feeling?"

"My throat still hurts a little but I'm okay," Maddie answered. "Where are you, Mama?"

Julia flashed a quick glance at him, then looked away. "Downstairs with W— Mr. Garrett. Didn't you see my note?"

"Yes, when I woke up. But I was just wondering if you were still down there."

"I am."

"Is Conan there with you?"

Will saw her sweep the room with her gaze until she found the dog still curled up by the couch. "He's right here. I'll bring him up with me if you want some company."

"Thanks, Mama."

She clipped the walkie-talkie to her belt, angled slightly away from him so he couldn't see her expression, then she seemed to draw another deep breath before she turned to face him.

"I...have to go up. Maddie needs me."

"Right." He ached to touch her again, just one more time, but he fiercely clamped down on the desire, wanting her gone almost as much as he wanted to sweep her into his arms again.

Without warning, he was suddenly furious. Damn her, *damn her,* for making him want again—for this churn of his blood pouring into the frozen edges inside him. Pain prickled through him, like he had just shoved frostbitten fingers into boiling water.

He didn't want this, didn't want to feel again. Hadn't he made that clear? So why the hell did she have to come in here, with her sweet smile and her warm eyes and her soft curves.

"Will—"

"Don't say anything," he bit out. "This was a mistake. It's been a mistake for me to spend even a minute with you since you came back to town."

At his sudden attack, shock and hurt flared in her green eyes and he hated himself all over again but that didn't change what he knew he had to do.

"You didn't think it was a mistake a moment ago," she murmured.

He couldn't deny the truth of that. "I'm attracted to you. That's obvious, isn't it? I have been since I was sixteen years old. But I don't want to be. You're in my way every single time I turn around."

He lashed out, needing only to make her understand even as he was appalled at his words, at the way her spine seemed to stiffen with each syllable.

Still, he couldn't seem to hold them back once he started. They gushed between them, ugly and harsh.

"You're always coming around to help me work, showing up at my house dragging your kids along, crowding me every second. Don't you get it? I don't want you around! Why can't you just leave me alone?"

Conan rose and growled and for the first time in Will's memory the dog looked menacing. At the same time, a branch outside Anna's apartment clawed and scratched against the window, whipped by a sudden microburst of wind.

Julia seemed to ignore all the external distractions. She drew in a deep breath, her face paler than he had ever seen it.

"That's not fair," she said, her voice low and tight.

He raked a hand through his hair, hating himself, hating her, hating Robin and Cara for leaving him this empty, harsh, cruel husk of a man. "I know. I know it's not fair. You don't deserve to bear the weight of all that, Julia. I know that, but I can't help it. I'm sorry, but it's the truth. I need you to leave me alone. Please. I can't do this anymore. I can't. Not with you. Not with anyone."

The branch scraped the glass harder and he made a mental note to prune it for Sage and Anna, even as he fought down the urge to pound something, to smash his fists hard into the new drywall he had put in a few months earlier.

She studied him for a long moment, her features taut.

"Okay," she finally murmured and headed for the door to Anna's apartment.

Before she left, she turned around to face him one last time. "I appreciate your frankness. Since I know you're a fair man, I'm sure you'll allow me the same privilege."

What the hell was he supposed to say to that? He waited,

though he wanted nothing more than to shove the door closed behind her and lock it tight.

"I have something I want to say, though I know it's not my place and none of my business. Still, I think you need to hear it from someone."

She paused, and seemed to be gathering her thoughts. When she spoke, her words sliced at him like a band saw.

"Will, do you really think Robin and Cara would want this for you?"

"Don't."

He couldn't bear a lecture or a commentary or whatever she planned. Not now, not about this.

She shook her head. "No. I'm going to say this. And then you can push me away all you want, as you've been doing since I came back to Cannon Beach. I want you to ask yourself if your wife and little girl would want you to spend the rest of your life wallowing in your pain, smothering yourself in it. From all I've heard about Robin, it sounds as if she was generous and loving to everyone. Sage has told me what a good friend she was to everyone, how people were always drawn to her because of her kindness and her cheerful nature. I'm sorry I never had the chance to meet her. But from what I've heard of her, I can't imagine Robin would find it any tribute to her kind and giving nature that you want you to close yourself away from life as some kind of…of penance because she's gone."

She looked as if she had more she wanted to say, but to his relief she only gave him one more long look then turned to gesture to Conan. The dog added his glare to hers, giving Will what could only be described as the snake-eye, then followed her out the door.

Will stood for a long moment, an ache in his chest and her scent still swirling around him. He closed his eyes, remembering again the sweetness of her touch, how fiercely he had wanted to hold on tight, to surrender completely and let her work her healing magic.

He had to leave.

That was all there was to it. He couldn't stay in Cannon Beach with Julia and her kids just a few houses away. There was no way in the small community of year-round residents that he could avoid her, and seeing her, spending any time with her, was obviously a mistake.

He had meant what he said. She crowded him and he couldn't deal with it anymore.

He knew after his outburst just now that she wouldn't make any effort to spend time with him, but they were still bound to bump into each other once in a while and he had just proved to himself that he had no powers of resistance where she was concerned.

He had no other option but to escape.

He pulled out his cell phone. He knew the number was there—he had dialed it only the night before but in the end he had lost his nerve and hung up.

With the wind still whipping the tree branches outside like angry fists, he found it quickly, hit the button to redial and waited for it to ring.

As he might have expected, he was sent immediately to voice-messaging. For a moment he considered hanging up again but the sweet scent of spring flowers drifted to him and he knew this was what he had to do.

He drew in a breath. "Eben, this is Will Garrett," he began. "I'd like to talk about your offer, if it's still open."

Chapter 12

"Simon, hands to yourself."

Her son snatched his fingers back an instant before they would have dipped into the frosting on the frill-bedecked sheet cake for Sage's wedding shower.

"I only wanted a little smackeral," he complained.

Julia sighed, even as she fought a smile. This was why she was destined to be a lousy mother, she decided. How on earth was she supposed to have the gumption to properly discipline her son when he knew he could charm her every time by quoting Winnie the Pooh?

"No smackerals, little or otherwise," she said as sternly as she could manage. "After the bridal shower you can have all the leftovers you want but Sage wouldn't want grimy little finger trails dipping through her pretty cake, would she?"

"Sage wouldn't mind," he grumbled.

All right, he was probably correct on that observation.

Sage was remarkably even-tempered for a bride and she adored Julia's twins and spoiled them both relentlessly.

But as their mother, it was Julia's responsibility to teach them little things like manners, and she couldn't let him get away with it, smackerals or not.

"I mind," she said firmly. "Tell you what, if you promise to help Anna and me put all the chairs and tables away after the shower, you can appease your sugar buzz with one of the cookies you and Maddie and I made last night."

He grinned and reached for one. "Can I take one to Mad? She's in her room."

"As long as you don't forget where you were taking it and eat that one too along the way."

"I would *never* do that!" he protested, with just a shade too much offended innocence.

Julia shook her head, smiling as she put the finishing touches on the cake.

Simon paused at the doorway. "Can we eat our cookies outside and play with Conan for a while since the rain *finally* stopped?"

"Of course," she answered. After an entire week straight of rain, she knew both of her children were suffering from acute cases of cabin fever.

A moment later, she heard the door slam then the pounding of two little sets of feet hurtling down the stairs, joined shortly after by enthusiastic barking.

Unable to resist, she moved to the window overlooking the backyard just in time to see Maddie pick up an armful of fallen leaves and toss them into the air, her face beaming with joy at being outside to savor the October sunshine. Not far away, Conan and Simon were already wrestling in the grass together.

The two of them loved this place—the old house, with

its quirks and its personality, the yard and Abigail's beautiful gardens, the wild and gorgeous ocean just a few footsteps away.

They were thriving here, just as she had hoped. They already had good friends at school, they were doing well in their classes. Maddie's health seemed to have taken a giant leap forward and improved immeasurably in the nearly two months they had been in Cannon Beach.

She should be so happy. Her children were happy, her job was working out well, they had all settled into a routine.

So why couldn't she shake this lingering depression that seemed to have settled on her shoulders as summer slid into autumn? She shifted her gaze from the Brambleberry House yard to another house just a few hundred yards up the beach.

There was the answer to the question of why she couldn't seem to shake her gray mood. Will Garrett. She hadn't seen him since their disastrous encounter nearly two weeks earlier but her insides still churned with dismay when she remembered his blunt words telling her to leave him alone, and then her own presumptuous reply.

She had been way out of line to bring Robin and Cara into the whole thing, to basically accuse him of dishonoring his wife and daughter's memory simply because he continued to push Julia away.

She had had no right to tell him how he ought to grieve or to pretend she knew what his wife might have wanted for him. She had never even met the woman.

Because of her lingering shame at her own temerity, she was almost grateful she hadn't seen him since, even to catch a glimpse of him through the pines as he moved around his house.

That's what she told herself, anyway. If she stood at her

window at night watching the lights in his house, hoping for some shadow to move across a window, well, that was her own pathetic little secret.

With one last sigh, she forced herself to move away from the window and return to the kitchen and the cake. A few moments later, with a final flourish, she judged it ready and carefully picked it up to carry it downstairs to Anna's apartment.

Since her arms were full, she managed to ring the doorbell with her elbow. Anna opened almost immediately. Though she smiled, Julia didn't miss the troubled expression in her eyes.

She was probably just busy setting up for the shower, Julia told herself. She knew Anna had been distracted with problems at her two giftshops as well, though she seemed reluctant to talk about them.

Julia smiled and held out the cake. "Watch out. Masterpiece coming through."

Anna's expression lifted slightly as she looked at the autumn-themed cake, with its richly colored oak and maple leaves and pine boughs, all crafted of frosting.

Sage wasn't one for frilly lace and other traditional wedding decorations. Given her job as a naturalist and her love of the outdoors, Julia and Anna had picked a nature theme for the shower they were throwing and the cake was to be the centerpiece of their decorations.

"Oh! Oh, it's beautiful!"

"Told you it would be," Julia said with undeniable satisfaction as she carried the cake inside Anna's apartment to a table set in a corner.

"You were absolutely right," Sage said from the couch. "I can't believe you did all that in one afternoon!"

Julia shrugged. "I don't have a lot of domestic skills but

I can decorate a cake like nobody's business. I told you I put myself through college working in a bakery, so if the teaching thing ever falls through, I've at least got something to fall back on."

She grinned at them both and was surprised when they didn't smile back. Instead, they exchanged grim looks.

"What is it? What's wrong? Is it the cake? I tried to decorate it just as we discussed."

"It's not the cake," Anna assured her. "The cake is gorgeous."

"Did somebody cancel, then?"

"No. Everybody's still coming, as far as I know." Sage sighed. "I just hung up the phone with Eben."

She frowned. "Is everything okay with Chloe?"

"No. Nothing like that. Julia, it's not Eben or Chloe or anything to do with the shower. It's Will."

Her stomach cramped suddenly and for a moment she couldn't seem to breathe. "What…what's wrong with Will?"

"He's leaving," Anna said, her usual matter-of-fact tone sounding strained.

"Leaving?"

Sage nodded, her eyes distressed. "Apparently he's taken a traveling job with Spencer Hotels. A sort of carpentry trouble-shooter, traveling around to their renovation sites and overseeing the work of the local builders. He's starting right after the wedding. He accepted the job a few weeks ago but apparently Eben didn't seem to think it was anything worth mentioning to me until just now on the phone, purely in passing."

She scowled, apparently at her absent fiancé. Julia barely noticed, too lost in her own shock. Two weeks ago. She didn't miss the significance of that, not for a minute.

They had kissed right here in this very living room and

she could think of nothing else but how he had all but begged her to leave him alone and then in her hurt, she had said such nervy, terrible things to him.

Ask yourself if your wife and little girl would want you to spend the rest of your life wallowing in your pain, smothering yourself in it.

Oh, what had she done? Now he had taken a traveling job with Eben's company and she could hardly seem to work her brain around it. He was leaving Cannon Beach—the home he loved, his friends, the business he had work so hard to build.

Because of her.

She knew it had to be so. What other reason could he have?

She had made him too uncomfortable, had pushed too hard.

I can't imagine Robin would find it any tribute that you want you to close yourself away from life as some kind of penance because she's gone.

Her face burned and her stomach seemed to twist into a snarled tangle. What had she *done?*

"What do you think, Julia?"

She jerked her mind back to the conversation to realize Sage was speaking to her and as her silence dragged on, both women were giving her curious looks.

It was obvious they expected some response from her but as she hadn't heard the question, she didn't know at all what to say.

"I'm sorry. What?"

"I said that you've known him longer than any of us. What could he be thinking?"

"Oh no. I don't know him," she murmured. "Not really."

Perhaps that was the trouble, she admitted to herself. She

had this idealized image of Will from years ago when she had loved him as a girl. Had she truly allowed herself to accept the reality of all the years and the pain between them?

She had pushed him, harder than he was ready to be pushed. She had backed him into a corner and he was looking for some way out.

This was all her fault and she was going to have to figure out a way to make things right. She couldn't let Will leave everything he cared about behind because of her.

The doorbell rang suddenly and Conan jumped up from his spot on the floor where he had been watching them. Now he hurried to Anna's open apartment door, his tail wagging furiously and for one wild moment her heart jumped at the thought that it might be Will.

Foolish, she realized almost instantly. Why would he be here?

More likely it was Becca Wilder, the teenager she had hired to corral the twins for the evening while she was busy with Sage's shower.

Her supposition was confirmed a moment later when Anna went to answer the door and Julia heard the voice of Jewel Wilder, Becca's mother and one of Sage's friends, who had offered to drop Becca off when she came to the shower herself.

She couldn't do anything about Will right now, she realized. Sage's bridal shower was supposed to start any moment now and she couldn't let the celebration be ruined by her guilt.

Three hours later, as Sage said goodbye to the last of her guests, Julia began gathering discarded plates and cups, doing her best to ignore her head that throbbed and pulsed with pain.

She knew exactly why her head was pounding—the same reason her heart ached. Because of Will and his stubborn determination to shut himself off from life and because of her own stubborn, misguided determination to prevent him.

For Sage's sake, she had done her best to put away her anxiety and guilt for the evening. She had laughed and played silly wedding shower games and tried to enjoy watching Sage open the gifts from her eclectic collection of friends.

Beneath it all, the ache simmered and seethed, like a vat of bitter bile waiting to boil over.

Will was leaving his home, his friends, his wife and daughter's resting places. She couldn't let him do it, not if he was leaving because of her.

She carried the plates and dishes into the kitchen, where she found Anna wrapping up the leftover food.

"It was a wonderful party," Julia said.

"I think everyone had a good time," Anna agreed. "But listen, you don't have to help clean up. I can handle it. Why don't you go on upstairs with the twins?"

"I just checked with Becca and they're both down for the night. She's heading home with her mom and is leaving the door open so we can hear them down here."

Anna stuck a plate of little sandwiches into her refrigerator, then gave Julia a placid smile.

"That's great. Since the twins are asleep, this would be the perfect chance for you to go and talk some sense into Will."

Julia stared at her, completely astounded at the suggestion. "Where did that come from?"

Anna smiled. "My brilliantly insightful mind."

"Which I never realized until this moment is a little on the cracked side. Why would he listen to me?"

"Well, somebody needs to knock some sense into him and Sage and I both decided you're the best one for the job."

"Why on earth would you possibly think *that?* You've both been friends with him for a long time. I just moved back. He'll listen to what you have to say long before he'll listen to me."

Not to mention the tiny little detail that she suspected *she* was the reason he was leaving in the first place—and the fact that he had basically ordered her to stay away from him.

She wasn't about to admit that to Anna, though.

"We're like sisters to him," Anna answered. "Naggy, annoying little sisters. You, on the other hand, are the woman he has feelings for."

She bobbled the plate she was loading into the dishwasher but managed to catch it before it shattered on the floor.

"Wrong!" she exclaimed. "Oh, you couldn't be more wrong. Will doesn't have feelings for me. He…he might, if he would let himself, but he's wrapped himself up so tightly in his pain he won't let anyone through. Or not me, at least. No, he absolutely doesn't have feelings for me."

Anna studied her for a long moment, then smiled unexpectedly. "Our mistake, then, I guess. Sage and I were quite convinced there was something between the two of you. Will's been different ever since you came back to Cannon Beach."

"Different, how?" she asked warily.

"I can't quite put my finger on how, exactly. I wouldn't say he's been happier, but he's done things he hasn't in two years. Going for ice cream with you and your kids. Coming to the barbecue with Eben and Chloe without putting up a fight. Sage and I both thought you were slowly dragging him back to life, whether he wanted you to or not, and we were both thrilled about it. He kissed you, didn't he?"

Julia flushed. "Yes, but he wasn't happy about either time."

Anna's eyebrow rose. "There was more than one time?"

She sighed. "A few weeks ago, when I helped him hang the new moldings in your living room. We had a fight afterward and I said horrible things to him, things I had no right to say. And now I find out he took a job with Eben's company, and accepted it two weeks ago. I just can't believe it's a coincidence."

"All the more reason you should be the one to convince him to stay," Anna said.

"He told me to stay away from him," Julia whispered, hurting all over again at the harshness of his words.

"Are you going to listen to him? Go on," Anna urged. "I'll keep an eye on Simon and Maddie for you. There's nothing stopping you."

Except maybe her guilt and her nerves and the horrible, sinking sensation in her gut that she was pushing a man away from everything that he cared about, just so he could escape from her.

Before she could formulate further arguments, a huge shaggy beast suddenly hurried into the room, a leash in his mouth and Sage right on his heels.

"Conan, what has gotten into you, you crazy dog?" she exclaimed. "I can put you out."

But the dog didn't listen to her. He headed straight to Julia, plopped down at her feet and held the leash out in his mouth with that familiar expectant look.

She groaned. "Not you, too?"

Sage and Anna exchanged glances and Julia was quite certain she heard Sage snigger.

"Looks like you're the chosen one," Anna said with a smile.

"You can't fight your destiny, Jules," Sage piped in. "Believe me, I've tried. The King of Brambleberry House has declared you're tonight's sacrificial lamb. You can't escape your fate."

She closed her eyes, aware as she did that the pain in her head seemed to have lifted while she was talking to Anna. "I suppose you're telling me Conan wants me to talk to Will, too."

"That's what it looks like to me," Sage said.

"Same here."

Julia stared at Anna—prosaic, no-nonsense Anna, who looked just as convinced as Sage.

"You're both crazy. He's a dog, for heaven's sake!"

Sage grinned. "Watch it. If you offend him, you'll be stuck for life giving him his evening walk."

"Rain or shine," Anna added. "And around here, it's usually rain."

She studied them all looking so expectantly at her and gave a sigh of resignation. "This isn't fair, you know. The three of you ganging up on me like this."

In answer, Sage clipped the leash on Conan's collar and held the end out for Julia. Anna left the room, returning a moment later with Julia's jacket from the closet in the entryway.

"What if Will doesn't want to talk to me?"

It was a purely rhetorical question. She knew perfectly well he wouldn't want to talk to her, just as she was grimly aware she was only trying to delay the inevitable moment when she had to gather her nerve and walk down the beach to his house.

"You're an elementary school teacher," Anna said with a confident grin. "You're good at making your students do things they don't want to do, aren't you?"

Julia snorted. "I have a feeling Will Garrett might be just a tad harder to manage than my fifth-grade boys."

"We all have complete faith in you," Sage said.

Before she was quite aware of how they had managed it, they ushered her and Conan out the front door and closed it behind her. She was quite surprised when she didn't hear the click of the door locking behind her. She wouldn't have put anything past them at this point.

Conan strained on his leash to be gone but she stood on the porch steps of Brambleberry House trying to gather her frayed nerves as she listened to the distant crash of the sea and the cool October breeze moaning in the tops of the pines.

Finally she couldn't ignore Conan's urgency and she followed the walkway around the house to the gate that opened to the beach.

It would probably be a quicker route to just take the road to his house but she wasn't in a huge hurry to face him anyway.

Conan seemed less insistent as they walked along the shoreline, after he had marked just about every single rock and tuft of grass they passed.

It gave her time to remember her last summer on Cannon Beach. She passed the rock where she had been sitting when he kissed her for the *last* time—not counting more recent incidences—the night before she left Cannon Beach when she was fifteen.

She paused and ran her finger along the uneven surface,

remembering the thrill of his arms around her and how she had been so very certain she had to be in love with him.

She'd had nothing to compare it to, but she had been quite sure at fifteen that this must be the real thing.

And then the next day her world had shattered and she had been shuttled to Sacramento with her mother, away from everything safe and secure in her life.

Still, even as her parents' marriage had imploded, she had held the memory of a handsome boy close to her heart.

At first she thought the moisture on her cheeks was just sea spray, then she realized it was tears, that she was crying for lost innocence and for the two people they had been, and for all the pain that had come after for both of them.

She wiped at her cheeks as she knelt and hugged Conan to her. The dog licked at her cheeks and she smiled a little at his attempts to comfort her.

"I'm being silly again, aren't I? I'm not fifteen anymore and I'm not that dreamy-eyed girl. I'm thirty-one years old and I need to start acting like it, don't I?"

The dog barked as if he agreed with her.

With renewed resolve, she squared her shoulders and stood again, gathering her courage around her.

She had to do this. Will's life was here in Cannon Beach. It had always been here, and she couldn't ruin that for him.

She swallowed her nerves and headed for the lights she could see flickering in his workshop.

Chapter 13

He would miss this.

Will stood in his father's workshop—his workspace now, at least for another few days—and routered the edge of a shingle while a blues station played on the stereo.

He had always found comfort within these walls, with the air sweet with freshly cut wood shavings and sawdust motes drifting in the air, catching the light like gold flakes.

He left the door ajar, both for ventilation and to let the cool, moist sea air inside. In the quiet intervals without the whine and hum of his power tools, he could hear the ocean's low murmur just down the beach.

This was his favorite spot in the world, the place where he had learned his craft, where he had forged a connection with his stern, sometimes austere father, where he had figured out many of his own strengths and his weaknesses.

Before Robin and Cara died, he used to come out here so he could have a quiet place to think. Sage probably would

have given it some hippy new age name like a transcen-
dental meditation room or something.

He just always considered it the one place where his
thoughts seemed more clear and cohesive.

He didn't so much need a place to think these days as
he needed an escape on the nights when the house seemed
too full of ghosts to hold anyone still breathing.

In a few days when he started working for Eben Spencer's company, everything would be different. He expected
his workspaces for the next few months would be any spare
corner he could find in whatever hotel around the globe
where Eben sent him to work.

Who would have ever expected him to become an itin-
erant carpenter? *Have tools, will travel.*

His first job was outside of Boston but Eben wanted to
send him to Madrid next and then on to Portofino, Italy
before he headed to the Pacific Rim. And that was only
the first month.

Will shook his head. Italy and Spain and Singapore.
What the hell was he going to do in a foreign country where
he didn't know a soul and didn't speak the language?

It all seemed wildly exotic for a guy who rarely left his
coastal hometown, who only possessed a current passport
because he and Robin had gone on a cruise to Mexico the
year before Cara came along.

The work would be the same. That was the important
thing. He would still be doing the one thing he was good at,
the one thing that filled him with satisfaction, whether he
was in Portofino or Madrid or wherever else Eben sent him.

Maybe those ghosts might even have a chance to rest if
he wasn't here dredging them up every minute.

He sure hoped he was making the right choice.

He set down the finished shingle and picked up another

one from the dwindling pile next to him. Only a few more and then he only had to nail them to the roof to be finished. A few more hours of work ought to do it.

Against his will, he shot another glance out the window at the big house on the hill, solid and graceful against the moonlit sky.

The lights were out on the second floor, he noted immediately, then chided himself for even noticing.

He was almost certain he wasn't really trying to outrun any ghosts by taking the job with Spencer Hotels. But he knew he couldn't say the same for the living woman who haunted him.

He sighed as his thoughts inevitably slid back to Julia, as they had done so often the last two weeks. Tonight was Sage's bridal shower, he knew. He had seen cars coming and going all night.

Julia was probably right in the middle of it all, with her sweet smile and the sunshine she seemed to carry with her into every room.

For a man who wanted to push her away, he sure spent a hell of a lot of time thinking about her. He sighed again, and could almost swear he smelled the cherry blossom scent of her on the wind.

But a moment later, when the router was silent as he picked up another shingle, he thought he heard a snuffling kind of noise outside the door, then a dark red nose poked through.

An instant later, Conan was barking a greeting at him and Julia was walking through the doorway behind him.

Will yanked up his safety glasses and could do nothing but stare at her, wondering how his thoughts had possibly conjured her up.

Her cheeks were flushed, her hair tousled a little by the wind, but she was definitely flesh and blood.

"Hi," she murmured, and he was certain her color climbed a little higher on her cheeks.

She looked fragile and lovely and highly uncomfortable. No wonder, after the things he had said to her the last time they had spoken.

"I'm sorry to bother you… I…we…" Her voice trailed off.

"Wasn't tonight Sage's big bridal shower?"

"It was. But it's over now and everyone's gone. After the shower, Conan needed a walk and he picked me to take him and Sage and Anna made me come down here to talk to you."

She finished in a rush, without meeting his gaze.

"They made you?"

Her gaze finally flashed to his and he saw a combination of chagrin and rueful acceptance. "You know what they're like. I have a tough enough time saying no to them individually. When they combine forces, I'm pretty much helpless to resist."

"Why did they want you to talk to me?" he asked, though he had a pretty strong inkling.

She didn't answer him, though, only moved past him into the workshop, her attention suddenly caught by the project he was working on.

Damn it.

He could feel his own cheeks start to flush and wished, more than anything, that he had had the foresight to grab a tarp to cover the thing the minute she walked in.

"Will," she exclaimed. "It's gorgeous!"

He scratched the back of his neck, doing his best to ignore how the breathy excitement in her voice sent a shiver rippling down his spine. "It's not finished. I'm working on the shingles tonight, then I should be ready to take it back up to Brambleberry House."

She moved forward for a closer look and he couldn't seem to wrench his gaze away from her starry-eyed delight at the repaired dollhouse he had agreed to work on the day she moved in.

"It's absolutely stunning!"

She drew her finger along the curve of one of the cupola's with tender care. Will could only watch, grimly aware that he shouldn't have such an instant reaction just from the sight of her soft, delicate hands on his work.

"You fixed it! No, you didn't just fix it. This is beyond a simple repair. It was such a mess, just a pile of broken sticks, when you started! And from that, you've created a work of art!"

"I don't know that I'd go quite that far."

"I would! Oh, Will, it's beautiful. Better than it ever was, even when it was new from my father."

To his horror, tears started to well up in her eyes.

"It's just a dollhouse. Not worth bawling about," he said tersely, trying to keep the sudden panic out of his voice.

She gave a short laugh as she swiped at her cheeks. "They're happy tears. Oh, believe me. Will, it's wonderful. I can't tell you how much this will mean to Maddie. She tried to be brave about it but she was so heartbroken when I told her the dollhouse hadn't survived the move. It was one of her last few ties to her father and she has always cherished it, I think because he gave it to her right after her diagnosis, a few days before he…"

Her voice trailed off for a moment and he thought she wasn't going to complete the sentence, but then she drew in a breath and straightened her shoulders. "Before he left us."

Will stared at her, trying to make sense of her words. "I didn't realize your husband died so soon after Maddie's cancer was discovered."

She sighed. "He didn't," she said slowly. "His car accident was eighteen months after her diagnosis but...we were separated most of that time. We were a few months shy of finalizing our divorce when he died."

She lifted her chin almost defiantly when she spoke the last part of the sentence.

He wondered at it, even as he tried to figure out how the hell a man with a beautiful wife and two kids—one with cancer—could walk away from his family in the middle of a crisis.

He left us, she had said quite plainly. He didn't miss the meaning of that now. The man had a daughter with cancer and he had been the one to walk away from them.

Will had a sudden fierce wish that he could have met her husband just once before he died, to teach the bastard a lesson about what it meant to be a man.

She was waiting for him to answer, he realized.

"I'm sorry," he finally said, wincing at the inane words. "That must have been hard on you and the kids during such a rough time."

She managed a wobbly smile. "You could say that."

"All this time, you never said anything about your marriage. I had no idea it was rocky."

She sighed and leaned against the work table holding the resurrected dollhouse.

"I don't talk about it much, especially when the kids are around. I don't want them thinking less of their father."

He raised an eyebrow at that, but said nothing. He had his own opinions about it but he didn't think she would be eager to hear them.

"Maddie's diagnosis kicked Kevin in the gut. The stark truth is, he just couldn't handle it. His mother died of cancer when he was young, a particularly vicious form that lingered for a long time, and I think he just couldn't bear the thought that he might lose someone else he loved in the same way."

What kind of strength had it taken her to deal with a crumbling marriage at the same time she was fighting for her daughter's life? He couldn't even imagine it.

He studied her there in his workshop and saw shadows in her eyes. There was more to the story, he sensed.

"Was there someone else?" Some instinct prompted him to ask.

She gave him a swift, shocked look. "How did you know that? I haven't told anyone else. Not even Sage and Anna know that part."

"I don't know. Just a guess." He couldn't very well tell her he was becoming better than he ought to be at reading her thoughts in her lovely green eyes.

She sighed, tracing a finger over one of the arched windows on the dollhouse. "A coworker. He swore he only turned to her after we separated—after Maddy's diagnosis—because he was hurting so much inside and so afraid for the future."

"That doesn't take away much of the sting for you, I imagine."

"No. No, it doesn't. I was angry and bitter for a long time. I mean, I was the one dealing with appointments and sitting through Maddie's chemotherapy with her and holding her when she threw up for hours afterward. I was scared, too. Not scared, I was *terrified*. I used to check on her dozens of times a night, just to make sure she was still breathing. I still do when she's having a rough night. It was a miracle I could function, most days. I was just as scared, but I didn't turn to someone else. I toughed it out by myself because I had no choice."

He couldn't imagine such a betrayal—more than that, he couldn't understand why she could seem to be such a happy person now after what she had been through.

Most women he knew would be bitter and angry at the world after surviving such an ordeal but Julia seemed to bubble over with joy, finding delight in everything.

She had been over the moon that he had repaired a dollhouse her bastard of an almost-ex-husband had worked on. He figured most betrayed women would have smashed the dollhouse to pieces themselves out of spite so they wouldn't have one more reminder of their cheating spouse.

"I don't know why I told you all that," she said after a moment, her cheeks slightly pink. "I didn't come here to relive the past."

Since she seemed eager to change the subject, he decided he wouldn't push her.

"That's right," he answered. "Sage and Anna sent you."

"I would have come anyway," she admitted. "They just gave me a push in this direction."

He found that slightly hard to believe, given his rudeness the last time they met.

"Why?" he asked.

She let out a breath, then confirmed his suspicion. "I... Sage just found out from Eben tonight that you're leaving."

He picked up another shingle, stalling for time. He did *not* want to get into this, especially not with her, though he had been half-expecting something like this for two weeks, since he accepted Eben's offer.

"That's right," he finally said. It would have been rude to

turn the router on again—not to mention, Conan wouldn't like it—but he was severely tempted, if only to cut her off.

She seemed to have become inordinately fascinated with one of the finials on the dollhouse.

"I know this is presumptuous and I have no real right to ask…"

Her voice trailed off and he sighed, yanking his safety glasses off his head and setting them aside. He had a feeling he wasn't going to be finishing the dollhouse anytime soon.

"Something tells me you're going to ask anyway."

She twisted her hands together, her color still high. "You love Cannon Beach, Will. I know you do."

"Yeah. I do love it here. I always have."

"Help me understand, then, why you would suddenly decide to leave the town you have lived in for thirty-two years. This is your home. You have friends here, a thriving business. Your whole life is here!"

"What life?"

He hadn't meant to say something that raw, that honest, but his words seemed to hang between them and he couldn't yank them back.

It was the truth, anyway.

He didn't have a life, or at least not much of one. Everything he had known and cared about was gone and he couldn't walk anywhere in Cannon Beach without stumbling over a memory of a time when he thought he had owned the world, when he was certain he had everything he could ever possibly want.

Since Julia came to town, everything seemed so much harder, his world so much emptier—something else he wasn't about to explain to her.

Her eyes were dark with sorrow and something else that looked suspiciously like guilt.

"Maybe I was ready for a change," he finally said. "You just said it yourself, I've lived here my entire life. That's pretty pathetic for a grown man to admit, that he's never been anywhere, never done anything. Eben offered me the job some time ago. I gave it a lot of thought and finally decided the time was right."

She didn't look convinced. After another long, awkward moment, she clenched her hands together and lifted her gaze to his, her mouth trembling slightly.

"Will you tell me the truth? Are you leaving because of me?"

He shifted his gaze away, wishing his hands were busy with the router again. Unfortunately, his gaze collided with Conan's, and the dog gave him an entirely too perceptive look.

"Why would you say that?" he stalled.

She stepped closer, looking again as if she wanted to weep. "I've been sick inside ever since Sage told me you were taking this job with Eben's company."

"You shouldn't be, Julia. This is not on you. Let it go."

She shook her head. "I pushed you too hard the other day. I said terrible things. I had no right, Will. I have a terrible habit of always thinking I know what's best for everyone else."

Her short laugh held no trace of humor. "I don't know why. I mean, I've made a complete mess of my own life, haven't I? So why would I dare think I have any right to tell anyone else what to do with their life? But I was wrong, Will. I shouldn't have said what I did."

"Everything you said was right on the money. I knew it even while I was reacting so strongly. I've thought the same things myself, deep in my subconscious. Robin wouldn't want me to hide away from life, to sit out here in my workshop and brood while the world carries on without me. That wasn't what she was about, what *we* were about. But even though I've thought the same thing, I can't deny that hearing it from you was tough."

"I'm so sorry."

He sighed at the misery in her voice and surrendered to the inevitable. He stepped forward and picked up her knotted fingers, feeling them tremble in his hands.

"I care about you, Julia, more than I thought I could ever care about anyone again. When I'm with you, I feel like I'm sixteen again, sitting on the beach with the prettiest girl I've ever seen. But it scares the hell out of me. I'm not ready. That's the bald, honest truth. I'm not ready and I'm afraid I don't know if I ever will be."

"That's why you're leaving?"

"I'd be lying if I said you had nothing to do with my decision to take the job with Eben. But leaving—trying something new—has been on my mind for some time. I was considering it long before you showed up again, back when you were just a distant memory of a past that sometimes feels like it should belong to someone else."

He paused, struck by the contrast of her soft, delicate hands in his fingers that were hard and roughened by years of work.

"I guess you could say you're part of the reason I'm leaving, but you're not the only reason. I need a change. If I stay here, buried under the weight of the past, I'm afraid I'll slowly petrify like a piece of driftwood."

She took a long time to answer. Just when he was about to release her hands and step away, she clutched at his fingers with hands that still trembled.

"Would it make any difference if I…if I were the one to leave?"

He stared at her, taken aback. "Where would you go? You love your new job, Brambleberry House. Everything."

Sadness twisted across her lovely features. "I do love it here and the twins are thriving. But I have much less invested in Cannon Beach than you do. I've only been here a short time. We started over here, we can start over somewhere else."

That she would even contemplate making such a sacrifice for his sake completely astounded him.

"You can't do that for me, Julia. I would never ask of it you."

"You didn't ask. I'm offering. I hate the idea that I had anything to do with your decision to leave. I blew in to town out of nowhere and ruined everything."

"You ruined nothing, Julia."

Whether he liked it or not, tenderness churned through him and he couldn't bear her distress. He lifted their joined hands and pressed his mouth to the warm skin at the back of her hand.

She shivered at his touch and he couldn't help himself. He pulled her into his arms, where she settled with a soft sigh.

"You ruined nothing," he repeated. "If anything, you made me realize I can't exist in this halflife forever. I have to move forward or I'll suffocate and right now taking this job with Eben feels like the best way to do that."

"I don't want you to leave," she murmured, her arms around his waist and her cheek against his chest.

He closed his eyes, stunned by the soft, contented peace that seemed to swirl through him. Right at this moment, he didn't want to think about leaving. Hell, he didn't want to move a muscle ever again.

They stood together for a long time, in a silence broken only by the sea outside the door and the dog's snuffly breaths as he slept.

When at last she lifted her face to his, he gave a sigh of surrender and lowered his mouth to hers.

Chapter 14

His kiss was slow and gentle, like standing in a torpid stream, and it seemed to push every single thought from her head.

After their last kiss and the words they had flung at each other afterward, she had been certain she wouldn't find herself here in his arms again.

The unexpectedness of it added a poignant beauty to the moment and she leaned into him, savoring his hard strength against her.

He kissed her for long, drugging moments, until her knees were weak and her mind a pleasant muddle.

Through the soft haze that seemed to surround her, she had a vague awareness that there a subtle difference this time, something that had been missing the other times they kissed.

It took her several moments to pinpoint the change. Those other times they had kissed, he had always held part of himself back and she had sensed the reluctance underlying each touch, even when she doubted he was fully aware of it himself.

This time, that hesitancy was gone. All she tasted in his kiss was tenderness and the sweet simmer of desire.

She smiled against his mouth, unable to contain the giddy joy exploding through her.

"What's so funny?" he murmured.

"Nothing," she assured him. "Absolutely nothing. It's just… I've just missed you."

He stared at her for a long moment, his face just inches from hers, then he groaned and kissed her again. This time his mouth was wild, urgent, and she responded eagerly, pouring all the emotions in her heart into their embrace.

She was in love with him.

Even as her body stirred to life, as their mouths tangled together, as she seemed to sink into the hard strength of his arms, the truth seemed to washed over her like the storm-churned sea and she reeled under the unrelenting force of it.

He was leaving in three days and had just made it quite plain he wouldn't change his mind. Nothing but heartache awaited her. She knew it, just as she knew she was powerless to change the inevitable.

But that didn't matter. Right here, right now, she was in his arms and she couldn't waste this moment by worrying about how much she would bleed inside when he walked away.

She tightened her arms around him and he made a low sound in the back of his throat and his arms tightened around her.

"Julia," he murmured. Just her name and nothing else.

"I'm here," she whispered. "Right here."

She brushed a kiss against the skin of his jawline, savoring the scent of sawdust and hard-working male. He made a low sound in his throat that sent an answering shiver rippling down her spine.

"You're cold."

"A little," she admitted, though her reaction was more from the desire spinning wildly through her system.

"I'm sorry. I like to keep it cool out here when I'm working, especially at night to keep me awake."

He paused for a moment, his gaze a murky blue. "We could go inside," he said, with a soberness that told her exactly what he meant by the words—and how much it cost him to make the suggestion.

A hundred doubts and insecurities zinged through her head. It would be tough enough for her to handle his departure. How could she possibly let him walk away after sharing such intimacies without her heart shattering into a million pieces?

But how could she walk away *now,* when he was offering her so much more of himself than she ever thought he would?

"Are you sure?" she asked.

He paused, taking his time before answering. "I'm not sure of anything, Julia. I only know I want you and this feels more right than anything else has in a long, long time."

"Oh, Will." She framed his face with her hands and kissed him again, pouring all her heart into the kiss.

When at last he drew back, both of them were trembling, their breathing ragged.

"I don't know if I can promise you anything," he said, his voice a low rasp in the night. "Hell, I'm almost a hundred percent certain I can't. But right now I can't bear the thought of letting you out of my arms."

"I'm not going anywhere," she said.

"Not even inside, where it's warmer and far more comfortable than my dusty workshop?"

She smiled, aware of the cold seeping through her jacket despite the heat of his embrace. "All right."

He returned her smile with one of his own and she shivered all over again at the unexpectedness of it. "I'm not going to let you freeze to death out here. Come on inside."

Conan was already standing by the door waiting for them, she saw when she managed to wrench her gaze away from Will's, as if the dog had heard and understood their complete conversation.

She shook her head at his spooky omniscience, but didn't have time to ponder it before Will was holding her hand and walking inexorably toward his house.

It had started to rain again while she was inside the workshop, a fine, cold mist that settled in her hair and made her grateful for the warmth that met them inside the house.

She hadn't been inside his home since that last summer so long ago, though she had seem glimpses of it through the window the day they had gone for ice cream, another lifetime ago.

She had the fleeting impression as she followed him inside of a roomy, comfortable place with a vaguely neglected air to it. He slept here but she had the feeling he spent as little time as possible within these walls.

Conan stopped in the kitchen and plopped down on a rug by the door but Will led her to a large family room with two adjoining deep sofas facing a giant plasma television on one wall.

"Are you still cold?" he asked. "I can start a fire. That should take the chill out of the air."

"You don't have to."

"It will only take a moment."

Without waiting for an answer, he moved to the hearth and started laying out kindling. She didn't mind, sensing he needed the time and space, just as she did, to regain a little equilibrium.

She shrugged out of her jacket and settled into one of the plump sofas, nerves careening through her.

It had been a long time for her and she hoped she wasn't unforgivably rusty. She would have been completely terrified if she didn't have the feeling he hadn't been with anyone since his wife's death.

"I imagine you have a spectacular view when it's daylight."

He gave her a rueful smile as he set a match to the kindling. "I guess. I've been looking at it every day of my life. I tend to forget how breathtaking it is. Maybe traveling a little—seeing other sights for a change—will help me appreciate what I've taken for granted all my life."

Somehow she didn't think the reminder of his imminent departure was accidental. She tried to pretend it didn't matter, even as sorrow pinched at her.

"Do you know where Eben's sending you first?"

"Outside of Boston. I'll be there for a few weeks then I guess I'm off to Italy. Quite a change for a guy who's never left the coast."

The tinder was burning brightly now so he added a heavier log. The flames quickly caught hold of it. Already, the room seemed warmer, though she wasn't sure if that was from the fire or from the nerves shimmering through her.

Will stood for a moment, watching the fire. When he seemed confident the log would burn, he turned back to her, his features impassive.

"Is something wrong?" she finally said, when the silence between them dragged on.

His sigh sounded deep, heartfelt. "You scare the hell out of me."

She tensed. "Do you want me to leave?"

"About as much as I want to take a table saw to my right arm," he admitted. "In other words, absolutely not."

Despite her nerves, she couldn't contain the laughter bubbling through her as he moved toward her and sat on the sofa beside her. He reached for her hand, but didn't seem in a rush to kiss her again.

This was lovely, she thought, sitting here gazing into the flickering firelight with a soft rain sliding against the window and his fingers tracing patterns on hers.

"I don't know if this is any consolation," she said after a moment, "but you're not the only one who's nervous. It's, uh, been a long time for me. I'd be surprised if you couldn't hear my knees knocking from there."

He gave her a careful look. "Do *you* want to leave?"

She mustered a shaky smile. "About as much as I want to *watch* you take a table saw to your right arm. In other words, absolutely not."

"Good," he murmured.

Finally he kissed her and at the delicious heat, the familiar taste and scent of him, her nerves disappeared. She was suddenly filled with the sweet assurance that this was right. She loved Will Garrett, had loved him since she was a stupid, naive girl.

She wanted this, wanted him, and even if this was all they would ever share, she wouldn't allow any regrets.

He kissed her until she was trembling, aching for more. She held him close, pouring all the emotions she couldn't verbalize into her kiss.

By the time he worked the buttons of her blouse, her head was whirling. When he pushed aside the lacy cups of her bra to touch her, she almost shattered apart right there as a torrent of sensations poured through her.

Oh, it had been far too long since she had remembered what it was to be touched with such heat and tenderness. She had forgotten this slow churn of her blood, the restless ache that seemed to fill every cell.

She arched against him, reveling in his hard strength against her curves, in his rough hands against her sensitive skin.

He groaned, low in his throat, and lowered his head to take her in his mouth. She clutched him close, her hands buried in his hair, as he teased and tasted.

His breathing was ragged when he lifted his clever, clever lips from her breast and found her mouth again while he shrugged out of his own shirt.

She couldn't help shivering as his hard strength covered her again.

"Are you still cold?" he murmured.

"Not even close," she answered, framing his face in her hands and kissing him fiercely. He responded with a groan and any tentativeness disappeared in a wild rush of heat.

In moments, they were both naked. Silhouetted in the dancing firelight, he was gorgeous, hard and muscled, ruggedly male.

"Okay, now I'm nervous again," she admitted.

"We can stop right now if you want," he said gruffly. "It might just kill me to let you out of my arms, but we don't have to go any further."

"No. I don't want to stop. Just kiss me again."

He willingly obeyed and for several long moments, only their mouths connected, then at last he pulled her close, trailing kisses from her mouth to the sensitive skin of her neck.

"Okay now?" he murmured, his body warm and hard against her.

"Oh, much, much better than okay," she breathed, her mouth tangling with his again as he pressed her back against the soft cushions of the sofa.

It was everything she might have dreamed—tender and passionate, sexy and sweet. When he filled her, she cried out, stunned at the emotions pouring through her, and she had to choke back the words of love she knew he wasn't ready to hear.

His mouth was hard and urgent on hers as he began to slowly move inside her and she lifted her hips to meet him.

Oh, she had missed this. She hadn't fully appreciated how much until right this moment.

How was she ever going to be able to go back to her solitary life?

She pushed the grim thought away, unwilling to let anything destroy the beauty of this moment.

He moved more deeply inside her and she gasped his name, feeling as breathless and shaky as the time she and Will had sneaked out to go cliff diving.

He withdrew then pushed inside her again and the contrast between the tenderness of his kiss and the wild urgency of his body sent her spinning and soaring over the edge.

With a groan, he joined her, his hands gripping hers tightly.

As they floated together back to earth, he shifted and pulled her on top of him, tugging a knit throw from the back of the sofa to cover them.

She nestled into his heat and his strength, a delicious lassitude soaking into her muscles, more content than she could ever remember being in her life.

* * *

She must have slept for a few moments, tucked into the safe shelter of his arms. When she blinked her eyes open, the grandfather clock in the hallway was tolling midnight.

Like Cinderella, she knew the spell was ending and she would have to slip away home.

She shifted her gaze to Will and found him watching her. Was he regretting what they had shared? To her frustration, she could read nothing in his veiled expression.

She sat up, reaching for her blouse as she went. "I need to go back to Brambleberry House. Sage and Anna are going to be sending a search party out after me."

He sat up and she had to force herself to look away from that broad, enticing expanse of muscles.

"Oh, somehow I doubt that. I have a feeling they know exactly where you are."

"You're probably right," she answered ruefully. "A little on the spooky side, those two."

He raised an eyebrow as he slid into his jeans. "A little?"

She smiled. "Okay. A lot. I should still go, much as I don't want to."

He was quiet for a long moment, watching out of those veiled features as she worked the buttons of her shirt.

"Julia, I can't promise you anything," he finally said.

She met his gaze, doing her best to keep the devastation at bay. "You said that earlier, and I understand, Will. I do. I don't expect anything."

He raked a hand through his hair. "I'm just so damn screwed up right now. I wish things could be otherwise. I'm just…"

She returned to him and cut his words off with a kiss, hoping he didn't taste the desperation in her kiss. This would be the one and only time for them, she knew.

He didn't have to say the words for her to accept the reality that nothing had changed. He was still leaving in a few days, and she would be left here alone with her pain.

"Will, it's okay," she lied. "My eyes were wide open when I walked into your house. No illusions here, I promise."

"I'm so sorry." His voice was tight with genuine regret and she shook her head.

"I'm not. Not for an instant."

She drew in a breath, gathering the last vestiges of courage left inside her for what somehow she suddenly knew she had to say.

"While we're tossing our cards out on the table, I think I should tell you why I'm here."

His expression turned wary. "Why?"

She sighed. "You haven't figured it out? I'm in love with you, Will."

The words hovered between them, raw and naked, and she had to smile a little at the sudden panic in his eyes.

"I know. It was a big shock for me, too. I'm not telling you that as some kind of underhanded tactic to convince you to stay. I know that nothing I say will change your mind and, believe me, I don't expect my feelings to change your decision in any way. I just felt that you should know. I wouldn't be here with you right now if I didn't love you— it's just not the kind of thing I do."

"I think some part of me guessed as much," he admitted.

"You've been in my heart for sixteen years, Will. Through my parents' divorce, through my own difficult teen years, through the breakup of my marriage, some part of me remembered that summer with you as a wonderful, magical time. Maybe the best summer of my life. You were my first love and I've never forgotten you."

"Julia…"

She shook her head, willing herself not to cry. Not now, not yet. "You don't have to say it. I know, we were different people then. And to be honest, the place you held in my heart was precious but only a tiny, dusty little spot, a corner I peeked into once in awhile with a smile and fond memories but then quickly forgot again."

She forced a smile. "And then I came back to Cannon Beach and here you were. As I came to know you all over again, I revisited those memories and realized that the boy I fell in love with back then had become a good, honorable man. A man who takes great pride in a job well done, who talks to dogs, who cares deeply about his neighbors and is kind to children…even when they make him bleed inside."

She touched his cheek, wishing with all her heart that he was ready to accept the precious, healing gift she so wanted to offer him.

Even as she touched him, though, she didn't miss his slight, barely perceptible flinch.

"Don't. Don't love me, Julia." His voice was ragged, anguished. "I'll only hurt you."

"I know you will." She managed a wobbly smile, even though she could swear she heard the sound of her heart cracking apart. "But I'll survive it."

She kissed him again, a soft, sincere benediction, then stepped away to shrug into her jacket. "I have to go."

He didn't argue, just pulled on his own shirt and boots. "I'll walk you back."

"I have Conan. I'll be fine."

"I'll walk you back," he said firmly.

She nodded, realizing that arguing with him would only be a waste of strength and energy, two commodities she had a feeling she would be needing in the days ahead.

In truth, she didn't mind. These were probably her last few moments with him and she wanted to savor every second.

Conan was again waiting expectantly by the back door. He cocked his head, his expression quizzical. She had no idea what he could read in their expressions but he whined a little.

More than anything, she wanted to bury her face in his fur and sob but she managed to keep her composure as Will handed her an umbrella and picked up a flashlight hanging on a hook by the door.

The slow, steady rain perfectly matched her mood. She shivered a little and zipped up her jacket, then headed toward Brambleberry House.

Will didn't share the umbrella—instead, he simply pulled the hood of his Gore-Tex jacket up, which given the dark and the rain effectively obscured his features.

They walked in silence and even Conan seemed subdued, almost sad. Instead of his usual ebullient energy, he plodded along beside her with his head hanging down.

As for Will, he seemed as distant and unreachable as the Cape Meares lighthouse.

She shouldn't have told him her feelings, she thought. He already carried enough burdens. He didn't need that one, too.

He finally spoke when they approached the gates of Brambleberry House, but they weren't words she wanted to hear.

"Julia, I'm sorry," he said.

"Please don't be sorry we made love. I'm not."

"I should be. Sorry about that, I mean. But I'm not. It was…right. That's not what I meant. Mostly, I guess I'm sorry things can't be different, that we have all these years and pain between us."

She touched his cheek. "The years and the pain shaped us, Will. They're part of who we are now."

He turned his head and kissed her fingers, then pulled her into his arms once more. His kiss was tender, gentle, with an underlying note of finality to it. When he drew away, her throat ached with unshed tears.

"You're not leaving until after the wedding, are you?"

He nodded. "Sage would kill me if I missed her big day. My flight leaves the next morning."

"Well, I'll see you then, anyway. Goodbye, Will."

She had a million things she wanted to say but this wasn't the time. None of them would make a difference anyway.

Instead, she managed one last shaky smile and tugged Conan up the stairs and into the entry, forcing herself not to look back as she heard his muffled footsteps on the sidewalk.

Anna's apartment door opened the moment Julia closed the front door behind her, and Sage and Anna both peeked their heads out into the entryway. They had changed into pajamas and she could smell the aroma of popcorn from inside the apartment.

Conan hurried inside as soon as she unclipped his leash, probably looking for any stray kernels that might have been dropped. She would have smiled if she thought she could manage it.

"So?" Sage demanded. "What happened? You were gone *forever*. Did you talk Will into staying?"

As much as she had come to love both the other women in just the few short months she had been in Cannon Beach, she couldn't bear their curiosity right now, not when her emotions had been scraped to the bone.

"No," she said, her voice low. "His mind is made up."

Sage made a sound of disgust but Anna gave her a searching, entirely perceptive look. She was suddenly aware that her hair was probably a mess and she no doubt had whisker burns on her skin.

"It's not your fault, Julia," she said after a moment. "I'm sure you tried your best."

She fought an almost hysterical urge to laugh. To hide it, she yanked off her jacket and hung it back in the closet. "He has his reasons. He didn't take the job with Eben on a whim, I can promise you that."

"That still doesn't make it right!" Sage exclaimed.

"As people who…who care about him, we owe it to Will to respect his decision, even if we don't agree with it or think it's necessarily the best one for him."

Sage looked as if she wanted to argue but Anna silenced her with a long, steady look.

"He won't change his mind?" Anna asked.

"I don't think so," Julia said.

To her surprise, though Sage was usually the demonstrative one, this time Anna was the one who pulled her into her arms for a hug. "Thanks for trying. I know it was hard for you."

You have no idea, she thought, even as Sage hugged her as well. For just a moment, Julia thought she smelled freesia and it was almost as if Abigail herself was there offering understanding and comfort.

"Don't badger him about it, okay?" she said. "It was a hard decision for him to make but I think taking the job is something he…he needs to do right now."

"Are you okay?" Anna murmured.

For one terrible moment, the sympathy in her friend's voice almost made her weep but she blinked away the tears. "Fine. Just fine. Why wouldn't I be?"

Anna didn't look convinced but to her immense relief, she didn't push. "You look exhausted. You'd better get some rest."

She nodded with a grateful look. "It's been a long day," she agreed. "Good night."

She quickly turned and hurried up the stairs, praying she could make it inside before breaking down.

After she closed the door behind her, she checked on the twins and found them sleeping peacefully, then returned to the darkened living room. Against her will, she moved to the windows overlooking his house and saw lights on again in his workshop.

The thought of him in his solitary workshop by himself, putting the finishing touches on Maddie's spectacular dollhouse was the last straw. Tears slid down her cheeks to match the rain trickling down the window and she stood for a long time in the dark, aching and alone.

Chapter 15

Three days later, he stood on the edge of the dance floor in the elegant reception room of The Sea Urchin, doing his level best not to spend the entire evening staring at Julia like the lovesick teenager he had once been.

He hadn't seen her since the night they had shared together but he was quite certain he hadn't spent more than ten minutes without thinking about her—remembering the softness of her skin, her sweet response to him, the shock that had settled in gut when she told him she loved him.

Just now she was dancing with her son, laughing as she tried to show him the steps of the fox-trot. She looked bright and vibrant and beautiful in a lovely, flowing green dress that matched her eyes. Despite her apparent enjoyment in the evening, he was almost certain he had caught a certain sadness in her eyes whenever their gazes happened to collide, and his heart ached, knowing he had put it there.

He couldn't stay much longer. He was leaving in the

morning and still had work to do packing and closing up his house for an indefinite time. Beyond that, it hurt more than he ever would have dreamed to keep his distance from Julia, to stand on the sidelines and watch her, knowing he could never have her.

He needed to at least talk to Sage before he escaped, he knew. When the music ended and she returned to the edge of the dance floor on the arm of ancient Mr. Delarosa, one of Abigail's old friends, he hurried to claim her before anyone else.

"Have any dances left for an old friend?"

Surprise flickered in her eyes, then she gave him a brilliant smile. "Of course!"

He wasn't much of a dancer but he did his best, grateful at least that it was another slow song and he wasn't going to have to make an idiot out of himself by trying to shake and groove.

"You make a stunning bride, kiddo," he said when they fell into a rhythm. "Who ever would have believed it?"

He gave an exaggerated wince when she punched him lightly in the shoulder.

"You know I'm teasing," he said, squeezing the fingers he held. "I'm thrilled for you and Eben, Sage. I really am. You're a beautiful bride and it was a beautiful ceremony."

"It was, wasn't it? I only wish Abigail could have been here."

"I don't doubt she was, in her own way."

She smiled, as he intended. "I think you're probably right. I was quite sure I smelled freesia at least once while Eben and I were exchanging our vows."

"I'm glad the weather held for you." It had been a gorgeous, sunny day, warm and lovely, a rarity on the coast for October.

"I thought for sure we were going to have to move everything inside for the ceremony but the weather couldn't have been more perfect."

"That's because Mother Nature knows she owes you big-time for all your do-gooder, save-the-world efforts. She wouldn't dare ruin your big day with rain."

She laughed softly then sobered quickly. "I forgot, I'm not supposed to be speaking to you. I'm still mad at you."

"Don't start, Sage. We've been over this. I'm going. But it's not forever—I'll be back."

"It won't be the same."

"Nothing will. Look at you, Mrs. Spencer. You're moving to San Francisco with Eben and Chloe. Things change, Sage."

"I'm going to miss you, darn it. You're the big, annoying, overprotective brother I've always wanted, Will."

He was more touched than he would dare admit. "And since the day you moved in to Brambleberry House, you've been like a bratty little sister to me, always sure you know what's best for everyone."

She made a harumph kind of sound. "That's because I do. For instance, I am quite certain you're making a huge mistake to leave Cannon Beach and a certain resident of Brambleberry House who shall remain nameless."

"Who? Conan?"

She smacked his shoulder again. "You know who I mean. Julia."

He shook his head. "Leave it alone, Sage."

"I won't." She stuck her chin out with a stubbornness he should have expected, knowing Sage. "If Abigail were here, she would tell you the exact same thing. You can't lie to me, you have feelings for Julia, don't you?"

"None of your business. This is a great band, by the way. Where did you find them?"

"I didn't, Jade Wu did. You know perfectly well she handled all the wedding details. And I won't let you change the subject. What kind of idiot walks away from a woman as fabulous as Julia, who just happens to be crazy about him?"

"I'm going to leave you right here in the middle of the dance floor if you don't back off," he warned her. Though he spoke amicably enough, he put enough steel in his voice that he hoped she got the message.

She gave him a piercing look and then her gaze suddenly softened. "You're as miserable as she is! You know you are."

He shifted his gaze to Julia, who was dancing and smiling with the owner of the bike shop—who just happened to be the biggest player in town.

"She doesn't look miserable to me."

They were several couples away from them on the dance floor, but just at that moment, her partner swung her around so she was facing him. They made eye contact and for one sizzling moment, it was as if they were alone in the room.

He caught his breath, snared by those deep green eyes for a long moment, until her partner turned her again.

"She does a pretty good job of hiding it, but she is," Sage said.

She paused, then met his gaze. "Did I ever tell you how I almost lost Eben and Chloe because I was too afraid of being hurt to let them inside my heart?"

"I don't think you did," he said stiffly.

"It's a long story but look at the happy ending, just because I decided Eben's love was worth far more to me than my pride. You're the most courageous man I know, Will. You've walked through hell these last few years. I know that, know that you've endured more than anyone should have to—a pain that most of us probably couldn't even guess at. Don't you think you've been through enough? You deserve happiness. Do you really think you're going to find it traveling around the world, leaving behind your home and everyone who loves you?"

"I don't know," he said, more struck by her words than he cared to admit. "But I'm going anyway. This is your wedding day. I don't want to fight with you about this. I appreciate your concern for me, but everything will be fine."

She sighed and probably would have said more but Eben came up behind them at that moment.

"What does a guy have to do to get a dance with his bride?"

"Just ask," Will said. "She's all yours."

He kissed Sage on the cheek and released her. "Thanks for the dance and the advice," he said. "Congratulations again to both of you."

Much as he loved her, he was relieved to walk away and leave her to Eben. He didn't need more of her lectures about how he was making a mistake to leave or her not-so-subtle hints about Julia.

What he needed was to get out of here, and soon. He couldn't take much more.

He made it almost to the door when he felt a sharp tug on his jacket. He turned around and found Maddie Blair standing beside him wearing a frilly blue party dress and a blazing smile.

His heart caught just a little but he probed around and realized he no longer had the piercing pain he used to whenever he saw Julia's dark-haired daughter.

"Hi," she said.

He forced himself to smile back. "Hi yourself."

"I had to tell you how much I love, love, *love* my dollhouse. It's the best dollhouse in the whole world! Thank you so much!"

"I'm glad you like it."

"Did you know it has a doorbell that really works? And it even has a secret closet in the bedroom that you open a special way."

"I believe I did know that."

He had finally finished the dollhouse late into the night two days before and had dropped it off at Brambleberry House, leaving it covered with a tarp on the porch for Julia to find. He knew it was cowardly to drop it off in the middle of the night. He should have picked a time when he could help carry it up the stairs for her, but he hadn't been able to face her.

"I would like to dance with you," Maddie announced, leaving him no room for arguments.

"Um, sure," he said, not knowing how to wiggle out of it. "I'd like that."

It wasn't even a lie, he realized to his surprise. He held out his arm in a formal kind of gesture and she grinned and slipped her hand into the crook of his elbow. Together they worked their way through the crowd to the dance floor.

While they danced, Maddie kept up an endless stream of conversation during the dance—about her dolls, about how she was going to go visit Chloe in San Francisco some time, about some mischief her brother had been up to.

He listened to her light chatter while the music poured around him, making appropriate comments whenever she stopped to take a breath.

"You're the best dancer I've danced with tonight," she said when the song was almost at an end. "Simon stepped on my toes a million times and I think he even broke one. And Chloe's dad wouldn't stop looking at Sage the whole time we danced. I think that's rude, don't you, even if they did just get married. Grown-ups are weird."

Will couldn't help it, he looked down at Maddie's animated little face and laughed out loud.

"You have a nice laugh," she observed, watching him through her wise little eyes that had endured too much. "I like it."

"Thanks," he answered, a little taken aback.

"You know what?" she whispered, as if confiding state secrets, and he had to bend his head a little lower to hear her, until their faces were almost touching.

"What?" he whispered back.

"I like you, too." She smiled at him, then before he realized what she intended, she stood on her tiptoes and kissed his cheek.

He stared at her as her words seemed to curl through him, squeezing the air from his lungs and sending all the careful barriers he thought he had built around his heart tumbling with one big, hard shove.

"Thanks," he finally said around the golf ball-size lump in his throat. "I, uh, like you, too."

It wasn't quite true, he realized with shock. His feelings for this little girl and her brother ran deeper than simple affection.

He had tried so hard to keep them all at bay but somehow when he wasn't looking, Julia's twins had sneaked into his heart. He cared about them—Simon, with his inquisitive mind and his eagerness to please, and Maddie with her unrelenting courage and the simple joy she seized from life.

How the hell had he let such a thing happen? He thought he had been so careful around them to keep his distance but something had gone terribly wrong.

He remembered Maddie offering to eat her ice cream

slowly so he could have a taste if he wanted, Simon talking about baseball and inviting him to watch a Mariners' game, budding hero worship in his eyes.

He loved Julia's children.

Just as he loved their mother.

He stopped stock-still on the dance floor. It *couldn't* be true. It couldn't. His gaze found Julia, standing at the refreshment table talking to Anna. She looked graceful and lovely. When she felt his gaze, she turned and gave him a tentative smile and he suddenly wanted nothing more than he wanted to yank her into his arms and carry her out of here.

"Are you okay, Mr. Garrett?" Maddie asked.

"I...yes. Thank you for the dance," he said, his voice stiff.

"You're welcome. Will you come play Barbies with me sometime?"

He had to get out of there, right now. The noise and the crowd were pressing in on him, suffocating him.

"Maybe. I'll see you later, okay?"

She nodded and smiled, then slipped away. On his way out the door, his gaze caught Julia's one more time and he hoped to hell the shock of his newfound feelings didn't show in his expression.

She gave him another tentative smile, which he acknowledged with a jerky nod, then he slipped out the door.

He climbed into his pickup in a kind of daze and pulled out of The Sea Urchin's parking lot in the pale twilight, not knowing where he was heading, only that he had to get away. He thought he was driving aimlessly, following the curve of the ocean, but before he quite realized it, he found himself at the small cemetery at twilight, just as the sunset turned the waves a soft, pale blue.

He parked outside the gates, knowing he didn't have long

since the cemetery was supposed to be closed after dark. Leaves crunched underfoot as he followed the familiar path, listening to the quiet reverence of the place.

He stopped at his father's grave first, under the spreading boughs of a huge, majestic oak tree. It was a fitting resting place for a man who could work such magic with his hands and a piece of wood. He stopped, head bowed, remembering the many lessons he had learned from his father. Work hard, play hard, cherish your family.

Not a bad mantra for a man to follow.

After long moments, he let out a breath and walked over a small hill to Abigail's grave, decorated with many tokens of affection. Sage had left her a wedding invitation, he saw, and a flower from her bouquet, and Will couldn't help smiling.

He saved the toughest for last. With emotion churning through him, he followed the trail around another curve, almost to the edge by the fence, where two simple headstones marked Robin's and Cara's graves.

He hadn't been here in a few months, he realized with some shock. Right after the accident he used to come here every day, sometimes twice a day. He had hated it, but he had come. Those visits had dwindled but he had always tried to come at least once a week to bring his wife whatever flowers were in season.

Like Abigail, Robin had loved flowers.

Guilt coursed through him as he realized how he had neglected his responsibilities.

He rounded the last corner and there they were, silhouetted in the dying sun. Two simple markers—Robin Cramer Garrett, beloved wife. Cara Robin Garrett, cherished daughter.

Emotions clogged his throat. Oh, he missed them. He

walked closer, then he blinked in shock, certain the dusky twilight must be playing tricks with his eyesight.

A few weeks after the accident, Abigail had asked him if she could plant a rosebush between Robin's and Cara's graves. He had been wild with grief, inconsolable, and wouldn't have cared whether she planted a whole damn flower garden, so he had given his consent.

He hadn't paid it much attention, other than to note a few times in the summer that if she had still been alive, Abigail would have been devastated to know she must have planted a sterile bush. He hadn't seen a single bloom on it in two years.

Now, though, as he stood in the cool October air, he stared in shock at the rosebush. It was covered in flowers—hundreds of them, in a rich, vibrant yellow.

This couldn't be right. He didn't know a hell of a lot about horticulture but he was fairly certain roses bloomed in summer. It was mid-October now, and had been colder than usual the last few weeks, rainy and dank.

It made absolutely no sense but he couldn't ignore the evidence in front of him. Abigail's roses were sending their lush, sweet fragrance into the air, stirring gently in a soft breeze.

Let go, Will. Life moves on.

He could almost swear he heard Abigail's words on the breeze, her voice as brisk and no-nonsense as always.

He sank down onto the wooden bench he had built and stared at the flower-heavy boughs, softly caressing the marble markers.

Let go.

His breathing ragged, he gazed at the flowers, stunned by the emotion pouring through him like a cleansing, healing rainstorm, something he hadn't known since his family was taken from him with such sudden cruelty.

Hope.

It was hope.

These roses seemed a perfect symbol of it, a precious gift Abigail had left behind just for him, as if she knew that somehow he would need to see those blossoms at exactly this moment in his life to remind him of things he had lost along the way.

Hope, faith. Love.

Life moves on.

Whether he was ready for it or not, he loved Julia Blair and her children. They had showed him that his life was not over, that if he could only find the courage, his future didn't have to be this grim, empty existence.

She had roared back into his life like a hurricane, blowing away all the shadows and darkness, the bone-deep misery that had been his companion for two years.

He couldn't say the idea of loving her and her kids still didn't scare the hell out of him. He had already lost more than he could bear. But the idea of living without them—of going back to his gray and cheerless life—scared him more.

He sat on the bench for a long time while the cemetery darkened and the roses danced and swayed in the breeze, surrounding him with their sweet perfume.

When at last he stood up, his cheeks were wet but his heart felt a million times lighter. He headed for the cemetery gates, with only one destination in mind.

Chapter 16

"Mama, I just love weddings." Though she was drooping with fatigue, Maddie's eyes were bright as Julia helped her out of her organza dress.

"It was lovely, wasn't it?"

"Sage was so pretty in her dress. She looked like an angel. And Chloe did a good job throwing the flower petals, didn't she? She didn't even look one bit nervous!"

Julia smiled at Maddie's enthusiasm. "She was the best flower girl I've ever seen."

"Do you think when you get married, I could wear a dress like Chloe's and throw flower petals, too?"

She winced, not at all sure how to answer. "Um, honey, I've already been married, to your dad," she finally said.

"But you could get married again, couldn't you? Chloe said you could because her dad was already married before, too, to her mom. Then her mom died just like Daddy and now her dad is married again to Sage."

Julia forced a smile. "Isn't it lucky he found Sage?"

She, on the other hand, had given her heart to Will Garrett, wholly and completely, and somehow she knew she would never be able to love anyone else. Will wasn't ready for it. For all she knew, he would *never* be ready. If Will couldn't bring himself to love her back, she was afraid she would spend the rest of her life alone.

But she wasn't about to confide her heartache to her daughter. "You need to get to sleep, kiddo. It's been a big day and I know you're tired. Simon's already in his bed, sound asleep."

She helped Maddie into her nightgown and was tucking her under the covers when Maddie touched her hand.

"Mama, I think you should marry Mr. Garrett."

Julia nearly tripped over Maddie's slippers in her astonishment. "Wh…why would you say that?"

"Well, lots of reasons. He smells nice and I just love the dollhouse he made me."

Not the worst reasons for a seven-year-old girl to come up with to marry a man, she supposed.

"And maybe if you married him, he wouldn't be so sad all the time. You make him smile, Mama. I know you do."

Tears burned in her eyelids at Maddie's confident statement and she knelt down to fold her daughter into her arms.

"Go to sleep, pumpkin," she said through the emotions clogging her throat. "I'll see you in the morning."

She turned off the light and closed her door, then moved to Simon's room to check on him. He was sleeping soundly, his blankets already a tangle at his waist. She tucked them back over his shoulders then returned to the living room, lit only by a small lamp next to her Stickley rocking chair.

Though she tried to fight the impulse, she finally gave

in and moved to the window overlooking Will's house. No lights were on there, she saw. Was he asleep already?

He was leaving in the morning. Maybe he intended to get a solid night's rest for traveling across the country.

The emotions Maddie had stirred in her finally broke free and she felt tears trickling down her cheeks. He hadn't said a word to her all day. She had felt his gaze several times, both during the ceremony and then after at the reception, but he hadn't approached her.

After his dance with Maddie, she had intended to track him down—if only to tell him goodbye before he left for his new job—but he had rushed out of The Sea Urchin so fast she hadn't had the chance.

She didn't need a pile of two-by-fours to fall on her head to figure out he didn't want to talk to her again.

She swiped at her tears with her palm. He hadn't even left town yet and she already missed him like crazy. Despite her determined claims to him that she wouldn't regret making love, she couldn't deny that the tender intimacy they had shared had only ratcheted up her pain to a near-unbearable level.

Sage's joy today had only served to reinforce to Julia that she was unlikely ever to know that kind of happiness with Will. He might have opened up his emotions to her a few nights ago but now they were as tightly locked and shoved away as they had been since she returned to town. If she needed proof, she only had to look at the careful distance he maintained at the wedding.

What a strange journey she had traveled since making the decision to return to Cannon Beach. She never would have guessed when she took that teaching job several months ago that she would find love and heartbreak all in one convenient package.

He was leaving in the morning and she could do nothing to stop him.

She sobbed, just a little, then the sound caught in her throat when she suddenly thought she smelled freesia.

"Oh, Abigail," she murmured. "I wish you were here to tell me what to do, how I can reach Will. I don't think I can bear this."

Silence met her impassioned plea, but an instant later she jumped a mile when she felt something wet brush her hand.

"Conan! You scared the life out of me! Where were you?"

The dog had followed her and the twins upstairs when they returned to Brambleberry House from the wedding, apparently needing company since Anna was still busy cleaning up at the reception and Sage and Eben were staying at The Sea Urchin for the night until they left for their honeymoon in the Galapagos in the morning.

He must have gone into her room to lie down, since she hadn't seen him when she came out of Simon's room and had forgotten he was even there. Still, she had to admit she was grateful for the company. The dog leaned against her leg, offering his own unique kind of support and sympathy.

"Thanks," she whispered, as they sat together in her dim apartment looking out at the lights of town.

But his steady comfort didn't last long. After a moment, his ears pricked up and he suddenly barked and rushed for the door, his tail wagging.

She sighed. "You want to go out *again?* We let you out when we came home!"

He whined a little and watched her out of those curiously intelligent eyes. With a sigh, she abandoned any fleeting hope she might have briefly entertained about sinking into a hot bubble bath to soak away her misery, for a while anyway.

"All right, you crazy dog. Just let me find some shoes first."

She had changed after the reception into worn jeans and her oldest, most comfortable sweater. Now she grabbed tennis shoes and headed down the stairs.

The moment she opened the outside door, Conan rocketed down the porch steps and toward the front gate, then disappeared from sight.

Oh rats. She forgot to check that the gate was still closed. Conan usually stuck close to home, preferring his own territory, but if he smelled a cat anywhere in the vicinity, all bets were off.

What was she supposed to do now? No one else was home, the twins were sleeping upstairs and the dog was loose. She couldn't let him wander free, though.

"Conan," she called. "Get back here."

He barked from what sounded like just the other side of the ironwork fence, but she couldn't see him in the darkness.

"Here, boy. Come on."

He didn't respond to the command and with a sigh, she headed down the sidewalk, hoping he wasn't in the mood for a playful game of tag. She wasn't at all in the mood to chase him.

"Come on, Conan. It's cold." She walked through the gate, then froze when she saw in the moonlight just why the dog hadn't answered her summons.

He was busy greeting a man who stood silent and watchful on the other side of the fence.

Will.

She stared at him, stunned to find him here, tonight, and wondering if she had left any evidence of the tears she had just shed for him. All those emotions just under the surface threatened to break through again—sorrow and regret, doubt, sadness.

Love.

Especially love.

She wanted to go to him, throw her arms around his waist and beg him not to leave.

"I didn't see you there," she said instead, hoping her emotional tumult didn't show up in her voice.

He said nothing, just continued to pet the dog and watch her. She walked a little closer.

"Is everything okay?"

"No." His voice sounded hoarse, ragged. "I don't think it is."

He stepped closer to her, so near she could smell the scent of his aftershave, sexy and male. Her heart, already pounding hard since the instant she saw him standing in the darkness, picked up a pace.

"What is it?"

He was quiet for a long time—so long she was beginning to worry something was seriously wrong. Finally, to her immense shock he reached out and grasped her fingers and pulled her even closer.

"I had to come. Had to see you."

"Why?"

His slow sigh stirred her hair. "I love you, Julia."

"Wh-what did you say?" She jerked her hand away and scrambled back. Her heartbeat accelerated and she couldn't seem to catch her breath as shock rippled through her.

He raked a hand through his hair. "I didn't mean to just blurt it out like that. I must sound like an idiot."

"I'm… I'm sorry. You don't sound like an idiot. I just… I wasn't expecting that. You're leaving tomorrow. Aren't you leaving?"

A tiny flutter of joy started in her heart but she was afraid to let it free, afraid he would only crush it and leave her feeling worse than ever.

"Yes. I'm leaving."

She expected his words but they still scored her heart. He said he loved her, but he was leaving anyway?

"I wish I didn't have to go but I gave my word to Eben and I'm committed, at least for a few weeks, until he can find someone else to take my place."

He reached for her hand again and she could feel her fingers trembling in his hard, callused palm. "And then I'd like to come back. To Cannon Beach and to you."

While she was still reeling from his words, he paused, then touched her cheek softly. "You were so right about everything you've said to me. I need to move forward, to give myself the freedom to taste all life has to offer again. It's time. I've known it's time, but I've been so afraid. That's a tough thing for a man to admit, but it's the truth. I was afraid to let myself love you, afraid I was somehow…betraying Robin and Cara by all the feelings I was starting to have for you."

She squeezed his fingers. "Oh, Will. You'll never stop loving them. I would never ask that of you. That's exactly the way it should be. But the heart is a magical thing. Abigail taught me that. When you're ready, when you need it to, it can miraculously expand to make room."

He studied her for a long moment and then suddenly he smiled. Only when she saw his mouth tilt, saw the genuine happiness in his expression, did she realize he truly meant what he said. *He loved her.* She still couldn't quite absorb it, but his eyes in the soft moonlight were free of any lingering grief and sorrow.

He loved her.

He cupped his hands around her face and kissed her then, soft and gentle in the cool October air. She wrapped her arms around his waist as a sweet, cleansing joy exploded through her.

"My heart has made room for you, Julia. For you and your beautiful children. How could it help but find a place? You already had your own corner there sixteen years ago. I think some part of me was just waiting for you to return and move back in."

His mouth found hers again, and in his kiss she tasted joy and healing and the promise of a sweet, beautiful future.

Not far away, a huge mongrel dog sat on his haunches watching them both with satisfaction in his eyes while the soft, flowery scent of freesia floated in the autumn air.

* * * * *

Also by Patricia Davids

HQN

The Amish of Cedar Grove

The Wish
The Hope
The Prayer

Love Inspired

North Country Amish

An Amish Wife for Christmas
Shelter from the Storm
The Amish Teacher's Dilemma

Brides of Amish Country

Plain Admirer
Amish Christmas Joy
The Shepherd's Bride
The Amish Nanny
An Amish Family Christmas: A Plain Holiday
An Amish Christmas Journey
Amish Redemption

Visit her Author Profile page at Harlequin.com,
or patriciadavids.com, for more titles!

KATIE'S REDEMPTION

Patricia Davids

This book is dedicated to my family.
You have supported me every step of the way
and I couldn't do it without you.

Even the sparrow has found a home,
and the swallow a nest for herself, where she
may have her young—a place near your altar,
O Lord Almighty, my King and my God.
—*Psalm* 84:3

Chapter 1

"Lady, you sure this is where you wanna get out?" The middle-aged bus driver tipped his hat back and regarded his passenger with worry-filled eyes.

"This is the place." Katie Lantz glanced from his concerned face to the desolate winter landscape beyond the windshield. A chill that owed nothing to the weather crawled over her skin.

It was her destination, but rural Ohio was the last place in the world she wanted to be. She had agonized over her decision for weeks. Now that she was here, the same worries that had robbed her of sleep for endless nights cartwheeled through her mind.

Would her brother take her in? What if Malachi turned her away? What would she do then? If he did allow her to return to his home would she ever find the strength to leave again?

"It don't feel right leaving a gal in your condition out here alone. You sure I can't take ya into town?"

"I'm sure." She pressed a protective hand to her midsection. Her condition was the only reason she was here. She didn't want to get off the bus, but what choice did she have?

None.

All her plans, her dreams and her hopes had turned to ashes. She took a deep breath and straightened her shoulders. "I'd just have to walk back if I went into Hope Springs. Thank you for letting me off. I know you aren't supposed to make unscheduled stops."

The driver pulled the lever to open the doors with obvious reluctance. "I don't make a habit of it, but I figured it was best not to argue with a gal that's as pregnant as you are."

A gust of wintry wind swirled in, raking Katie's face with icy fingers. A tremor raced through her body. She turned up the collar of her red plaid coat, prolonging the moment she would have to actually step out of the bus and back into the life she dreaded.

The driver seemed to sense her unwillingness to leave. "Is someone meeting you?"

She hadn't bothered to write that she was coming. Her previous letters had all been returned unopened. Proof, if she needed any, that her family hadn't forgiven her for turning her back on her Amish heritage.

She lifted her chin.

I don't have to do this. I can stay on the bus and go to the next town.

And then what?

As quickly as her bravado appeared it evaporated. She closed her eyes. Her shoulders slumped in defeat.

All she had in her pocket was twelve dollars. All she

owned was in the suitcase she clutched. It wasn't enough, not with her baby due in three weeks. For her child's sake, returning home was her only option.

For now.

Clinging to that faint echo of resolve, she drew a steadying breath, opened her eyes and faced her bleak future. "My brother's farm is just over the hill. It's not far. I'll be fine."

Oh, how she hoped her words would prove true.

She didn't belong in this Amish world. She had escaped it once before. She would do so again. It would be harder with a baby, but she would find a way.

With no money, without even a driver's license and nothing but an eighth-grade education, the English world was a hard place for an ex-Amish woman on her own.

Matt had taken her away and promised to take care of her and show her the wonders of the modern world, but his promises had been empty. He'd disappeared from her life three months ago, leaving her to struggle and fail alone.

The bus driver shrugged. "All right. You be careful."

"*Danki.* I mean…thank you." When she was upset the language of her childhood often slipped out. It was hard to remember to speak English when the words of her native Pennsylvania Dutch came to mind first.

Gripping her small case tightly, Katie descended the steps and walked toward the edge of the roadway. The doors slammed shut behind her. The engine roared as the driver pulled away, followed by a billowing cloud of diesel fumes.

There was no turning back—nowhere left to run.

Shivering as the frigid air found its way inside the coat she couldn't button over her bulging stomach, she pulled at the material to close the gap. Now she was truly alone. Except for the child she carried.

Standing here wasn't helping. She needed to get moving. Switching her suitcase to her other hand, she arched her back to stretch out a persistent cramp. When it eased, she turned and glanced up the long lane leading over the hill. For her baby she would do anything. Endure anything.

With the late-March sky hanging low and gray overhead, Katie wished for the first time that she had kept some of her Amish clothing. If she at least looked the part of a repentant Plain woman, her family reunion might go better.

She had left before her baptism—before taking her vows to faithfully follow the Plain faith. She would be reprimanded for her errant behavior, but she might not be shunned if she came asking forgiveness.

Please, God, don't let them send me away.

To give her child a home she would endure the angry tirade she expected from her brother. His wife, Beatrice, wouldn't intercede for Katie. Beatrice would sit silent and sullen, never saying a word. Through it all Malachi wouldn't be able to hide the gloating in his voice. He had predicted Katie would come to a bad end out among the English.

How she hated that he had been right.

Still, she would soon have the one thing her brother and her sister-in-law had been denied in their lives—a baby. Was it possible the arrival of her child might heal old wounds? Or would it only make things worse?

An unexpected tightening across her stomach made her draw in a quick breath. She had been up since dawn, riding for hours on the jolting bus. It was no wonder her back ached almost constantly now. She started toward the lane that led north from the highway. There could be no rest until she reached her brother's house.

The dirt road running between twin fences made for rough and treacherous walking. Buggy wheels and horse's hooves had cut deep ruts in the mud that was now frozen. Tiny, hard flakes driven by the wind stung her cheeks and made it difficult to see. She shivered and hunched deeper into her too-small coat.

As much as she wanted to hurry toward the warm stove she knew was glowing in her brother's kitchen, she couldn't. She had to be careful of each step over the rough ground. The last thing she wanted to do was fall and hurt the child that meant everything to her. When her son or daughter arrived, Katie would have the one true thing she had always longed for—a family of her own.

Her stomach tightened again. She had to stop to catch her breath. Her pain deepened. Something wasn't right. This was more than fatigue. Had her long day of travel hurt the baby? She'd never forgive herself if something happened to her child.

After a few quick, panting breaths the discomfort passed. Katie straightened with relief. She switched her suitcase to her other hand, pushed her frozen fingers deep into her pocket and started walking again. She hadn't gone more than a hundred yards when the next pain made her double over and drop her case.

Fear clogged her throat as she clutched her belly. Breathing hard, she peered through the blowing snow. She could just make out the light from a window up ahead. It wasn't much farther. Closing her eyes, she gathered her strength.

One foot in front of the other. The only way to finish a journey is to start it.

With grim determination, she pressed on. Another dozen yards brought her to the steps of the small front porch. She sagged with relief when her hand closed over the railing. She was home.

Home. The word echoed inside her mind, bringing with

it grim memories from the past. Defeat weighed down her already-low spirits. She raised her fist and knocked at the front door. Then she bowed her head and closed her eyes, grasping the collar of her coat to keep the chill at bay.

When the door finally opened she looked up slowly past the dark trousers and suspenders, past the expanse of pale blue shirt to meet her brother's gaze.

Katie sucked in a breath and took a half step back. A tall, broad-shouldered Amish man stood in front of her with a kerosene lamp in his hand and a faint puzzled expression on his handsome face.

It wasn't Malachi.

Elam Sutter stared in surprise at the English woman on his doorstep clutching a suitcase in one hand and the collar of her coat with the other. Her pale face was framed by coal-black hair that ended just below her jawline. The way the ends of it swung forward to caress her cheeks reminded Elam of the wings of a small bird.

In his lamplight, snowflakes sparkled in her hair and on the tips of her thick eyelashes. Her eyes, dark as the night, brimmed with misery. She looked nearly frozen from her head…to her very pregnant belly.

He drew back in shock and raised the lamp higher, scanning the yard behind her for a car, but saw none. Perhaps it had broken down on the highway. That would explain her sudden appearance.

The English! They hadn't enough sense to stay by a warm fire on such a fierce night. Still, she was obviously in trouble. He asked politely, "Can I help you?"

"Would you…" Her voice faltered. She swallowed hard then began again. "I must speak with Malachi."

"Would you be meaning Malachi Lantz?"

She pressed her lips together and nodded.

"The Lantz family doesn't live here anymore."

Her eyes widened in disbelief. "What? But this is his home."

"*Jah,* it was. He and his wife moved to Kansas last spring after he sold the farm to me. I have his address inside if you need it."

"That can't be," she whispered as she pressed a hand to her forehead.

"Who is it, Elam?" his mother, Nettie, called from behind him.

He spoke over his shoulder, "Someone looking for Malachi Lantz."

A second later his mother was beside him. She looked as shocked as he at the sight of a very pregnant outsider on their stoop, but it took only an instant for her kindheartedness to assert itself.

"Goodness, child, come in out of this terrible weather. You look chilled to the bone. Elam, pull a chair close to the fireplace." She nudged him aside and he hurried to do as she instructed.

Grasping the woman's elbow, Nettie guided her guest into the living room and helped her into a straight-backed seat, one of a pair that flanked the stone fireplace.

"*Ach,* your hands are like ice." Nettie began rubbing them between her own.

The young woman's gaze roved around the room and finally came to rest on Elam's mother's face. "Malachi doesn't live here anymore?"

Nettie's gaze softened. "No, dear. I'm sorry. He moved away."

Pulling her hands away from the older woman's, she

raked them through her dark hair. "Why would he move? Was it because of me?"

Elam exchanged puzzled glances with his mother. What did the woman mean by that comment? Nettie shrugged, then took the girl's hands once more. "What's your name, child?"

The dazed look on his visitor's face was replaced by a blankness that troubled him. "My name is Katie."

"Katie, I'm Nettie Sutter, and this is my son, Elam."

Katie bent forward with a deep moan. "I don't know what to do."

"Don't cry." His mother patted the girl's shoulder as she shot Elam a worried glance.

After several deep breaths, Katie straightened and wiped her cheeks. "I have to go."

"You haven't thawed out yet. At least stay for a cup of tea. The kettle is still on. Elam, bring me a cup, too." Nettie caught his eye and made shooing motions toward the kitchen with one hand.

He retreated, but he could still hear them talking as he fixed the requested drinks. His mother's tone was calm and reassuring as she said, "Why not stay and rest a bit longer? It's not good for your baby to have his mother turning into an icicle."

"I need to go. I have to find Malachi." Katie's voice wavered with uncertainty.

"Is he the father?" Nettie asked gently.

Elam didn't want to think ill of any man, but why else would a pregnant woman show up demanding to see Malachi months after he had moved away?

"No. He's my brother."

Elam stopped pouring the hot water and glanced toward the living room. He had heard the story of Malachi's willful sister from the man's own lips. So this was the woman that had left the Amish after bringing shame to her family. At least she had done so before her baptism.

Elam placed the tea bags in the mugs. Malachi had his sympathy. Elam knew what it was like to face such heartbreak—the talk, the pitying looks, the whispers behind a man's back.

He pushed aside those memories as he carried the cups into the other room. "I didn't see your car outside."

She looked up at him and once again the sadness in her luminous eyes caught him like a physical blow. Her lower lip quivered. "I came on the bus."

Elam felt his mother's eyes on him but he kept his gaze averted, focusing instead on handing over the hot drinks without spilling any.

Nettie took a cup from Elam and pressed it into Katie's hands. "Have a sip. This will warm you right up. You can't walk all the way to Hope Springs tonight. Elam will take you in the buggy when you're ready."

Katie shook her head. "I can't ask you to do that."

"It's no trouble." He tried hard to mean it. He'd already finished a long day of work and he was ready for his bed. He would have to be up again before dawn to milk the cows and feed the livestock.

Returning to the kitchen, he began donning his coat and his black felt hat. It was a mean night for a ride into town, but what else could he do? He certainly couldn't let her walk, in her condition.

Suddenly, he heard Katie cry out. Rushing back into the room, he saw her doubled over, the mug lying broken on the floor in a puddle at her feet.

Chapter 2

Through a haze of pain, Katie heard Elam ask, "What is it? What's wrong?"

She felt strong arms supporting her. She leaned into his strength but she couldn't answer because she was gritting her teeth to keep from screaming.

"I believe her baby's coming," Nettie replied calmly.

Panic swallowed Katie whole.

This can't be happening. Not here. Not with strangers. This isn't right. Nothing is right. Please, God, I know I've disappointed You, but help me now.

A horrible sensation settled in the pit of her stomach. Was this her punishment for leaving the faith? She knew there would be a price to pay someday, but she didn't want her baby to suffer because of her actions.

She looked from Elam's wide, startled eyes above her to his mother's serene face. "My baby can't come now. I'm not due for three weeks."

Nettie's smile was reassuring. "Babies have a way of choosing their own time."

Katie bit her lower lip to stop its trembling. She'd never been so scared in all her life.

"Don't worry. I know just what to do. I've had eight of my own." Nettie's unruffled demeanor eased some of Katie's panic. Seeing no other choice, Katie allowed Nettie to take charge of the situation.

Why wasn't Matt here when she needed him? It should have been Matt beside her, not these people.

Because he'd grown tired of her, that's why. He had been ashamed of her backward ways. Her pregnancy had been the last straw. He accused her of getting pregnant to force him into marriage, which wasn't true. After their last fight three months ago, he walked out and never came back, leaving her with rent and bills she couldn't pay.

Nettie turned to her son. "Elam, move one of the extra beds into the kitchen so Katie has a warm place to rest while you fetch the midwife."

"Jah." A blush of embarrassment stained his cheeks dark red. His lack of a beard proclaimed his single status. Childbirth was the territory of women, clearly a territory he didn't want to explore. He hurried away.

Nettie coaxed Katie to sit and showed her how to breathe through her next contraction. When Elam had wrestled a narrow bed into the kitchen and piled several quilts on one end, Nettie helped Katie onto it. Lying down with a sigh of relief, Katie closed her eyes. She was so tired. "I can't do this."

"Yes, you can. The Lord will give you the strength you need," Nettie said gently.

No, He won't. God doesn't care what happens to a sinner like me.

"Is the midwife okay, or will you be wanting to go to a hospital?" Elam's voice interrupted her fatalistic thoughts.

She turned her face toward the wall. "I can't afford a hospital."

"The midwife will do fine, Elam. I've heard good things about Nurse Bradley from the women hereabouts. Go over to the Zimmerman farm and ask to use their phone. They'll know her number. What are you waiting for? Get a move on."

"I was wondering if there was anyone else I should call. Perhaps the baby's father? He should know his child is being born."

"Matt doesn't care about this baby. He left us," Katie managed to say through gritted teeth. The growing contraction required all her concentration. The slamming of the outside door signaled that Elam had gone.

When her pain eased, Katie turned back to watch Nettie bustling about, making preparations for her baby's arrival. The kitchen looked so different than it had during the years Katie had lived here. She could see all of the changes Elam and his mother had made. She concentrated on each detail as she tried to relax and gather strength for her next contraction.

Overhead, a new gas lamp above the kitchen table cast a warm glow throughout the room. As it had in her day, a rectangular table occupied the center of the room. The chairs around it were straight-backed and sturdy. The dark, small cabinets that once flanked the wide window above the sink had been replaced with new larger ones that spread across the length of the wall. Their natural golden oak color was much more appealing.

Setting Katie's suitcase on a chair, Nettie opened it and

drew out a pink cotton nightgown. "Let's get you into something more comfortable."

Embarrassment sent the blood rushing to Katie's face, but Nettie didn't seem to notice. The look of kindness on her face and her soothing prattle in thick German quickly put Katie at ease. Elam's mother seemed perfectly willing to accept a stranger into her home and care for her.

Dressed in a dark blue dress covered by a black apron, Nettie had a sparkle in her eyes behind the wire-rimmed glasses perched on her nose. Her plump cheeks were creased with smile lines. No one in Katie's family had ever been cheerful.

Nettie's gray hair was parted in the middle and coiled into a bun beneath her white *kapp* the way all Amish women wore their hair. Katie fingered her own short locks.

Cutting her hair had been her first act of rebellion after she left home. Amish women never cut their hair. It had been one way Katie could prove to herself that she was no longer Amish. At times, she regretted the loss of her waist-length hair. She once thought she despised all things Amish, yet this Amish woman was showing her more kindness than anyone had ever done. Only one person Katie knew in the neighborhood where she'd lived with Matt would have taken her in like this, but that friend was dead. The English world wasn't always a friendly place.

After she had changed into her nightclothes, Katie settled back into bed. Nettie added more wood to the stove. The familiar crackle, hiss and popping sounds of the fire helped calm Katie's nerves. Until the next contraction hit.

Elam wasted no time getting Judy hitched to the buggy. In spite of her master's attempts to hurry, the black mare balked at the wide doorway, making it clear she objected to leaving her warm barn. Elam couldn't blame her. The wind-blown sleet felt like stinging nettles where it hit his face. He pulled the warm scarf his mother had knitted for him over his nose and mouth, then climbed inside the carriage.

The town of Hope Springs lay three miles to the east of his farm. He had Amish neighbors on all sides. None of them used telephones. The nearest phone was at the Zimmerman farm just over a mile away. He prayed the Mennonite family would be at home when he got there or he would have to go all the way into town to find one.

Once he reached the highway, he urged Judy to pick up her pace. He slapped the reins against her rump and frequently checked the rectangular mirror mounted on the side of his buggy. This stretch of curving road could be a nerve-racking drive in daylight. Traveling it in this kind of weather was doubly dangerous. The English cars and trucks came speeding by with little regard for the fact that a slow-moving buggy might be just over the rise.

Tonight, as always, Elam trusted the Lord to see him safely to his destination, but he kept a sharp lookout for headlights coming up behind him.

It was a relief to finally swing off the blacktop onto the gravel drive of his neighbor's farm. By the time he reached their yard, his scarf was coated with ice from his frozen breath. He saw at once that the lights were on. The Zimmermans were home. He gave a quick prayer of thanks.

Hitching Judy to the picket fence near the front gate, he bounded up the porch steps. Pulling down his muffler, he rapped on the door.

Grace Zimmerman answered his knock. "Elam, what on earth are you doing out on a night like this?"

He nodded to her. "*Goot* evening, Mrs. Zimmerman. I've come to ask if I might use your telephone, please."

"Of course. Is something wrong? Is your mother ill?"

"*Mamm* is fine. We've a visitor, a young woman who's gone into labor."

"Shall I call 911 and get an ambulance?"

"*Mamm* says the midwife will do."

"Okay. Come in and I'll get that number for you."

"My thanks."

The midwife answered on the second ring. "Nurse Bradley speaking."

"Miss Bradley, I am Elam Sutter, and I have need of your services."

"Babies never check the weather report before they decide to make an appearance, do they? Has your wife been into the clinic before?"

"It is not my wife. It is a woman who is visiting in the area, so she hasn't been to see you."

"Oh. Okay, give me the patient's name."

He knew Katie's maiden name, but he didn't know her married name. Was the man she spoke of her husband? Deciding it didn't matter, he said, "Her name is Katie Lantz."

"Is Mrs. Lantz full term?"

"I'm not sure."

"How far apart are her contractions? Is it her first baby?"

"That I don't know. My mother is with her and she said to call you," he stated firmly. He was embarrassed at not being able to answer her questions.

"Are there complications?"

"Not that I know of, but you would be the best judge of that."

"All right. How do I find your place?"

He gave her directions. She repeated them, then cheerfully assured him that she would get there as fast as she could.

As he hung up the phone, Mrs. Zimmerman withdrew a steaming cup from her microwave. "Have a cup of hot cocoa before you head back into the storm, Elam. Did I hear you say that Katie Lantz is having a baby?"

"*Jah*. She came looking for her brother. She didn't know he had moved." He took the cup and sipped it gratefully, letting the steam warm his face. Mrs. Zimmerman was a kindhearted woman but she did love to gossip.

"Poor Katie. Is Matt with her?" She seemed genuinely distressed.

"She's alone. Is Matt her husband? Do you know how to contact him?"

Mrs. Zimmerman shook her head. "I have no idea if they married. Matt Carson was a friend of my grandson's from college. The boys spent a few weeks here two summers ago. That's how Katie met Matt. I'll call William and see if he has kept in touch with Matt or his family."

"Thank you."

"I never thought Katie would come back. Malachi was furious at the attention Matt paid her. If he hadn't overreacted I think the romance would have died a natural death when Matt went back to school. I don't normally speak ill of people, but Malachi was very hard on that girl, even when she was little."

"'Train up a child in the way he should go: and when he is old, he will not depart from it.' *Proverbs* 22:6," Elam quoted.

"I agree the tree grows the way the sapling is bent, but not if it's snapped in half. I even spoke to Bishop Zook about Malachi's treatment of Katie when she was about ten but I don't think it did any good. I wasn't all that surprised when she ran off with Matt."

Elam didn't feel right gossiping about Katie or her family. He took another sip of the chocolate, then set the cup on the counter. "*Danki,* Mrs. Zimmerman. I'd best be getting back."

"I'll keep Katie in my prayers. Please tell her I said hello."

"I will, and thank you again." He wrapped his scarf around his face and headed out the door.

By the time Elam returned home, the midwife had already arrived. Her blue station wagon sat in front of the house collecting a coating of snow on the hood and windshield.

He lit a lantern and hung it inside the barn so his mother would know he was back if she looked out. He took his time making sure Judy was rubbed down and dry before returning her to her stall with an extra ration of oats for her hard work. When he was done, he stood facing the house from the wide barn door. The snow was letting up and the wind was dying down at last.

Lamplight glowed from the kitchen window and he wondered how Katie was faring. He couldn't imagine finding himself cast upon the mercy of strangers at such a time. He had seven brothers and sisters plus cousins galore that he could turn to at a moment's notice for help. It seemed that poor Katie had no one.

Knowing his presence wouldn't be needed or wanted in the house, he decided he might as well get some work done if he wasn't going to get any sleep. Taking the lantern down, he carried it to the workshop he'd set up inside the barn. Once there, he lit the gas lamps hanging overhead. They filled the space with light. He turned out the portable lamp and set it on the counter.

The tools of his carpentry and wooden basket-making business were hung neatly on the walls. Everything was in order—exactly the way he liked it. A long, narrow table sat near the windows with five chairs along its length. Several dozen baskets in assorted sizes and shapes were stacked in bins against the far wall. Cedar, poplar and pine boards on sawhorses filled the air with their fresh, woody scents.

Only a year ago the room had been a small feed storage area, but as the demand for his baskets and woodworking expanded, he'd needed more space. Remodeling the workshop had been his winter project and it was almost done. The clean white walls were meant to reflect the light coming in from the extra windows he'd added. When summer took hold of the land, the windows would open to let in the cool breezes. It was a good shop, and he was pleased with what he'd accomplished.

Stoking the coals glowing in a small stove, he soon had a bright fire burning. It wasn't long before the chill was gone from the air. He took off his coat and hung it on a peg near the frost-covered windows. Using his sleeve, he rubbed one windowpane clear so he could see the house.

Light flooded from the kitchen window. They must have moved more lamps into the room. Knowing he couldn't help, he pick up his measuring tape and began marking sections of cedar board for a hope chest a client had ordered last week.

He didn't need to concentrate on the task. His hands knew the wood, knew the tools he held as if they were extensions of his own fingers. His gaze was drawn repeatedly to the window and the drama he knew was being played out inside his home. As he worked, he prayed for Katie Lantz and her unborn child.

Hours later, he glanced out the window and stopped his work abruptly. He saw his mother hurrying toward him. Had something gone wrong?

Chapter 3

"You are so beautiful," Katie whispered. Tears blurred her vision and she rapidly blinked them away.

Propped up with pillows against the headboard of her borrowed bed, she drew her fingers gently across the face of her daughter where she lay nestled in the crook of her arm. Her little head was covered in dark hair. Her eyelashes lay like tiny curved spikes against her cheeks. She was the most beautiful thing Katie had ever seen.

Amber Bradley, the midwife, moved about the other side of the room, quietly putting her things away. Katie had been a little surprised that the midwife wasn't Amish. That the women of the district trusted an outsider spoke volumes for Amber. She was both kind and competent, as Katie had discovered.

When Amber came over to the bed at last, she sat gently on the edge and asked, "Shall I take her now? You really do need some rest."

"Can I hold her just a little longer?" Katie didn't want to give her baby over to anyone. Not yet. The joy of holding her own child was too new, too wonderful to allow it to end.

Amber smiled and nodded. "All right, but I do need to check her over more completely before I go. We didn't have a lot of time to discuss your plans. Maybe we can do that now."

Reality poked its ugly head back into Katie's mind. Her plans hadn't changed. They had simply been delayed. "I intend to go to my brother's house."

"Does he live close by?"

"No. Mr. Sutter said Malachi has moved to Kansas."

"I see. That's a long way to travel with a newborn."

Especially for someone who had no money. And now she owed the midwife, as well. All Katie could do was be honest with Amber. She glanced up at the nurse. "I'm grateful you came tonight, but I'm sorry I can't pay you right now. I will, I promise. As soon as I get a job."

"I'm not worried about that. The Amish always pay their bills. In fact, they're much more prompt than any insurance company I've dealt with."

Katie looked down at her daughter. "I'm not Amish. Not anymore."

"Don't be worrying about my fee. Just enjoy that beautiful baby. I'll send a bill in a few days and you can pay me when you're able."

The outside door opened and Nettie rushed in carrying a large, oval wooden basket. She was followed by Elam. He paused long enough to hang his coat and hat by the door, then he approached the bed. "I heard it's a fine, healthy girl. Congratulations, Katie Lantz."

"Thank you." She proudly pulled back the corner of

the receiving blanket, a gift from Amber, to show Elam her little girl.

He moved closer and leaned down, but kept his hands tucked in the front pockets of his pants. "*Ach,* she's *wundascheen!*"

"Thank you. I think she's beautiful, too." Katie planted a kiss on her daughter's head.

Nettie set the basket on the table, folded her arms over her ample chest and grinned. "*Jah,* she looks like her Mama with all that black hair."

Reaching out hesitantly, Elam touched the baby's tiny fist. "Have you given her a name?"

"Rachel Ann. It was my mother's name."

Nodding his satisfaction, he straightened and shoved his hand back in his pocket. "It's a *goot* name. A plain name."

Katie blinked back sudden tears as she gazed at her daughter. Even though they would have to live with Malachi for a while, Rachel would not be raised Amish as Katie's mother had been. Why did that make her feel sad?

Amber rose from her place at the foot of the bed. "I see you've got a solution for where this little one is going to sleep, Nettie."

"My daughter, Mary, is expecting in a few months. She has my old cradle, but a folded quilt will make this a comfortable bed for Rachel. What do you think, Katie?"

"I think it will do fine." All of the sudden, Katie was so tired she could barely keep her eyes open.

"I will make a bassinet for her," Elam offered quickly. "It won't take any time at all."

Overwhelmed, Katie said, "You've been so kind already, Mr. Sutter. How can I ever thank you?"

"Someday, you will do a kindness for someone in need.

That will be my thanks," he replied, soft and low so that only she could hear him.

Katie studied his face in the lamplight. It was the first time she had really looked at him. He was probably twenty-five years old. Most Amish men his age were married with one or two children already. She wondered why he was still single. He was certainly handsome enough to please any young woman. His hair, sable-brown and thick, held a touch of unruly curl where it brushed the back of his collar.

His face, unlike his hair, was all chiseled angles and planes, from his broad forehead to his high cheekbones. That, coupled with a straight, no-nonsense nose, gave him a look of harshness. Until she noticed his eyes. Soft sky-blue eyes that crinkled at the corners when he smiled as he was smiling now at the sight of Rachel's pink bow mouth opened in a wide yawn.

"Looks like someone is ready to try out her new bed." He stepped back as Amber came to take Rachel from Katie.

"I know her mother could use some rest," Amber stated with a stern glance in Katie's direction.

Katie nodded in agreement, but she didn't want to sleep. "If I close my eyes for a few minutes, that's all I need."

"You're going to need much more than that," Nettie declared, placing the quilt-lined basket on a kitchen chair beside Katie's bed.

Amber laid the baby on the table and unwrapped her enough to listen to her heart and lungs with a stethoscope. Katie couldn't close her eyes until she knew all was well. After finishing her examination, Amber rewrapped the baby tightly and laid her in the basket. "Everything looks good, but I'll be back to check on her tomorrow, and you, too, Mommy. I'll also draw a little blood from her heel tomorrow. The state requires certain tests on all newborns.

You'll get the results in a few weeks. I can tell you're tired, Katie. We'll talk about it tomorrow."

Katie scooted down under the covers and rolled to her side so that she could see her daughter. "Will she be warm enough?"

"She'll be fine. We'll keep the stove going all night," Nettie promised.

"She's so sweet. I can't believe how much I love her already." Sleep pulled Katie's eyelids lower. She fought it, afraid if she slept she would wake and find it all had been a dream.

The murmur of voices reached her. She heard her name mentioned and struggled to understand what was being said.

"I'm worried about Katie." It was Amber talking.

"Why?" came Elam's deep voice.

Opening her eyes, Katie saw that everyone had gone into the living room. She strained to hear them.

Amber said, "It's clear she hasn't been eating well for some time. Plus, her blood loss was heavier than I like to see. Physically, she's very run-down."

"Do you think she should go to the hospital?" Elam asked. Katie heard the worry behind his words.

He was concerned about her. She smiled at the thought. It had been a long time since anyone had worried about her. As hard as she tried, she couldn't keep her eyes open any longer.

Concerned for his unexpected guest's health, Elam glanced from the kitchen door to the nurse standing beside his mother.

Amber shook her head. "I don't think she needs to go to the hospital, but I do think she should take it easy for a few days. She needs good hearty food, lots of rest and plenty of fluids. I understand she was on her way to her brother's home?"

"Jah," Nettie said. "When she realized he wasn't here, she said she was going to the bus station."

Amber scowled and crossed her arms. "She shouldn't travel for a while. Not for at least a week, maybe two. If having her here is an inconvenience, I can try to make other arrangements in town until her family can send someone for her."

Elam could see his mother struggling to hold back her opinion. He was the man of the house. It would have to be his decision.

At least that was the way it was supposed to work, but he had learned a valuable lesson about women from his father. His *dat* used to say, "Women get their way by one means or another, son. Make a woman mad only if you're willing to eat burnt bread until she decides otherwise. The man who tells you he's in charge in his own house will lie about other things, too."

His father had been wise about so many things and yet so foolish in the end.

Elam's mother might want Katie to remain with them, but Elam was hesitant about the idea. The last thing he needed was to stir up trouble in his new church district. Katie wasn't a member of his family. She had turned her back on her Amish upbringing. Her presence might even prompt unwanted gossip. His family had endured enough of that.

"I certainly wouldn't mind having another woman in the house." It seemed his mother couldn't be silent for long.

This wasn't a discussion he wanted to have in front of an outsider. He said, "Nothing can be done tonight. We'll talk it over with Katie in the morning."

The faint smile that played across Nettie's lips told him she'd already made up her mind. "The woman needs help. It's our Christian duty to care for her and that precious baby."

Mustering a stern tone, he said, "You don't fool me, *Mamm*. I saw how excited you were to tell me it was a little girl. The way you came running out to the barn, I thought the house must be on fire. You're just happy to have a new baby in the house. I've heard you telling your friends that you're hoping Mary's next one is a girl."

His mother raised one finger toward the ceiling. "*Gott* has given me five fine grandsons. I'm not complaining. I pray only that my daughters have more healthy children. If one or two should be girls—that is *Gotte wille,* too, and fine with me. Just as it was *Gotte wille* that Katie and her baby came to us."

Her logic was something Elam couldn't argue with. He turned to the nurse. "She can stay here until her family comes to fetch her if that is what she wants. She can write to Malachi in the morning and tell him that she's here."

Amber looked relieved. "Wonderful. That's settled, then."

For Malachi's sake and for Katie's, Elam prayed that she was prepared to mend her ways and come back to the Amish. If she was sincere about returning, the church members would welcome her back with open arms.

Amber gathered up her bag. "I'll come by late tomorrow afternoon to check on both of my patients. I'm going to leave some powdered infant formula with you in case the nursing doesn't go well, but I'm sure you won't need it. Please don't hesitate to send for me if you think something is wrong. Mrs. Sutter, I'm sure you know what to look for."

"Thank you for coming, Miss Bradley."

"Thank you for calling me."

Elam hesitated, then said, "About your bill."

She waved his concern aside. "Katie and I have already discussed it."

After she left, a calm settled over the house. Nettie tried to hide a yawn, but Elam saw it. The clock on the wall said it was nearly two in the morning. At least it was the off Sunday and they would not have to travel to services in the morning. "Go to bed, *Mamm*."

"No, I'm going to sleep here in my chair in case Katie or the baby needs me."

He knew better than to argue with her. "I'll get a quilt and a pillow from your room."

"Thank you, Elam. You are a good son."

A few minutes later he returned with the bedding and handed it to her. As she settled herself in her favorite brown wingback chair, he moved a footstool in front of it and helped her prop up her feet, then tucked the blanket under them. She sighed heavily and set her glasses on the small, oval reading table beside her.

When he was sure she was comfortable, he quietly walked back into the kitchen. Before heading upstairs to his room, he checked the fire in the stove. It had died down to glowing red coals. The wood box beside it was almost empty. The women must have used most of it keeping the room warm for Katie's delivery. Glancing toward the bed in the corner, he watched Katie sleeping huddled beneath a blue-and-green patterned quilt.

She looked so small and alone.

Only she wasn't alone. Her baby slept on a chair beside the bed in one of his baskets. And what of the child's father? Katie had said he didn't care about them, but what man would not care that he had such a beautiful daughter?

There was a lot Elam didn't know about his surprise guest, but answers would have to wait until morning.

Quietly slipping into his coat, he eased the door open and went out to fetch more wood. He paused on the front steps to admire the view. A three-quarter moon sent its bright light across the farmyard, making the trees and buildings cast sharp black shadows over the snow. High in the night sky, the stars twinkled as if in competition with the sparkling landscape.

Elam shook his head. He was being fanciful again. It was a habit he tried hard to break. Still, it had to be good for a man to stop and admire the handiwork of God. Why else did he have eyes to see and ears to hear?

Elam's breath rose in the air in frosty puffs as he loaded his arms with wood and returned to the house. He managed to open the door with one hand, but it banged shut behind him. He froze, hoping he hadn't disturbed his guests or his mother. When no one moved, he blew out the breath he'd been holding and began unloading his burden as quietly as he could.

After adding a few of his logs to the stove, he stoked up the blaze and closed the firebox door. He had taken a half-dozen steps toward the stairs and the bed that was calling to him when the baby started to fuss. He spun around.

Katie stirred but didn't open her eyes. He could hear his mother's not-so-soft snoring in the other room. The baby quieted.

He took a step back and grimaced as the floorboard creaked. Immediately, the baby started her soft fussing again. Elam waited, but neither of the women woke. The baby's cries weren't loud. Maybe she was just lonely in a strange new place.

He crossed the room. Squatting beside the basket, he

rocked it gently. The moonlight spilling in through the kitchen window showed him a tiny face with bright eyes wide open.

"Shh," he whispered as he rocked her. Rachel showed no inclination to go back to sleep. Her attempts to catch her tight fists in her mouth amused him. What a cute little pumpkin she was. Another of God's wonders.

Glancing once more at Katie's pale face, he picked the baby up. She immediately quieted. He crossed the room and sat down at the table. "Let's let your mama sleep a bit longer."

He disapproved of the choices this little one's mother had made, but none of that disapproval spilled over onto this new life. Settling her into the crook of his arm, he marveled at how tiny she was and yet how complete. The cares and worries of his day slipped away. A softness nestled itself around his heart. What would it be like to hold a child of his own? Would he ever know? Rachel yawned and he smiled at her.

"Ah, I was right. You just wanted someone to cuddle you. I know a thing or two about wee ones. You're not the first babe I've held."

Babies certainly weren't new to him. He'd rocked nephews aplenty. He raised her slightly to make her more comfortable.

"My sisters think nothing of plopping a babe in my arms so they're free to help *Mamm* with canning or gardening, but I know what they're up to," he whispered to the cute baby he held.

"They think if I'm reminded how wonderful children are I'll start going to the Sunday night singings again and court a wife of my own. They don't see that I'm not ready for that."

He wasn't sure he would ever be ready to trust his heart to someone again. If that time did come, it would only be with a woman he was certain shared his love of God and his Plain faith.

"Once burned, twice shy, as the English say," he confided to his tiny listener.

He waited for the anger to surface but it didn't. For the first time in over a year he was able to think about his broken engagement without bitterness. Maybe the sweet-smelling babe in his arms had brought with her a measure of God's peace for him. To her, life was new and good and shouldn't be tainted with the sins of the past.

He began to sing a soft lullaby in his native tongue. Rachel stared back at him intently for a few minutes, but she eventually grew discontent with his voice and the fingers she couldn't quite get in her mouth. Her little fussing noises became a full-fledged cry.

"I guess I can't fix what ails you after all. I reckon I'll have to wake your mother."

"I'm awake." Katie's low voice came from the bed.

He looked over to find her watching him with dark eyes as beautiful and intense as her daughter's. How long had she been listening to him?

Chapter 4

Katie met Elam's gaze across the room. Moonlight streaming through the windows cut long rectangles of light across
the plank floor. It gave her enough light to see the way
Elam held her daughter. With confidence, caring and gentleness. Would Matt have done the same? Somehow, she
didn't think so.

Her boyfriend's charm had evaporated quickly, once the
novelty of having an Amish girlfriend wore off. When he
found himself stuck with a "stupid Amish bumpkin" who
couldn't use a microwave and didn't know how to work a
cell phone, he reverted to his true nature. The harder Katie
tried to make him happy, the more resentful he became. The
harder she tried to prove her love, the louder he complained
that she was smothering him. Looking back, it seemed that
their relationship had been doomed from the start.

Her elderly landlady back in Columbus once said,

"Honey, that man's a case of bad judgment. Dump him before he dumps you."

Katie hadn't wanted to believe Mrs. Pearlman, but it turned out she knew what she was talking about.

Elam spoke as he rose to his feet, yanking Katie's attention back to the present. "I was trying to get Rachel to go back to sleep without waking you."

"The song you were singing, what's it called?"

"You don't know *In der Stillen Einsamkeit?*" He sounded genuinely surprised.

"No."

"I thought every Amish child had heard it. My mother sang it to all of us and still sings it to her grandchildren."

"There wasn't a lot of singing in my house. I don't remember my mother ever singing. I have very few clear memories of my family. My father died before I was born in some kind of farm accident. I do remember my brother Hans playing with me. He was always laughing. He gave me a doll that I loved, and he gave me piggyback rides. I remember someone scolding him to be careful. I think it was my mother."

"What happened to your family?"

"Everyone except Malachi and I died in a fire when I was four."

"I'm sorry."

Katie shrugged off his sympathy. "It was a long time ago."

Rachel gave another lusty cry. Elam said, "I think she's telling me I make a poor substitute for her mother."

Katie shifted into a sitting position in the bed and held out her arms. When Elam laid her daughter in her embrace, she said, "I'm afraid she's going to think I'm a poor substitute for a mother when she gets to know me."

"My sisters all worried that they wouldn't make good mothers, but they learned. You will, too."

"I hope you're right." He sounded so matter-of-fact. Like it was a done deal. She wanted to believe him, but she had made such a mess of her life up to this point.

"My mother will help as long as you're here. If you let her."

"I'm not sure I could stop her. She's something of a force of nature."

Chuckling softly, he nodded. "*Jah,* that is a good description of *Mamm.*"

As their eyes met, Katie experienced a strange thrill, a sizzling connection with Elam that both surprised and delighted her. Rachel quieted. Elam's expression changed. The amusement left his gaze, replaced by an odd intensity that sent heat rushing to Katie's cheeks.

Since the baby had quieted, Katie simply held and admired her. Stroking one of her daughter's sweetly curved brows, Katie said, "This wasn't the way I planned for you to come into the world."

Elam folded his arms. "Our best laid plans often come to naught."

"My landlady used to say, 'Man plans, God laughs.'" Katie tried to imitate her friend's broad Yiddish accent.

"She sounds like a wise woman."

Katie nodded sadly. "She was a very wise woman."

If Mrs. Pearlman had lived, Katie wouldn't be in this mess. Her kind landlady would have taken her in until she found a job. God had once again taken away the person who truly cared about her, leaving Katie where she had always been. Alone, unwanted, belonging nowhere.

She glanced up at Elam as he towered over her bed.

"Your mother reminds me of my friend. She had the same kind eyes."

When he didn't say anything, Katie sighed. "I know what you're thinking."

Frowning slightly, he asked, "And what would that be?"

"You're thinking I didn't plan very well at all."

He crossed his arms and looked at the floor. "I didn't say that."

"No, you didn't, but it's the truth. I kept thinking that Matt would come back for me. For us."

"How long ago did he leave you?"

"Three months. After that I got a part-time job working for our landlady, but she died and the place was sold. I waited for him to come back until my rent ran out. I only had enough money left to buy a bus ticket here."

"Your husband should not have left you."

It was her turn to look away. The shame she'd tried so hard to ignore left a bitter taste in her mouth. "Matt Carson wasn't my husband."

"Ah." It was all Elam said, but to her ears that one syllable carried a wealth of condemnation and pity.

After a long moment, he said, "You should know that Grace Zimmerman mentioned Matt was a friend of her grandson when I went there to use the phone. She said she would have her grandson try and contact Matt. Perhaps he will come for you when he finds out you are here."

Rachel began to fuss again. Katie bounced her gently. "Matt had plenty of time to come for us when we were in the city. I don't expect he will come now. We won't be a burden to you or your family any longer than necessary."

"We will not turn you out. That is not our way. The Bible commands us to help those in need."

"I'm grateful for all you've done, but I'll go on to my brother as soon as possible."

Nettie appeared in the living room doorway rubbing her neck. "There's no need to speak of traveling yet. The nurse says you're to rest. You can write to Malachi and tell him your situation, but you will stay here for a few days. Or more if you need it."

Katie bit her lip. Writing her brother would not be enough. She had to go to Malachi in person. He'd made that abundantly clear the day she left with Matt. His angry words still echoed inside her head.

"You ungrateful harlot, you've brought shame on me since the day you were born. You'll not last six months out in the English world. When you come to your senses you'll be back. But know this. You are dead to me until I see you kneeling in front of me and begging my forgiveness."

At the time, she felt only relief at getting away from her brother's strict control. In the months that followed, when it became clear that running away with Matt had been a bad decision, Katie came to realize that she did still care about her brother and she was sorry for the way she'd left.

Matt laughed at her and called her spineless when she decided to try and mend things with her only sibling. She had written several long letters of apology, but each one came back unopened. After two months, she gave up trying. When Matt left she didn't bother writing to her brother. She knew he meant what he'd said.

Rachel started crying again. Nettie waved a hand to send Elam on his way. "We'll talk about this tomorrow. Right now this little one is hungry and she doesn't want to wait any longer."

Elam bid her good-night, then turned away and headed for the stairs leading to the upper story.

Katie was sorry their quiet talk had ended. She would have enjoyed spending more time with him.

As soon as the thought occurred, she chided herself for such feelings. The last thing she needed was to complicate her life with another man. She appreciated Elam's kindness, but she wouldn't mistake those feelings for anything more.

After that, all Katie's attention was taken up trying to satisfy her daughter's hungry demands. Later, as Katie fell asleep again, she dreamed about Elam rocking her baby in his arms and singing a soft lullaby. In her dream, the sound of his voice soothed her spirit and brought with it a quiet peacefulness.

For most of the next two days all Katie did was doze and feed the baby. Nettie took over the job of nursemaid, in addition to running her household, without missing a beat and with undisguised gentle joy. At her insistence, Katie was allowed to rest, drink plenty of hearty chicken soup, nurse her baby and nothing else.

Elam had moved a folding screen into the kitchen and placed it in front of her bed to give her and the baby some privacy, then he vanished for most of the day to do his chores and work in his woodshop.

Katie saw so little of him that she began to wonder if he was deliberately trying to avoid spending time with her. When he was in the house, she felt none of the closeness they'd shared the night Rachel was born. She began to think she'd simply imagined the connection they had shared.

The midwife returned as promised to check on Katie and the baby. Amber came bearing a gift of disposable diapers, several blankets and baby gowns which she insisted were donations made by the community for just such an occasion. While Rachel scored glowing marks and was pronounced as healthy as a horse, Amber wasn't quite as pleased with Katie's progress.

"At least another day of bed rest is in order. If your color and your blood pressure aren't better by tomorrow, I may send you to the hospital after all."

"I promise I will take it easy," Katie assured Amber. It was an easy promise to keep. Deep fatigue pulled at her limbs and made even the simplest task, like changing diapers, into an exhausting exercise.

"Mrs. Sutter will tell me if you aren't." Amber glanced at Nettie, who stood at the foot of the bed with her arms folded and a look of kindly determination on her face.

Amber was on her way out the door when another car pulled into the drive. She said, "Looks like you have more company. Don't overdo it."

"I'm sure they aren't here to see me."

Looking out the door, Nettie said, "I believe that is Mrs. Zimmerman talking to Elam."

Katie sat up as hope surged in her heart. Had Mrs. Zimmerman been able to contact Matt? Was he on his way here? "Is she coming in?"

"No. It looks like she's leaving, but Elam is coming to the house."

Unwilling to let hope die, Katie threaded her fingers together and held on tight. As soon as Elam walked in and she saw his face, her last tiny reservoir of hope faded into nothingness. "He's not going to come, is he?"

Elam shook his head. "Mrs. Zimmerman's grandson says the family has gone abroad. He sent a computer message to Matt, but he hasn't answered."

Katie nodded. "I think I'd like to rest now."

She slipped down under the covers and turned her back on the people standing beside her bed.

From her place inside her small alcove in the corner of the kitchen, Katie could hear Nettie and her son speaking in hushed tones, and the sounds of housework taking place, but she was simply too tired to care what they were saying.

Her beautiful daughter was her whole world now. Rachel was all that mattered.

It was the smell of cinnamon bread baking that woke Katie on the morning of the third day. She opened her eyes to the sight of bright morning light pouring in through the kitchen windows. Someone, Nettie perhaps, had moved the screen aside. Warm and comfortable beneath the quilts, Katie rested, feeling secure and safe for the first time in weeks. She knew it was an illusion, but one she desperately wanted to hold on to.

Nettie was busy pulling a pan of steaming hot bread from the oven with the corner of her apron. The mouth-watering smell was enough to make Katie's empty stomach sit up and take notice with a loud rumble. Nettie glanced her way and began to chuckle. "I reckon that means you feel *goot* enough to have a bite to eat."

"If it tastes as good as it smells, I may wolf down the whole loaf."

"You'll have to fight Elam for it. This is his favorite."

Katie sat up and swung her bare feet to the cool plank floor. As she did, the room dipped and swirled, causing her to shut her eyes and clutch the side of the mattress.

"Are you all right?"

Katie opened her eyes to find Nettie watching her with deep concern. "Just a touch of dizziness. It's gone now."

"You sit right there until I get a cup of hot coffee into you. I don't want you fainting when you stand up."

Katie took several deep breaths and waited for the room

to stop spinning. When everything settled into place, she looked down at her daughter sleeping quietly in her basket. The sight brought a thrill of delight to Katie's heart. This was her child, her gift. Matt had been wrong when he said a baby would only be a burden.

If he saw Rachel now, would it change how he felt? The thought pushed a lump of regret into her throat. She had made so many bad decisions.

Nettie, having poured the coffee from a dark blue, enameled pot on the back of the stove, laced it liberally with milk from a small pitcher on the table and added a spoonful of sugar before carrying the white earthenware mug to Katie.

Katie didn't take her coffee sweetened, but she didn't mention the fact. Nettie had done far too much for her. Grasping the cup, Katie sipped the hot drink slowly, feeling the warmth seep into her bones.

Nettie stood over her with her hands fisted on her hips. Looking up, Katie said, "I'm fine. Really."

"I will tell you when you are fine. When the color comes back to those cheeks you can get up. Not before. Now drink."

"Yes, ma'am." Katie blew on the cup to cool the beverage and took another sip.

Nettie nodded, then left the room. She returned a few minutes later with a large black shawl, which she wrapped around Katie's shoulders. That done, Nettie turned back to the stove.

Upending the bread pan, she dumped the loaf onto a cutting board and pulled a knife from a drawer. Cutting off thick slices, she transferred them to a plate. Setting the dish aside, she began breaking eggs in a bowl. "Are you drinking?" she asked without looking.

"Yes." Katie took another quick sip and pulled the shawl tighter, grateful for its soft warmth.

She thought she detected a smile tugging at the corner of the older woman's mouth, but she didn't have a clear view of Nettie's face.

After a few minutes of silence, Nettie asked, "How's the coffee?"

"It's good. Better than my sister-in-law ever made on that stove. I used to think her bitter coffee gave Beatrice her sour face."

"You don't like your sister-in-law?"

"She's okay." It was more that Beatrice didn't like her. Katie had felt Beatrice's resentment from the moment she came to live with them, although she never understood why.

"I've got a sister-in-law I don't care for. It's not right to speak ill of her, but she thought my brother married up when he married into her family. That, and she claims her peach preserves are better than mine. They aren't. I use my mama's recipe."

"And riper peaches?"

Nettie's eyes brimmed with humor as she shot a look in Katie's direction. "Can you keep a secret?"

Taken aback slightly, Katie replied, "I guess. Sure."

"I use canned, store-bought peaches."

Katie laughed, feeling oddly pleased to be let in on a Sutter family joke.

Chuckling, Nettie continued. "I hate to think of the hours that woman has slaved over a hot stove stewing her fresh fruit and trying to outdo me. It's prideful, I know. I reckon I'd better confess my sin before next communion."

Katie's mirth evaporated. She bowed her head. She had so much more than a little false pride to confess. What must Nettie think of her?

If Mrs. Sutter hoped her admission would prompt Katie to seek acceptance back among the Amish, she was sadly mistaken. Katie had no intention of talking to a bishop or anyone else about the choices she'd made in her life. She had made them. She would live with them.

After a few minutes of silence, Nettie said, "It must feel strange to see another family living in your childhood home."

Relieved by the change of subject, Katie looked up to find her hostess watching her closely. "It was a bit of a shock."

"It's a good house, but I'd like a bigger porch. Elam has promised to build it this summer. I love to sit outside in the evenings and do my mending. That way I can enjoy a cup of coffee and the flowers in my garden while I watch the sun go down. Speaking of coffee, are you finished with yours?"

"Almost. Do you miss the home you left behind?"

"*Jah,* at times I do, but my oldest son and his wife still live on our farm in Pennsylvania, so I can go back for a visit as often as I like."

"What made you leave?"

A fleeting look of sadness crossed Nettie face. "Elam wanted to come west. There's more farm ground out here and it's cheaper than back home. That, and there was some church trouble."

Nettie busied herself at the stove and began scrambling eggs in a large cast-iron skillet. Katie waited for her to elaborate, but she didn't. Although Katie found herself curious to hear more of the story, it was clear Nettie wasn't willing to share.

Suddenly, Nettie began speaking again. "My daughter-in-law's parents were talking about moving into the *dawdy haus* with one of their children. I would have welcomed the company, but then Elam told me he'd found this property."

The Amish welcomed their elderly relatives and nearly all Amish farms had a second, smaller, "grandfather house" connected to the main home. Grandparents could live in comfort and remain a part of the family, helping to care for the children or with the farm work if they were able.

"Elam is my youngest, you know, and he's without a wife yet. All my others are married. It just made sense for me to come with him and to keep house for him until he finds a wife of his own."

"Not all men want to get married." Katie was thinking more of Matt than Elam, but she did wonder why Nettie's son was still single. Besides being a handsome man, he was kind, gentle and seemed to love children.

Nettie stopped stirring and stared out the window. "Elam was betrothed once."

Katie recalled Elam's comment about "once burned, twice shy" the first night when he was holding Rachel. Now she knew what he meant. "What happened?"

Nettie began stirring her eggs again. "Salome wasn't the right one for him. It was better that they found it out before they were married, because she left the church."

"After her baptism?"

"Jah."

Katie knew what that meant. "She was shunned."

"It was very hard on Elam. Especially after…" Nettie paused and stared out the kitchen window as though seeing unhappy things in the past.

"You don't need to explain anything to me," Katie said, gently. She considered Nettie a friend, and she was willing to respect her privacy.

Nettie glanced her way. The sorrow-filled look in her

eyes touched Katie's heart deeply. "It is no secret. You may hear it anyway. I'd rather you heard it from me. My husband also left the church a few months before he died."

While the Amish religion might not be something Katie wanted for herself, she understood how deeply spiritual true believers were and how painful such an event would be to Nettie's entire family. "I'm so sorry."

"*Danki.* How are you feeling?"

"Better."

It was true. Katie finished her drink, rose and carried her cup to the table, happy to find her dizziness didn't return. As she sat down she thought she understood better why Elam disliked that she had left the faith. "That can't have been easy for Elam or for any of you."

Nettie looked over her shoulder with a sad little smile. "Life is not meant to be easy, child. That is why we pray for God's strength to help us bear it."

Katie didn't want to depend on God for her strength. She had made her own mistakes. She was the one who would fix them.

The front door opened and Elam came in accompanied by a draft of chilly air. In his arms he held a small bassinet. He paused when he caught sight of Katie at the table. She could have sworn that a blush crept up his neck, but she decided she was mistaken. He nodded in her direction, then closed the door.

Nettie transferred her eggs from the stove top to a shallow bowl. "I was just getting ready to call you, Elam. Breakfast is ready."

"*Goot,* I could use some coffee. The wind has a raw bite to it this morning. March is not going out like a lamb. At least the sun is shining. The ground will be glad of the moisture when this snow melts. It will help our spring planting."

He hung his coat and black felt hat on the row of pegs beside the door, then he approached Katie. "I made your Rachel a better bed. It'll be safer than setting her basket on a chair and it will keep her up off the drafty floor."

The bassinet was about a third the size of the ones Katie had seen in the stores in the city when she had gone window-shopping and dreamed about things she could never afford for her baby. The picnic basket-size bed was finely crafted of wooden strips sanded smooth and glowing with a linseed oil finish. It had a small canopy at one end. "It's lovely. You didn't have to do this."

"It was easy enough to make out of a few things I had on hand. It has double swing handles and the legs fold up so you can take it with you when you leave. Have you had time to write a letter to your brother? I'll carry it to the mailbox for you."

He wasn't exactly pushing her out the door, but he was making it plain she couldn't expect to stay longer than necessary.

She didn't blame him. Katie knew she had been dependent on the Sutters' charity for too long already. She'd never intended to take advantage of them and yet she was.

How could she explain that her brother—her only family—wouldn't come to her aid? She might find shelter for herself and her baby at his home, but it would be on his terms and his terms alone.

Elam was waiting for her answer. She wouldn't lie to him. Nor could she write and pretend she was waiting for an answer when she knew full well the letter would come back unopened.

She glanced at Elam. Two important people in his life had betrayed the faith and he had shunned them.

If he knew her brother had disowned her would he allow her to stay?

Chapter 5

"Let the girl get a little food in her before you start pestering her, Elam."

Elam didn't miss the grateful look Katie flashed at his mother. He kept silent, but only out of respect for Nettie. His unexpected visitor had aroused his curiosity and a niggling sense of unease. Katie didn't seem at all eager to contact her brother. That bothered him.

That and Grace Zimmerman's comments about Malachi's harsh treatment of his young sister.

Elam was well aware that some men held to the idea that being the head of the house gave them the right to be stern, even cruel. He also knew such behavior was against God's teaching.

If Katie had been subjected to that type of treatment in the past, it might explain a lot. But even if her life had been difficult, it was no excuse for turning her back on her religion.

Nor was it his place to pass judgment on her or on her brother, he reminded himself sternly. He stepped up to the sink and began to wash. When he was finished, he pulled a white towel off the hook on the end of the counter and dried his hands.

Whatever troubles Katie had, she would take them with her when she left. Then the peace he tried so hard to cultivate would once again return to his life.

Nettie set a bowl in the center of the table. "Take a seat, both of you. Don't let my eggs get cold."

Elam took his place at the head of the table, and Nettie sat in her usual spot at his right. Katie was already seated in the chair to his left. In the morning light her color was still pale, made more so by the black woolen shawl she had wrapped about her shoulders. The dark circles under her eyes added to the impression of sadness he saw in her face.

Her dark eyes looked too big for her thin face. What she needed was some of his mother's good cooking to put a little meat on her bones. He wasn't a man who liked scrawny women.

She quietly clasped her hands together and bowed her head. The movement sent the ends of her short hair swinging against her cheeks. The sight brought a sudden tightening to his chest. She might be a thin waif, but she was also a woman. There was no mistaking that or the odd pull of attraction he felt when she was near.

He tore his gaze away. He'd made a fool of himself over a woman once before and once was enough. Closing his eyes, he bowed his head as a signal to the others, then he began a silent blessing over the meal.

When he was finished, he cleared his throat to signal the prayer was done, then reached for the cinnamon bread. Katie stretched out her arm at the same moment and their hands touched. He felt the shock of the contact all the way up his arm.

She jerked her hand back as quickly as he did. A flush stained her cheeks, giving her back some much-needed color.

"I'm sorry," he mumbled. "Help yourself."

"You first. You've been out working already."

"And you're eating for two."

Following their exchange neither of them moved. Finally Nettie pushed the plate closer to Katie. "I thought you were starving?"

Katie smiled shyly at her. "I am."

"Then eat," Elam added sternly. When Katie still didn't move he took her plate and loaded it with scrambled eggs, two sausage patties and two thick slices of cinnamon bread. When the plate was filled to his satisfaction, he set it in front of her and folded his arms over his chest.

Her blush deepened, but she picked up her fork and began eating. She kept her head down and her gaze focused on her meal so she didn't see the look of triumph on his mother's face, but Elam did.

He had seen just that look when his mother had convinced his oldest sister that her two boys needed and deserved to keep the muddy stray puppy they'd found in the orchard on their last visit. His mother had a big heart and she often thought she knew what was best for everyone.

In the case of the puppy she had been right, but her desire to mother Katie and her little girl wasn't the same thing at all. Having Katie in their home could easily bring the censure of the community to bear on them. Katie's rejection of her faith placed all of them in an awkward position. He and his mother had few friends among their new acquaintances who would speak up for them.

His mother had endured enough heartache back in Pennsylvania. He wanted it to be different here.

From the far corner of the room, Rachel began crying. Katie quickly started to rise, but Nettie stopped her by saying, "I'll get her this time. You finish your meal."

Katie sank back into her seat. "Thank you."

Elam noticed she didn't take her eyes off Rachel as his mother picked the child up. Nettie said, "I see what's wrong, *moppel*. You need your diaper changed."

She carried the child to her bedroom as she crooned, "We had better send Elam to the store for more."

Elam turned his attention back to Katie. "If you make a list of things you need I'll be happy to make a trip into town."

She stared at her plate and pushed a piece of sausage around with her fork. "I don't have the money to repay you."

"I asked for a list, not for money. Your brother will settle with me when he comes for you. I'm not worried about it."

When she made no comment, he resumed eating, but she didn't. The silence in the room lengthened uncomfortably. Every time he brought up the subject of her brother she clammed up. He wasn't sure what to make of her withdrawal. He wasn't sure what to make of Katie Lantz at all.

He could understand her reluctance to admit to her family how far she had fallen, but the time for such false pride was past. She had a child to care for now and no way that he could see to support herself, let alone her baby. If she couldn't bring herself to write her brother then Elam would do it for her.

That might be best. He could mail a letter today.

He would not include the details of her plight. That would be for Katie to do. He'd only say that she had come looking for her family and that she needed her brother's assistance to get home.

When Katie found the courage she could say what she needed to say to her family, but the sooner they came for her the better it would be for everyone.

Elam studied her as she picked at her food. He'd heard not one word of complaint from her. She didn't bemoan her fate, that was commendable. She was certainly attentive to her baby. The love she had for her child shone in her eyes whenever she looked upon her babe's face. There was much he liked about Katie. It was a pity she had turned her back on the Plain life.

As if aware of his scrutiny, she self-consciously tucked her hair behind her ear, then gave up any pretense of eating. She laid her fork down and folded her hands in her lap. "I'll make a list of things the baby needs. It won't be much."

"*Goot*. Now eat or my mother will scold us both." He gestured toward her plate with his fork.

A hint of a smile tugged at her lips, but it vanished quickly. She picked up her slice of cinnamon bread and took a dainty bite.

A few minutes later, Nettie returned with a quiet baby nestled in her arms. Katie started to rise. "I'll take her."

Nettie waved her away. "I can manage. You've barely touched your food."

"And you haven't eaten a thing," Katie countered.

Elam pushed his empty plate aside. "I'll take her, then you can both eat."

"Very well." Nettie handed Rachel over reluctantly.

Elam took her and settled her upright against his shoulder. He liked holding her. Leaning back in his chair, he glanced down at her plump cheeks and tiny mouth. Each day it was easier to see the resemblance between her and her mother, except Katie's cheeks were hollow, not plump and healthy-looking. They shared the same full bottom lip, but Rachel's curved naturally into a sweet smile.

His gaze was drawn to Katie's face. She was watching him, an odd expression in her eyes. What would it take to make her smile as freely as her baby did?

Katie returned to her bed for the rest of the day. Physically she was stronger, but when night finally came the hopelessness of her situation pulled her spirits to a new low. She was homeless and penniless with a new baby to care for and a growing debt to the people that had befriended her.

The memory of Nettie and Elam's tender care of Rachel brought tears to her eyes. For one horrible instant she wondered if her baby wouldn't be better off without her.

Turning over, she muffled her sobs in the pillow as she gave in to despair.

The following morning she stayed behind the screen until Elam had gone outside. She didn't want to answer his questions about why she hadn't written to Malachi. It was cowardly and she knew she couldn't avoid the subject much longer, but she didn't know how to explain.

She had been a trial to Malachi and his wife all her life. Even though the Sutters were aware she had made bad choices, she didn't want them to know Malachi had disowned her. She was too ashamed to admit it. If she had to grovel before Malachi, for her child's sake she would, but what little pride she had left kept her from admitting as much to the Sutter family.

The day passed slowly, but when Elam came in for supper he didn't mention her brother or ask her for a letter. Relieved, but puzzled, she was able to eat a little of Nettie's excellent beef stew and listen as Elam talked about plans for planting pumpkins to sell in addition to their normal produce.

"Pumpkins?" Nettie cocked her head to the side. "Would you sell them through the organic farming co-op?"

"*Jah.* The demand is growing."

Katie's curiosity was aroused. She knew most of the area's Amish farmers sold their produce from roadside stands and at the local produce auctions. Every year her brother had complained bitterly about how hard it was to earn a living competing against the large, mechanized English farms. She asked, "What's an organic co-op?"

Nettie passed a bowl of her canned pears to Katie. "Last year Elam persuaded several dozen farmers to switch from conventional agriculture to organic, using no chemicals, no antibiotics, none of those things."

Katie could see the spark of interest in his eyes. "There's a good market for organic vegetables, fruits and cheeses. I had heard about such a co-op near Akron. Aaron Zook and I contacted them. They helped us find a chain of grocery stores in Cleveland that were interested in selling our crops. They even helped us obtain our organic certification from the U.S.D.A."

"The government men came and inspected the barns and the fields of everyone involved," Nettie added.

Frowning slightly, Katie asked, "Isn't it more expensive to farm that way?"

He gave a slight shake of his head. "Not if it's done right."

"Elam attended seminars on soil management to learn what organic products would give our soil the best nutrients. He learned how to make the plants strong, so they wouldn't fall prey to insects and disease without chemicals to protect them. It has already saved two of our families from losing their farms." Nettie beamed, clearly pleased with her son's accomplishments.

It seemed there was more to Elam than the stoic farmer Katie had assumed he was. The Amish were known as shrewd businessmen, but it was plain Elam was also forward thinking.

Nettie picked up her empty plate and carried it to the sink. "If our people can make a living from the farms and not have to work in factories, then our families will stay intact. It's a win-win situation."

After the meal was over Nettie retired to her sewing room, and in what seemed like no time she emerged with a stack of baby gowns for Rachel and two new cotton nightgowns for Katie.

"You shouldn't have." Katie managed to speak past the lump of gratitude in her throat.

Nettie smiled. "You might as well accept them. They're much too small for me and I'm not going to rip out all those stitches."

It seemed that every minute Katie stayed here she became more indebted to Elam and his mother. She needed to be on her way. It was doubtful that Malachi would pay back any of the money the Sutters had spent on her or Rachel. In time, when she found a job, she would make sure she repaid them herself as soon as possible.

The following days passed in much the same fashion. Katie took care of Rachel and tried to regain her strength. Nettie fussed over the both of them.

Whatever Elam thought of Nettie's pampering, he kept it to himself, but Katie could tell he was ready for her to be on her way. Elam had done his Christian duty by taking her in, but he wanted her out of his home. He avoided looking at her when he was in the same room. A faint scowl creased his brows whenever his gaze did fall on her.

Nearly a week after her arrival, Katie was helping clear the lunch dishes when Nettie announced that she and Elam were driving her out to her daughter Mary's farm some five miles away. That explained why Nettie had been baking all morning.

"Mary is pregnant and expecting in a few months. She's been feeling low. I've several baskets of baked goods and preserves I want to take her and her family. Nothing makes a person feel more chipper than a good shoofly pie they didn't have to bake themselves."

Grateful as Katie was for Nettie's care and mothering, she was excited to hear she would finally have some time alone. "When will you be back?"

"I think about four o'clock. Will you be okay without us? I could have Elam stay with you."

"No, I'll be fine."

"I'm sure you will. You should rest. You still look washed-out."

"Oh, thank you very much." Katie rolled her eyes, and Nettie chuckled.

Thirty minutes later, with Rachel asleep and the quietness of the house pressing in, Katie put down the book she couldn't get into and began looking for something to do. Memories of her life in this same house crept out without Nettie's happy chatter to keep them at bay.

It wasn't so much that her brother had been cruel. It was that he had been cold and devoid of the love she saw so freely given by Nettie to her son. The Sutters were the kind of family Katie longed to be a part of. Malachi and his wife hadn't given her that. Neither had Matt.

With sudden clarity, Katie realized she would have to

see that Rachel grew up knowing she was loved, knowing happiness and hearing laughter. A new determination pushed aside the pity she had been wallowing in. She would raise her child on her own. She would get a job and make a life for the two of them. They would have to live with Malachi for a while, but it wouldn't be any longer than absolutely necessary.

Katie walked into the kitchen with a new sense of purpose. In her rush to leave, Nettie had left a few pots and pans soaking in the sink. Smiling, Katie pushed up the sleeves of her sweater and carried a kettle to the sink. She filled it with water and put it on the stove to heat. It was time to stop feeling sorry for herself and do something for someone else.

It wasn't long until she was putting the last clean pot in the cupboard and closing the door. Looking around the spotless kitchen, she bit the corner of her lower lip. Would Nettie think it was clean enough? Would Elam?

That was a silly thought. Why should she want to impress Elam with how well she could manage a home? He wouldn't care. He wasn't at all like Malachi.

Many was the time she'd scrubbed this same kitchen until her hands were raw only to have her brother come in, look around and begin shouting that she couldn't do anything right, that if she wanted to live in filth she could live in the barn.

How many nights had she spent locked inside the feed room listening to the sounds of scurrying mice in the darkness? Too many to count.

She pressed a hand to her lips to hide the tiny smile that crept out of hiding. Malachi would have been furious to know she hadn't really minded sleeping there. The old sheet she had been given was much softer stuffed with hay than the thin mattress in her room upstairs. The mice had been quieter than her brother's heavy snoring in the room next to hers. She often wondered how her sister-in-law ever got a wink of sleep.

Folding the dish towel carefully, Katie hung it on the towel bar at the end of the counter. Nettie and Elam were not like Malachi. She didn't have to be afraid while she was here.

Two hours later Katie's solitude was interrupted when Amber arrived to check on her patients. To Katie's chagrin, the nurse caught her sweeping the porch and steps free of the mud that clung to everything now that the weather had warmed up enough to melt the snow.

Amber advanced on Katie and took the broom out of her hands. "What do you think you're doing? I gave you strict orders to rest."

Katie sighed. "I'm not used to lying around. Besides, I wanted to repay Nettie's kindness in some small fashion. She and Elam have gone to visit his sister and I thought I'd clean up a little while she was gone."

"I understand, but you won't repay her if you overdo it and get sick. That will just make more work for her. Come inside and have a seat. I want to check your blood pressure. At least your color is better today."

"I feel fine." Maybe if she kept repeating the phrase it would remain true.

Inside the house, Katie hung up her coat and took a seat at the kitchen table. Amber did the same and opened the large canvas bag she carried slung over one shoulder. "How's your appetite?"

"It's good."

Amber narrowed her eyes as she wrapped the black cuff around Katie's arm. "If I ask Nettie, what will she say?"

"She'll say I pick at my food like a bird."

"I thought so." Placing her stethoscope in her ears, Amber inflated the cuff and took her reading.

"Well?" Katie asked when she was done.

"It's good, and your pulse is normal, too. You Amish women amaze me the way you bounce back after child-birth."

"I'm not Amish."

"I'm sorry. That was thoughtless of me." Amber leaned back to regard Katie intently. "I know you grew up here and I've lived in Hope Springs for almost six years, yet I don't remember seeing you."

"How can you tell us apart in our white caps and dark dresses?" Katie didn't mean to sound bitter, but she couldn't help it.

"I think I would have remembered you. There aren't too many women in this area with black hair and eyes as dark as yours. I don't think I remember your brother and his wife."

"They didn't have any children."

"Then they'll be excited to have a baby in the house."

"I'm not so sure."

Amber leaned forward and placed a hand on Katie's arm. "I will tell you something I've learned in my years as a nurse midwife. No matter how upset a family may be at the circumstances surrounding the arrival of a baby, once that child is born…the love just comes pouring out. It's the way God made us."

Would that be the case for her and Rachel? Would her daughter bring love and happiness to her brother's home? Would Rachel help her mother find the sense of belonging she craved?

They were big hopes to pin on such a small baby.

One step at a time, Katie cautioned herself. First, she

had to get home, and soon. She had been a burden on the Sutters long enough.

"Amber, do you know what day the bus leaves that I'd need to take to go to Kansas?"

"As a matter of fact I keep copies of the bus schedule in my car. You have no idea how often I'm asked about that when people want to make plans for family members to come see a new baby. I should just memorize it. It isn't like Hope Springs is a major hub. I think we only get four buses a week through here."

After she checked on Rachel, Amber went out to her car and returned with a laminated sheet of paper. "It looks like the bus going west leaves on Monday and Friday evening at six-ten. The buses going east leave on Wednesday and Saturday afternoon at five forty-five. There's no Sunday service."

Today was Friday. Katie glanced at the clock. It was half past two now. If she hurried, she could make today's bus. Otherwise, she wouldn't be able to leave until Monday. As much as she had grown to like Nettie and even Elam, she didn't want to burden them with her presence for three more days.

The only problem was that she was broke. She didn't have enough money to pay for a ticket to the next town, let alone to go across four states.

Amber tucked the sheet in her bag. "Actually, the bus isn't the best way for you to travel. The best thing would be if your brother could arrange to send a car."

The Amish often hired drivers for long trips. It was a common occurrence in a society devoted to the horse and buggy. One was permitted to ride in an automobile for such things as doctor visits or to travel to see relatives that lived far away. One could even take an airplane if they obtained the bishop's permission.

Katie had heard that a few Amish churches permitted owning and driving a car, but that certainly wasn't accepted by her brother's church. "Hiring a driver to come all this way would be expensive."

Amber fisted her hands on her hips. "True, but you can tell your brother that's what the nurse recommends."

Katie forced a smile, but she knew her brother wouldn't send anyone for her. She would have to make her own way home.

Only…what if she didn't go. What if she stayed in Hope Springs?

The kindness and caring she'd been shown over the last few days had given her a different vision of what her life could be like. A new sense of energy swept through her. "Amber, do you know of any jobs in the area?"

"For you?"

"Yes. Perhaps someone who needs live-in help. I'm not afraid of hard work. I can clean and cook. I know my way around a farm. I'll take anything."

"I don't know of any work right offhand, but I'll keep my ears open. Are you thinking of returning to Hope Springs?"

"I just need a job as soon as possible."

Stepping close, Amber laid a hand on Katie's arm. Her eyes softened. "If you're worried about paying me, don't be. I can wait."

She pulled a card from her coat pocket. "This is my address. Just send what you can…when you can."

Katie took the card, but her heart sank. It seemed that God wanted her to return to her brother's house after all. She considered asking Amber for the loan of enough money to reach her brother's but quickly discarded the idea. She already owed the woman for her midwife services. She couldn't ask for anything else. Except perhaps a ride into town.

"Amber, are you heading back to Hope Springs now?"

Taking her coat from the hook by the door, Amber slipped it on and lifted her long blond hair from beneath it, letting it spill down her back. "No, I've got a few more visits to make. I'm on my way to check on Mrs. Yoder and her new baby. I'm worried that the child is jaundiced. I may end up sending them to the hospital. Why? Was there something you needed in town?"

Katie shook her head. "It's nothing that can't wait until the Sutters get home."

"Are you sure?"

"I'm sure."

After Amber left, Katie pulled out the newspaper that Nettie had finished reading that morning. Quickly, she looked over the help wanted ads in case there was something listed that Amber didn't know about. As she read the few listings her heart sank. There were few jobs available, and none for a woman without education or skills.

Folding the paper, Katie returned it to Nettie's reading table. Rachel began crying in the other room. Katie picked her up and sat on the edge of her bed. "I feel like crying, too."

So much for her renewed sense of optimism.

Looking around the room, Katie couldn't believe how much she had dreaded coming to this place. Now she dreaded leaving. In a strange way her arrival here had turned out to be a blessing. What else could she call this family's kindness?

Cradling her baby, she looked down at her child's wonderful bright eyes and beautiful face. "I just have to believe that God has more blessings in store for us when we reach Malachi's new home."

Reaching that home would require money they didn't have. Besides her clothes and shoes, she didn't own anything of value. As much as she dreaded it, she would simply have to tell Elam why she hadn't yet written to Malachi.

Perhaps Elam and Nettie knew of some work she could do to earn her bus fare. No doubt Nettie would offer to pay Katie's way home, but she couldn't take advantage of the woman's kind heart any more than she already had.

After feeding her daughter, Katie laid the baby in her bassinet. "At least you own a fine place to sleep. Never take it for granted."

Lifting the handles, Katie started to carry the baby's bed into the living room, but stopped in the doorway and looked down. She did own something of value. The bed Elam had made for Rachel was beautifully crafted, but was it worth more than a bus ticket out of town?

Could she bring herself to sell it?

No, Elam had made it clear that it was a gift to Rachel. He'd even made it to travel, so Katie could take it with her.

She bit her lip. Selling it would solve her immediate problem. Should she?

The memory of Elam gently holding her baby in the moonlight came rushing to mind.

His kindness to her daughter had touched something deep inside Katie. Thoughts of him stirred vague longings, but she refused to examine those feelings. She had no right to be thinking about her own happiness. Rachel was her first priority.

Malachi would give them a home where Rachel would be safe. She'd have a roof over her head and food to eat. What did it matter that her mother had coldhearted relatives? Rachel would be taken care of and one day soon they would both leave again. For good.

Katie sat in the chair before the fireplace and considered her options. The weather was decently warm today. She would make sure Rachel was snugly dressed and wrapped in one of Nettie's old but warm quilts. As soon as she could, Katie would send the quilt back with a letter of thanks for its use.

It was only a three-mile walk into town. She could easily get there before the bus left that evening. Unless things had changed drastically in Hope Springs, there were several stores in town that catered to the tourist trade by selling Amish furniture, gifts and quilts. The thought of parting with Elam's beautiful gift gave Katie pause, but she didn't see any other choice.

No. This was the only way.

Chapter 6

It was nearly four o'clock in the afternoon when Elam and his mother returned home. Leaving Judy tied up near the gate, he helped his mother unload her empty baskets and carried them up the steps for her. Inside the front door, he stopped. The house had an odd, empty feel to it.

He glanced around the kitchen. The folding screen had been pushed back against the wall. Katie's bed was stripped and empty. The quilts and sheets sat neatly folded at one end. Rachel's cradle was gone along with Katie's suitcase. It was clear they had left.

His heart sank. He'd tried not to become attached to them, but it seemed that he had failed.

Nettie came in behind him. "Just set those baskets on the table, son. I'll get them washed in a few minutes. Are you still planning to go to the lumberyard?"

He didn't move, couldn't take his eyes off the empty

corner. "Yes. I need to pick up some more cedar to finish the chest I'm working on."

Where had she gone? Had she found someone to take her to her family or was she going back to the city and Rachel's father?

"What's wrong?" Nettie asked as she stepped around him.

"I think our little birds have flown." He couldn't believe how disappointed he was. In only a few days he'd become deeply attached to little Rachel…and to her mother, although he hated to admit that, even to himself.

Walking to the table, he set the baskets on it and slipped one hand into his pants pocket. He withdrew the pink-and-white wooden baby rattle he'd made and simply stared at it.

"She can't be gone." His mother's distress was clear as she carried her burdens in and set them next to his. A letter sat in the middle of the table. Nettie picked it up and read it.

She pulled her bonnet from her head and laid it and the note on the table, then turned to Elam. "That girl doesn't have a lick of sense. She isn't strong enough to be gadding about. She's gone to the bus station. You have to go after her."

That was exactly what he wanted to do. He wanted to bring her back where she and her baby would be safe, but perhaps this was for the best. Perhaps it was better that Katie went away before he grew any fonder of her and her child. He knew what heartbreak lay in that direction.

"She's a grown woman, *Mamm*. She has made up her mind."

"She's not thinking straight. She's putting herself and her baby in danger."

"What do you mean?"

"The baby blues have muddled her thinking. Tell me

you didn't notice how depressed she has been. What if she collapses on the way, or worse?"

"The town is only three miles away. Amish children walk that far to school every day." He slipped the rattle back in his pocket.

"Please, take the buggy and fetch her back. It will get cold as soon as the sun goes down."

"By then she'll be on a bus headed for Kansas. She will be happier with her own family."

Nettie paced the length of the kitchen and back with her hands pressed to her cheeks. "I'm not sure that's true."

He frowned. "Do you know something you aren't telling me?"

"It's not what I know. It's what I feel. She didn't want to write to her brother. Why? Something isn't right."

"You can't know that."

"Even if I'm wrong, we at least need to make sure she made it to the bus depot. I couldn't rest without knowing that she and that precious baby are all right. Katie isn't strong enough to be traveling. What will become of Rachel if anything happens to her mother?"

Everything Nettie said was an echo of his own concerns, but still he hesitated. "Katie has the right to live her own life as she sees fit. She has made her choice. She chose to leave us."

He turned to the bed in the corner and began dragging off the mattress.

"Elam, what are you doing?"

"I'm putting the bed back in the spare bedroom. We have no need of it in here anymore."

The little bassinet, which seemed like such a wonderful way to carry Rachel, had become horribly heavy long before Katie had finished the first mile. By the time she reached the outskirts of town she'd already stopped to rest a dozen times. Now, outside the Amish Trading Post, she simply had to stop again.

After setting Rachel down gently on the sidewalk, Katie used her suitcase as a seat. Rubbing her aching arms, she willed her nagging dizziness away. She was stronger than this. She had to be.

The hollowness in the pit of her stomach made her wish she'd had the forethought to bring something to eat. The sun was low in the western sky and the chill had returned to the air. She had no idea what time it was, but it was getting late. She couldn't rest for long. She had to make it to the bus station on time.

Glancing down, the sight of her sleeping daughter brought a little smile to Katie's lips. At least the baby had slept the whole trip. Lifting Rachel from the bassinet, Katie swaddled her tightly in her blanket. Rising, she pushed her suitcase beneath the branches of a nearby cedar tree, picked up Elam's gift and crossed the street to the store.

At the door, she hesitated. Rachel's bed was the only thing she owned that had been given to her out of kindness. Keeping it meant hanging on to a small part of Elam.

No, I've already been over this. It has to be done. Open the door and go in.

Selling the bassinet proved to be easier than she had hoped. In fact, the woman behind the counter asked if Katie could supply her with several more. Pocketing the cash, Katie thanked the saleswoman and gave her Elam's name. If she helped him earn some extra income, it might make up in some small way for the fact that she'd had to part with his gift like this.

Once outside the building, Katie retrieved her suitcase

and hurried toward the bus station. Main Street in Hope Springs ran north and south past shops, a café and small, neat homes with drab winter yards. Traffic was light. Only an occasional car passed her. Each time she heard the fast clip-clop of a buggy coming up behind her she couldn't help but think of Elam and Nettie and how kind they had been to her.

In a secret place in her heart, Katie foolishly wished that Elam would come after her. She knew better, but the wish remained.

She prayed he and his mother were not offended by her abrupt departure. She'd tried to explain herself in the note she'd left, but words were inadequate to thank them for all they had done.

The bus depot lay at the far side of town just off the highway. Relief flooded through her when she saw the large blue and gray vehicle still idling beneath the corrugated iron awning outside the terminal. A man in a gray uniform was stowing a green duffel bag in the luggage compartment. She stopped beside him. "Is this the bus going west?"

"It is."

"Can I still get a ticket?"

He slammed the storage lid shut. "If you hurry. I'm pulling out in five minutes."

"I'll hurry."

Inside, she rushed to the ticket window, but had to wait for a couple, obviously tourists, to finish first. She glanced repeatedly at the large clock on the wall.

When it was finally her turn, she said, "I need a ticket to Yoder, Kansas."

The short, bald man with glasses didn't look up, but typed away at his keyboard. "We don't have service to

Yoder. The nearest town is Hutchinson, Kansas. You'll have to make connections in St. Louis and Kansas City."

"That will be fine. How much is it?" She pulled the bills from her pocket.

"One hundred and sixty-nine dollars."

Her heart dropped to her feet. That was thirty dollars more than she had. This couldn't be happening. She'd come so far. She'd even sold Elam's gift to her child. Rachel began squirming and fussing. Tightening her grip on her daughter, Katie said, "Are you sure it's that much?"

He looked over his glasses. "I'm sure. Do you want a ticket or not?"

"I don't have enough, but I have to get on this bus." What was she going to do?

"We take credit cards."

"I don't have one," she admitted in a small voice.

"Then I can't sell you a ticket. I'm sorry."

"Please, I have to get on this bus today."

"Do you want to buy a ticket to St. Louis instead of Hutchinson?" he suggested.

"No." What good would it do to arrive in a strange city with no money and no one to help her? It would be jumping from the frying pan into the fire. She turned to look over the waiting room. Besides the tourist, there were two Amish men, both in black suits with wide-brimmed, black felt hats and long gray beards. The only other person waiting to board was a young soldier in brown-and-green fatigues.

Rachel began crying in earnest. Any pride that Katie had slid away in the face of her growing desperation. She left the ticket counter and approached the Amish men first praying they would treat her with the same kindness the Sutter family had shown her.

"Sirs, I must get on this bus, but I don't have enough

money to reach my destination. Could I beg you for the loan of thirty dollars? I will pay you back, I promise."

The men stared at her a long moment, then one spoke to the other in German, but Katie understood them. "She looks like a runaway. We shouldn't help her. We should send her back to her family."

"Jah."

The bus driver pushed open the outside door and said, "All aboard."

Katie clutched the black gabardine sleeve of the Amish elder. "I'm not a runaway. I mean… I was, but I'm trying to reach my brother's home. Malachi Lantz. Perhaps you knew him before he moved away from here."

"We are not from Hope Springs. We came on business and now we must go home." They picked up their satchels and moved toward the doorway.

Katie spun around to face the English tourists. "Please. I only need thirty more dollars to get home. Won't you help me?"

The man hesitated, then started to pull his wallet out of his pocket, but his wife stopped him. "She probably wants it for drug money. I've heard plenty stories about these Amish teenagers. Let's go."

Tears filled Katie's eyes as she watched them leave. The young soldier stopped at her side. "I've only got ten bucks on me, but you're welcome to it. I won't need it. I'm headed back to my post."

She shook her head. "It's not enough, but bless you."

He shrugged and said, "Good luck."

As the people filed up the steps of the bus outside, Katie sank onto one of the chairs. Exhaustion rushed in to sap what little strength she had left.

The man behind the ticket counter came out and began

turning off the lights. "We're closing, ma'am. You'll have to leave."

Rising, she picked up her small suitcase and walked out with lagging steps.

The bus pulled away in a cloud of diesel fumes. The sight reminded her so much of her arrival only days ago that she started to laugh. Only her chuckle turned into a broken sob. She couldn't do anything right. Everything she touched turned to ashes. She couldn't run away. She couldn't even run home. How was she going to take care of her daughter?

Dropping her suitcase, she sat on it and leaned back against the wall of the depot. She pressed a hand to her lips to stifle the next sob.

Rachel began crying but Katie was too tired to do more than hold her. Closing her eyes, she rocked back and forth. "What will become of us now?"

Chapter 7

Elam finished loading the lumber he needed into the back of his farm cart. His gray Belgian draft horse, Joey, stood quietly, his head hung low, waiting to carry the load home. As Elam closed the tailgate of the wagon, he heard some-one call his name. Turning, he saw Bishop Joseph Zook approaching.

"Good evening to you, Elam." The bishop touched the brim of his black felt hat.

"And to you, Bishop," Elam replied, feeling uneasy at the man's intense scrutiny.

"Mrs. Zimmerman mentioned that Katie Lantz has been staying with you. I didn't know she was a friend of the family."

"She returned expecting to find her brother still farming here. The shock of finding him gone brought on her labor and she delivered a little girl, but they left today."

"She's gone, then?" The bishop seemed relieved.

"*Jah,* she's gone." Saying the words made it seem so final. Katie had dropped into his life without warning. She had stirred up feelings he'd tried to keep buried. Now she was gone and he felt her loss keenly.

He hesitated, then asked, "Did you know her well, Bishop?"

"I did not. Once she was of age, she rarely attended services or gatherings. Her brother used to lament how stubborn and how selfish she was, how she thought herself better than the others in our Plain community. He expressed much worry that she meant to leave us and to entice other youth away, as well."

Her brother's description didn't match the quiet, meek woman that had come to Elam's door. Still, her family would know her best.

Bishop Zook hooked his thumbs in his suspenders. "I wish that I might have spoken to her to see if she has come back to the faith. My cousin lives near Malachi in Kansas and he has written that they are happy in their new home. It would be good news for them to hear Katie has found redemption."

Elam shook his head. "She was in trouble and seeking her family's help, but I fear she does not mean to stay among the Plain people."

"It was commendable that you rendered her assistance, but it is better that she has left your home if she has not repented. Perhaps she will see the error of her ways. Until then all we can do is pray for her."

"*Jah,* we can do that. I'd best be getting on my way or it will be dark before I get home." Elam nodded toward the bishop and climbed up to his seat.

"Please tell your mother I send my regards."

"I will. She's looking forward to holding church services at our home come Sunday."

"I know God will bless the gathering. It will not be long until spring communion is upon us. We must select a new deacon before then."

"I was sorry to hear of Deacon Yoder's passing. I did not know him well, but I'm told he was a good man."

"He is with God now, and we must all rejoice in that."

Besides the bishop, Elam's church district had two preaching ministers and one deacon. The deacon's responsibilities included helping the bishop and preachers at church services and assisting needy members of the community, such as widows, by collecting alms. It was also the duty of a deacon to secure information about errant members of the community and convey those to the bishop.

It had been the deacon in Elam's old church that had brought the pronouncement of Elam's father's excommunication and later the news of his fiancée's shunning.

"You are new to our congregation, Elam. If you feel you don't know our men well enough to nominate someone for the office, I can offer you some guidance. My cousin in Kansas writes that they too have lost their deacon and that Malachi Lantz has been chosen to take his place."

Being single, Elam knew he was ineligible to be nominated, and for that he was glad. Only married men could serve. A deacon would be chosen by lots from among the nominated men. It was a lifelong appointment.

Nodding to the bishop, Elam said, "I will visit with you after services this Sunday."

Slapping the lines against Joey's broad rump, Elam left the lumberyard and headed down Lake Street toward Main. Pulling to a halt at the traffic light, he glanced up Main toward the bus depot at the other end of town. Had Katie already left? Was she on her way to her brother's or was she going back to the city and Rachel's father?

Either way it was none of his business, so why did he care so much? The light turned green, but he didn't notice until a car honked behind him. The English, always in such a hurry.

He clucked his tongue to get Joey moving, but as they entered the intersection Elam suddenly turned the horse left instead of right.

What would it hurt to make sure Katie had gotten on the bus? If he could tell his mother he knew for certain Katie had left town Nettie might feel better and give up worrying over Katie and Rachel. He didn't closely examine his own motives for going out of his way. He simply assumed he wanted the chance to say goodbye.

As he neared the station, he saw the lights were off and the closed sign had been hung on the door. Sadness filled him. The bus had already gone, taking puzzling, pretty Katie Lantz with it.

Pulling on the reins, he started to turn around when he caught the sound of a baby crying. Drawing closer to the building, he saw Katie sitting huddled against the side of the depot. She had her head down, her face buried in one hand as she cradled her baby with the other. Her shoulders shook with heavy sobs.

He stopped the wagon and jumped down. Reaching her in three long strides, he dropped to his haunches beside her.

Her head jerked up and he found himself looking at her red-rimmed eyes and tearstained face, partially obscured by the curtain of her dark hair. Even in her pitiful state he couldn't help but think how beautiful she was. Reaching out with one hand, he gently tucked her hair behind her ear. "Ah, Katie, why couldn't you have been on that bus."

"I tried…but I didn't have…enough money."

Her broken sobs twisted his heart like a wet dishrag. He had no business caring so much about this woman. He said, "Mother wants me to bring you home."

"I can't…go with you. I've been…too much trouble… already. We'll be…fine."

"You are a prideful woman, Katie. Would you stop me from doing what the Bible commands of me?"

At her look of confusion, he said, "It is my duty to care for anyone who is destitute and in need, even if it be my bitter enemy—which you are not. Now, let me have Rachel." He eased the baby from her arms.

"Besides, if Mother found out that I left you and Rachel here alone she would tan my hide. Or make me do my own cooking, which would be worse." His attempt at humor brought a fresh onslaught of crying.

"Don't cry, Katie." Slipping his free hand under her elbow, he helped her to her feet. She swayed, and for a second he feared she would crumple to the sidewalk. He pulled her close to steady her, wondering how he could manage to carry both of them to the wagon.

"Be strong just a little longer," he whispered.

She nodded and moved away from him, but he didn't let go of her arm. Helping her up onto the wagon seat, he glanced toward the street as a horse and buggy trotted past. What kind of rumors would soon be flying about him and the weeping English woman he'd picked up at the bus station? Hope Springs was a small town with a well-oiled rumor mill. By tomorrow, speculation would be flying over the fences.

More gossip was the last thing he wanted for his family in their new community, but leaving Katie and her baby on the side of the road was out of the question. He briefly considered taking them to the medical clinic and leaving them in the care of the midwife and the town doctor, but he dismissed the idea.

He hadn't been kidding when he said his mother would be upset if he didn't bring Katie back. It was easier to blame her than to admit he wanted Katie and Rachel back under his roof as much as his mother did.

When Katie was settled on the seat, he handed her the baby, then picked up her suitcase and swung it into the wagon bed. After glancing around, he asked, "Where is Rachel's *babybett?*"

"I sold it," Katie answered, her voice low and filled with anguish.

"You did what?"

"I sold it to the woman who runs the Amish Trading Post to pay for my ticket but it wasn't enough. I'm so sorry. I had to do it."

And you left Rachel without a place to lay her head.

He bit back the comment he wanted to make and climbed onto the seat beside Katie. Picking up the reins with one hand, he clucked to Joey.

The big Belgian swung the wagon around and began plodding toward the edge of town. Before long, a line of cars started stacking up behind them, but he didn't care.

At the Trading Post, Elam drove into the parking lot and stopped near the front of the store. Katie withdrew a wad of bills from her pocket and silently held them out. He ignored her.

He jumped down from the wagon without saying a word and entered the building. The bassinet was on display near the counter. He picked it up, haggled the outrageous price down to one he could afford and left the store with the bed slung over his arm and his anger simmering low and hot.

Outside, he climbed onto the wooden bench and set the basket between them.

As soon as Joey had them back out on the highway, Katie said. "I'm sorry. It was all I had. Please take the money."

He glanced at her from the corner of his eye. Her lips trembled pitifully. Her face was pale, her eyes red-rimmed and swollen from crying. His anger evaporated. How could he stay angry with her in the face of her obvious distress?

"Keep your money."

"But you bought back the bed."

"I bought it for Rachel, not for you. It is hers. Put your money away."

Katie extended the bills toward him. "I can't let you do that."

"Repay me by explaining why you ran off today."

Her eyes widened. She looked like a rabbit caught in the open, with nowhere to hide and a hawk swooping in for the kill.

"I wanted to reach my brother. The next bus wasn't until Monday. I didn't want to impose on you for that long."

"Since you have not given me or my mother a letter to mail to your brother, I'm going to ask why not."

She looked down at the child she held in her arms. "I have to go to Malachi in person."

"What are you not telling me, Katie Lantz?" Elam's firm tone demanded a truthful answer.

She looked away and stared at the barren fields awaiting their spring planting. "I am dead to my brother until I kneel in front of him and beg his forgiveness."

Elam could only wonder at the behavior that had forced her brother to make such a pronouncement. Church members who had committed serious offences were required to kneel in front of the congregation or the bishop and confess their sins before they could be forgiven. Her brother was not a bishop.

"Surely a letter would suffice under these circumstances," Elam said. "Had you written to him when you first came to us, you might have a reply by now."

"I wrote my brother several times in the first months after I left home. I was sorry for the things I said and the way we parted. He sent my letters back unopened. After that, I stopped trying."

"So that's why you didn't know he had sold the farm and moved away."

"Yes."

"He will open a letter from me," Elam stated firmly.

Katie said nothing. Her eyes were closed and she swayed on the seat. She looked utterly exhausted. He said, "Why don't you put the baby in her bassinet before you drop her."

Katie's eyes shot open. "I won't drop her."

"You're both bone tired. I think she'll rest better in her bed."

"She does seem to like it. The woman at the Trading Post wanted you to make more of them."

"Is that so?" Some additional orders for his work would be welcome. He hadn't considered making baby beds. Perhaps Katie's actions would bring some good after all.

Elam let the lines go slack, but the horse continued on his way without faltering. He needed no urging to head home where there would be hay, grain and a rubdown at the end of the trip. Elam held the baby bed steady while Katie laid her daughter in it. Rachel made little grunting noises as she squirmed herself into a comfortable position and drifted off to sleep.

Once he was sure she wasn't going to start fussing again,

he carefully set her bed on the floorboard under the seat, where she would be out of the wind.

"She's beautiful, isn't she?" Katie asked, her voice barely audible. "I don't know what I did to deserve her."

"*Jah,* she's a right pretty baby." A baby with a young and foolish mother and a father who didn't want her. As Elam picked up the reins again, he prayed that Rachel and her mother would come to know God's love in their lives.

They rode on in silence as the last rays of sunlight cast long shadows toward the east. Elam began to make an inventory of the supplies he'd need to make more beds like the one Rachel slept in.

Suddenly, Katie slumped against Elam. He grabbed her to keep her from tumbling forward off the wagon seat and jerked Joey to a halt.

"Katie! Are you all right?"

He cupped her chin and lifted her face so he could see her. She was deathly pale. Dark circles under her eyes stood out like vivid bruises. Her eyelids fluttered open and she tried to focus on his face.

"I'm…so tired…." Her words trailed off and her eyes closed again.

Poor thing. She was all done in. It was no wonder. She'd had a rough time of it today. He shifted his weight and settled her head against his shoulder, keeping one arm around her to hold her steady.

Elam spoke softly. "Hup now, Joey. Get along."

The horse moved forward once more. Elam tried to concentrate on the road ahead, but the feel of Katie's slender body nestled against him drove all coherent thoughts out of his head. How could something that felt so right be so wrong? She wanted no part of his faith or his way of life. He knew that, but he couldn't deny the attraction he felt for her.

He'd only held one other woman this way. Salome, the night he'd asked her to marry him. The memory of that day came rushing back.

He had nervously proposed marriage as he was driving her home in his buggy after the barn raising at Levi Knopp's farm. She'd said yes as she sat bolt upright beside him, looking straight ahead. He'd draped his arm around her shoulder wanting to hold her close.

Instantly he'd sensed her withdrawal. At the time, he put it down to her modesty and promptly withdrew his arm. It wasn't until much later that he understood she didn't return his regard. If only she'd been able to confide in him that night, a great deal of heartbreak could have been avoided.

He glanced down at Katie. She and Salome were nothing alike. Where Katie was small, slender and dark-haired, Salome had been tall, blonde and sturdy. A hardworking farm girl, she and Elam had known each other their entire lives, attending the same church and sitting on opposite sides of the one-room schoolhouse until they'd finished the eighth grade.

As with all Amish children the eighth grade was the end of their formal education. Salome had cried inconsolably the final day of school. A year later, he took her home after Sunday singing. He had only been sixteen, but he knew then that he was going to ask her to marry him someday.

Joey turned off the highway into Elam's lane and picked up the pace without urging. Katie moaned softly when the wagon wheels hit a deep rut in the dirt road.

Pushing the painful memories of Salome to the back of his mind, he again pondered Katie's situation. Why had Malachi cut her out of his life? Had it been because he felt the censure of the community over Katie's rejection of her Amish heritage? Elam found that hard to believe.

The community of Hope Springs had been welcoming and supportive. A few Amish families in the area had children who didn't follow the faith. His uncle Isaac had two children out of ten that had never been baptized. They maintained cordial relations with their parents and visited back and forth often. Uncle Isaac referred to them as his English sons. He loved and enjoyed seeing his English grandchildren.

Not all Amish felt that way. Many families simply couldn't come to terms with children who jumped the fence and never reconciled with them. Yet, for Malachi to move to another state without leaving a way for his sister to contact him spoke of a very serious breach. There had to be more to the story than Katie had told them. Perhaps his letter to Malachi would bring some answers in the return mail.

Would Katie be angry that Elam had written to her brother without her consent? He suspected she might, and that made him smile down at her. If he had learned anything about Katie Lantz, it was that she had a large measure of pride. Perhaps today's troubles had shown her the error of such thinking. Perhaps—but he doubted it.

As the wagon rolled into the farmyard, his mother rushed out of the house. "You found them. Thanks be to God. Are they all right? Where is the baby?"

"She's sleeping in her bed under the seat. Can you get her? I'm afraid to let go of Katie."

Looking up at him, Nettie seemed to notice for the first time that he had his arm around Katie. A quick frown put a crease between her brows. "Is she ill?"

"I think she's just exhausted."

Nettie stepped up to the side of the wagon and extracted the baby and her bed. "Come here, precious one. I've missed you."

Elam shook his passenger. "Katie, wake up. We're home."

"We are?" she muttered against his shoulder. Sitting up straighter, she wavered back and forth, but didn't open her eyes.

"We are. If I let go of you, will you fall off the wagon?"

It took her a long moment to reply. She pushed her hair out of her eyes and blinked hard. "I'm fine. Where's Rachel?"

"I have her," Nettie said.

Elam stepped down and held up his arms to Katie. At first he thought she intended to refuse his help, but she changed her mind. Leaning toward him, she braced her hands on his shoulders as he lifted her out of the cart.

Her knees buckled when her feet hit the ground. He scooped her up into his arms to keep her from falling.

"Put me down. I'm fine." Her slurred words and drooping eyelids said otherwise.

He shifted her higher. The feel of her slight body in his arms made him catch his breath. She was a woman who made him all too aware that he was a flesh-and-blood man. The last thing he wanted was to become involved with a woman outside his faith.

She put her arms around his neck and laid her head on his shoulder. "I said I'm fine, Elam."

She wasn't, but neither was he. Without replying, he turned and carried her into his home.

Chapter 8

Katie woke in a familiar room. Her own room. The room she'd slept in all through her childhood. The same white-painted, unadorned walls surrounded her. The ceiling over the bed sloped low because of the roof's pitch. The series of cracks that had developed in the plaster over her head hadn't changed. When she was little, they had reminded her of stair steps leading to heaven, the place where her parents had gone.

It had been a comfort to a lonely little girl to believe that she might be able to follow them up those steps someday. Now Katie knew they were only cracks in the plaster.

She turned her head. Sunlight was streaming through the tall, narrow window because the green shade was up. It must be late.

She sat up. The room was chilly but not unbearable. The heat from the stove in the kitchen below had always kept this room warmer than any of the other upstairs bedrooms.

She winced as she threw off the covers. Rubbing her aching arms, she quickly realized almost every part of her body throbbed with dull pain. She felt as if she'd been run over by a bus.

The bus! She'd missed the bus.

And Elam had found her weeping in the terminal parking lot.

Embarrassment flooded every fiber of her being as she recalled being carried up the narrow stairs in his arms, followed by Nettie's gentle scolding as she had readied Katie for bed.

Where was Rachel? Where was her baby?

Katie quickly checked the room, but her daughter was nowhere in sight. She noticed her suitcase beside a dark bureau along the opposite wall. Rising, she dressed quickly in a red cable-knit sweater and dark skirt, then ran her fingers through her tousled hair.

At the top of the stairs she heard women's voices. As she descended the steps, she heard laughter and banter exchanged in German. Stepping into the kitchen, she saw Nettie and three other Amish women all hard at work cleaning the room.

Nettie was the first to catch sight of Katie. "You're up. How are you feeling?" she asked in English.

Instantly, Katie found herself the focus of the other women's attention. "I'm feeling much better. Where is Rachel?"

"Elam is keeping the little ones entertained in the living room while we get our work done. Katie, these are my daughters, Ruby and Mary, and this is Ruby's sister-in-law, Sally. All of them work with Elam in his basket business."

Although farming was considered the best work, Katie knew many Amish families needed more than one income and small, home-based businesses were the norm.

Katie glanced around the room. The two women in their late twenties to early thirties were carbon copies of their mother, with blond hair, apple-red cheeks and bright blue eyes. Katie thought the youngest woman must be fifteen or sixteen. She had ginger red hair parted in the middle beneath her white *kapp* and a generous sprinkling of freckles over her upturned nose.

One of the older women stepped forward. Katie saw she was pregnant. "I'm Mary. My mother has told us about your daughter's unexpected and exciting arrival."

Mary glanced over her shoulder toward her mother then leaned closer. "I shouldn't say this, but I'm grateful you've given her something to do besides hover over me and fuss."

"I don't hover or fuss," Nettie declared.

The two sisters looked at each other and burst into giggles.

"When one of us is pregnant that's exactly what you do," Mary countered.

"*Ach,* pay them no mind, Katie. Would you like something to eat? You must be starving. You've nearly slept the clock around." Without waiting for a reply, Nettie began gathering a plate and silverware to place on the table.

Katie frowned. "I'm okay, but Rachel must be starving."

"No need to worry," Nettie answered. "I gave her some infant formula the nurse left with us. Rachel took it fine."

"I could use a bite to eat. I'm as hungry as a horse," Mary interjected.

"And as big as one," Ruby added, then ducked away from her sister's outrage.

"You just wait. Your turn will come round again, sister."

"Everyone sit down," Nettie commanded. "I have cinnamon rolls, and I can fix coffee in a jiffy."

Mary eased into a kitchen chair at the table. She looked

at Katie and patted the seat beside her. "*Mamm* tells us you used to live here."

"I did. My mother died in a fire when I was just a toddler. My brother Malachi and his wife took me in. This was his house."

Before Katie sat down to eat she had to check on Rachel. She moved to the living room doorway. Looking in, she saw Elam with the baby in his arms and three little boys playing with blocks around his feet. Elam hadn't noticed her as he was trying to keep the oldest boys from squabbling over the ownership of a carved wooden horse.

Her daughter looked so tiny balanced against his broad chest. For Katie, it was odd to see a man who wasn't intimidated by a newborn baby. Elam firmly but kindly settled the brewing quarrel and sat back in his chair to keep a watchful eye on the bunch. Rachel looked quite content where she was, so Katie returned to the table and sat down.

She was hungry so she made short work of the delicious cinnamon bun and the glass of milk Nettie placed in front of her.

While Mary and Ruby seemed at ease with their mother's houseguest, Sally remained quiet. She had a hard time meeting Katie's eyes. The young Amish girl obviously hadn't had much exposure to the English or an ex-Amish who was trying to be English.

Finally, Sally worked up the nerve to speak. "Did you really live in Cincinnati? What was it like in such a big city?"

How do I answer that question? My experience was colored by so many different things, Katie thought.

She smiled at Sally. "When I first moved there it was very exciting. Especially at night. You can't imagine the lights. They glow from every tall building and many stay on all night long."

"It sounds so exciting." Sally's tone was wistful.

Katie knew just how it felt to wonder about forbidden things so far away. "Although it can be pretty, it was also terrifying. It was far, far different than I imagined."

Sally leaned forward eagerly. "Are you going back there?"

"I'm not sure what I'm going to do."

"I would like to see the city. My *dat* sometimes travels there for his furniture business, but he's never taken me. Are the buildings really so tall that they block out the sun?"

"It's a place filled with wickedness ready to ensnare the unwary." Elam spoke from the doorway to the living room. He still held Rachel in his arms.

Katie felt the heat rising in her cheeks. He was talking about her. She raised her chin, refusing to give in to the need to keep her head down. Amazed at her own daring, she replied, "Wickedness can ensnare the unwary no matter where they are. Even on the family farm."

He met her gaze, then nodded slightly. "That is true."

An awkward silence ensued until Sally asked, "Elam, my *dat* wants to know when you need me to start weaving again."

"I'll be ready to start the middle of next week, if that's okay with everyone."

All the women nodded. One of the boys, the littlest one, who looked to be about a year old, crawled over to Elam's leg and pulled himself upright and babbled away. Elam reached down to steady the child. "Monroe thinks he is hungry, Ruby."

Nettie came and took the boy from him. His older brother wriggled between Elam's leg and the doorjamb. "I'm starving, *Mamm*."

"You don't fool me, Thomas. You heard the words *cinnamon roll*."

A wide grin split his cheeks, and he bobbed his blond head.

Elam rubbed his stomach. "I'm hungry, too. It's hard work watching the children. I've worked up an appetite."

Ruby threw up her hands. "That's what I tell my Jesse, but he doesn't believe me."

A shout from outside drew everyone's attention. Elam looked out the window. "The bench wagon is here."

Nettie, dishing out rolls to each of the women at the table and their assorted children, said, "Oh, my, and I'm not done with the cleaning."

Katie realized the arrival of the bench wagon meant that the family was making preparations for the *Gemeesunndaag*, the church Sunday, to be held in their home.

The Amish had no formal house of worship. Instead, a preaching service was held every other Sunday in the home of one church family. Up to a hundred and twenty people had attended services in the house when Katie was growing up. In fact, the wall between the kitchen and the living room was constructed so that it could be moved aside to make more space for the benches that were lined up for the men on one side and the women on the other.

In their district, the church owned the benches required to seat so many people and transported them from home to home for each service as they were needed. In the summertime, church was occasionally held in the cool interiors of large barns in the area.

"I'll have the men stack the benches on the porch." Elam approached Katie and handed over the baby. She took care not to touch him, as her heart skipped a beat and then raced ahead of her good sense at his nearness. When he was close, the memory of his strong arms around her brought the heat of a blush rushing to her face. She glanced around covertly, hoping no one noticed her reaction.

There was something about Elam that stirred feelings she didn't want to acknowledge. What a fickle woman she must be. Once she'd imagined herself in love with Matt. Now she was wrestling with those same emotions when Elam was near.

No. These were not the same emotions.

Elam was kindness and charity. He was strength and faith. He was as different from Matt as day was from night.

How had she been fooled into thinking that what she felt for Matt was love? It had been a shallow substitute. She understood that now. Why hadn't she been smart enough to see it before she'd made such a mess of her life?

With her daughter in her arms, Katie rose, wanting to escape the turmoil of her own thoughts. "I'll feed Rachel and then I'll be back to help you get ready for church."

Nettie shook her head. "We can do this. You need to rest."

"I've already slept the clock around. How much more rest do I need?" Katie countered.

"A lot. You go take it easy," Ruby said, gathering up the plates.

What Katie really wanted to do was race up to her room and hide under the warm quilt on her bed. It would have been easy to withdraw and hide, but she couldn't do it. She wanted to earn the respect this family was showing her. And she wanted to show Elam that she was more than a helpless, sobbing woman in need of rescue.

Elam escaped outside and drew a deep breath—one filled with the smell of a muddy farmyard, not with the sweet, womanly scent that was so uniquely Katie's.

What was wrong with him? Why did his thoughts continually turn to her? The memory of carrying her in his arms had haunted him long into the night and came rushing back the moment he'd seen her today.

Was he so weak in his faith that he was only attracted to the forbidden fruit? Katie had chosen to be an outsider. He should have nothing to do with her.

Be ye not unequally yoked together with unbelievers: for what fellowship hath righteousness with unrighteousness? And what communion hath light with darkness?

The Plain people were to live apart from the world. He must harden his heart against Katie's dark eyes so full of pain and loneliness. He had to resist the need to make her smile. To touch her soft skin, to kiss her full lips. She was not for him.

Eli Imhoff stepped down from the bench wagon. "*Goot* day, Elam. Jacob and I have brought the benches for your house."

"*Danki,* Mr. Imhoff, and my thanks to you, as well, Jacob." Elam nodded to the teenage boy sitting on the back of the wagon.

The boy nodded and held out a bundle of letters and the newspaper. "The mailman was dropping this off as we came by. I thought I'd save you a trip down the lane."

"*Danki,* Jacob." Elam took the mail and laid it on his mother's rocker near the front door.

Walking to the back of the wagon, Mr. Imhoff lowered the tailgate. "Shall we get started?"

Elam hurried to join them. "*Jah,* and then you must stay for a cup of coffee. My mother has just made some."

Mr. Imhoff, a widower, glanced toward the house. "How is your mother getting along? Is she liking Hope Springs?"

Perhaps it was his awareness of Katie's effect on him

that made Elam notice the odd quality in Mr. Imhoff's simple questions.

"Mother is well. She misses her friends back home, but I think she likes the area well enough."

"*Goot.* Very *goot.*" Mr. Imhoff grinned and began pulling off the first seat. After unloading the sturdy wooden benches and stacking them together on the porch, Elam invited Mr. Imhoff and his son into the house.

Elam picked up the mail as he followed them inside. He laid the letters on the counter, more interested in the looks and shy smiles that passed between his neighbor and his mother. How long had this been going on? His mother had been a widow for three years now, but he'd never considered that she might be interested in another man.

After accepting a cup of coffee, Mr. Imhoff said, "I was just asking your son if you're adjusting to our community."

"I find it much to my liking, especially since two of my daughters and my son are here."

"It's a blessing to have your family close by." Mr. Imhoff blew on his coffee to cool it.

Jacob was drawn into the other room by Elam's nephews. The next time Elam glanced that way, the strapping boy was down on the floor with them. Mr. Imhoff followed Elam's gaze. "He's used to having little ones underfoot."

The sound of someone descending the stairs made Elam tense. He hadn't thought of how he would introduce Katie to the members of his church.

She came through the door holding Rachel on her shoulder. Her English clothing and uncovered head made her stand out in the room filled with Plain women. She nodded politely at the visitors.

Elam's mother stepped in to fill the awkward silence.

"This is our visitor. Mr. Imhoff, perhaps you remember Katie Lantz."

He nodded in her direction. "Quiet little Katie with the dark eyes? I do, but you are much changed. How is your brother? Is he happy in Kansas? My cousin moved there a few years ago. He says a man can own land and not farm it, but make a living by renting his grass out for other men's cows to graze on."

"I have not seen my brother in quite a while," Katie admitted.

"I'm sorry to hear that. Family is so very important."

Katie looked lovingly at the child she held. "I'm beginning to understand that."

Mr. Imhoff sighed. "I wish God had seen fit to leave mine with me longer."

Nettie laid a hand on his arm. "We take comfort in knowing they are with God."

He patted her hand, allowing his fingers to linger on hers longer than Elam thought necessary.

Elam knew that Mr. Imhoff's wife and three of his seven children had been killed when a car struck their buggy several years ago. His oldest daughter, Karen, had taken over the reins of the family and was raising her younger siblings.

Nettie caught her son looking her way and withdrew her hand. Mr. Imhoff said quickly, "My daughter wants you to know she'll be happy to help with the meal and the cleanup after church if you wish it."

Nettie cast a sly look at Elam before she replied. "Tell Karen her help will be most welcome."

Even his sisters exchanged speaking looks and little smiles. Mary said, "*Jah,* we always welcome Karen's help."

A possible reason for their covert glances suddenly dawned on him. Karen was single and close to his own age. Had the women of his family decided on some match-making?

Shaking his head, he turned away and picked up the mail. Sorting through it, he froze when his glance fell on a long white envelope. The return address was Yoder, Kansas. It was an answer from Malachi Lantz.

Elam's heart dropped to his boots. He glanced to where Katie was happily showing her daughter to Mr. Imhoff.

Her brother had written. That meant she would be leaving soon.

Elam leaned back against the counter. That was what he wanted, wasn't it? So why wasn't he glad?

Chapter 9

When Mr. Imhoff and his son left, Katie excused herself from the group in the kitchen and carried Rachel into the living room where the bassinet was set up. When Katie attempted to put her down, her daughter displayed an unusual streak of bad temper and threw a fit. The young boys were immediately intrigued by the baby and crowded around, their toys forgotten.

"Why is she crying?" the older boy asked in Pennsylvania Dutch. He, like all Amish children, would not learn more than a few words of English until he started school.

She answered him in kind. "I think she is tired, but she's afraid she'll miss something interesting if she goes to sleep."

"Can I hold her?"

"If you sit quietly on the sofa, you may."

The boys scrambled onto the couch and sat up straight. Katie laid Rachel in Thomas's arms. The baby immediately fell silent as she focused on the unfamiliar face. The difference between her dark-haired baby and the boys with their white-blond hair was striking.

Thomas grinned at Katie. "She likes me."

Katie smiled back at him. "I think she does."

She was sitting beside Thomas showing him how to support Rachel's head, when Elam came into the room. Katie looked up and froze when she saw the expression on his face. He drew a chair close and sat in front of her.

He glanced at the boys. "Thomas, I need someone to gather the eggs today. Can you boys do that?"

Thomas puffed up. "Sure."

Katie took Rachel from the boy. Clearly Elam wanted to talk to her without the children in the room. A sense of unease settled in the pit of her stomach.

"*Gut.* Get a basket for the eggs from your grandmother." Elam ruffled Thomas's hair. The boy hurried to do the chore with his younger cousin following close behind.

Katie held Rachel and rocked her gently, waiting for Elam to speak.

"I wrote to your brother shortly after you came to us."

Her heart sank. "You did what?"

"It was clear you couldn't find the words. I did not tell him anything about Rachel. I only said that you were staying with us, but had not the means to get to Kansas."

"I wish you hadn't done that, Elam."

"I know. I'm sorry I didn't tell you sooner." After a moment, he held out a white envelope. "This came this morning."

Katie tried to hide her trepidation, but she could feel Elam's gaze on her as she stared at the envelope without moving. She asked, "What does he say?"

"I haven't opened it. I thought perhaps you would like to do that."

"It's addressed to you. You should read it." She lifted her chin, expecting the worst but praying for the best.

"All right."

She struggled to maintain a brave front. He tore open the envelope and read the short note inside.

His expression hardened. He pressed his lips together.

"Well?" Katie asked.

He read aloud. "'Dear Mr. Sutter, I am sorry to hear Katie has burdened your family with her presence. Please understand it is with a heavy heart that I tell you she is not welcome in our home.'"

Elam stopped reading to look at her. "Perhaps it would be better if you read the rest in private."

She shook her head and clutched Rachel more tightly. "No, go on."

Swallowing hard, Elam resumed reading. "'I will not make arrangements for Katie to travel here. Beware of her serpent's tongue. She has fooled us too often with her words of repentance uttered in falsehood. I pray God will take pity on her soul. She is no longer kin of mine. Your friend in Christ, Malachi Lantz.'"

Katie cringed as Elam lowered the letter. Though she had tried to prepare herself for Malachi's response, it still hurt. She turned her face away as tears stung her eyes.

She was disgraced with nowhere to go. All her struggles to reach her family had been in vain.

Looking into Elam's sympathetic eyes, she said, "I had hoped Malachi would take us in, but if he has publicly disowned me…he won't. I did not believe he would do this."

"Perhaps when he learns you have a child."

She shook her head. "I don't see how that will make him think better of me."

"What about Matt's family?"

"I never met any of them. I think Matt was too ashamed of me."

"Ashamed or not, he has a duty to provide for his child."

"I don't know how to reach him or his family. Mrs. Zimmerman said they were out of the country."

Katie looked up at Elam through her tears. "I truly had nowhere to go."

Elam longed to gather her into his arms and comfort her, but he couldn't. It wouldn't be right. How could a brother be so coldhearted? And Matt! To cast aside a woman and ignore his own child. What kind of man could do that? Elam wanted to shake them both.

Now was the time for her family to show Katie compassion, to welcome her back as the prodigal child and show her the true meaning of Christian forgiveness.

While he had no way of knowing what had transpired between the siblings before Katie left home, this didn't seem right. Many young people made mistakes and fell away from the true path during their *rumspringa,* the "running around" time of adolescents, but it was unusual for a person to be disowned by their family because of such activity.

Elam stared at Katie, trying to see her as her brother saw her. Tears stained her cheeks. She couldn't disguise the hurt in her eyes. She was simply a young woman struggling to find her way in life.

"Is what your brother said true?"

"About my serpent's tongue? Maybe it is. I was ready

to pretend to be Amish again so that Rachel and I would have somewhere to live."

"So you were going to lie to your brother when you faced him."

"I don't know what I would have done. I was so desperate."

Would she have lied? Elam wanted to believe she would have found the strength to tell the truth. "What will you do now?"

"I'll find work. I'll take care of Rachel."

"What if you can't find work?"

She managed a crooked half smile. "I have a little money put back that I won't have to use on a bus ticket. If I can't find work here, then I'll go to the next town and the next one until I do find something."

"You can't wander the country with a baby."

She shot to her feet. "I'll do whatever I have to do to take care of my child."

Elam stared at her dumbfounded as she stormed out of the room and up the stairs.

A few minutes later, his mother came in the room and began picking up toys. "Your sisters are leaving. Ruby has some baby clothes for little Rachel. I thought Katie was in here? Where did she go?"

Elam held up Malachi's letter. "I heard from her brother today."

Nettie's happy smile faded. "Oh. I knew she wouldn't be with us long, but I had hoped she could stay a few more days. I've grown so fond of her and of that baby. How soon is Malachi coming?"

"He's not."

"What?"

"He says that she is no longer kin of his."

"That's ridiculous."

Elam held out the paper. "Read for yourself."

Taking the note, Nettie settled herself in the chair beside him and adjusted her glasses. After reading the short missive she handed it back. "Well, I never. His own sister is destitute and begging for his help and he is refusing to acknowledge her. No wonder *Gott* sent that child to us."

"Her brother may have his reasons. We can't know his heart, only God can."

"You think this is right?"

"No, but what we think isn't important."

Nettie stood. "She is going to need friends now that she has no family."

His mind told him he could be a friend to Katie, but he realized in his heart he wanted to be much more. Unless she gave up her English ways, that would never happen.

Sunday morning dawned overcast and gray. The warm spell had come to an end. Winter reclaimed the land for a little while longer, sending a cold, drizzling rain that fit Katie's mood. She would have to make some kind of decision soon. Without her brother, she had no one to turn to now. She needed a new plan.

As much as she wanted to be angry with Malachi, she couldn't. She'd never felt like she belonged in his home.

Gazing at her baby sleeping sweetly in her arms, Katie tried to block out the despair that threatened to overwhelm her. She was bone tired. Between Rachel's frequent night feedings and the lingering effects of her hike into town, she could barely keep her eyes open. Any sleep she did get was filled with nightmares of what would happen to them now. No matter what, she had to protect her child.

Outside, buggy after buggy began to arrive. Katie

watched the gathering from her upstairs window. Families came together, the men and boys in their black suits and hats, the girls and women in dark dresses with their best black bonnets on their heads.

While most came in buggies, a number of people arrived on foot. Before long the yard was filled with black buggies and the line stretched partway down the lane. The tired horses, some who'd brought a family from as far away as fifteen miles, were unhitched and taken to the corrals.

Nettie had invited Katie to attend services, but she had declined. She didn't belong among them. She didn't belong anywhere.

What was she going to do? How would she take care of Rachel? How would they live?

Why had God sent her this trial?

She turned her limited options over and over in her mind. Perhaps Amber had learned of a job Katie could take? It didn't matter what it was. She'd do anything. Anything.

She turned away from the window. Knowing that the services would last for several hours, she was prepared to stay in her room the entire time. What she wasn't prepared for was the tug of emotion she felt when the first familiar hymn began.

Downstairs, the slow and mournful chanting rose in volume, as voices blended together in one of the ancient songs that had been passed down through the generations. No music accompanied the singing. The Amish needed only the voices of the faithful.

Listening to the words of sorrow, hope and God's promise of salvation, Katie felt a stirring deep within her soul. She knew sorrow, she needed hope, but she was afraid to trust God's mercy.

Moving to the door, Katie opened it a crack. The song

continued for another few minutes, then silence fell over the house. She opened the door farther and caught the sound of a man's voice. The preaching had begun, but she couldn't quite make out the words.

Moving outside her room, she stopped at the top of the stairwell where she could hear better. Standing soon grew tiring and she sank down to sit on the top riser.

Cuddling Rachel close to her heart, Katie closed her eyes and listened to the words of the preacher. The scripture readings and preaching were in German, but she had no trouble understanding them.

When the second hymn began, Katie found herself softly singing along as she pondered the meaning of the words for her own life.

When the three-hour service concluded, she heard the rustling of people rising and the flow of social talk getting underway. Shortly, the gathering meal would start.

Suddenly, an Amish woman started up the stairs. When she looked up, Katie recognized Sally.

The young woman stopped a few steps below Katie. "Nettie says you have to eat and it's time to come down. She won't take no for an answer."

Nodding, Katie rose. It was time to face the community she had turned her back on.

She had no illusions that everyone would be as welcoming as Elam and his mother had been. Drawing a deep breath, she descended the stairs with Rachel in her arms.

When she came out of the stairway, she saw Elam off to one side of the room with several other men who were rearranging the benches and forming tables by stacking them together. Not knowing what to do, Katie simply stood out of the way.

It wasn't long before Nettie caught sight of her. "Katie, come help me set the tables."

Sally returned to Katie's side and reached for Rachel. "I'll take her."

Handing over her daughter, Katie smiled at Sally. "Thanks."

Now that she had two free hands, Katie joined Nettie and her daughters in the kitchen. Other women came in carrying hampers laden with fresh breads, meat pies, homemade butter and jams as well as cheeses. Many covert glances came Katie's way, but no one made comments.

Katie and Ruby began setting a knife, cup and saucer at each place around the tables. Since there wasn't enough room to feed everyone at once, the ordained and eldest church members would eat first. The youngest among them would have to wait until last.

Katie was amazed at how natural it felt to be doing such an ordinary task with Nettie and her family. No one chided her or scolded her for sloppy work. She laughed in response to some story Ruby relayed about her boys. Looking across the room, she met Elam's gaze. He gave her a small smile and a nod. She felt the color rush to her cheeks, but she smiled back.

Looking down, she laid another knife by a cup and saucer. She could almost pretend this was her family and this was where she belonged.

When she looked up again, Elam stood across the table from her. He said, "It is good you're not hiding anymore."

She glanced toward the women gathering in the kitchen. "I'm not sure the worst is over."

"I pray that it is, Katie." It seemed as if he wanted to say more, but he didn't.

She watched as he went out to the barn to wait his turn

to eat with the other young men. She couldn't help but wonder how he would explain her presence to his friends.

Elam stood just inside the wide-open barn doors amid a group of ten other young men near his age. He was the only clean-shaven one in the group. They were all farmers and his neighbors, and all were married with growing families. A number of those children raced by playing a game of hide-and-seek in the barn. The dreary weather hadn't put a damper on the jovial mood of those around Elam.

"Heard you planned on planting pumpkins this year," Aaron Zook remarked. The bishop's son farmed sixty acres across the road from Elam's place.

Aaron had been the one to help Elam develop the area's newly formed organic food cooperative. Limited to small acreages by their reliance on horses, the local Amish farmers had been struggling to compete with the commercial produce farms in the area. But thanks to Aaron and Elam's efforts, they were finding a niche in a new, fast-growing market as certified organic farmers.

"Prices aren't what they were last year," Samuel Stutzman cautioned.

Elam fought back a smile. Samuel always thought last year's prices were better. "I'm going to try a small field of pumpkins. They're a good fall cash crop, but mostly I'll be sticking to cabbage, potatoes and onions."

Aaron pushed aside his black coat to hook his thumbs in his suspenders. "I'm going to plant more watermelon and cantaloupe. They did the best for me."

Elam kept one ear in the conversation, but planting and cash crops weren't what was foremost on his mind. He looked past the array of black coats, beards and black hats to the house. He had no trouble picking Katie out among the throngs of women on the porch waiting their turn to eat.

Her simple gray skirt and red sweater made her stand out like a sore thumb. The women of his family surrounded her.

They were making it plain that Katie was a friend and accepted by them. Part of him was proud of their actions, but another part feared their public display of support would bring disapproval down on them. Katie's history would keep many of the women from acknowledging her.

His mother was talking to Karen Imhoff. Karen's father, rather than gathering with the men, was helping move the tables where Elam's mother directed him.

"Elam, might I have a word with you?"

He turned to find Bishop Zook at his elbow. "Of course, Bishop."

"Come. Walk with me."

Chapter 10

Elam walked silently alongside the bishop until they were out of earshot from the men in the barn.

The bishop spoke at last. "I see that Katie Lantz is still with you."

"*Jah*. She missed the bus."

"I had hoped to hear she was turning from her English ways?"

"Not yet, but my mother is a good influence on her."

"Let us pray so." He took a deep breath and then continued. "There has been talk, Elam. I tell you this because I value you as a member of the church. You have done much to preserve our way of life."

"I can assure you that nothing unacceptable has happened in my home."

The bishop stopped walking and turned to face him. "I believe you. You are an upright man, but such talk can take on a life of its own. Some are saying that your family cares more about outsiders than our own people."

Anger rose up in Elam, but he worked to suppress it. "Because of my father?"

"Word has reached us of your troubles back in Pennsylvania. Perhaps that is why members of the district have scrutinized you so closely. Taking in this woman wasn't a good idea. We must limit our contact with those who do not believe as we do."

"What would you have me do? Turn her and her child out to beg on the roadside?"

"Of course not, but surely you could arrange for her to travel to her brother's home."

"He has disowned her. The baby's father has abandoned her. She has nowhere to go."

The bishop frowned as he rubbed his neck. "Malachi has disowned his own sister? I had not heard this."

"The letter came yesterday. My mother is only doing her Christian duty in caring for Katie and her baby. Perhaps you can stem this gossip."

"I will do what I can, but I can only do so much."

Elam nodded, but his frustration boiled beneath the surface. It was so unfair. He hadn't lived a blameless life, but he had always loved his faith and tried to do God's will. His mother was a good and kind woman. That should not be held against her.

The bishop began walking back toward the house. "If Katie's brother would change his mind it might solve this problem."

"She does not believe he will. From the tone of his letter, I fear she is right."

"I will write to Malachi and the bishop of his district and explain the situation. Perhaps Malachi can be persuaded to listen to wiser counsel. So you are thinking of planting pumpkins. I've been considering that myself."

Elam followed the bishop's lead and changed the subject back to spring planting.

As they walked back to the gathering, Elam related what he knew about the new variety of pumpkins available, but inside he was deeply worried.

He would not turn Katie and Rachel out of his home, but neither could he stand by and watch his family be shunned again.

Katie was acutely aware that she was the focus of much speculation among the district members. A few of the younger women, friends of Mary and Ruby, came up to be introduced. Some of them Katie remembered from her school days. For the most part, the older women of the group ignored her. Katie recognized many of them as friends of her sister-in-law, Beatrice.

From the covert glances cast her way, she knew most, if not all, were aware that she was an unwed mother.

Another poor Amish girl come to no good in the English world. They would point her out to their teenage daughters as an example of why English men weren't to be trusted.

She glanced toward Elam. Did he see her as spoiled goods?

As she watched, Bishop Zook left Elam's side and came toward her. The bishop looked pensive, but Elam had a deep scowl on his face. Apprehension crawled across her skin.

She folded her hands and lowered her gaze. "Hello, Bishop Zook."

"Hello, Katie. It's been a long time."

"Yes, it has."

"Might I have a word with you in private?"

"Of course." She folded her arms to keep her hands from trembling.

They left the porch and walked to where a large oak tree provided some shelter from the light mist.

"I'm sorry to hear of your troubles. What are your plans now that you are back in Hope Springs?"

"I will be looking for work."

"I see. It won't be easy with a new baby to take care of."

Katie glanced toward the house. "Life is not meant to be easy. That is why we pray for God's strength to help us bear it."

"That is true."

She studied Bishop Zook's lined face and saw only kind concern. His long gray beard was considered a sign of wisdom. She hoped that was true. "Is my presence causing trouble for the Sutters?"

"You wish to protect them?"

"I would not hurt them for the world."

"Let me ask you this. Do you plan to join the church?"

If she gave the bishop that impression, would it prevent the censure of Elam and his family? She didn't want to lie. She chose a middle ground and hoped it would be enough.

"I have been gone a long time. I need to reaccustom myself to the community before making a decision. Joining the church is not a step to be taken lightly."

He rocked back on his heels. "That is wise. Since you were not a member when you left, you will not be expected to make a confession to the church should you decide to begin instructions for baptism. Don't hesitate to come to me if you feel you are in need of guidance."

Relief swept over her. She had bought herself more time without an outright lie. "I will keep that in mind."

As the bishop walked away, Katie headed back to the

house. She reached the steps just as Mrs. Zook and several women came out after having finished their meal. The stark expressions on their faces sent a bolt of apprehension through Katie.

Lifting her chin a notch, Katie nodded toward the bishop's wife. "Good day, Mrs. Zook."

She didn't reply. She and the other women turned their faces aside. The brims of their black bonnets effectively blocking their faces from Katie's view as they walked past her without a word.

Katie's smile slipped as humiliation drained the blood from her face. She could feel the eyes of everyone watching her. Glancing across the yard, she saw Elam staring at her. He stood without moving for a long moment, then he turned away. Her whole body started shaking.

A second later, Nettie was at her side. "Sally says that Rachel is getting fussy. Why don't you take her upstairs and I'll bring you something to eat."

Grateful for Nettie's quick intervention, Katie tried to smile, but her throat ached with unshed tears. She quickly fled into the house where Sally was watching Rachel in Nettie's room.

"I tell you, Elam, I was shocked. The bishop's wife snubbed Katie in front of everyone."

Sitting in his living room that evening, Elam pondered what to tell his mother about his conversation with the bishop. He glanced at the ceiling. Katie had gone to her room and hadn't come down.

Sighing deeply, he said, "The bishop told me talk is already circulating in the community. Some people are saying we are going against the *Ordnung* by allowing Katie to stay here."

"Are you worried about a few gossips who have nothing better to do? And the bishop's wife is the worst offender."

"Which means her words will carry much weight with him. You must take care."

"Are you trying to protect me or yourself? Search your heart, Elam. Katie is a lost sheep, but she wants to find her way back to God."

"I have not heard her say this."

"That's because you aren't listening. We must be a light for her, Elam. We can show her God's goodness and His kindness. If we send her away, we only prove that she doesn't belong here. That child wants so much to belong somewhere. She has been made to feel apart her whole life. Her heart is crying out for someone to care about her, but she is afraid."

"Afraid of what?"

"She's afraid of the same thing that frightens you. She's afraid that she doesn't deserve to be happy."

"I'm not afraid."

She took his hands between her own. "I know your heart has been broken. I know your trust was betrayed. None of it was your fault, Elam. You must forgive."

"I have."

"You say that, but I think there is still bitterness in your heart."

There was, and he hated himself for it. "Have you forgotten how much we all suffered when we had to shun *Dat?* How we begged and pleaded with him to come back to God? Do you remember how your friends stopped seeing you? Of standing on the porch and hearing Deacon Hertzler tell both of you that you were excommunicated because you could not bear to shun your own husband. I heard your weeping, *Mamm,* night after night."

"I have not forgotten, Elam," she answered quietly. "But I made my confession, and I was welcomed back into the church after your father died."

He struggled to bring his agitation under control. "But it was never the same. It must be different here or we have uprooted our lives for nothing."

"And Katie? What part did she play in those sorrows?"

The breath whooshed out of his lungs. He hung his head. "None."

"She has been abandoned by everyone she loved. You and I, we know the pain of that. Of trusting and loving someone only to find that love isn't enough."

"What would you have me do?"

"I would have you show her the compassion I know lives in your heart."

Chapter 11

"What will you do now?" Nettie hung a pair of Elam's pants on the clothesline and secured them with wooden clothespins. Monday was wash day.

Beside her, Katie hung up one of Rachel's gowns and reached into the basket for another. "I can't continue living on your charity."

"Don't worry about that," Nettie mumbled around the clothespin she held in her mouth. She secured another pair of pants and said, "You've been a help to me. My wash is going twice as easy with your help."

Katie rolled her eyes. "You could do Monday wash with one hand tied behind your back."

Chuckling, Nettie said, "I've done it with one toddler on my hip and two at my ankles, but I appreciate your help anyway. I'm not as young as I used to be."

Picking up a pair of her own slacks, Katie said, "All I've done is add to your work."

"Your few pants and blouses add very little to my work-load. You need more clothes."

Katie was thankful she had packed a few of her pre-pregnancy outfits in her suitcase. "If I keep eating your good cooking, I'm going to have to start wearing my ma-ternity pants again."

"You don't eat enough to make a mouse fat. I would loan you some of my dresses, but they'd be much too big. You are welcome to borrow some things from my daughters. Mary will be happy to loan you a few dresses. The two of you are about the same size."

She'd sworn she would never wear Plain clothes again. After shaking the wrinkles out of one of Nettie's navy dresses, Katie pinned it to the line. The simple designs and solid colors didn't seem as restrictive as she'd once thought them. Wearing sweatshirts and jeans hadn't made her happy or made her feel she belonged in the English world.

She picked up a white sheet. Tossing it over the cord, she adjusted it until it hung evenly. The wind that set it to flapping was cold. The sun played peekaboo behind low gray clouds.

Securing the sheet, Katie said, "Thanks for the offer, but what I need is to get a job. Then I can buy my own clothes and pay rent on my own place."

"Who will take care of Rachel while you work?"

"I'll find someone. There must be a day-care center in Hope Springs."

"It's not right to let others raise your child."

Katie sighed. "What choice do I have?"

"Perhaps your brother will reconsider." Elam's deep voice startled Katie and she nearly dropped the pillowcase she was holding.

Why did he have such an effect on her? She took a deep

breath to quiet her rapid pulse. "He might if I go to him in person."

"And if he won't take you in, then you've gone all the way to Kansas for no reason and you'll be worse off than you are now because you'll not have a single friend there." Nettie scowled at her son.

Nettie pulled a shirt from the laundry basket at her feet and shook it vigorously. "What your brother needs is a serious attitude adjustment!"

Katie's mouth fell open. She looked at Elam and they both started laughing. He said, "*Mamm,* where did you hear such talk?"

Her gaze darted between their startled faces. "I heard Jacob Imhoff say it about his little brother. Why? Doesn't it mean he must change his mind?"

Smiling at her, Katie said, "It means you'd like someone to beat him up and change his mind for him."

Taken aback, Nettie raised her eyebrows. "Is that what Jacob meant? Well, I hope and pray your brother finds it in his heart to offer you aid, but I certainly don't wish him harm."

Neither did Katie. With her limited options, she knew she needed to find work as soon as possible. "Would it be all right if I borrowed the buggy this afternoon?"

Elam nodded. "I won't be using it."

"I'd like to see if I can find work in town."

"I will drive you." Elam started to leave.

Katie stopped him by saying, "I can drive myself. I've not been among the English so long that I've forgotten how to handle a buggy."

He scowled at her. "Very well. Have it your way. What time will you be wanting to leave?"

She gestured toward the baskets of laundry waiting to be hung on the clotheslines. "As soon as we are done here."

"Then I'll get Judy hitched up now."

As he strode away, Katie said, "I'm sorry if I made him angry."

"He doesn't know how to handle a woman who wants to make her own way in life."

"I've spent my whole life waiting for a man to take care of me. I thought that was the way it should be, but if I hadn't been so dependent on Matt, and on my brother before that, I wouldn't be in this situation. I'm not going to blithely put my life in the hands of another man. I'm going to take care of myself and I'm going to take care of Rachel."

"I believe you will," Nettie said.

Katie's irritation faded. "It's just bold talk. I haven't a clue how to take care of myself or a baby. Nettie, what am I going to do?"

"Pray to God for guidance and take things one day at a time."

One day at a time. Nettie's advice repeated itself over and over in Katie's mind as she drove toward Hope Springs an hour later. There was little else she could do.

On Main Street, people turned to stare as she drove past. A woman dressed in a red plaid coat and blue jeans driving an Amish buggy was an odd sight to say the least.

At the Trading Post, the same woman that had bought Elam's bassinet was rearranging items on a clearance rack. She looked up at the sound of the bell over the door. "Welcome to the Trading Post. Is there something I can help you with? Oh, you're the young woman who came in with that adorable little bassinet. I sold it the very same day. I don't suppose you've brought more, have you?"

Katie decided not to tell her she'd sold it to the man who made it. "Actually, I've come looking for a job."

"I'm sorry. We aren't hiring now, but we usually take on summer help starting about mid-May. If you want, I can give you an application."

Hiding her disappointment, Katie said, "That would be great."

"I'm sure I can sell more of those baby carriers."

"I'll tell the man who made mine." Katie filled out the application and left it with the woman, but the idea of waiting another month and a half for a job was discouraging.

The responses at the other merchants and eateries in town were pretty much the same. No one needed help, but most said they would be hiring when the tourist season got underway.

Dejected, Katie left a half-dozen applications with various merchants and turned Judy toward home.

Katie was unhitching the horse when Elam appeared at her side. He said, "Let me give you a hand with that."

"I can manage."

"I know you can, but I'm going to help anyway." He took the heavy harness out of her hands. "How did your job hunting go?"

"Not well. You may be stuck with me until the tourists arrive."

"I thought as much."

Katie pulled off Judy's headstall and paused to draw her hand down the horse's silky black neck. Unlike her brother and some Amish, Katie knew Elam took good care of his horses. He was kind to animals and stray women. She shouldn't read anything into the way he'd cared for her and her baby. "I'm sorry, Elam. If I didn't have Rachel, I'd just go, but I have to think of her welfare."

"You are being foolish to worry about this. God will provide."

"He hasn't done such a good job so far."

"Do not mock Him. He brought you to my mother, didn't He? What better care could He have provided than that?"

"I'm sorry. I'm just frustrated and angry."

"Angry about what?"

"Everything. I'm angry with Matt for leaving me. I'm angry with my brother for disowning me. I'm angry at the people in town who don't need help until summer."

"Are you angry with me?"

She turned to face him. "Of course not. You and your mother have been kindness itself."

"But you still wish to leave and go back among the English."

Did she? There were times when her previous life seemed like an unreal dream. She hadn't truly been happy on this farm, but she hadn't been happy in the city, either. What was wrong with her? What was missing inside her that made her feel she was always on the outside looking in?

Katie led Judy into her stall, turned the mare loose and closed the gate. Facing Elam, Katie knew only the truth would satisfy him.

"I don't belong here, Elam. I never fit in, not with my family, not with the other Amish kids. I was always different. Sometimes I used to wonder if I'd ever find a place where I did belong."

"Would staying here really be so bad?" he asked softly.

Did she imagine the soft pleading in his voice? She must have. It was only wishful thinking on her part. He had no interest in her as a woman. She wasn't of his faith. It was foolish to consider there could be anything between them.

Katie moved to hang up the harness, needing to put some

distance between herself and the man who disturbed her peace of mind. She needed to get a handle on her wayward emotions. "I don't want to be a burden on anyone. I need to make a life of my own. To do that, I must find work."

He was silent for so long that she thought he'd gone. When she turned around, he was standing with his hands in his pockets and his head bowed.

Finally, he said, "I've been thinking of hiring more help for my woodshop. I've been getting a fair number of orders for my baskets. More than I'll be able to fill once spring planting starts. Ruby, Mary and Sally all work with me in the business."

"Why haven't I seen them working?"

"I've been remodeling my workroom, but it's done now. They'll all be back to work the day after tomorrow. Of course, once Mary has her baby she'll be at home, but by then you should be able to pick up her slack. Would you be interested in work like that?"

Katie couldn't believe her ears. "Are you offering me a job?"

"You will get paid a commission for each piece you make. It won't be much to start with. Not like the jobs you could get in Cincinnati."

"A woman with nothing but an eighth grade education doesn't earn much, even if she can *find* a job in the city."

"So, do you want to work for me?"

Katie hesitated. "Aren't you afraid of what people will say?"

He sighed deeply. "Katie, I'm sorry about yesterday."

"I was expecting it from people like Mrs. Zook and her friends." She just hadn't expected it from him. It hurt, but she couldn't sustain the anger she wanted to feel. She knew he was simply protecting his family.

"I should have shown you the same support my mother did. Let me make up for my lapse of courage. Come work for me."

She needed work, but she hadn't planned on having to work beside Elam. She was already much fonder of him than was good for her. Whenever he was near, her heart charged into a gallop that left her feeling elated and breathless. Hopefully he didn't suspect. She would die of mortification if he realized how often her thoughts turned to him.

She glanced at his face as he waited for her reply. "I'll have to think on it. I've never done any weaving. I might not be any good at it."

"I can teach you what you need to know. You'll get the hang of it in no time. Come. I'll show you how it's done." He turned on his heels and strode toward the front of the barn. Surprised by his confidence in her ability to learn a new skill, Katie followed him.

He opened a door and stood aside for her to enter. Katie paused at the doorway. She rubbed her hands on her jeans. "This used to be the feed room."

"*Jah,* I turned it into my workroom because it had a good big window."

"Wasn't the window nailed shut?"

"I took the old one out and added more. Come in and see what else I have done. Here is where I keep the wood I use for the baskets. I like working with poplar. There's a big stand of them around the pond, so I don't have to buy the wood." His voice brimmed with eagerness to show her his work.

"I remember the poplars." She recalled their shiny green leaves reflected in the calm waters of the pond in the summertime.

"I also use brown ash. These are some of my finished baskets." He gestured toward a bin beside the window.

Katie stepped inside the room. The aromatic scent of cedar and wood shavings enveloped her. Elam had painted the walls a bright white. Tools hung from pegs neatly arranged on one wall. A nearly completed cedar chest sat on a worktable. Its lid and a long hinge lay beside it waiting for him to assemble them. In the far corner of the room a tall cabinet stood open.

On the top shelf, Katie spied an Amish doll in a faded purple gown and black apron. It looked out of place among the tools and baskets.

She crossed the room and picked up the doll. Once she'd had one just like it. It had been a gift from her brother Hans. One of her few memories of him.

As she stared at the toy she noticed a small burn hole in the hem of the dress. Her doll's dress had had just such a hole. A burst of excitement sent her pulse racing. It couldn't be. Not after all these years. With shaky fingers she turned back the edge of the bonnet.

Thrilled, she spun around clutching the doll to her chest. "You found Lucita."

The delight in her voice and the happiness shining in her eyes took Elam's breath away. He'd once wondered what it would take to make her smile at him. It seemed that he'd found the answer.

"Clearly, she must be one of your long-lost toys."

"It's my Lucita. Where did you find her?"

"She had been stuffed inside the wall through a gap in the boards. I found her when I was remodeling the place."

She was still hugging the toy. "My brother Hans gave her to me. It's the only thing I have from before the fire."

Elam stepped closer, happy that he had found the toy and kept it all these months. It was a simple Amish doll. The absence of facial features and hair was in keeping with the Amish obedience to the biblical commandment that forbade the creation of an image. It was dressed in typical Amish clothing, a deep purple gown that had faded over the years and a black apron and bonnet.

He said, "Lucita is an odd name for an Amish doll."

"Hans named her."

"Hans was the brother who died in the fire?"

She smiled sadly. "Yes. Hans saved my life that night. He carried me out wrapped in a blanket. I had Lucita in my arms. I suffered a few burns on my legs, but Hans was badly injured. Malachi told me he died a short time later."

"I'm sorry."

She shrugged. "It was a long time ago."

"How can you be sure it's your doll?"

She gave a guilty grin and pulled back the doll's bonnet to reveal a secret. "Hans used a marker to give her black hair like mine. I wanted someone who looked like me. All my family had blond hair. I always felt like I stuck out."

"Now you can give the toy to your daughter."

"I will, and I'll tell her it's a gift from her uncle Hans." Katie's smile was bright as the summer sun, and Elam basked in its warmth.

"You must tell her to take better care of Lucita than you did and not lose her."

Katie's smile faded. "Malachi took her away from me when I was seven. He said I was too old to play with dolls. He told me he threw her in the rubbish fire. Why would he hide her inside the wall?"

"I don't know. Perhaps he meant to give her back to you one day."

"I'd really like to believe that, but I don't think I can. He used to make me sleep out here when I did something that upset him. I think he enjoyed knowing he'd hidden the one thing that could give me comfort just out of sight."

"Why would your brother do something so cruel?"

"Because I caused the deaths of our whole family."

He stared at her in shock. "How could you? You were only a child."

"Malachi said I was the one who knocked over a kerosene lamp and set the house on fire. I don't remember doing it, but I remember seeing flames everywhere and screaming for help. Besides my mother, I lost Hans and two sisters, Emma and Jane. I can barely remember their faces. Malachi had recently married and had moved into this place. If he hadn't, he might have died, too."

Elam was deeply affected to hear how much she had suffered. He wanted to comfort her, but wasn't sure how. "Such things happen. It was a terrible tragedy, but it was God's will. It was not your fault. Your brother was wrong to blame you."

She straightened the bonnet on her doll's head. "I know. I tried so hard to earn his forgiveness when I was little. As I grew older, I resented his coldness and pretended I didn't care what he thought. The sad thing is… I really did care. I still do."

"Forgiveness is our way, Katie. Even if your brother cannot forgive you, you must forgive him."

"Easier said than done."

How could he ask it of her if he had not been able to do it himself? He sighed and smiled gently. "I know that well. But it does not change what is right."

Katie Lantz had brought turmoil into his orderly world, but she'd brought something else, too. She had a way of making him take a closer look at his own life, his own shortcomings. He strongly suspected that by the time she left, he would be a better man for having known her.

She drew a deep breath and looked up. "You were going to show me how to weave a basket."

He allowed her to change the subject, but he would always remember the sadness in her voice. It touched a place deep inside him. A place that he'd kept closed off after the death of his father and Salome's excommunication. He wasn't the only one who had suffered a loss.

Katie moved about the room looking at the tools. She stopped at the stove. "What are these trays for?"

"For soaking the wooden strips so they can be bent easily."

"Tell me everything I need to know." She gestured toward the stacked poplar logs.

He focused on his work and pushed his need to comfort her to the back of his mind. "My baskets are unique. They're handmade from strips of wood. I buy the plywood for the base, but I do all the cutting here. After a log is trimmed and the bark stripped off, I pound the log with a mallet to loosen the growth rings."

"Will I be hammering logs?"

"No."

"I'm stronger than I look."

"I've seen baby barn swallows hanging out of their nests who look stronger than you."

She opened her mouth to reply, but seemed to think better of it. Instead, she turned back to the wood on the sawhorse. "What do you do next?"

"Then I peel off splints, or strips. The splints are then shaved to get rid of the fuzzy layer between the growth rings. They are rolled up in coils and stacked here. I cut them to size when I'm ready to start a basket."

Picking up a splint, she laid it on the workbench. "Now what?"

"This is one of the forms we use." He began setting the strips in place to form the ribs of the basket. Katie moved to stand close beside him. The top of her head barely reached his shoulder. She tucked her hair behind her ear and leaned over his work to inspect it.

Among his people women never cut their hair. Out of modesty and reverence, they wore it in a bun under a *kapp.* Katie's head was uncovered. She had cut her hair.

She was not Amish. He had to remember that. He had to harden his heart against the influence of this woman who chose to be an outsider.

Only the more he was near her, the more impossible that became. How was he going to work with her day after day?

Chapter 12

Two days later, Katie found herself seated at the long table in Elam's workshop. The air, already filled with the smell of fresh-cut wood and simmering dyes, was being flooded with giggles. Mary, Ruby and Sally sat at the same table watching Katie's fledgling attempts to weave.

"I thought you were making a candy basket." Ruby picked up Katie's project to examine it.

"I am."

"Aren't you afraid the candy will fall though the gaps?" Ruby chuckled as she pushed her fingers through the loose slats and wiggled them at Katie.

Snatching her work away from Elam's oldest sister, Katie said, "Very funny. It's better than my last one."

Sally rose to Katie's defense. "I'm sure she'll improve in time."

"Before I run out of trees?" Elam came in carrying an armload of freshly cut wooden splints.

Katie rolled her eyes. "Another comedian in the family."

After slipping the poplar pieces into a large vat of warm water, he came to stand at Katie's elbow. "You aren't doing so badly. You should have seen Ruby's first piece. In fact, I think *Mamm* still has it in the attic. Shall I go get it?"

Ruby wove another band between the upright stakes of her heart-shaped basket. "Go. You can spend all day looking through that dusty place. I don't care."

"Because she burned it." Mary's honesty was rewarded with an elbow to the ribs. She promptly swatted her sister with a long wand of reed. Ruby grabbed it. The ensuing tug-of-war ended when the reed broke in two.

"Oops." Ruby held out her broken half to Elam.

He sighed and grinned at Katie. "See what I've had to put up with all my life? It's no wonder this venture isn't making much money."

"But it keeps you close as a family," Sally said.

"*Jah*. It does that." Mary snatched the reed from her sister and tossed both pieces in the trash.

Elam moved to the stove. "The poplar should be ready."

The women all rose to select the plywood bases and molds for the unit they would be working on. Katie didn't bother to get up. Working with the woods instead of the more pliable reeds required some skill. Looking at her poor example, she knew she wasn't ready to tackle a complicated piece, but she was determined to learn.

She watched closely as Elam and Mary began to construct large hampers. Ruby and Sally both worked on picnic baskets. Their labors didn't stem the flow of chatter. More than once Katie found herself chuckling at the women's stories of family life.

"Just the other day, Thomas smeared mud all over Monroe so he could stick straw on him and make him look like a porcupine crawling across the floor." Ruby added a double band of scarlet color to the middle of her piece.

Mary smothered a laugh. "Now where did he get such an idea?"

Ruby shot a look at her brother. "It seems *Onkel* Elam told the boys a story about finding a porcupine in the wood-pile."

"I didn't tell Thomas to make Monroe into one."

Pointing at him, Ruby said, "No, but you told me to drop an egg on *Dat's* hat from the haymow. Do you remember that?"

"I remember scrubbing milk cans for a month because you hit Bishop Stulzman."

Ruby held up her hands. "How was I to know the bishop had come to talk to Papa? Besides, from the hayloft door I could only see the hat, not the man. I shouldn't have let you take the blame for that one."

"It *was* my idea. You just had better aim."

Mary began cutting the top of her basket ribs in preparation for setting the rim in place. "No wonder your boys are so ornery."

Sally began looping strands of rattan over her rim. "*Jah,* Jesse says they get their high jinks from their mother."

Ruby's eyebrows shot up. "Oh, he does, does he?"

Startled by her tone, Sally looked up to find her sister-in-law scowling at her. She opened her mouth, but closed it again.

A smile tugged at the corner of Elam's lips. "I didn't realize your husband was so smart, Ruby."

Ruby's jaw dropped. Mary snickered.

Katie, quietly turning and tucking the ribs of her basket, said, "He must be smart. He married Ruby."

Ruby's eyes lit up. "That's right." She poked her brother's arm.

Elam's face reflected his surprise. "I did not know you could be so sassy, Katie."

Sitting back with satisfaction, Ruby grinned. "I like you, Katie Lantz. You're a quick wit."

"But not a quick basket weaver. I'm stumped. How do I attach the rim?" Katie was amazed at how easily she fit in with this family, and how accepting of her they were.

Sally moved her chair closer to Katie. "Use the thicker strips of flat, oval reed. One on the inside and one on the outside."

"I don't have enough hands to hold it all in place."

From her pocket, Ruby pulled a half-dozen wooden clothespins and slid them across the table. "Use these to clip the reed in place. They'll be your extra hands."

Sally demonstrated and Katie leaned in to watch as the younger woman used dyed sea grass to lash the rim pieces to the top row of the basket. When Sally was done, she handed it to Katie. "It's yours to sell now."

Katie looked at Elam. "Speaking of selling, how does that work?"

"Once a month, I take our products to a shop in Millersburg. The owner sells them for us. He takes orders at his shop and from mail catalogs and also from their internet site, then he gives them to me to be filled."

"How many kinds of baskets do you make?" She looked at the variety in the bins.

"We have twenty different types, from laundry hampers to little trinket boxes." Mary stood and placed her hand in the small of her back as she stretched.

"Our best sellers are these picnic baskets. What do you think?" Ruby held up her finished container. It was the fanciest piece on the table, with double bands of scarlet color in the middle and a strip of scarlet rattan lashed around the top.

Katie tipped her head to the side. "It's very nice, but not plain."

Ruby smiled. "It's for the tourists."

Elam took it from his sister. "They come to see us Plain folk, but they like bright colors in their quilts and souvenirs. I'll put a lid and handles on this."

As Elam went to work with his small hand drill at the adjacent workbench, Katie couldn't help but admire the view of his broad shoulders, slim waist and trim hips. His homemade dark trousers and shirt accentuated his physique. She especially liked the way his hair curled in an unruly fashion, defying the typical "bowl style" haircut Amish men wore.

"He is a fine-looking man," Sally said quietly.

Katie, feeling the heat of a blush in her cheeks, glanced at Sally. Both Mary and Ruby were busy teasing each other and hadn't heard the remark. "He's well enough, I guess."

That produced a smothered giggle. "Far better than some I've met here. He will make a fine husband."

Katie tried to sound nonchalant. "Is there someone special?"

"Elam doesn't attend the singings on Sunday nights. Ruby and Mary fear he plans to remain single. They are hoping he'll be interested in Karen Imhoff, but I don't think he will be," Sally said.

"Why not?"

"She's *en alt maedel,* an old maid. She's twenty-five and never been married."

At twenty-two, Katie didn't consider twenty-five to be

that old. Katie decided it was best to steer the subject away from Elam's single status. "Do you attend the singings?"

"*Jah*. I'll be seventeen next month. My mother says it's time I started looking for a husband."

"Don't be in a big hurry to give up your freedom."

Sally scooted her chair closer. "I'm not. I want to see and do things before I settle down. You've lived among the English. What was it like? Tell me about the music and dancing and movie stars."

Katie glanced at Elam's back. "I don't think I should."

"You're the only one I know who has lived away from this place."

It was hard to ignore the pleading in Sally's eyes. Katie, too, had dreamed about a world beyond the farm and the endless work. "I understand how you feel. Believe me, I do."

The door opened and Nettie came in, a bright smile on her face. "Rachel is awake and she wants her mama."

"I'm coming." Happy for any excuse to leave, Katie rose and left Sally's questions unanswered.

While she wouldn't mind satisfying Sally's curiosity, she knew Elam would object. The last thing she wanted was to upset the man who was giving shelter to her and her child.

"How goes life on the Sutter farm?"

Katie smiled at Amber as she began undressing Rachel for her one month examination.

"It's okay, I guess."

Elam had insisted on bringing her and the baby into Hope Springs for Rachel's visit with the doctor. Katie had enjoyed the ride seated beside him, but they had both remained silent. It seemed whenever they were together a kind of tension filled the air between them.

Amber glanced at Katie closely. "You don't sound like it's okay."

"You mustn't think I'm ungrateful. I can't begin to repay the Sutters for all they have done for me."

"So what's the problem?" Amber placed Rachel, naked and kicking, on the infant scale. The baby promptly voiced her disapproval with a piercing cry.

Katie leaned forward. "How much does she weigh?"

"Eight pounds nine ounces."

"That's good, right?"

"Very good. She's passed her birth weight. The doctor will be in in a few minutes." After measuring the baby, Amber swaddled her in a blanket and handed her back to her mother.

Katie shouldered the baby and patted her until she stopped fussing. "Amber, did you learn of any work in the area?"

Picking up a spray bottle of antiseptic, Amber misted the scale and then wiped it down with a paper towel. "I thought you were working for Elam Sutter and his mother?"

"I am, but I thought maybe I could find something else."

Amber regarded Katie closely. "Is Mr. Sutter working you too hard? Because if he is…"

Katie quickly shook her head and looked down. She couldn't stop the soft smile that curved her lips. "No, it's nothing like that. Elam has been very kind."

"Is Nettie chafing to have you out of the house?"

"Not that I can tell. She spoils the baby every chance she gets."

The puzzled expression on Amber's face changed to a look of understanding. "Oh. I see how it is. You poor thing."

Katie frowned at her. "What's that supposed to mean?"

"Elam's very kind, but you don't want to work for him.

His mother adores your baby and spoils her, but you don't want to live with her. I'm getting the picture."

"I don't know what you're talking about."

"You know, it shows when you say his name."

Katie dropped her gaze. "You're talking nonsense."

"I don't think I am. Your eyes light up when you say Elam."

"They do not. You're being ridiculous."

"No, I'm not. Say his name."

"Stop it."

Amber propped her hands on her hips. "You can't do it without blushing."

"Because you're embarrassing me."

Pulling over a chair, Amber sat beside Katie. "I'm sorry to tease you. Are you thinking of joining the Amish church?"

"I've considered it, but I'm not sure. Sometimes I think it would make things easier."

"Don't do it if you're not certain that's where your heart lies."

"It's hard to know what to do. I wanted to get away from here so badly, yet now that I'm back things are different. No matter what I want, I have to think of what's best for Rachel. It isn't that I want material things for her. I want her to know she is loved and accepted. I want her to feel safe and secure."

"She can have those things in the Amish world or in the English one."

"I'm not sure that's true. I couldn't have given her any of that without Matt to help me in the city. Here, you've seen how Nettie dotes on Rachel. It's the same with everyone in the Sutter family. Rachel will be taken care of in this community. She will belong."

"Joining a church for your daughter's sake isn't the same as doing it because you feel God has called you to that life. Do you feel called?"

It was a question Katie couldn't answer. Was she being called or was she just searching for something she'd never had?

The outer door opened. Katie looked up in relief as a white-haired man in a pale blue lab coat walked in. His smile was kindly and vaguely familiar. "Good afternoon. I'm Dr. Harold White. You must be Katie Lantz."

Katie shook the hand he held out. "It's nice to meet you, Dr. White."

He sat down on a metal stool and rolled it close. "I remember you now. You were only three or four at the time, so I shouldn't be surprised if you don't remember me. I treated your burns after your family's house fire. Terrible, sad business that was."

Katie still bore the scars on her legs. "I think I remember you. Did you know my family well?"

"Not really. Your mother hadn't been in the area very long. I do remember hearing that she had immigrated to the United States from Belize."

This was the first that Katie had heard of such a thing. "My family came from Central America?"

"I believe so. I know several colonies of Old Order Amish exist in Belize."

Amber handed Dr. White Rachel's chart, then grinned at Katie. "That's the fun thing about working with Dr. White. You learn something new every day."

He chuckled. "A day I don't learn something new is a wasted day."

Katie smiled, but her mind was reeling. Why hadn't Malachi told her this? Was it possible she still had family in another country? She'd often wondered why she didn't have grandparents and cousins when everyone else at school had such big extended families. All Malachi ever said was that all her family was gone. If they had come from Central America, her doll's Spanish name made much more sense.

Dr. White placed his stethoscope in his ears and directed his attention to Rachel. "Let's have a listen to this little one."

After he had checked her over and pronounced her in excellent health, Katie asked, "Dr. White, is it possible to find out exactly where my family came from?"

He rubbed his chin. "I reckon the State Department would have to have some kind of records. Would you like me to check into it for you? I know a fella that used to work for them."

"I don't want to make extra trouble for you." Katie wasn't going to get her hopes up. Surely, if they had family anywhere Malachi would have mentioned it.

Dr. White chuckled. "I enjoy a challenge. It keeps me young. Besides, everything can be done on computers these days. Amber, have you drawn blood from Rachel?"

"Not yet, Doctor."

Katie frowned. "Why does she need blood drawn?"

Turning aside to make a note on the chart, Dr. White said, "It's just routine newborn screening."

"Shall I do the extended panel?" Amber asked.

He looked at Katie. "Is the baby's father of Amish or Mennonite descent?"

Katie shook her head. "No. What difference does that make?"

Gathering her supplies and pulling on a pair of latex gloves, Amber said, "Because the Amish and Mennonites are almost all descended from a relatively small group of ancestors, there are some inherited diseases that show up more frequently in their children."

Dr. White closed the chart and rose. "It's unlikely that you'll have to worry about any of those. Just do the regular lab, Amber. I'd like to see Rachel again in three months and at six months."

"I may not be here then."

"Where will you be?" he asked.

"I'm not sure."

"Well, wherever you settle, she needs her well-baby checkups at least that often."

Katie had been focused on earning enough money to pay back the people who had helped them. She hadn't considered where she would go if she left Hope Springs.

Where did she want to settle?

Out in the waiting room, Elam put down the gardening magazine he'd been leafing through and glanced at the clock. What was taking so long? Rachel was a happy, healthy baby. Surely there wasn't anything wrong with her.

He had work to do. If he'd been thinking clearly, he would have let his mother bring Katie and the baby to town. The truth was, he hadn't been able to pass up this chance to spend time alone with Katie.

He had no idea how long she'd be staying with them. He had begun to cherish the minutes and hours he spent in her company, knowing it would end soon. It was foolish—he knew that—but his heart could not be persuaded otherwise.

He heard a door open and glanced toward the hallway leading back to the exam rooms. Katie came out with Rachel in her arms. Amber walked beside her. The two women exchanged hugs and Katie turned to him. She was grinning from ear to ear.

He smiled back as his heart flipped over in his chest. No amount of rationalization or denial could change the fact that he was falling for this woman. And those feelings were growing every day.

Rising to his feet, he waited until she reached him. "You look happy about something."

"I've been learning so much about my family. My mother brought us here from Central America."

With her at his side, they left the doctor's office. He helped her into the buggy, using the excuse to hold her hand as she stepped up. "Your brother never mentioned this?"

"No, and I can't imagine why not. Dr. White is going to find out exactly where we came from and if any of my family still live there. I could have aunts, uncles and cousins I never knew about." Her eyes sparkled with exhilaration.

"I suppose it's possible." If she found she had family in Central America, would she travel there? Sending her to Kansas would be hard enough, but he at least had some hope of seeing her again if she stayed with her brother.

She gripped her hands together. "It's so exciting."

He hated to burst her bubble, but he didn't want her getting her hopes up. "It's possible, but don't you think it's unlikely?"

As he feared, the excitement drained from her face. "I guess it is. I'm being silly, aren't I?"

"No. I don't think you're silly at all." He maneuvered Judy out into traffic.

She looked at him and said, "I am being silly. It's just—"

"Just what?" he prompted.

She blushed and looked down. He longed to lift her chin and see what was in her eyes, but Judy shied at a passing car and he turned his attention back to his driving.

Sitting up straighter, she asked, "When will you start planting your pumpkins?"

"In the next week or two."

The rest of the way home, they talked about everything from pumpkins to his mother's interest in Mr. Imhoff. It was a pleasant journey, but he got the feeling Katie was deliberately steering him away from her conversation with Dr. White.

Chapter 13

Over the next weeks, Elam found himself constantly making excuses to spend time with Katie and Rachel. Holding the baby and playing with her became his normal evening pastime. He was pleasantly surprised by Katie's aptitude and fast-growing skill at weaving. She had a good eye for color combinations and weaving patterns, and she had nimble hands. Some of her pieces were as good as Ruby's, and his sister had been weaving for over a year.

Late one evening, he was leaving the barn after tending to a sick colt when he passed the workroom and saw a light shining from under the door. He opened it to find Katie seated at the table with pen and paper in front of her, making a sketch. He almost left without disturbing her, but something drew him in.

"What has you up so late, Katie?"

Her gaze shot toward him. She laid both hands over her

drawing. "I couldn't sleep. I had an idea and I wanted to see if I could make it work."

"Let me see this idea." He entered the room, but she snatched the paper and held it behind her back before he could get a peek.

"It's nothing. You'll think it's silly."

"I've been making baskets for many years. If the idea has merit, I will know."

He approached the table and took a seat across from her. It was just the two of them. The lamp made a cozy circle of light. For an instant, it was almost possible to believe they were alone in the world. She was so beautiful it hurt his heart to look at her, but neither could he look away.

Nervous under his scrutiny, she licked her lips.

Ah, Katie. You have no idea how much I want to kiss you.

He forced his eyes away from her full red lips and held out his hand. "Let me see it. I may save you hours of frustration later."

Unfortunately, there would be no one to save him from the frustration of having her near and not being able to touch her. He'd been foolish to give her this job, to let her stay in his home. The price he would have to pay for such foolishness was becoming more apparent day by day. His heart was breaking by inches.

She smiled shyly and pushed the paper across the table. On it he saw a sketch of a bowl basket with a spiral weave curving around the sides like the stripes on a peppermint candy. "I saw one like this a long time ago and never forgot it. Is it possible to make one like this?"

As he studied it, he could see how a new mold would need to be made to shape the bowl just so. It might take some trial and error to find the right angle to form up the ribs. "What type of wood are you planning to use?"

"I don't know. What do you think?"

"Maybe a mix of light and dark maple. I could make a solid wood lid with a wooden knob on it for a top. It would be very fancy."

"Too fancy?" She reached to take the paper from him, but he held on to it.

"Not too fancy to sell."

It was definitely different from anything he'd seen in the gift shops. It was an eye-catching piece. "If they do well, I'll have to give you a larger commission."

"You really think it's *goot?*" The delight in her eyes shone as bright as the lamp.

He couldn't believe how happy it made him to see her smile. "*Jah,* Katie. It is very *goot.*"

She dipped her head. "*Danki,* Elam. More money is what I need."

His smile faded. Allowing Katie to earn more money meant that she would leave that much sooner.

It was the thing he wanted...and the thing he now dreaded.

Katie watched the play of emotions across Elam's face. What was he thinking? She knew the local gossips were linking his name with hers. His mother and his sisters tried to downplay the impact of the talk, but she wasn't fooled. They were beginning to worry. The family had suffered so much when their father was shunned. She didn't want to cause more pain.

He rose to his feet and picked up the lamp. "It is late. You should get some rest."

She stood and walked to the door with him. "Rachel will be awake soon. Once I've fed her I'll go back to bed and try to sleep."

"What troubles your sleep? Or is it that our beds are not as soft as the English like."

"The bed is fine. I just have a lot on my mind."

"Give your cares over to God."

Pulling her coat from a peg by the door, she slipped into it. "Good advice, but hard to follow."

As she walked out the door he nodded. It was true for him, as well.

At the house, they found Nettie reading her Bible in the living room. She held Rachel in the crook of one arm. Peering over the top of her glasses at them, she asked, "What have you two been up to?"

"Katie has been drawing up plans for a new basket design."

Blushing, Katie said, "I was just playing with an idea. Elam saw how to make it work."

"I'd like to see this plan. Elam, would you take this child. She's put my arm to sleep."

He lifted Rachel from his mother and carried her to the sofa where he sat down. "You are getting heavy. What are we going to do about that? Oh, I see. It's your eyelids that are getting heavy. Well, don't mind me. Go back to sleep."

Katie smiled at the pair. Elam was so good with Rachel. He was never impatient, always gentle. It was easy to see he cared a great deal for her daughter. He would make a good father someday.

He glanced up at her. As their eyes met, an arch of awareness passed between them. She knew by the look in his eyes that he felt it, too. How had this happened? When had she fallen in love with Elam?

On the last Saturday in April, Elam packed his baskets into the back of the buggy and prepared for the three-hour round trip into Millersburg. He wasn't surprised when Nettie announced that she and Katie would be joining him.

Attired in her newest dress and her Sunday bonnet and cape, Nettie climbed into the buggy. "What a nice spring day we have for our trip. I can't believe it's already the middle of April."

Elam found it hard to believe that Katie and Rachel had been with them for over a month. Katie had proven herself to be a hard worker and he knew she was making his mother's life easier by helping her with household chores. "I'll be able to get started with planting soon if the weather holds."

"And I need to get my garden in, but first we'll have a fine shopping trip. I want to go to the superstore and then I may need to stop at the fabric store. What are you needing, Elam?"

"Some new drill bits and blades for my wood plane. I also want to pick up some new dyes and coils of maple splints."

"Maple?" His mother looked at him in surprise. "I thought you only used poplar and ash in your baskets."

"We are trying something new with Katie's design. What about you, Katie? What are you needing in town?" Taking the baby from her, he helped her in and then handed up Rachel when Katie was settled.

"A few things for Rachel and a new pair of jeans. It shouldn't take me long to find what I need."

"*Goot,* then we will not have to spend much time in the city."

The buggy rocked in his direction when he stepped in, tipping Katie toward him. With Rachel in her arms, she couldn't catch herself. He threw up a hand to steady her. It landed at her waist. Her cheeks flamed crimson. When she regained her balance he withdrew his hand, but the feel of her slender torso remained imprinted in his mind.

Katie moved as far over as she was able, but it was still a tight fit with her sandwiched between him and his mother. It was going to be a long ride. He didn't know how he'd keep his attention on the road with her soft body pressed against his.

Each jolt in the road threw them against one another and sent waves of awareness tingling along his nerve endings. The sweet fragrance of her hair was like a tempting flower beside him. Judy tossed her head anxiously each time a car passed them, and he knew he was communicating his nervousness to the animal. Fortunately, they soon turned into the lane leading to Ruby's home.

Ruby had volunteered to keep Rachel so Katie would be free to enjoy her shopping trip. She came out of the house to meet them. "Sally is wanting to go with you, Elam. Do you mind one more?"

Sally came flying out of the house. "Please say I can go!"

Elam cast his gaze skyward. "What do you need in the city?"

"Some new shoes."

He frowned at her. "You can't find them in Hope Springs?"

"They'll be cheaper in Millersburg. I won't be any trouble. I promise."

"You'll have to squeeze in back with my cargo."

"That's fine. Thank you." She quickly climbed in the backseat, pushing aside several of the baskets.

Ruby moved to stand beside Elam. "Thanks for taking her. Can I have that fine baby girl now?"

Katie handed Rachel to him, a look of apprehension on her face. "I've never left her for so long."

Elam knew exactly how she felt as he handed the baby to his sister. "Don't let the boys turn her into a porcupine."

Gathering Rachel close, Ruby smiled at her. "Don't worry. I'll keep a good eye on her."

Katie handed out a bag with diapers and formula in it. "I know you will. Thanks again for watching her."

"My pleasure." Ruby waved as Elam turned Judy and drove out of the yard.

Back on the highway, the mare managed a brisk trot, but she was no match for the cars that went zinging past. It wasn't the local drivers he minded. They shared the road with only occasional complaints. It was the out-of-towners and teenagers he worried about. The ones who didn't know enough to slow down when they crested a hill, in case a buggy was just over the rise and out of sight. At fifty-five miles an hour, a car could run up on an Amish vehicle before the driver knew it. In such crashes, the car always won.

They had been on the road for an hour when a white van came flying past and honked loudly. The noise spooked the horse, but Elam was able to keep her under control. His temper was harder to hold in check. "Foolish English. They're looking to get someone killed."

"Calm yourself, Elam," his mother said.

She was right. What good did it do to show his temper to his family?

The next car that passed them slowed when it drew alongside. As soon as he saw the camera aimed his way, he pulled off his hat to shield his face. The Plain People felt photographs were graven images and forbidden by the Bible. His mother turned away, as well. To his surprise, so did Katie. As the car sped on, he looked at Katie with a new respect. It was good to see she still practiced some of the Amish ways.

After another half hour of travel, Sally, sitting behind him, leaned forward. "Does anyone know some new jokes?"

For the next mile they exchanged funny stories and jokes that had all the women laughing. Elam put up with it.

Finally, Katie prodded Elam with her elbow. "Knock, knock."

"This is silliness," he stated firmly.

"'A merry heart doeth good like a medicine: but a broken spirit drieth the bones,'" his mother quoted from *Proverbs*.

Katie repeated, "Knock, knock."

He rolled his eyes heavenward. "Who's there?"

"Amish."

He glared at her from the corner of his eye. "Amish who?"

She playfully draped her arm around his shoulders. "Ah, I miss you, too."

Katie regretted her impulsive hug the moment she felt Elam stiffen. Self-consciously, she withdrew her arms and folded her hands in her lap. Nettie and Sally were laughing, but he wasn't. Had she made him angry with her forward behavior?

"That's a good one," Nettie declared.

"A bunch of silliness," Elam stated again, but as Katie glanced his way she saw the corner of his mouth twitching.

She said, "The English don't think the Amish have a sense of humor."

"Oh, but we do," Nettie declared, still chuckling.

"Have you heard the one about the Amish farmer with twin mules?" Elam asked.

"No." Katie relaxed and listened to his joke with a light heart. It felt good to be included and accepted by Elam and his family. The trip into town became a happy jaunt as they all tried to outdo each other with funny stories. Katie was sorry when the outskirts of Millersburg came into view.

The first stop was a busy gift shop where Elam carried in his baskets. Katie followed, eager to see how her weaving design would be greeted. Of course, it had been Elam who perfected the pieces, but she had had a hand in their creation. The owner showed enough interest to order a dozen more bowls and to add a photo of one to his online catalog.

With the cargo disposed of, Katie joined Sally in the backseat. Sally, eager to see as much of the small city as possible, rolled up the rear flap and was almost hanging out. "Did you see the dresses in that store window?"

"I saw them." Katie was sure the prices were well above what she could afford.

Sally checked to make sure Nettie and Elam weren't listening. In a low voice she said, "My friend Faith has clothes like that. She sneaks out of the house and goes out on dates with English boys. They go to movies and smoke cigarettes. Faith says she's going to make the most of her *rumspringa*."

It was a common enough occurrence in Amish communities. Teenagers often rebelled against their strict upbringing. Most families in Katie's more liberal district tolerated such behavior and waited for it to end. When the teenagers reached marrying age, most settled down, made their baptisms and led quiet lives. Most, but not all.

"Is that what you want to do?" Katie asked.

Sally averted her gaze. "I don't know. It sounds like fun, but my folks would be so disappointed and ashamed if I was caught doing something like that."

"Only if you were caught?"

Sally's eyes snapped to meet Katie's. She didn't reply, but her mood became pensive. After a while, she said, "I noticed you weren't at the last church service. Will you be going tomorrow?"

"I'm not sure." Katie had been considering it but she

didn't know if she was ready to face Bishop Zook again. He was sure to ask if she was ready to start instructions for baptism.

At the superstore, Elam secured Judy to one of the dozen hitching rails in a special section of the parking lot, and the group headed through the large sliding glass doors. By unspoken consent, the women became reserved and quiet. When they were out in the English world, they did nothing to attract attention to themselves.

Inside, Elam turned to his mother. "I will not be long. I know where the tools are. Where shall we meet?"

Sally turned around slowly, awe written on her face.

Nettie pulled a red shopping cart from the line. "I may be a while. I need several bolts of fabric and some thread. Hopefully they will have the sewing machine needles I need here and we won't have to go to another store."

Spinning to face her, Sally said, "I don't mind if we have to visit more stores."

"I'm sure it won't take me long to find things for Rachel. Why don't we meet in the food court," Katie suggested, gesturing to a collection of booths and fast-food counters off to the side of the doorway.

Elam smiled and rubbed his stomach. "*Jah,* a cheese-burger and French fries sounds yummy."

Katie grinned. Eating out was a rare treat. One enjoyed by every member of the family.

Nettie took Sally's hand. "Let's see if we can find you some shoes that fit. Then you can help me pick the fabric for my new dresses."

Elam strode toward the hardware department as Nettie and Sally went in the other direction. Left alone, Katie strolled through the store. Row after row of bright summer clothes in every color of the rainbow beckoned her. After trying on several pairs of jeans and finding one that fit, Katie draped them over her arm and left the dressing room.

A pair of teenage girls were holding up tank tops and shorts in front of a mirror. Katie stopped beside them to hang up a pair of pants she didn't want. As she did, one of the girls began snickering and pointing. Katie followed their gaze to see what was so funny. She saw Sally admiring the shimmering material of a dress on one of the mannequins.

What a contrast. Sally wore a simple dark blue dress beneath her black cape. Black stockings and sturdy black shoes with little heels adorned her feet. Her head was covered with a wide-rimmed bonnet. They were the same style of clothes every Amish woman wore. Yet so much more than clothes separated Sally from these other young women.

Katie's thoughts turned to Rachel. Which world did she want for her daughter? Until Katie had met Elam and his family, her choice seemed simple. Now she was seeing the Amish in a new light. Her brother's views weren't the views of all Plain people. Malachi was an unhappy man who took his sour mood out on those around him. She understood that now.

One of the shopping teens pulled out her cell phone and snapped a picture of Sally. "Why do they dress so stupid?"

Katie answered the girl, although she knew the question hadn't been directed at her. "They dress that way because they wish to be separate from the world. Their clothing and even the shape of their head coverings identify them as part of a special group."

"What does being separate from the world mean?" the other girl asked.

"That they have chosen to live a life they believe is pleasing to God. To do that, they must reject worldly things such as electricity and cars, bright colors and jewelry, even phones."

"No electricity, no TV, no iPods—that's just dumb." The taller girl shook her head and the two of them laughed as they resumed their shopping.

Katie threaded her way between racks of clothes on her way to the infant department. How funny was it that she should be the one explaining about Amish practices? Matt would be laughing his head off if he were still around.

With a start, she realized she hadn't thought about Matt in days. The man occupying her thoughts lately had been Elam. She thought about his ready smile, the way he was always willing to help his mother or his sisters with their work in addition to his own. The way he enjoyed talking to and rocking Rachel in the evenings. He was so different from her brother. So different from Matt.

Katie had to admit she was falling hard for Elam. Her head told her there was no future there, but the heart rarely paid attention to what was smart.

As Katie rounded the corner into the infant section, she stopped short at the sight of a beautiful baby dress on display. Pink satin with short, puff sleeves trimmed with lace, it had a row of pearl buttons and bows down the front. Katie reached out to finger the silky cloth.

"Is that how you want Rachel to grow up?"

She turned to see Elam leaning on a shopping cart behind her.

He nodded toward the dress. "Do you want her to value fancy clothes, to think our ways are stupid?"

"Of course I don't."

But once she had felt that way. Until a few weeks ago Katie had been determined to return to the outside world. She had a choice now.

Elam straightened and stepped closer. "I heard what you said to those young women. You said we have chosen to live a life that is pleasing to God."

"That's what I was taught."

"But is it what you believe?"

Was it? It was hard to put into words what she believed. No one had ever asked her that question. Elam stood quietly waiting for her answer. She said, "I believe people of all faiths can choose to live a life that is pleasing to God."

His eyes bored into hers. "Is that what you are doing, Katie? Are you living a life that pleases God?"

Chapter 14

Katie had no answer for Elam's questions. Instead, she said, "It won't take me long to get what I need for Rachel, then I'll be ready to leave."

"All right. I'll wait for you in the food court." As he turned away, she glimpsed a deep sadness in his eyes and couldn't help wondering why he cared so much.

When she had what she needed, she crossed the store to the sewing center. She found Nettie talking to another Amish woman next to a table of solid broadcloth bolts in an array of colors. Lavenders, purples, darker greens, mauves and even pinks were all acceptable colors for dresses in their church district.

Nettie caught sight of Katie and nodded in her direction. The other woman glanced her way, said something else to Nettie and then walked off without acknowledging Katie.

Nettie held up a length of green fabric. "What do you think of this one?"

"I like the mauve better."

"For me, yes, but for you this dark green would be a good color."

"You don't need to make me a dress."

"No, but I want to. I'm tired of seeing you in those jeans all the time. Now don't argue with me."

Katie debated a moment, then said, "All right."

Nettie's brows shot up in surprise. "You aren't going to argue?"

"If you want to make me a dress, I won't stop you."

A slow smile spread across Nettie's features. "And you will wear it to church services tomorrow?"

So that was the hitch. Katie's conversation with the young shoppers and with Elam came to mind. Perhaps it was time she started living a better life and not just existing in her present one.

Anyway, just because I go to a church service doesn't mean I'm thinking of joining the Amish faith. Does it?

Was she really considering returning to the strict, devout life she once hated? To her surprise, she found that she was.

She met Nettie's hopeful gaze and nodded. "*Jah.* I will wear the dress to tomorrow's preaching."

"*Wundervoll.* I was worried you would refuse." Nettie's relief was so evident that Katie instantly became suspicious.

"Who was the woman you were talking to when I came up?"

Nettie busied herself with choosing thread to match her fabric. "Oh, that was the new deacon's wife."

"What did she want?"

"Eada was shopping for fabric, the same as me."

"But she said something that upset you. I saw your face."

"Eada likes to repeat gossip, that's all."

"And the gossip was about me." A horrible sensation settled in the pit of Katie's stomach.

"It's nothing. Nothing. Where did I put my purse?"

"Nettie, you don't lie well."

Sighing in resignation, Nettie said, "Some of the elders don't like that you are staying under the roof of an unmarried man. I said, 'What am I? A doorpost?' I chaperone you."

"Oh, Nettie, the last thing I want is to make trouble for you and Elam."

"Talk will die down when they see what a fine woman you have become."

Katie wasn't so sure. Her old insecurities raised their ugly heads. She'd never fit in before. What made her think she could fit in now?

The following morning Katie was the last one to leave the house. Nettie was already waiting in the buggy. Elam stood at the horse's head.

Katie slanted a glance in his direction. He gave her a gentle smile. "You look Plain, Katie Lantz."

From Elam, it was a wonderful compliment. She knew she had to be blushing.

The dark green dress and white apron she had on fit her well enough. Made without buttons or zippers, the dress required pins to fit it to the wearer. To Katie, it felt strangely comforting to be back in Plain clothes. It was the only thing comforting about the morning. Worrying about how she would be accepted at the service had her stomach in knots.

Katie handed Rachel up to Nettie. The baby, swaddled in a soft, white woolen blanket, wore a small white bonnet. Katie had borrowed a *kapp* from Nettie for herself, but wisps of her short hair kept escaping her hairpins. She might pass for an Amish woman to an outsider, but the church members would know differently.

The trip to services took nearly half an hour. With each passing mile Katie became more nervous. When the farm came into view, she drew a deep, ragged breath and tried to brace her failing courage.

Suddenly, she felt Elam's hand on hers. He didn't say anything, but the comfort in his simple touch gave her the strength she need. After a long moment, he let go to guide the horse into the yard. When he pulled the horse to a stop, Katie was ready.

She took her place beside Nettie and her daughters on one side of the room. After the first hymn the preaching started. As she listened to the minister, she noticed two little girls in front of her squirming on hard benches. Some things never changed.

At one point, Katie left to nurse her baby. In one of the bedrooms at the back of the house, a second young mother on the same mission joined her.

Katie learned the woman was Bishop Zook's daughter-in-law, the wife of Aaron Zook and a neighbor of Elam's. As the two of them exchanged pleasantries, Katie learned their children were almost the same age. Discussing their infant's temperaments, their funny quirks and motherly concerns made Katie see she wasn't that different from any mother, Amish or otherwise.

When Rachel was satisfied, Katie returned to her place beside Nettie. The second sermon, conducted by Bishop Zook, was heartfelt and moving.

A great sense of peace came over Katie. She held tight to the presence of Christ in her heart for the first time in a long, long time. All that she had worried about drifted away. She was one of God's children and she had been called to this place by His will.

Throughout the long service, Elam was constantly aware of Katie across the room from him. What was she thinking? Was she only pretending piety to stem the gossip or to appease his mother? He didn't want to believe it, but how could he be sure?

In spite of his best intentions, he had grown fond of Katie and Rachel. In his mind, it was easy to see them all becoming a family. What would it be like to spend a lifetime with Katie at his side? To see her bear his children? How he wanted to watch Rachel grow into a young woman, to see her marry and have children of her own.

These were things he wanted, but he kept them closed off inside his heart. He didn't dare give voice to them for if Katie took Rachel and left their community, he would grieve their loss more deeply than any other in his life.

When church came to an end, he followed the other men outside. It was warm enough that the homeowners had decided to set out the meal picnic style in the yard.

A volleyball net was soon up in place between two trees on the lawn. Several dozen of the younger boys and girls quickly began a game. The cheering and laughter from participants and onlookers filled the spring afternoon with joyous sounds.

Elam spied Katie watching the game, a wistful look on her face. She stood on the edge of the lawn by herself, except for Rachel in her arms.

Elam loaded two plates with fried chicken, coleslaw, pickled red beets, fresh rolls and two slices of gooey shoofly pie. He carried them to where she stood. "I've brought you something to eat."

She smiled and rolled her eyes. "What is this *thing* you have about feeding me?"

"I don't like skinny women." He held out one plate.

Lowering herself to the ground, she leaned back against the trunk of the tree and placed Rachel on her outstretched thighs.

"If you think I'm going to get fat just to make you happy, think again."

"One plate of food will not make you fat."

"Ha! Do you know how many calories are in that peanut butter and marshmallow spread?"

He sat beside her. "No, and I don't want to know."

She took the plate from his hand, set it on the grass and picked up the slice of homemade bread covered with the gooey spread. She bit into it and moaned. "Oh, this is good."

The words were no sooner out of her mouth than the volleyball came flying toward them. Elam threw out his hand to protect Rachel as the ball landed beside her. Katie caught it on the bounce. Holding her chicken between her teeth, she threw the ball back to the players.

Elam sat back, relieved they were both okay.

"Nice toss," Sally said as she dropped down at Katie's feet.

"It was a fluke. I don't have an athletic bone in my body."

"You didn't play ball when you were younger?" Elam asked.

"No." Shaking her head, Katie took another bite of her meal.

Sally scowled. "Why not?"

"Malachi didn't like it."

"Your brother sounds…*premlijch*."

Katie laughed. "Yes, *grumpy* is a good word for him."

Sally shot to her feet and grabbed Katie's arm. "Well, he's not here, so come and play."

"I can't. I have a baby to watch."

Laying his plate aside, Elam held out his arms. "I'll watch her."

"There! Now you have no excuse." Sally clapped her hands together.

After a moment of hesitation, Katie gathered Rachel close and turned toward Elam, a look of uncertainty in her eyes. "Are you sure you don't mind?"

In that moment, he knew Katie had wormed her way past all the defenses he'd set around his heart. He smiled and said, "Go."

Grinning, she handed him the baby and shot to her feet. Elam leaned back against the tree with Rachel propped against his shoulder as Katie joined the game in progress.

She missed the first ball that came her way. Hiding her face behind her hands, she doubled over laughing at her own foolishness. The second time the white ball came flying toward her, she hit a creditable return.

Hearing cheering for her, he twisted his head to see his mother and sisters sitting on a bench near the house. Nettie and Ruby, their hands cupped around their mouths, were yelling instructions.

It seemed that Katie had wormed her way into more hearts than just his.

He glanced down at Rachel's sleeping face. "What have I let myself in for, little one?"

There was no help for it now. He was well and truly on his way to falling in love with Katie Lantz.

Katie felt like a kid again. No, she felt like the kid she'd never been allowed to be.

Racing over the fresh new grass, she chased a ball that

she'd hit out of bounds. It rolled to a stop at the feet of Bishop Zook.

He said, "You are out of practice, Katie."

Breathless, she scooped up the ball and nodded to him. "*Jah,* I am."

"When your game is over, come and speak with me for a little while."

She felt her smile slip away. "Should I come now?"

Shaking his head, he said, "No, it will wait. Go and enjoy this beautiful day that God has made."

Katie returned to the game, but some of her enjoyment was lost. At the end of the match, she checked to see that Elam was still okay holding Rachel, then she excused herself and went to seek the bishop. She found him loading a large picnic basket into the back of his buggy.

"Are you leaving?" Maybe she could put off this conversation.

"In a little while. My wife and I are taking some food to Emma Wadler. Her mother is recovering from a broken hip and Emma is having a tough time running the inn and taking care of her."

"I think I remember Mrs. Wadler." It was easier to make small talk than to find out why the bishop wanted to see her.

"It was good to see you back among us, Katie, dressed Plain and attending services. It makes my heart glad. For we know there is more rejoicing in Heaven over one sinner who repents than over ninety-nine righteous ones who do not need to repent."

She looked down, unable to meet his gaze. "Thank you, Bishop."

"Many of us have doubts about the path God wishes us to follow."

Looking up, she asked, "Even you?"

"You have no idea how I struggled with my decision to become baptized."

"Really?"

He smiled at her. "Really."

"But you're a bishop."

"It was a path I never wished to trod, but *Gott* chose me. Without His help, I could do none of this. Let *Gott* be your help, Katie. Be still. Be at peace and listen with your heart to His council."

"I'm trying to do that."

"If you find *Gott* wishes for you to stay among us, we shall welcome you with open arms." He began rolling down the rear flap on his buggy.

Katie glanced to where Elam sat talking to Aaron Zook and his wife. Both men held the babies while the women of the congregation were busy packing up their hampers of leftover food. Numerous children, reluctant to give up their games, were kicking the ball across the grass with shouts of glee.

Wasn't this what she wanted? Didn't she long to be a part of a family, a part of a community? It wouldn't be an easy life, but it would be a life of belonging.

Impulsively, she turned back to the bishop. "When does *die Gemee nooch geh* begin?"

He paused in the act of fastening the leather flaps. "The class of instruction to the faith will be starting after the next church day."

"Thank you, Bishop."

He looked over her head. "Ah, here is my wife. I believe there is something she wishes to say to you."

Chapter 15

Elam unharnessed his draft horses on Monday evening and led them to the corral beside the barn. Turning them loose, he watched as they each picked a spot and began to turn around with their nose at ground level. Finally, they dropped to their knees, then rolled their massive bodies in the dirt. Wiggling like puppies, they thrashed about to scratch their backs and shake off the sweat of their long day in the fields.

Elam spared a moment to envy them. Planting was hard work, and he still had things in the woodshop waiting for him. After hanging and cleaning his harnesses, he strode to the front of the barn and opened the workroom door. Katie was seated at the table with a small heart-shaped basket in front of her.

He saw she had finished several already. "You are getting faster?"

"But am I getting better?" She held up one for inspection. He examined it closely *"Jah,* you are getting better."

Handing it back, he moved to his workstation and selected the tools he needed. A nearly finished rocking chair was waiting for him to carve a design into the headrest. He glanced over his shoulder. The frown of concentration on Katie's face made him smile.

Was she happy here? He wanted to ask, but he was afraid of the answer. Although she rarely talked about leaving any more, he'd never heard her mention another plan.

Would she stay if he asked her to? He looked back to the wood in front of him. He was afraid to ask. Afraid she might say no, and equally afraid she might say yes for all the wrong reasons. Instead, he said, "I thought Bishop Zook did a good job of preaching yesterday."

"He did. It was long and the benches haven't gotten any softer since I left, but I did find it comforting."

"I saw Mrs. Zook talking to you. Was she rude again?"

"No. She apologized for her earlier behavior."

He picked up his chisel. "Did she?"

"I can tell you I was stunned."

He chuckled. "You and me both."

"She said she'd let hearsay form her opinions and that she was aware that people could change."

"I reckon they can. What did you think of the service?"

"I enjoyed it."

"Enough to attend again?"

"I'm thinking about it."

He spun around to look at her. "You are?"

"*Jah.* I can tell you're stunned."

Moving to stand beside her, he said, "Maybe a little stunned but mostly happy."

They stood staring at each other for a long time. He wanted so badly to kiss her. He sucked in a quick breath and moved back to his workbench.

"Elam, can I ask you a personal question?"

"Jah."

"What was she like, the girl you were betrothed to?"

He leaned forward and pushed his gouge into the wood, wondering how to answer that. "She was quiet. A hard worker."

"Was she pretty?"

"Yes." He kept his eyes on his task.

"How did you meet?"

"We grew up together. How did you meet Matt?"

"Matt and I met at the drugstore in Hope Springs. He was visiting some friends in the area. They were sitting at a booth and making fun of a young Amish boy who had come in."

"Is that what you liked about him? That he poked fun at us?"

"No. I felt sorry for the boy and I told Matt and his friends to stop it. I know I shouldn't have. We are to turn the other cheek."

"Rude behavior doesn't have to be tolerated."

"Anyway, after I left, Matt followed me and apologized. I thought it was very fine of him."

Her voice took on a soft quality. "He could be like that. One moment a good man, the next moment a spoiled child. I don't know what it was about him that blinded me to his true self."

"It is our own feelings that blind us."

"Were you blind to Salome's feelings?"

"Jah. When I finished school, my parents sent me to my uncle Isaac in Ontario to learn the woodworking trade. During those years I wrote to Salome every week. I told her about my plans for our life together."

"And she wrote back?"

"She did, but her letters were filled with the day-to-day things. I should have known then that something was wrong, but I wasn't looking for the signs." It was the first time in a long time that he was willing to examine his feelings about those days.

"I know what you mean. Matt seemed so interested in me. The more I resisted his advances, the more interested he became. I was so flattered. I snuck out of the house to see him. Malachi caught us together one night. He was furious. He grabbed my arm and ordered Matt to leave. That's one thing about Matt—he hates to have anyone tell him what to do."

"And so it is with you, too."

"Perhaps that's true. To be honest, I jumped at the chance to defy Malachi."

"So you left with Matt."

"I did. I was honestly determined to make our relationship work, but he wasn't. He soon grew tired of being saddled with a stupid Amish girlfriend who couldn't drive a car or work the DVD recorder."

He turned around and came to sit beside her. Taking her hand, he said, "You aren't stupid."

She stared into his eyes for a long time. She had such beautiful dark eyes. He could almost see his future in them. Finally, she looked down. "It took me a while to start believing that. What happened between you and Salome?"

"It isn't important anymore." He started to rise, but she laid a hand on his arm and stopped him.

"It is important. Past wrongs have the power to hurt us if we don't let go of them."

The warmth of her small, soft hand on his skin sent a wave of awareness coursing through his body. He focused on her concerned face. "What makes you think I haven't let go?"

She tipped her head to the side. "Have you?"

"Perhaps not."

He longed to reach out and touch her face. How would she react? Would she pull away?

Such thoughts were folly. He should go. He had work to do. But he didn't rise. He sat there looking into her eyes and he saw himself as he had been when he was young and impressionable and sure of his place in the world. He wanted to share that part of his life with Katie.

"I returned home from my uncle's at the age of twenty-one, ready to settle down, start my own business…and marry. That spring I was baptized and took my vows to the church. Salome did the same. If only she had waited until she was certain of what she wanted."

"Don't judge her too harshly."

"I've begun to forgive her." As he said it, he realized it was true. She had hurt him, but how much more would they both have suffered if she had gone ahead with the wedding?

Glancing sideways at Katie seated beside him, he said, "When the date for our marriage approached she finally admitted the truth. She had used our engagement to keep her parents from pressuring her into marrying anyone else. She didn't love me."

"I'm so sorry."

"I thought maybe she saw some flaw in me."

"I don't see how. You're a good man, Elam."

She thought he was a good man. Well, he wasn't, Elam reflected bitterly. He struggled every day to live a life pleasing to God. Perhaps she understood that better than anyone, for she openly admitted her own struggles.

Katie said, "Why did she leave the church?"

"All the time I had been working for my uncle, Salome had been working for an English family as a nanny. I believe she tried to give up her life among the English, but she couldn't do it. Not when her employer offered to help her further her education. She told me she longed to go back to school, to learn things beyond what she needed to know to keep house and rear children."

Salome had turned her back on her family, on Elam and on his hopes and dreams. "My family, her family, we all tried to reason with her, but after several months it was clear that she wasn't going to return to the church. She was shunned, not because we didn't love her anymore, but in the hopes of making her reconsider her choices."

"Your mother told me your father also left the faith."

Elam bowed his head. "He did. I had to shun my own father. My mother couldn't bear it and asked to be excommunicated, too, so that they could live together as man and wife. It was a dark time."

Katie's heart went out to Elam. She squeezed his hand. "I'm so sorry. Was that why you moved to Ohio?"

"After *Dat* passed away, my mother came back to the church, but it was not the same for us. I saw an ad in the paper for farms for sale in Ohio. My brothers-in-law and I came to look the places over. Your brother was eager to sell to me. I got the land for a good price. We were blessed that Mary and Ruby found homes here, as well."

Katie hesitated before voicing the question she couldn't ignore. Finally, she asked gently, "Elam, was your mother wrong to leave the church to stay with your father?"

The sadness in his eyes was replaced by anger. "My father was wrong to leave the church."

"Your mother must have loved him very much."

"*Jah,* she loved him, but did he love her? I'm not so

sure. What kind of love is it to make another suffer for your own doubts?"

He shot to his feet and left. Katie didn't try to stop him. She was happy that he'd been able to share this much about himself. All she wanted was to be near him and to make him happy.

She loved him, but loving a person was not enough. They had both learned that the hard way. He wasn't indifferent to her. She was woman enough to read the signs in his eyes, but he never spoke of it. She knew why.

Even if she found the courage to tell him of her love, she knew he'd never consider marriage to someone outside his faith. If she became Amish would it change how he felt about her? Or was she breaking her own heart by staying here?

The following afternoon, Katie was working in the woodshop when Elam poked his head in the door. She laid the basket aside, loving the way her heart skipped a beat each time he was near.

He said, "Katie, you have a visitor. Dr. White is here."

She frowned. "Dr. White? Why has he come to see me?"

Elam stepped closer, a look of concern on his face. "I don't know. Is Rachel okay?"

Katie rose to her feet. "He did take a blood test from her."

Had the results been serious enough to bring him out to the farm? She was aware that some Amish children suffered from inherited birth defects, but she hadn't seen any signs that Rachel was sick.

Please, God, don't let there be anything wrong with my baby.

Katie darted past Elam and hurried toward the house. Inside, Nettie had the good doctor settled at the kitchen table with a cup of coffee and a slice of her homemade cherry pie in front of him. He already had a forkful in his mouth.

Katie halted inside the door, striving to keep calm. Elam came in and stood behind her. To her surprise, she felt his hands on her shoulders offering comfort and support.

She said, "Dr. White, what brings you out here?"

He finished chewing, then tapped his plate with his silverware. "If I had known that there was pie this good here, I've have come much sooner."

Nettie beamed. "I'm glad it's to your liking."

"If your family ever has need of medical care, you may pay the bill with pies, Mrs. Sutter."

Katie took a step forward. "Is there something wrong with Rachel's tests?"

The doctor shook his head. "No, everything is fine. After your visit, I got to thinking about your family and I did a little investigating with the help of my old college roommate. He's retired from the State Department, but he still has connections there. It turns out your family immigrated from a place called Blue Creek in Belize. Unfortunately, that's all my friend could find out. There isn't anyone left in the area with the name of Lantz or Eicher, which was your mother's maiden name. I'm sorry. I know you were hoping for a different answer."

Katie struggled to hide her disappointment and hold back tears. She knew the chances of finding more of her family had been remote, but she couldn't help getting her hopes up.

After the doctor thanked Nettie for her hospitality, he donned his hat and headed outside to his car. He opened the car door, then stopped. "I almost forgot. Nettie's pie drove it right out of my mind. Amber said to tell you she found a job you might like."

"She has? Where?"

"At the Wadler Inn. Now, it's only a temporary position, but it could turn into more. Emma Wadler is needing help because her mother has broken her hip, and Amber thought of you."

"I'll go and see her today."

As the doctor drove away, Katie heard the screen door slam. She looked toward the house to see Elam approaching. When he was close enough, he said, "I'm sorry, Katie. I know how much finding more of your family meant to you."

She turned and began walking toward the bench beneath the apple tree at the back of the yard. "It's just that I've wanted to be a part of a real family for as long as I can remember. I wanted to be a part of a family like yours. A place where people laugh and talk about their worries and their hopes. Where they get together on Sundays and travel to visit each other in their homes. I took that away from Malachi. I have to accept that he is my only family."

Elam grasped her arm and turned her to face him. "Katie, you can't keep blaming yourself."

"Oh, I know. I used to think I didn't deserve a family after what I'd done. I just needed to know there was someone out there who wanted me."

He opened his arms and she went to him. "Katie, you are already a part of a family. You are one of God's children. That makes you a part of His family. Wherever you go, no one can take that from you."

Wherever I go. He doesn't believe I will stay here.

She laid her cheek against his chest, drawing strength from him and comfort from his embrace. "You are a good man, Elam."

"And you're a good woman, Katie."

Giving a tiny shake of her head, she said, "A lot of people will disagree with that."

From the porch, his mother called his name. He slowly drew away from Katie. She missed his warmth like a physical ache. He gazed at her intently. "I stand by what I said."

She watched him walk to the house. She had been searching for a place to belong somewhere in the world, but what she really wanted was to belong here.

Was it possible? Elam's embrace had just given her a bright ray of hope.

Chapter 16

"What is that long face for?" Nettie demanded as she sprinkled a packet of flower seeds into the freshly turned earth bordering the walkway.

On her knees clearing away last year's old growth, Katie sighed. How was she going to break the news to her friend? Pulling out a few early weeds, Katie said, "What if I told you I was moping because… I'm moving out."

"What is this? Where are you going?" Nettie propped her fists on her hips.

"I have a job at the Wadler Inn starting the day after tomorrow. Emma Wadler also owns a small apartment that I can rent starting in two weeks."

Turning away, Nettie wiped at her eye with her forearm. "I'm happy for you, but I will miss you."

"I'll come to visit often and you will see me at church. I've already talked to Bishop Zook about taking instructions."

Nettie turned back, a wide smile on her face. "That's wonderful news."

"I thought you'd be happy to hear that."

"Have you told Elam?"

"Not yet." Katie looked down. She wasn't sure how Elam would take the news. Would he think she was only doing it because of her feelings for him?

There had been no repeat of the closeness they'd shared the day the doctor came to see her. She was half-afraid her growing love was making her see things that weren't there. Did Elam care for her the way a man cared for a woman, or was she reading what she wanted to see into his simple kindness?

Nettie brought up a hand to shade her eyes. "It looks like Elam is home from town."

Sitting back on her heels, Katie dusted off her hands and tried to calm her rapidly beating heart. She was surprised when he stopped the buggy in front of the house instead of driving it to the barn.

Stepping down, Elam came toward her, a pensive expression on his face. She stood, a sense of unease tickling the back of her neck. He held out a thick white envelope. "This came for you in the mail today."

"For me?" She took a step closer.

"It's from your brother."

Stunned, she took the letter from him and stared at the return address. Why had Malachi written? What did he want?

"Aren't you going to open it?" Elam prompted.

"Yes." She turned away and walked across the new green grass to the bench beneath the blooming apple tree. The pink flowers of the tree scented the air with their heady perfume. The drone of bees inspecting each open bud mingled with the soft sighing of the breeze in the branches.

Sitting down, she opened the envelope with trembling hands and began to read.

Dear Katie,

I hope this letter finds you well. We are settled in Kansas. Beatrice finds it too hot and dusty here in the summer.

I have been asked by my bishop and by Bishop Zook to seek a mending between us. Bishop Zook has written to tell me you have a daughter named Rachel, for our mother. When I heard this I knew God had chosen this time for me to reveal the truth to you, Katie. Rachel was not your mother's name.

Katie stared at the words in shock. What did he mean? Fearfully, she continued reading.

Our family farm was in the hill country of Belize. A young native woman, an orphan named Lucita, worked for us. She was much loved by my mother. One day she came to my mother to confess she was pregnant. She did not want the child. She asked my mother to take you and raise you. We never learned who your father was. Lucita died when you were born and my mother took you in as Lucita had wished and raised you as her own.

Because my father was dead, speculation began to circulate in the church that the child was Mother's. Such gossip caused her great distress. She denied it, but some women who did not like her kept the gos-

sip alive. The bishop asked Mother to repent, she refused and was shunned. It finally drove us to leave.

Katie laid the letter down without reading more. Her
mind reeled. She wanted to pinch herself and wake from this
bad dream. No wonder she'd never felt as if she fit in. She
wasn't a Lantz. She wasn't Amish. Her black hair and eyes
were a gift from a mother she'd never known. She stared at
the grass littered with apple blossoms in front of her without seeing it. After a few minutes, she began reading again.

I did not wish to leave Belize. There was someone
I planned to marry there, but as father was dead, I
was the head of the house. It was my responsibility
to take care of my mother and the rest of the family.
When everyone died in that fire, I could not look upon
your face without seeing all I had lost because of you.

Perhaps I was too hard on you when you were
growing up. If I was, it was because I saw your mother's wildness in you and wished to stem it.

Beatrice and I have come, at last, to accept that
God does not mean to bless us with children of our
own. It will not be easy for you, an unwed mother,
to raise a child by yourself. Please consider letting us
raise her for you. We have a good home. She will not
want for anything. You may see her often if you wish.
I know of work nearby if you choose to move here.

As I told you the day you left, if you had come to
me in person, Katie, and shown repentance, I would
have taken you in. I shall now tell my bishop all is
mended between us.

Malachi Lantz

Katie wadded the letter up and threw it into the grass. How dare Malachi offer to take her baby after making her miserable her entire life! Rising to her feet, she paced back and forth. Pausing to calm herself, she saw Elam watching her.

Elam asked, "What does he say?"

She wanted to run to Elam's embrace and cry out her heartache, but something held her back. "He told me the truth. Finally. Read it for yourself." She turned away instead and began walking out into the fields to be alone.

She had no family. She didn't belong anywhere.

Elam came out of the house and leaned a hip against the porch railing later that evening. Katie sat on a rocker on the front porch with Rachel in her arms. He had found the letter from her brother and read it. His heart ached for what she must be going through. He studied Katie's faraway look. "You barely touched your supper."

"I'm not hungry."

"*Mamm* has a custard pie cooling on the counter. If you'd like a slice, I can fetch one for you."

Katie smiled. "I imagine when you were a boy you brought home all manner of birds with broken wings and stray kittens."

"A few," he admitted.

"I'm fine, Elam. I don't need to eat."

"You must keep up your strength for your daughter's sake."

Kissing the baby's forehead, Katie then leaned her cheek against her child's head. "Yes, she's all I have now."

He sat down in the rocker next to her. "I'm sorry for the way Malachi delivered this news, but isn't it best to know the truth?"

"I guess you're right. I just feel so lost. All my life I wanted my family back. I hated that God took them all from me, and now I find out they weren't my family at all. My mother gave me away. I have no idea who my father is. I'm truly without any ties to this world."

"A family is more than blood, Katie. You know this. Those who live in our hearts are our family." He reached across and laid a hand on her arm.

He longed to ask her to become part of his family, to marry him, but fear held back his words. He had asked Salome to marry him and she had taken her vows to the church without meaning them. The result was that she was shunned by her family and friends for the rest of her life. He couldn't bear to have that happen to Katie.

She seemed so remote, as though she needed to separate herself from all that had gone on. Rocking back and forth, she held her baby, looking as lost and alone as she had that day at the bus station.

"It's going to be all right, Katie."

She didn't seem to hear him. He moved his hand to her cheek. "What can I do to help you?"

Pulling away, she said, "Nothing. I just want to be alone for a little while."

He stood but couldn't bring himself to leave her. "I wish you would not take this so hard."

Rising to her feet, she gave him a brave smile. "I'm not. I'm going to stop dreaming of things that can't be and make my own way in the world. It will be Rachel and me and that will be enough."

She left him and went into the house, closing the door softly behind her.

Elam sat back down in the rocker. It might be enough

for her, but it would not be enough for him. He wanted to be included in their lives. He loved them both.

Katie was on the right path. When she had made her baptism and her hurts had healed, he would offer her his heart, his home and his family as her own.

His mother had told him about Katie's job and her plan to move into town. He was prepared to bide his time. Katie Lantz was a woman worth waiting for.

Kate's first day of working for Emma Wadler proved to be easier than she expected. The Wadler Inn sat at the west end of town, overlooking a valley dotted with white Amish farmsteads. The view was unspoiled by power lines, as none of the families beyond the edge of the city in that direction used electricity.

Emma's rooms were small and quaint. The beds were covered with bright Amish quilts, and the furniture had all been made by local craftsmen. Her large gathering room boasted a wide, brick fireplace and soft sofas that the tourists seemed to love.

Katie's duties were to answer the phone, to take reservations and to keep Grandma Wadler company. The latter proved to be the easiest task of all. Grandma Wadler had made it her mission in life to spoil Rachel the moment she met her.

Knowing she was lucky to find a job where she could keep Rachel with her, Katie allowed the wheelchair-bound woman to hold and rock the baby whenever Rachel was awake.

Emma's current group of guests were a family from Arizona. They were genuinely interested in learning about Amish culture. Katie was happy to answer their questions. They were disappointed to learn that they should avoid photographing the Amish, but heartily promised to drive slowly and watch out for buggies on the area's winding, narrow roads.

When five o'clock rolled around, Katie was ready to go home and put her feet up. When she walked outside with Rachel in her bassinet, Elam was waiting to take her home.

"How was it?" he asked, as she climbed in the buggy.

"It wasn't bad. Emma is very nice and her mother is easy to please."

After guiding the horse into the traffic, he settled back and took a peek at Rachel. "How did *moppel* like being a working woman?"

"She isn't a fat baby. I wish you and your mother wouldn't call her that."

"Ach, she's just plump enough to suit me."

"That's right. You don't like skinny women."

He eyed Katie up and down. "I make an occasional exception."

She felt the blood rush to her cheeks. Was he implying he found her attractive? Perhaps there was hope for her after all.

Before she could think of a comeback, he changed the subject.

"Mr. Imhoff is bringing over one of his ponies and a cart for you to use until you move into town."

"That's very kind of him."

"*Jah,* it's kind but we both know why he's doing it." Elam rolled his eyes and grinned.

Katie giggled. "To impress your mother."

"She was baking a lemon sponge cake when I left the house."

"Let me guess. It's Mr. Imhoff's favorite."

They looked at each other and both ducked their heads

as they began laughing. Still smiling, Katie studied the man beside her. It felt good to laugh with him. She'd shared so many things with him that she hadn't shared with anyone else.

She loved his quiet strength, his bright eyes and ready smile. He was a good man. She was blessed to be able to call him a friend.

Content to ride beside Elam, Katie enjoyed the rest of the trip home. As Judy turned into a lane, Katie tucked the memory of her time with Elam into a special place in her heart. When she had her own place, these rides with him would stop. But until then, she would cherish their time alone.

The following day was "off" Sunday, a day of rest, but without a preaching service. It was a day normally devoted to reading the Bible and visiting among friends. Katie was reading from the German Bible and struggling a bit with the language. Elam was helping her. She was determined to finish the chapter while Rachel was napping.

"Is that a car I hear?" Nettie looked over the top of her spectacles toward the door.

Katie glanced up. "Maybe Amber has come for a visit."

Rising, Katie walked to the screen door to look out. Her heart jumped into her throat and lodged there. It wasn't Amber.

Matt stepped out of a dark blue sedan in front of the house.

Chapter 17

Shocked beyond words, Katie could only stare. What was Matt doing here?

Elam, sipping a cup of coffee, didn't bother looking up. "Amber is always welcome."

"It's not Amber." Katie didn't explain. She simply opened the door and walked outside.

Matt had changed a bit in the four months since she'd last seen him. Had it only been four months? It seemed like a lifetime.

He was still good-looking in a reckless sort of way. His long, dark hair had been cut and was neatly styled now. The diamond earring he normally wore was missing from his earlobe. His clothes were casual and expensive.

She hadn't realized until this moment how much better looking Elam was than her former boyfriend. Elam's goodness came from within. His clothes might be homemade and simple, but his heart was genuine.

Matt's face brightened when he caught sight of Katie. He held out his arms. "I found you at last."

When she didn't move, he slowly lowered his arms and slipped his hands in the pockets of his pants.

Katie found her voice at last. "What do you want, Matt?"

"What do I want? I've come to bring you home. I see your brother's got you wearing one of those sacks again."

She smoothed the front of her apron. "I chose to dress Plain, Matt. My brother had nothing to do with it."

"You're still mad at me, aren't you?" He sent an apologetic look her way, then approached.

When he was standing in front of her, he said, "I've come to say I'm sorry for the way I left you. I can explain everything, and I've come to see our baby."

Katie heard the screen door open behind her. Elam said, "Who is it, Katie?"

A big smile creased Matt's face. He held out his hand to Elam. "Hello. I'm Katie's partner, Matt Carson."

When no one said a word or took his hand, Matt let it fall. "I know my showing up like this must be something of a shock to you. Is it a boy or a girl?"

"It's a girl," Katie answered. "I named her Rachel."

Matt smiled. "I like it. Can I see her?"

Katie glanced toward Elam. Should she refuse? How could she?

Before she could form a reply, Elam stepped forward and squared off with Matt. "You are not welcome here."

Matt took a step backward. "I think that's up to Katie."

"She has nothing to say to you."

Katie laid a hand on Elam's tense arm. "I will talk to him, Elam, and then I will send him away."

His jaw tensed, she could see the muscles twitch as he

held back his anger. Finally, he nodded once. "I will be in the workshop if you need me."

Elam crossed the yard with angry strides. Matt took a step forward and blew out a breath. "Wow, I thought the Amish were nonviolent."

"We are."

Matt nodded toward the house. "I'm not sure about *him*."

"Elam would rather die than harm another human being. That doesn't mean he doesn't feel anger or annoyance. It just means he will not act on them."

"Good to know. Look, Katie, I know I have a lot to apologize for, but there is a lot you don't know. Let me explain before you kick me off the place."

She glanced toward the house where Nettie stood watching them. Katie said, "Why don't we take a walk?"

As they strolled side by side down the lane, Katie worked to keep her anger in check. Matt seemed to sense her feelings and said, "Katie, I was stupid. I shouldn't have left you when I did. I got scared. I didn't want to be a father. I'd never even told my parents about you."

"Because you were ashamed of me," she bit out.

"Like I said, I was stupid. Anyway, my folks were taking this trip to Italy. I got my dad to spring for my ticket and I joined them. They were thrilled because I hadn't seen them in almost a year. I honestly intended to tell them about you and the baby and then come back in a week."

Was he telling the truth? She found herself believing him. "So what happened?"

"My dad had a stroke the night we arrived in Rome. He lingered for another two months in the hospital, but then he died. He never even knew he was going to be a grandfather." The quiver in his voice wasn't faked. Katie could see the sorrow in his eyes.

"I'm sorry, Matt."

"I really messed up. Mom was a basket case. She'd never done anything without dad. By the time we flew the body home and arranged a funeral, you had already left the apartment."

"I was kicked out because I couldn't pay the rent…three weeks before our baby was due. You could have called."

"I know, I know. None of this was your fault. I messed up. I messed up big time, and I've come to ask your forgiveness."

Katie sucked in a deep breath. She had to forgive him. It was a fundamental part of being Amish. She searched her heart for God's grace and found the words she needed. "I forgive you, Matt."

Hope filled his eyes. "Do you? Do you really?"

"Yes."

Stepping forward, he took hold of her hand. "I want my mother to meet you and to meet the baby. You and I and our child are all the family she has left. She was lost without my dad, but as soon as she learned about the baby, the light came back into her eyes."

"Matt, don't do this to me." Katie pushed him away gently. "I have learned to get along without you. You didn't care enough to see that we had a place to live, or food, or medical care."

"I can keep saying I'm sorry for the rest of my life if that will help. Give me another chance, Katie. I'm begging you. We can make it work. Will you marry me?"

Shaking her head, she turned away. "It's getting late. We should get back."

"Think about it, Katie. Think about Rachel and what it will mean to her if you come with me. We can be a family."

"Please, Matt. I need some time to think."

She left him and hurried toward the barn, but she didn't go to Elam's workshop. Instead, she climbed the ladder that led to the hayloft, looking for solitude. Matt's arrival had been completely unexpected. He was asking for a second chance. He was Rachel's father. He was offering her everything Katie once thought she wanted.

Reaching the loft floor, she moved toward the dim interior at the back of the barn where bales of hay were stacked to the rafters. Dust motes drifted in lazy arcs across the bands of sunlight that streamed from the double doors at the end of the loft. Overhead, pigeons fluttered about in the rafters, disturbed by her presence.

Matt had come back for her. He had asked for her forgiveness and she had forgiven him. Now what? He was offering her something she'd never truly had—a family. But a family away from the Amish life she had finally grown to love.

She had a choice. Go with Matt or stay near Elam. Elam, a devout man of the Plain faith. Would he be able to return her love? Would Elam trust that she had truly found her way back to God?

She heard a rustling behind her and turned to see Elam, pitchfork in hand, standing at the wide doors.

He said, "I'm sorry if I frightened you."

She smiled at him. "You could never frighten me."

He came toward her. Laying the pitchfork aside, he took a seat beside her in the hay. His hand lay close to hers but not touching. She wanted him to hold her hand. She wanted him to kiss her and wipe away this feeling of being alone.

"I saw you out walking with Matt. Will he be staying long?"

She sighed. "That depends."

"On what?"

"On me." Suddenly, she couldn't stand it any longer. She grasped his hand. "Elam, I don't know what to do."

He didn't draw her close, didn't kiss her, didn't promise to make everything all right. Some of the hope she'd held in her heart began to fade.

"What are you doing, Katie?"

A chorus of chirping began overhead. Katie looked up to see a mother swallow returning to her mud nest in the rafters. Katie held on to Elam's hand. "I am like that swallow. I had a home here once but I couldn't stay. My life was like a long winter. I wanted someone to show me the sun."

"So you flew away."

"I never planned to come back."

"Yet like the swallow, you did return and you began to raise your young one. The swallow will nest here, but she won't stay. When the days grow short and winter comes and her little ones no longer need her—she'll fly away again. Is that what you will do, Katie?"

She turned so she could face him. "I don't know."

"Do you love Matt?" he asked quietly.

"I did. I think I did, but maybe he was just a means to an end. I felt used when he left me, but maybe I was using him, too. To escape Malachi's strictness. I'm so confused. Why couldn't it be simple?"

"It is simple, Katie."

"How can you say that?"

He looked away. "Because it is simple."

"I don't want to go, Elam. I want to stay here with you and your family."

"Do you?"

"Give me a reason to stay, Elam."

Sadness filled Elam's eyes. "Ah, Katie. Have you learned nothing?"

"I don't know what you mean."

"I wish with all my heart that I could give you a reason to stay, but I can't. The reason must come from your own heart or it won't be strong enough to withstand the trials that will come your way in life."

"I could withstand them if you were beside me."

"Only faith in God can give you that strength, Katie. I love you, but I will not use that love to bind you to a faith you have not accepted with your whole heart."

"My faith can grow." He was breaking her heart.

Leaning forward, he kissed her forehead and whispered, "I pray that it will."

Rising to his feet, he left her alone in the loft. When she was sure he was gone, she broke down and cried.

Elam walked sightlessly between the rows of ankle-high new corn. He wasn't ready to face anyone yet. He couldn't believe how close he had come to gathering Katie in his arms and telling her nothing mattered but their love.

If only it could be that simple.

Perhaps for the English it was. He wanted Katie. He wanted her in his life, wanted her to be his wife and he wanted to raise Rachel as his own child.

The temptation to race back to Katie was almost unbearable. Why had God laid this burden upon him again?

If she chose to return to the outside world with Matt, Elam didn't think he could bear it.

The Lord never gave a man more than he could bear; yet if that were true why did his heart ache like it was being torn in two? He could barely draw a breath past the pain. Tears filled his eyes and he stumbled on the rough ground. Pressing the heels of his hands to stem the flow of tears, he dropped to his knees in the rich earth.

"Why, God? Why didn't You send me a woman of my own faith to love? Why must You test me? What have I done to deserve this sorrow?"

If he had given in to the pleading in Katie's eyes and asked her to stay, how much worse would it be to lose her later?

Elam sank back onto his heels. How could it be worse than this?

I could go with her into the English world.

Even as the tiny voice in his mind whispered the words, Elam knew he could not act upon them. He had made a vow to God and before the members of his church. If he broke that promise, what value would any promise he made in the future hold?

He tipped back his head and blinked away the tears to stare at the blue sky. "Your will be done, Lord. Give me Your strength, I beseech You."

When Katie came out of the barn, she saw Matt smoking a cigarette while leaning on the railing of the front porch. He held up the butt. "I'm trying to quit. Don't tell my mom. She thinks I already have."

Katie stared at him a long moment.

Poor Matt. He's trying to become a better man, but he's still willing to backslide and deceive others.

A passage from *Luke* 16 flashed into her mind.

He that is faithful in that which is least is faithful also in much: and he that is unjust in the least is unjust also in much.

Matt bent forward to look at her more closely. "Have you been crying?"

How can I judge him harshly when I am guilty of the same thing? Forgive me, Father, for failing You in so many ways. She drew a deep breath. "I was, but I'm fine now. You should be truthful with your mother."

"You're right."

"Matt, we need to talk."

He ground the cigarette butt beneath the toe of his shoe. "That's why I'm here."

"I can't go back with you."

"Katie, I know I treated you badly, but it won't happen again. My father's death made me see things in a different light. I'm all the family my mother has. I want you and Rachel to become part of that. She's beautiful, by the way. She has your eyes and your hair. Mrs. Sutter let me hold her."

"I'm Amish, Matt." As she said the words, she knew in her heart that they were true. She was Amish. Not by blood or because of her family, but by choice.

He looked at her funny. "I know."

"That means so many different things that I don't expect you to understand it all, but one thing it means is that marriage to someone outside of my faith is forbidden."

"I thought you had to go through some kind of baptism for that to happen."

"I will be baptized in a few months."

"How can this be the life you want? It's crazy. Are you sure?"

"I'm sure. This is the Plain life. Each day I will try to make my life pleasing to God. That is what I want."

"And what about Rachel? What about my daughter? What if she doesn't want to live in the Stone Age?"

"Matt, she will be loved, cherished and accepted among the Amish."

He paused, at a loss for words, but then he said, "She'll only get an eighth-grade education."

"She'll read and speak two languages. She'll know everything there is to know about running a household, raising a happy family and running a farm or a business."

"And what if that's not enough for her? What if she wants to be a doctor or a lawyer?"

"Then she will not stay among the Plain people." She reached out to lay a hand on his face. "And she will have a father to go to who can show her a bigger, if not a better world."

"Why do you have to sound so rational?"

"Because that's the way it is. You didn't really want to marry me, did you? Let's be honest with each other."

He looked taken aback. "I came here to do just that."

"You came to appease your conscience and because you wanted to offer your mother the comfort of having a grandchild. It was a good thing, but it isn't reason enough to marry me."

"So you're going to stay and marry the Amish farmer, is that it?"

"No."

He drew back, a look of confusion on his face. "I don't get it. You just said that's what you want."

"I love Elam and his family. I always wanted a loving family, but it wasn't until I met Elam that I came to understand I've always had one. I belong to the family of God. Elam helped me to see that I am Amish."

"Okay, I'm missing something. Why don't you want to marry him?"

"I do, but Elam doesn't believe that I'm staying out of my love for God. I didn't know it myself until a little while ago."

"What are you going to do?"

"I'll go to Malachi in Kansas. I can stay with him until I find a job and a place of my own."

"You'll be getting child support from me. That should make things a little easier."

"Thank you, Matt."

"It's the right thing to do. I just wish I hadn't blown my chances with you."

"You and I weren't meant to marry. We should both thank God we didn't get the chance to make each other miserable for fifty years."

"You're probably right."

"I know I'm right. Matt, I promise I will bring Rachel to visit both of you as often as I can."

He smiled for the first time since he had arrived. "That'll give us both something to look forward to. How soon will you be heading to Kansas?"

"The bus doesn't leave until tomorrow evening. I have a friend in town I can stay with until then." The memory of Elam finding her at the bus station threatened to bring on her tears again, but she fought them back. She was sure Amber would put her up for the night.

"Can I give you a lift to your friend's place?"

"That would be great." Katie glanced over her shoulder, but there was no sign of Elam. Perhaps that was for the best. In her heart, she knew they had already said their goodbyes.

Katie led Matt inside the house where she told Nettie her plans and had a tearful farewell.

Chapter 18

"They have only been gone a day and yet I can't believe how quiet the house is without them." Nettie sighed heavily at the kitchen sink.

"You said that already." Elam sipped his coffee without tasting it. Katie was gone and so was the sunshine that warmed his soul.

"I just can't get over what a difference it made having them here."

He wouldn't mourn something that was never meant to be. "We got on well enough before they came. Mary will have her babe in another month. You'll be so busy helping her you won't notice that Katie and Rachel aren't around."

If only he had some way to block out his thoughts of them. Had he been right to rebuff Katie or had he pushed her into Matt's arms?

She said she wanted a reason to stay. He could have given it to her. Setting his cup down, Elam rested his elbows on the table and raked his fingers through his hair. Why didn't he give her that reason?

She might have been content, even happy with him. With his help she might have had a chance to grow in her faith and understanding of God's will. He glanced at his mother slowly drying the supper dishes and putting them away. Her boundless energy seemed as lacking as his. Katie and Rachel had taken the life from this home.

"*Mamm,* can I ask you a question?"

"Of course." She set the last glass in the cupboard and closed the door.

"When did you first know that *Dat* had lost his faith?"

She turned around, a look of shock on her face. "Why are you asking about that now?"

"I have wondered for a long time if there were signs."

She came and sat beside him at the table. "You know that our first child died when she was only two months old. She was such a beautiful babe. It broke our hearts to lay her in the cold ground. Your father struggled mightily with his faith after her illness and death."

"It must have been terrible."

"It was *Gotte wille.* He needed her in Heaven more than we needed her here on earth, although we cannot understand why. You father never got over her loss."

"But he was a good and faithful servant all the years I was growing up."

"He went through the motions for me. There were times I almost believed he had found his way back to God, but then I would see something in his eyes and I would know he had not. I was not surprised the day he announced that he wouldn't go to the preaching anymore. He could not forgive God for taking his baby girl from him."

"Do you wish he'd gone on pretending?"

"No. I wish he could have opened his heart to God's healing power the way Katie was able to. I'm sorry it did not work out for the two of you. I thought you cared for each other."

Elam set his cup on the table. "She was only pretending or she would not have gone back to the English."

"What do you mean? She has not gone back to the English."

He looked up sharply. "She left with Matt. I saw them."

Cocking her head to the side, Nettie said, "Yes, he gave her a ride to Amber Bradley's place. She's taking the bus to her brother's. She plans to stay with him only until she can get a job. I thought you knew this."

Elam jumped to his feet. "She's taking the bus?"

"Did I not just say that?"

She hadn't left with Matt. He still had a chance. "I must get to the bus station."

"Why?"

"Because I love her. I drove her away with my false pride instead of believing she was the one God chose for me."

He snatched his hat from the peg and jammed it on his head on the way out the door.

Katie sat in the front seat of Amber's car as she drove them to the bus station. Rachel slept quietly in the infant seat in the back. "Thanks for giving me a lift."

"No problem. Are you sure you won't change your mind and stay in Hope Springs?"

It would be too painful to live in the same community with Elam. To see him at worship and at gatherings and to know he didn't trust that her faith was genuine.

"I think it's better that I go to Malachi. He will take care of us until I can manage on my own."

"I'm going to miss you and Rachel."

"We will miss you, too."

When they reached the station, Amber carried Katie's suitcase to the pile waiting to be loaded on the bus. The two women faced each other then hugged one another fiercely. "Take care of yourself and that beautiful baby," Amber whispered.

"I will. God bless you for all you've done for us." Drawing away, Katie straightened her bonnet and picked up Rachel, now sleeping in her bassinet. She entered the bus station with tears threatening to blind her.

The same thin, bald man stood behind the counter. Katie wondered if he would remember her. She said, "I'd like to purchase a ticket to Yoder, Kansas."

He didn't glance up. "We don't have service to Yoder. The nearest town is Hutchinson, Kansas. You'll have to make connections in St. Louis and Kansas City."

"That will be fine. Is it still one hundred and sixty-nine dollars?"

He looked up at that. "Yes, it is. Do you have enough this time?"

"I do." She laid the bills on the counter.

"No, you don't," a man said behind her.

She recognized the voice instantly. It was Elam.

"I have enough." She didn't turn around. She didn't trust herself not to start crying.

"You haven't paid me for Rachel's baby bed." He was right behind her. She could feel the warmth of him through the fabric of her Amish dress.

Reaching around her, he took the money from the counter. "Now you cannot leave."

"I don't have a reason to stay." Her heart was beating so hard she thought it might burst.

Quietly, he said, "God willing, I shall spend my life giving you a thousand reasons to be glad you stayed."

She turned at last to face him, the love she'd tried to hide shining in her eyes. "Malachi says it's very hot and dusty in Kansas."

Elam covered her hands with his own. She could feel him trembling. He said, "It doesn't sound like a good place for Rachel."

Behind her, the man at the counter said, "Do you want a ticket or not?"

She smiled at Elam. "It seems I can't afford one."

Elam drew a deep breath. "Come. I'll give you a ride home."

Outside, Katie climbed sedately into the buggy, although she was so happy she wanted to shout. Elam helped her in, then handed her the baby and climbed up after them. With a cluck of his tongue he sent Judy out into the street.

They rode in silence until they were past the outskirts of town. As the horse trotted briskly down the blacktop, he turned in the seat to face Katie. "I ask you to forgive me. I judged you unfairly, Katie. I pushed you away when you needed my counsel."

"I forgive you as I have been forgiven."

"Will you marry me, Katie Lantz?"

Her heart expanded with happiness and all the love she'd kept hidden came bubbling forth. "*Jah,* Elam Sutter. I will marry you—on one condition."

His smile widened. "I knew it could not be so easy. What is your condition?"

"I want Rachel to be able to visit her English family."

His grin faded. His gaze rested on the sleeping baby. "And what if she is tempted to leave us and go into the English world when she is older?"

"Then we will face that together, and we will pray that she finds God in her own way."

"This is a hard thing to ask, Katie. I love her like my own child."

"And she will love you and honor you as her father. Just as I love you and will honor you as my husband."

He was silent for a time and Katie waited, not daring to hope. The clop-clop of Judy's hooves and the jingle of her harness were the only sounds on the empty highway. At last Elam said, "And you will obey me in all things and without question."

She heard the hint of teasing in his tone and all her fear vanished. With a light heart and prayer of thanks she leaned close to him. "You will be in charge of the house. It shall be as you say."

Elam chuckled. "A man who claims he's in charge of his own home will lie about other things, too. When do you want the wedding to take place?"

"Tomorrow."

He slanted a grin her way. "Be sensible, Katie."

"If tomorrow isn't possible, then I think a fall wedding will be good. How about the first Tuesday in November?"

"Tomorrow sounds better, but November will do. It can't come soon enough to suit me."

Happier than she had ever imagined she could be, Katie linked her arm through his and looked out at the passing landscape. The once-empty fields were springing to life with new green crops. Wildflowers bloomed in the ditches and along the fencerows. Larks sang from the fenceposts and branches of the trees. Her life, once bleak and empty, was now full to overflowing.

She laid her head against Elam's strong shoulder. "It's a beautiful evening, isn't it?"

"Beautiful," he replied, happiness welling up in his voice. He wasn't looking at the countryside. He was smiling down at her.

She smiled at him. "Do you think your mother and Mr. Imhoff will see more of each other when you marry?"

"I think that's a good possibility. Mother deserves to be happy. She would like having stepgrandchildren to raise."

"Who knows, maybe there will be more than one wedding this fall in your family."

"It will be hard to keep our betrothal a secret. Do you know how much celery I'll have to plant for two weddings? The whole township will know something is going on."

"I can live with that if you can."

He nodded. "*Jah,* I can."

When they finally reached the lane, Judy turned off the highway and picked up her pace. As the farmhouse came into view, Katie thought back to the night she'd arrived.

How she had dreaded returning here. Now the farm had become something different, something it had never been before. It was a place of joy. A place where she could raise her child to know God. A place where she and her family would work together and pray together as God intended.

She said, "'Even the sparrow has found a home, and the swallow a nest for herself, where she may have her young—a place near your altar, O Lord Almighty, my King and my God.'"

"*Psalms* 84:3, I think," Elam said quietly. At the top of the rise, he pulled the horse to a halt. Katie looked up at him, at the love shining in his eyes, and she knew she was truly blessed.

"Why are we stopping?" she asked, hoping she already knew the answer.

He drew his fingers along her jaw and cupped her cheek

with his hand. "Because I've been wanting to kiss you since the first time I picked you up at the bus station."

"Then you've waited long enough. Don't waste another minute." She raised her face to him and closed her eyes.

As Elam's lips touched hers with gentleness and love Katie knew in her heart that God had truly brought her home.

* * * * *

We hope you enjoyed reading

His Second-Chance Family

by *New York Times* bestselling author

RaeAnne THAYNE

and

Katie's Redemption

by *USA TODAY* bestselling author

PATRICIA DAVIDS.

Both were originally Harlequin® series stories!

From passionate, suspenseful and dramatic
love stories to inspirational or historical,
Harlequin offers different lines to
satisfy every romance reader.

New books in each line are available every month.

LOVE INSPIRED
INSPIRATIONAL ROMANCE
Uplifting stories of faith, forgiveness and hope.

Harlequin.com

SPECIAL EXCERPT FROM

LOVE INSPIRED
INSPIRATIONAL ROMANCE

Can newborn twins bring two grieving people together?

Read on for a sneak preview of
An Amish Mother for His Twins *by Patricia Davids,*
available July 2021 from Love Inspired.

His head was ready to explode.

Nathan Weaver sat at the kitchen table in his one-room cabin with his hands pressed to his throbbing temples. He had come to Maine to live a quiet life and to forget. For six months he'd done just that. In less than a week his peace was gone. He'd never know solitude again.

Both babies were crying at the top of their lungs in their Moses baskets near his feet. His hound, Buddy, howled in accompaniment. The yellow cat, yowling to be let out, had crawled to the top of the screen door and hung splayed like a pelt on the wall. The kettle's piercing whistle was close to drowning out everything. He closed his eyes and moved his hands to cover his ears. It didn't help.

Buddy stopped howling and started barking a challenge. The abrupt change made Nathan look up. An Amish woman stood outside the screen door. For a moment his heart froze. It wasn't possible.

"Annie?" he croaked.

Was he hallucinating? It couldn't be her. Annie had died in childbirth six days ago.

The woman opened the screen door. His cat launched himself into the night, just missing her head. "Not Annie, Nathan. It's Maisie Schrock."

He blinked hard. Maisie? Annie's twin sister? She was a widow who lived in Missouri caring for their ailing father. What was she doing in Maine?

She gazed inside, an expression of shock on her face. She held a suitcase in her hand. Buddy stopped barking and went to greet her with his tail wagging. The babies continued to cry.

"Annie died." Nathan swallowed against the pain. Saying the words aloud still didn't make it feel real.

"I know. The hospital told me yesterday," Maisie said with a catch in her voice.

"I can raise them by myself." But could he?

"You don't have to, Nathan. I'm here now. We can get through our loss together."

Don't miss
An Amish Mother for His Twins
by USA TODAY *bestselling author Patricia Davids,*
available July 2021 wherever Love Inspired books and ebooks
are sold.

LoveInspired.com

LIEXP75861MAX

LOVE INSPIRED
INSPIRATIONAL ROMANCE

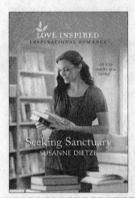

Save **$1.00**
on the purchase of **ANY**
Love Inspired book.

Available wherever books are sold, including most bookstores, supermarkets, drugstores and discount stores.

Save **$1.00**
on the purchase of ANY Love Inspired book.

Coupon valid until August 31, 2021. Redeemable at participating outlets in the U.S. and Canada only. Not redeemable at Barnes & Noble stores. Limit one coupon per customer.

52617081

5 65373 00076 2   (8100)0 12500

BACCOUP20995MAX

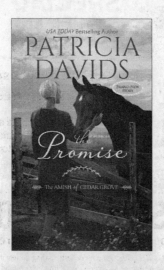

SPECIAL EXCERPT FROM

◆HARLEQUIN
SPECIAL EDITION

Rosa Galvez's attraction to Officer Wyatt Townsend is as powerful as the moon's pull on the tides. But with her past, Rosa knows better than to act on her feelings. But her solo life slowly becomes a sun-filled, family adventure—until dark secrets threaten to break like a summer storm.

Read on for a sneak peek at
the next book in The Women of Brambleberry House miniseries,
A Brambleberry Summer,
by New York Times *bestselling author RaeAnne Thayne.*

"Everyone has secrets, do they not? Some they share with those they trust, some they prefer to keep to themselves."

He was quiet for a long moment. "I hope you know that if you ever want to share yours, you can trust me."

She trusted very few people. And she certainly wasn't going to trust Wyatt, who was only a temporary tenant and would be out of her life in a few short weeks.

"If I had any secrets, I might do that. But I don't. I'm a completely open book."

She tried for a breezy smile but could tell he wasn't at all convinced. In fact, he looked slightly disappointed.

She tried to ignore her guilt and opted to change the subject instead. "The lightning seems to have stopped for now. I am sure the power will be back on soon."

"No doubt."

"Thank you again for coming to my rescue. Good night. Be careful going back down the stairs."

"I will do that. Good night."

He studied her, his features unreadable in the dim light of her flashlight. He looked as if he wanted to say something else. Instead, he shook his head slightly.

"Good night."

As he turned to go back down the stairs, the masculine scent of him swirled to her. She felt that sudden wild urge to kiss him again but ignored it. Instead, she went into her darkened apartment, her dog at her heels, and firmly closed the door behind her. If only she could close the door to her thoughts as easily.

Don't miss
A Brambleberry Summer *by RaeAnne Thayne,*
available July 2021 wherever
Harlequin Special Edition books and ebooks are sold.

Harlequin.com